Congratulations to

Samantha Hunt

Winner of the

2010 Bard Fiction Prize

Samantha Hunt, author of
The Invention of Everything Else, joins previous
winners Nathan Englander, Emily Barton,
Monique Truong, Paul La Farge, Edie Meidav,
Peter Orner, Salvador Plascencia, and Fiona Maazel.

The Bard Fiction Prize is awarded annually to a
promising emerging writer who is an American citizen
aged thirty-nine years or younger at the time
of application. In addition to a monetary award
of $30,000, the winner receives an appointment
as writer in residence at Bard College for one semester
without the expectation that he or she will teach
traditional courses. The recipient will give at least one
public lecture and meet informally with students.

For more information, please contact:

Bard Fiction Prize
Bard College
PO Box 5000
Annandale-on-Hudson, NY 12504-5000

COMING UP IN THE SPRING

Conjunctions:54
SHADOW SELVES

Edited by Bradford Morrow

The mirror is our most devious invention. When we look into it, do we see ourselves or an other? If we see an other, is that other a lie or some complex extension of a truth we don't quite grasp? And when we set down the mirror and imagine ourselves to be one or the other or some combination of both, who have we become?

For our spring issue, the very idea of self is tackled in fiction, poetry, and essays that investigate everything from innocent misperception to studied deception, delusion to fraud, mad misdemeanor to careful crime. The venerable theme of the doppelgänger has preoccupied the likes of Dostoevsky and Abraham Lincoln, Shakespeare and Buffy the Vampire Slayer. *Shadow Selves* offers a spectrum of permutations on this theme, which is central not just to classical literature but to postmodernism and post-Freudian psychoanalysis from Lacan forward.

Acclaimed writers such as Elizabeth Hand, Jonathan Carroll, Rikki Ducornet, Frederic Tuten, Peter Straub, and Rick Moody will join newcomers like J. W. McCormack, Jess Row, and Michael Sheehan in an issue that confronts the intricate nature of identity itself.

Subscriptions to *Conjunctions* are only $18 for more than seven hundred pages per year of contemporary and historical literature and art. Please send your check to *Conjunctions*, Bard College, Annandale-on-Hudson, NY 12504. Subscriptions can also be ordered by calling (845) 758-1539, or by sending an e-mail to Michael Bergstein at Conjunctions@bard.edu. For more information about current and past issues, please visit our Web site at www.Conjunctions.com.

CONJUNCTIONS

Bi-Annual Volumes of New Writing

Edited by
Bradford Morrow

published by Bard College

* * *

New Work

"The past is never dead.
It's not even past."
—William Faulkner
Requiem for a Nun

EDITOR'S NOTE

NOT EVEN PAST: HYBRID HISTORIES is decidedly hybrid. Works in which past moments in history play a centralizing role. Works that can now take their places in the history of contemporary literature. And three other works by and about several of the most historically significant, eloquent voices in world literature, writing in French, German, Spanish, and even in English—Beckett, Bernhard, Bolaño. Together, a gathering of those near the beginnings of their writing lives, many well into their life's work, and three in the pantheon.

A note, above all, about Barney Rosset, the fourth "B" *Conjunctions* is so privileged to publish here. Founder, publisher, and editor of Grove Press and *The Evergreen Review,* Barney has made a contribution to the shape and direction of twentieth-century world literature that cannot be overstated. Nobody has worked with greater courage, acumen, and plain old-fashioned hardheaded diligence than Barney Rosset to push back the philistines and open the way for so many of us who follow in the footsteps of his seven-league boots. His First Amendment battles are the stuff of legend, taking him to the Supreme Court for the right to publish, unexpurgated, *Lady Chatterley's Lover* and *Tropic of Cancer,* and clearing the way for him to bring out William Burroughs's controversial *Naked Lunch,* which celebrates its fifieth anniversary this year. He's the living epitome of a man you can't keep down. To read his moving memoir of Samuel Beckett is to glimpse why so many of the most groundbreaking authors of the last century embraced him, and why so many readers and writers still do. I would like to thank Barney and Astrid Rosset, Edward Beckett, Joanna Marston, and Lisa Gilbey for making it possible to publish Barney's account of Beckett, along with previously unpublished correspondence about *Waiting for Godot.* Also, heartfelt thanks to Barbara Epler and everyone at New Directions, as well as Petra Hardt at Suhrkamp Verlag, for helping us bring these translations of Roberto Bolaño and Thomas Bernhard into print here for the first time. And though it goes unsaid, it must be said: Continued gratitude, as ever, to Bard College, our own undaunted publisher of many years.

—Bradford Morrow
October 2009
New York City

7

*Samuel Beckett and Barney Rosset on the occasion of
Beckett's eightieth birthday, Paris, April 1986.*
Photograph © Bob Adelman. Used with permission.

Remembering Samuel Beckett
Barney Rosset

SYLVIA BEACH WROTE TO ME in New York, asking for an appointment. For many years she had been the famous proprietor of Shakespeare and Company, the leading and legendary English-language bookstore in Paris. She had been the close friend and publisher of James Joyce. She had also known Sam Beckett for many years. During our meeting she spoke about Beckett in the warmest terms as a writer of great importance whose day would surely come.

Sylvia Beach's words sounded a magical note.

When I had read Beckett's pieces in *Transition Workshop*, edited by Eugene Jolas in Paris, I was still a student at the New School. Jolas had Beckett listed under the category of "paramyths." Other writers listed in the same genre included Kay Boyle, Ernest Hemingway, James Joyce, Franz Kafka, Katherine Anne Porter, Gertrude Stein, and Dylan Thomas. And of course there was also Henry Miller, represented by pieces from *The Cosmological Eye* and *Tropic of Cancer*—the very books I had written a term paper about as a freshman at Swarthmore College in 1940–41.

One day in 1953, I saw a small item in, I believe, *The New York Times*. It told of the opening in Paris on January 5th of that year of a play by Samuel Beckett. It was called *Waiting for Godot*. I somehow got a copy of *Godot*—it had only been published in French, the language in which Beckett had written it—and read it. My immediate response was, here was a kind of human insight that I had never experienced before. I wanted to publish it. I set about finding Beckett's New York agent, Marian Saunders, and made one of the earliest Grove Press contracts. The contract itself was with Beckett's French publisher, Éditions de Minuit, the first of many I was to sign with them. It called for an advance of $1,000 against royalties, which might become due not only on *Godot* but also on Sam's novels, *Molloy*, *Malone Dies*, and *The Unnamable*.

About this time, after I had read *Godot*, I asked Wallace Fowlie, a specialist in French literature who had been one of my professors as well as my friend at the New School, to give me his opinion of it. I believed him to be a far more conservative reader than I. But he more than confirmed what Sylvia Beach had said to me and what I myself had concluded. He said, "Beckett will come to be known as one of the greatest writers of the twentieth century."

I had the same sort of feeling about two more "French" writers we contracted for in that same year: Eugène Ionesco and Jean Genet.

* * *

June 18, 1953
New York

Dear Mr. Beckett,

It is about time that I write a letter to you—now that agents, publishers, friends, etc., have all acted as go-betweens. A copy of our Grove Press catalogue has already been mailed to you, so you will be able to see what kind of a publisher you have been latched onto. I hope that you won't be too disappointed.

We are very happy to have the contract back from Minuit, and believe me, we will do what we can to make your work known in this country.

For me, the first order of the day would appear to be the translation. I have just sent off a letter to *Merlin* editor Alex Trocchi telling him that the difficulties did not seem as ominous from here as they evidently do from there, to him at least.

If you would accept my first choice as translator the whole thing would be easily settled. That choice of course, being you. That already apparently is a satisfactory solution insofar as the play is concerned.

As for translation of the novels, I am waiting first, to hear from you, what you advise, and whether or not you will tackle them yourself. If your decision is no, and I do hope that it won't be, we can discuss between us the likely people to do it.

Sylvia Beach is certainly the one you must blame for your future appearance on the Grove Press list. After she talked of you in beautiful words I immediately decided that what Grove Press needed most in the world was Samuel Beckett. I told her that, and then she suggested that I make a specific offer. I certainly had not thought of that up to the very moment she took out a piece of paper and pencil and prepared to write down the terms.

A second person was also very important—Wallace Fowlie. At my request he read the play and the two novels with great care, and came back with the urgent plea for me to take on your work. Fowlie is also on our list. His new translation of Rimbaud's

10

Illuminations, and a long study of them, is just now coming out. This would seem to be an already indecently long letter, so I will close. If you would give me your own address we might be able to communicate directly in the future.

Sincerely,
Barney Rosset

* * *

June 25, 1953
Paris

Dear Mr. Rosset

Thank you for your letter of June 18. Above my private address, confidentially. For serious matters write to me here, for business to Lindon, Ed. de Minuit, please.

Re: translations. I shall send you to-day or to-morrow my first version of *Godot.*

This translation has been rushed, but I do not think the final version will differ from it very much. With regard to the novels my position is that I should greatly prefer not to undertake the job myself, while having the right to revise whatever translation is made. But I know from experience how much more difficult it is to revise a bad translation than to do the thing oneself. I translated myself some years ago two very brief fragments for Georges Duthuit's *Transition.* If I can get hold of the number in which they appeared I shall send it to you.

With regard to my work in general I hope you realize what you are letting yourself in for. I do not mean the heart of the matter, which is unlikely to disturb anybody, but certain obscenities of form which may not have struck you in French as they will in English, and which frankly (it is better you should know this before we get going) I am not at all disposed to mitigate. I do not of course realize what is possible in America from this point of view and what is not. Certainly as far as I know such passages, faithfully translated, would not be tolerated in England.

Sylvia Beach said very nice things about the Grove Press and that you might be over here in the late summer. I hope you will.

Thanking you for taking this chance with my work and wishing us a fair wind, I am

Yours sincerely
Samuel Beckett

11

* * *

July 13, 1953
New York

Dear Mr. Beckett,

It was nice to receive your letter of June 25 and then your letter of July 5.

First I must tell you that I have not received your translation of *Godot*. I am most anxious to see it. I would like to plan on publication of the play for 1954, either in the first or second half of the year, depending entirely upon completion date of the translation. I would think the ideal thing would be to coincide publication with performance, but that is ideal only and I would not think it wise to indefinitely postpone publication while waiting for the performance.

As to the translation of the novels, I am naturally disappointed to hear that you prefer not to undertake translation yourself. I can well see your point, however, and it would seem a little sad to attempt to take off that much time to go back over your own books but I hope that you will change your mind.

As to the obscenities within the books, my suggestion is that we do not worry about that until it becomes necessary. Sometimes things like that have a way of solving themselves.

I do hope you locate a copy of *Transition* with the fragments translated by yourself.

I do plan on going to Europe in the fall, and I will certainly look forward to meeting you then.

Yours sincerely,
Barney Rosset

* * *

July 18, 1953
Paris 15me

Dear Mr. Rosset

In raising the question of the obscenities I simply wished to make it clear from the outset that the only modifications of them that I am prepared to accept are of a kind with those which hold for the text as a whole, i.e. made necessary by the change from one language to another. The problem therefore is no more complicated than this: Are you prepared to print the result? I am convinced you will agree with me that a clear understanding on this matter before we set to work is equally indispensable for you, the translator and myself.

Herewith *Transition* with my translation of fragments from *Molloy* and *Malone*.

> Yours sincerely
> Samuel Beckett

* * *

July 31, 1953
New York

Dear Mr. Beckett,

Your translation of *Godot* did finally arrive. I like it very much, and it seems to me that you have done a fine job. The long speech by Lucky is particularly good and the whole play reads extremely well.

If I were to make any criticism it would be that one can tell that the translation was done by a person more used to "English" speech than American. Thus the use of words such as "bloody"— and a few others—might lead an audience to think the play was originally done by an Englishman in English. This is a small point, but in a few places a neutralization of the speech away from the specifically English flavor might have the result of enhancing the French origins for an American reader. Beyond that technical point I have little to say, excepting that I am now extremely desirous of seeing the play on a stage—in any language.

I read the fragments by you in *Transition*, and again I must say that I liked them very much, leading to the continuance of my belief that you would be the best possible translator for the novels. I really do not see how anybody else can get the sound quality, to name one thing, but I am willing to be convinced.

By all means, the translation should be done with only those modifications required by the change from one language to another. If an insurmountable obstacle is to appear, let it first appear.

I will look forward to hearing about progress towards a translation.

> Yours sincerely,
> Barney Rosset

* * *

13

August 4, 1953
New York

Dear Mr. Beckett,

I am putting aside *Watt*, which I received this morning, to write this letter. Fifty pages poured over me and I will inundate myself again as soon as possible. After the sample of *Godot* went back to you, the first part of *Molloy* arrived and I was most favorably impressed with it. I remember Bowles's story in the second issue of *Merlin* and it does seem that he has a real sympathy for your writing. If you feel satisfied, and find it convenient to work with him, then my opinion would be to tell you to go ahead. Short of your doing the work yourself the best would be to be able to really guide someone else along—and that situation you seem to have found.

Again a mention of words. Those such as "skivvy" and "cutty" are unknown here, and when used they give the writing a most definite British stamp. That is perfectly all right if it is the effect you desire. If you are desirous of a little more vagueness as to where the scene is set it would be better to use substitutes which are of common usage both here and in Britain.

I am happy to be reading *Watt* and I hope to see more of *Molloy* soon.

With best regards,
Barney Rosset

* * *

September 1, 1953
Paris 15me

Dear Mr. Rosset

Thank you for your letters of August 4th and July 31st both received yesterday only.

It is good news that my translation of *Godot* meets with your approval. It was done in great haste to facilitate the negotiations of Mr. Oram and I do not myself regard it as very satisfactory. But I have not yet had the courage to revise it.

I understand your point about the Anglicisms and shall be glad to consider whatever suggestions you have to make in this connection. But the problem involved here is a far-reaching one. Bowles's text as revised by me is bound to be quite un-American in rhythm and atmosphere and the mere substitution here and there of the American for the English term is hardly likely to improve matters, on the contrary. We can of course avoid those words which are incomprehensible to the American reader, such as "skivvy" and "cutty," and it will be a help to have them pointed out to us. In *Godot* I tried to retain the French atmosphere as much as possible and you may have noticed the use of English and American place-names is confined to Lucky whose own name might seem to justify them.

Yours sincerely
Samuel Beckett

* * *

Shortly after this exchange of letters, my wife Loly and I went to Paris for the first of many meetings with Sam Beckett. Loly and I were married at New York City Hall on September 15, 1953, and the next day we embarked for Europe on the small but elegant French liner *Le Flandre*. I was seasick before we got out of New York Harbor.

Our first meeting took place at the bar of the Pont Royale Hotel on Rue Montalembert, almost next door to France's largest literary publisher, Gallimard. Beckett came in, tall, trench coated, and taciturn, on his way to another appointment. He said he had only time for one quick one. "He arrived late," Loly remembered. "He looked most uncomfortable and never said a word except that he had to leave soon. I was pained by his shyness, which matched Barney's, and, in desperation, I told him how much I had enjoyed reading *Godot*. At that, we clicked, and he became warm and fun."

The other appointment forgotten, the three of us went to dinner and to various bars, ending up at Sam's old hangout, La Coupole, on Boulevard Montparnasse at three in the morning, with Beckett ordering champagne.

* * *

14/12/Paris
15me
(1953)

Dear Barney and Loly

Sorry for the no to design you seem to like. It was good of you to consult me. Don't think of me as a nietman. The idea is all right. But I think the variety of symbols is a bad mistake. They

15

make a hideous column and destroy the cohesion of the page. And I don't like the suggestion and the attempt to express it of a hierarchy of characters. A la rigueur, if you wish, simple capitals, E. for Estragon, V. for Vladimir, etc., since no confusion is possible, and perhaps no heavier in type than those of the text. But I prefer the full name. Their repetition, even when corresponding speech amounts to no more than a syllable, has its function in the sense that it reinforces the repetitive text. The symbols are variety and the whole affair is monotony. Another possibility is to set the names in the middle of the page and text beneath, thus:

ESTRAGON
I'd rather he'd dance, it'd be more fun.
POZZO
Not necessarily.
ESTRAGON
Wouldn't it, Didi, be more fun?
VLADIMIR
I'd like well to hear him think.
ESTRAGON
Perhaps he could dance first and think afterwards,
if it isn't too much to ask him.

But personally I prefer the Minuit composition. The same is used by Gallimard for Adamov's theatre (1st vol. just out). But if you prefer the simple capitals it will be all right with me. Could you not possibly postpone setting of galleys until 1st week in January, by which time you will have received the definitive text? I have made a fair number of changes, particularly in Lucky's tirade, and a lot of correcting would be avoided if you could delay things for a few weeks.

The tour of Babylone *Godot* mostly in Germany (including the Grundgens theatre in Düsseldorf), but also as far as the Milan Piccolo, seems to have been successful. Marvellous photos, unposed, much superior to the French, were taken in Krefeld during actual performance. One in particular is fantastic (end of Act 1, Vladimir drawing Estragon towards wings, with moon and tree). It is the play and would make a remarkable cover for your book. I shall call at the theatre this afternoon before posting this and add address of photographer in case you are interested in purchasing the set.

Best wishes for Xmas and the New Year.
Sam

That was the same Beckett who a year later would write me: "It's hard to go on with everything loathed and repudiated as soon as formulated, and in the act of formulation, and before formulation . . . I'm horribly tired and stupefied, but not yet tired and stupefied enough. To write is impossible, but not yet impossible enough."

It was the same lovely, courtly Beckett who had written:

ESTRAGON: I can't go on.
VLADIMIR: That's what you think.

The problem of who was going to translate *Godot* into English was a thorny one. Perhaps when Beckett wrote in French, no one looked over his shoulder, and he could achieve a more dispassionate purity. Perhaps he was also angry at the British for failing him as publishers. His novel *Murphy* and a short-story collection, *More Pricks Than Kicks*, had achieved little notice in England. Perhaps Beckett felt he was too lyrical in English. He was always striving to take away as many of his writer's tools as possible before having to cease writing—taking away tools as you'd take away a shovel from a person who wants to dig.

Beckett had never been truly satisfied with any of his English translators, and I constantly tried to persuade him to do the translation job himself. I think he always wanted to go back to writing in English, which he did, mostly, from then on. But I felt he needed to be encouraged. Sam finally came to the only possible conclusion. He did the translation of *Godot* himself. The novels trailed behind.

"It's so nice where we are—snowed-in, quiet, and sootless, that I think you might like it," I wrote my new author in January 1954 from our East Hampton bunkerlike Quonset-hut home. The letter concerned the page proofs of *Waiting for Godot*, the work that would change the course of modern theater.

Our correspondence, formal at first, warmed quickly. Sometimes Beckett typed, at my rather brash request, and sometimes letters were written in his almost indecipherable script. "You know, Barney, I think my writing days are over," Beckett wrote in 1954. And later: "I'm sick of all this old vomit and despair more and more of even being able to puke again. . . . Perhaps I can feel a little bit of what you are going through." In a world where writers switch publishers at the first shake of a martini pitcher, our transatlantic communications seemed to float on a sea of tranquility and trust.

Grove published *Waiting for Godot* in 1954 and Genet's *The Maids* and *Deathwatch* as well.

* * *

Suzanne Deschevaux-Dumesnil, who finally became Sam's wife in 1961, had been his strongest supporter for many years. She was his manager and practical organizer, tending to his every need, protecting him from the world, and vigorously promoting his career. Tall, handsome, and austere, she was even more reclusive than he, never, as far as I know, learning English, and walling herself off from his friends. I remembered her making an attempt to study English at Berlitz when we first met, but it seemed to go against her grain, and I never actually heard her speak anything but French.

During the German occupation of Paris, Sam and Suzanne, who were part of the Resistance and were in danger of arrest by the Gestapo, went to the South of France and hid out on an isolated farm near Roussillon, in the Vaucluse, to which Beckett specifically refers in *Godot* as well as mentioning one of the local farmers by name. There in the Vaucluse the emptiness and monotony of the days stretched on until it must have seemed like an eternity to Beckett.

For three years in the Vaucluse, Beckett and Suzanne were mostly alone, and I get the feeling of their being bored with each other, and not knowing how to pass the time, and wondering what they were doing there and when the hell they were going to get out, and not wanting ever to see each other again, and yet not being able to leave one another. The heart of *Godot* must be inextricably intertwined with all of this. In one exchange between the protagonists Estragon has gone off and is beaten up. Upon his return there is this exchange:

VLADIMIR: You again! . . . Come here till I embrace you . . . Where did you spend the night?

ESTRAGON: Don't touch me! Don't question me! Don't speak to me! Stay with me!

VLADIMIR: Did I ever leave you?

ESTRAGON: You let me go.

18

While Beckett clearly indicates an all-male cast for *Godot*, and refused permission to two top American actresses, Estelle Parsons and Shelley Winters, to perform it in 1969, writing Ms. Parsons that "theater sex is not interchangeable," I believe he'd taken that very real situation—he and Suzanne on a farm, waiting—and converted it into an eternal predicament, a universal myth. I thought the latent sexuality became much clearer in the New York 1988 Lincoln Center production of *Godot* with Robin Williams as Estragon and Steve Martin as Vladimir. They pushed forward the male/female sides of their characters.

Beckett's life with Suzanne seemed to have had the despairing yet persevering, separate yet joined quality of many of his other plays as well. In *Endgame:*

HAMM: Why do you stay with me?

CLOV: Why do you keep me?

HAMM: There's no one else.

CLOV: There's nowhere else.

Beckett was extremely precise about his stage directions, including the look and size of the sets, and I believe that the configuration of his and Suzanne's two Paris apartments reflected their deepening impasse as graphically as did his instructions for the settings of his plays.

Their first apartment, at 6 Rue des Favorites, was in a fairly lively neighborhood. It was a tiny duplex, two small rooms, one above the other, the lower one sparsely furnished with just enough chairs for a few people to sit down, and a couple of paintings. It had a claustrophobic feeling, but at least it was close to friendly restaurants and bars once you got outside. I never saw the upstairs bedroom, but cannot imagine it to have been particularly sybaritic. When Sam and Suzanne fled Paris to escape from the Nazis, the latter did them an accidental favor. Their apartment was locked up and left that way so that after the war they were able to reoccupy it without anything having been changed.

One night when they still lived there, Sam and I spent an evening together. I was driving and I remember that the dawn was just coming up as we got to Rue Fremicourt. Then something happened. All the streetlights went out. It was not because dawn was breaking. An electricity strike had just started. In Paris, at least at that time, you got into your house by pushing a button, on the outside, to get your door to open. Without this *minuterie* functioning you could not get in or even warn somebody inside that you were there.

So Sam and I drove to my hotel, Le Pont Royal. There the front door was open but the elevator was not working. We trudged up seven floors to my isolated room at the top, briefly looked at the sun rising over Paris, and then climbed into bed, a nice big double one. Now I could say that I had been to bed with Samuel Beckett.

When Sam and Suzanne moved, it was to an even more appropriate setting for Beckett. It was right across from the Santé prison, with a view down into the exercise yard. Sam had a deep identification with prisoners, so this flat was made to order. The neighborhood, near the outskirts of Paris where the Metro emerges from the underground to run down the middle of Boulevard St. Jacques (he lived at No. 38), was grim, impersonal, as bleak as any Beckett setting. It's hard to find a place like that in Paris, a *banlieu* where there are hardly any bars or restaurants or little shops or people in the streets. The building in which Beckett lived had several floors, a cramped entryway, and the usual tiny French elevator. On his landing, small in itself, were two doors leading to two separate apartments. To reach Sam's, you turned right, and he let you in. To the left you would find Suzanne. There were two rooms in Sam's part, a small study with a lot of books and papers very neatly arranged, and a bedroom with a skinny cot and an ordinary bureau. Then there was a narrow little kitchen placed horizontally in the rear. It was rather like a corridor that connected the two apartments from the rear. So the living spaces were connected but you could close them off, with doors placed at each end of the kitchen. Her friends could come and go to her place, and his friends could visit his place, but they didn't have to see one another if they didn't feel like it. It was a unique, chilly arrangement, and I never saw Suzanne again after the move. Of course, that might have been because I fell asleep at the Paris opening of *Endgame* sitting beside her. I'd just flown in from New York and was half dead of jet lag—I heard she never forgave me for that. Later I understand that she became ill, and increasingly difficult and withdrawn, and perhaps saw no one. Sam and she were in Tunisia, the land of her birth, when it was announced that he had won the Nobel Prize in Literature.

Beckett had at least one close woman friend I know of during this lifetime with Suzanne. She was an English woman, Barbara Bray, a translator who had worked for the BBC in London. Previously married, with two children, Barbara was nearly thirty years younger than Beckett. She moved to France in the early 1950s, and has lived there ever since. She was very attractive, slim, dark haired, as I remember, and pretty in an English way. She was extremely intelligent and quite similar to Beckett: laid-back, and concerned with accuracy in translation. She was very close to him, and she may well have been one of the strongest attachments during the period I knew him. I remember several instances when he and I had been out drinking and it was late, but not so late for us—only about three in the morning. I'd offer to walk him home, and he would say something like: "No, I'm going to stop by and see Barbara."

During this period Beckett continued to live with Suzanne. When he finally married her in Folkestone, England, in 1961, he was fifty-four, she sixty-one.

Barbara's close friendship with Beckett continued. I remember one evening in particular in 1965 when Harold Pinter was in Paris for the opening of the French production of his plays *The Collection* and *The Lover*. Barbara, Harold, Sam, my girlfriend at the time, Nicole Tessier, and I were at a bar right off Boulevard Montparnasse where Beckett liked to go. It was called the Falstaff and featured beer. To me, except for the name, it was as French as anyplace else.

We occupied a narrow table that butted up against a wall, Barbara and Harold seated opposite each other, then Sam and my girlfriend next to each other, with me at the end. I began to notice that Barbara and Harold were discussing Sam, very admiringly, but sort of as if he were a sacred object they were having an academic chat about, not involving him in the conversation at all. I could see that he was getting increasingly irritated, and finally Sam took his stein and banged it on the table hard enough to spill some beer. Then he got up and walked across the room in the ungainly gait he had before his cataract operation, which gave people the impression that he was drunk when he was just having difficulty seeing. I watched him slowly climb the narrow stairs to the men's room and disappear. A hush fell over our table. Then he reappeared and seemed to be making his way back to us when he stopped about twenty feet away and sat down at another table with two people whom I slowly realized were total strangers to him. He stared at us for a few minutes, then rejoined us without comment or excuse. That was one of his rare shows of anger. Perhaps a touch of jealousy could enter the head of even a great psychoanalyst.

Similar moments of passion appear here and there in the emotional texture of Beckett's work, sudden oases of piercingly romantic fulfillment and loss in which the prose becomes suffused with sensuality and then with tears. I felt this most in *Krapp's Last Tape*, my favorite Beckett play, a monologue written in English in 1958. In it, a ruined old man plays and replays tapes from his younger days, trying to find some meaning in his life. One passage is excruciatingly passionate. The affair between Krapp and his lover has now been destroyed beyond retrieval.

> *We drifted in among the flags and stuck. The way they went down, sighing, before the stem! (Pause.) I lay down across her with my face in her breasts and my hand on her. We lay there without moving. But under us all moved, and moved us, gently, up and down, and from side to side.*
>
> *Then: . . . Scalded the eyes out of me reading Effie again, a page a day, with tears again. Effie . . . (Pause.) Could have been happy with her, up there on the Baltic, and the pines, and the dunes.*
>
> *Then the previous tape is replayed.*

Led to it by Beckett, I searched for the nineteenth-century German novelist Theodor Fontane's *Effi Briest* for clues to this passage. Finally Beckett revealed to me that it related to a summer with his cousin Peggy Sinclair in 1929 at a small resort on the Baltic Sea, where Peggy was engrossed in Fontane's novel about a young girl's calamitous life that ended with her death from tuberculosis. Although Beckett was only twenty-three at the time, his feeling for Peggy Sinclair, and the memory of their being together, survived her engagement to another man and her death in 1933, ironically also of tuberculosis.

The story struck an incredibly strong chord in me. It reopened my suffering of the loss of a young love, my Nancy Ashenhurst. I still grieve for Nancy, and have dreams about her. This bond of early bereavement led me to find other references to Peggy Sinclair in Beckett's later works, particularly in *Ohio Impromptu*, a short play of extraordinary lyricism that was published by Grove in 1981 in a collection called *Rockaby*. In *Ohio Impromptu* the protagonist seeks relief from the memory of "the dear face" by moving to an unfamiliar place, "back to where nothing ever shared." However, there is no relief until a man sent by "the dear name" comes to comfort him by reading and rereading "a sad tale from a worn volume."

Finally the messenger says he has had word from "the dear name" that he (the messenger) shall not come again:

> So the sad tale, they stayed on as though turned to stone . . . what
> thoughts who knows. Thoughts, no, not thoughts. Profounds of
> mind. Buried in who knows what profounds of mind.

Beckett often sat "as though turned to stone" during his long silences. I remember him "buried in who knows what *profounds* of mind."

His friendship with Barbara Bray, I think, may well have given inspiration for a short, extremely bitter 1963 work called *Play* in which a husband, wife, and mistress, encased up to their necks in urns, are trapped in an eternal triangle, condemned endlessly to repeat the details of the husband and mistress's affair under the glare of a harsh, inquisitorial spotlight.

Shortly after completing *Play*, which Alan Schneider directed at the Cherry Lane Theatre in Greenwich Village, Beckett made his only trip to the United States. It was in the summer of 1964, and he came to be here for the shooting in New York of his motion picture *Film*, which I had commissioned him to write.

* * *

In 1962 I had started a new unit to produce films outside of Grove Press—called Evergreen Productions—but with Grove people, specifically Fred Jordan and Dick Seaver, and one outsider who was by then a close friend, Alan Schneider, whom I had come to know because of Sam Beckett.

Very ambitiously, I made a list of writers—with the help of my associates—whom we asked to write scripts for us to produce. Those writers were, first and foremost, Samuel Beckett, as well as Harold Pinter, Eugène Ionesco, Marguerite Duras, and Alain Robbe-Grillet. They all said yes to our request and all of them wrote their scripts. Duras and Robbe-Grillet both wrote full-length scenarios for us. We envisaged the Beckett, Ionesco, and Pinter scripts as constituting a trilogy.

These five were all Grove Press authors. I invited three more authors to contribute. Another Grove author, Jean Genet, was asked. Fred Jordan and I went to London to make the request, but he said no. (Strangely, years later we bought the rights and became the U.S.

23

distributor of the one film he wrote and directed himself—a wonderful silent black-and-white film, *Un Chant d'Amour.*)

The last two authors we asked to write scripts for us (they were not Grove Press authors) were Ingeborg Bachmann and Günter Grass. I trailed Bachmann to Zurich (I think) to get her no, and I went to Berlin to see Grass. He lived in what I recall as being a sort of bombed-out area, in a precarious, small building. You reached its second floor if he wanted you to, via a ladder that he extended down to you in lieu of a staircase. Grass was completely charming and friendly, but the outcome was the same as with Bachmann.

Out of the five scripts we did get, we were able only to produce Samuel Beckett's *Film.*

I set out to create a production team to turn Beckett's script into a motion picture. The most important member of that team was Sam himself. He wrote, he guided, and he kept the ship afloat. Alan Schneider had had no previous film experience but had done a great deal of successful theater directing, including plays by Pinter, Albee, and especially Beckett. There was no doubt in my mind that we could overcome that problem. The other top two people on the team were Sidney Meyers and Boris Kaufman.

Sidney Meyers was an acclaimed veteran filmmaker. In 1960 he had been awarded the Flaherty Documentary Award for *Savage Eye* (which he shared with Joseph Strick and Ben Maddow). Haskell Wexler and Helen Levitt were the cinematographers. Meyers was nominated for both the Venice Film Festival Golden Lion Award in 1949 and for an Academy Award for *The Quiet One* in 1950.

He was also a consummate musician, a self-effacing, literate, and intelligent man, and he got along beautifully with Sam. And, not incidentally, he had helped me in a very important and selfless way at the end of the production work on an earlier film project of mine, *Strange Victory.*

And then there was Boris Kaufman. He was the brother of the famous Soviet directors Dziga Vertov and Mikhail Kaufman. Also, unbeknownst to me, he had won the Academy Award in 1954 for *On the Waterfront.* But it was very important for me that he was the cinematographer on Jean Vigo's great films *L'Atalante* (1934), *Zéro de Conduite* (1933), and *À Propos de Nice* (1930). These were perhaps my favorite films above all others. The filmmaker I had felt most akin to was Vigo.

Amos Vogel, in his book *Film as a Subversive Art,* said about Vigo's *Zéro de Conduite:* "In this anarchist masterpiece—a poetic, surreal portrayal of revolt in a boys' school—Vigo also summarizes the suffocating atmosphere of French petty bourgeoisie life, seen, as the rest of the film, through a child's eyes: the *pater familias* who never emerges from his papers, the kitsch décor, the girl, her underwear showing: though the hero is blindfolded, we know he sees it all."

Our crew was now complete.

Judith Schmidt, my invaluable assistant, retyped the script after conferences held and audiotaped in East Hampton. We had brought Beckett to stay there when he first arrived from Paris. He arrived at night at the little East Hampton airport. It was a very dramatic landing—they had thrown on some searchlights and it all reminded me of *Casablanca*. Several days later, we went back to New York City to shoot *Film*.

Alan Schneider had suggested Buster Keaton for the lead role in *Film* and Sam liked the idea. So Alan flew out to Hollywood to attempt to sign up Buster. There he found the great silent star living in extremely modest circumstances. On arrival, Alan had to wait in a separate room while Keaton finished up an imaginary (perhaps drunk) poker game with, among others, the legendary but long-dead Hollywood moguls Louis B. Mayer and Irving Thalberg. Keaton took the job. He would die a year and half after completing the shooting of *Film*.

Sometime after *Film* was finished and being shown, Kenneth Brownlow, a Keaton/Chaplin scholar, interviewed Beckett about working with Keaton. Beckett had said, "Buster Keaton was inaccessible. He had a poker mind as well as a poker face. I doubt if he ever read the text—I don't think he approved of it or liked it. But he agreed to do it and he was very competent. He was not our first choice. It was Schneider's idea to use Keaton, who was available. . . . He had great endurance, he was very tough, and, yes, reliable. And when you saw that face at the end—oh." He smiled. "At last."

When Brownlow asked Beckett if he had ever told Keaton what the film was about, Sam said:

> I never did, no. I had very little to do with him. He sat in his dressing room, playing cards . . . until he was needed. The only time he came alive was when he described what happened when they were making films in the old days. That was very enjoyable. I remember him saying that they started with a beginning and an end and improvised the rest as they went along. Of course, he

25

tried to suggest gags of his own. . . . His movement was excellent—covering up the mirror, putting out the animals—all that was very well done. To cover the mirror, he took his big coat off and he asked me what he was wearing underneath. I hadn't thought of that. I said, "The same coat." He liked that. The only gag he approved of was the scene where he tries to get rid of the animals—he puts out the cat and the dog comes back, and he puts out the dog and the cat comes back—that was really the only scene he enjoyed doing.

Brownlow asked Sam what the film meant, what it was about, and he replied, "It's about a man trying to escape from perception of all kinds—from all perceivers, even divine perceivers. There is a picture which he pulls down. But he can't escape from self-perception. It is an idea from Bishop Berkeley, the Irish philosopher and idealist. 'To be is to be perceived'—'*Esse est percipi.*' The man who desires to cease to be must cease to be perceived. If being is being perceived, to cease being is to cease to be perceived."

Beckett went on to say that distinguishing between the modes of being perceived was a major technical roadblock: "There was one big problem we couldn't solve—the two perceptions—the extraneous perception and his own acute perception. The eye that follows sees him and his own hazy, reluctant perception of various objects. Boris Kaufman devised a way of distinguishing between them. The extraneous perception was all right, but we didn't solve his own. He tried to use a filter—his view being hazy and ill defined. This worked at a certain distance but for close-ups it was no good. Otherwise it was a good job."

Besides the problem of capturing the two perceptions there was another technical problem. It was when we attempted to use "deep focus" in the film. Originally, *Film* was meant to run nearly thirty minutes. Eight of those minutes were to have been used in one very long shot in which a number of actors would make their only appearance. The shot was based on a technique developed by Samuel Goldwyn and his great cameraman Greg Toland to achieve deep focus. A little later it was used to stunning effect by Orson Welles, with Toland as cameraman, in *Citizen Kane.* Even when panning their camera, deep focus allowed objects from as close as a few feet to as far as several hundred feet to be seen in the same shot with equal clarity. Toland's work was so important to Welles that he gave his cameraman equal billing. Sad to say, our deep focus work in *Film*

26

was unsuccessful. Despite the abundant expertise of our group, the extremely difficult shot was ruined by a stroboscopic effect that caused the images to jump around.

We went on without that shot. Beckett averted this incipient disaster by removing the scene from the script.

In his book *Entrances* Alan Schneider says, "Sidney [Meyers] proceeded to do a very quick, very rough cut for Sam to look at before taking off for Paris. And that first cut turned out to be not far off from what we finally used. The editing was painstaking—and painful, Sidney always gently trying to break the mold we had set in the shooting, and Sam and I in our different ways always gently holding him to it. There was no question of sparring over who had the legal first cut or final cut or whatever. We talked, argued, tried various ways, from Moviola to screen and back again, to make it come out as much the film that Sam had first envisioned as we could."

In New York, Sam and Alan stayed with me and my new wife, Cristina, in our house on Houston Street in Greenwich Village. When the shooting stopped, all Beckett wanted to do was get back to France as soon as possible so we booked an early morning flight, set our alarm, and I promised to wake him at 7:30 a.m. in time to get to the airport. At 9:00 a.m. Cristina and I woke up, horrified to find that we had overslept, and we were appalled to stumble over Beckett sitting outside our bedroom door, wearing his overcoat even though it was July. He had his packed bag on the floor next to him and was sound asleep. It never occurred to him to knock on our door. I made another airline reservation for 5:00 p.m., and the three of us spent the day at the New York World's Fair in Flushing Meadows, wandering among the exhibits. We somehow managed to lose our homesick writer along the way. After a frantic search we found him, on a bench, sound asleep again. We revived him enough for him to buy two knitted Greek purses—one for Cristina and one for Suzanne—whereupon we escorted him to an air-conditioned bar at what was then Idlewild Airport for drinks until departure time. "This is somehow not the right country for me," Sam said at the bar. "The people are too strange." Then he said, "God bless," got on the plane, and was gone, never to return again.

* * *

27

Once Sam was back in Paris, things went on as before—I continued to visit him there. Since both he and I had been deeply involved in school athletic competition, I as cocaptain of my high school football team and Beckett the leader of his school cricket squad, we found a common ground in sports. I tried my hand at Beckett's favorite pastimes, chess and billiards, but found them too maddeningly demanding of precision. Beckett, for his part, enjoyed playing my more slapdash table tennis. As a spectator sport we settled on tennis, which we both had once played, and now we often attended matches at Roland Garros stadium outside Paris. I remember one time in particular, a match between the great American Pancho Gonzales and Lew Hoad, the Australian champion of the time. The referee was a Basque and an admirer of Beckett's. As he mounted his tall chair courtside, he waved enthusiastically at Sam. A couple of sets later, before a booing crowd, the referee was ejected at Gonzales's request after making a number of quite legitimate calls against him. He paused to chat for a moment in the midst of his forced exit.

Usually, however, Sam the writer and I the publisher just went out eating and drinking and talking. Beckett always had very set ideas about where to go and what to eat. At first his tastes were quite broad, but as the years went by they narrowed down, exactly like his writing, and the choices got fewer and fewer. In the beginning Beckett favored the Closerie des Lilas on Boulevard Montparnasse, where Hemingway had liked to go, and where names of famous writers were embossed on the tables. There was also the grandiose La Coupole, a small bar called Rosebud, and the allegedly English pub Falstaff. But especially congenial was a seafood brasserie in a tough, nightlife neighborhood nearby called Ile des Marquises where *le patron* revered Beckett and had a photograph of him on the wall along with huge glossies of Marcel Cerdan (the Algerian boxer and world middleweight champion killed in a transatlantic crash), the great American boxer Sugar Ray Robinson, and other assorted personalities. Beckett's photo was between the two fighters.

One New Year's Eve, probably in the early seventies, Cristina, her mother, and our children—my daughter, Tansey, and son, Beckett, a namesake—were in Paris with me. Beckett was vacationing in Morocco with Suzanne. That night the phone rang in our hotel room. It was Matthew Josephson, the famed Hollywood agent, calling to say he was representing Steve McQueen, who desperately wanted to make a film of *Waiting for Godot*. Money was no object,

Beckett could have complete control and any other actors he chose: Laurence Olivier, Peter O'Toole, and Marlon Brando—who was then about to do *Apocalypse Now*—were mentioned. After I ascertained that the agent was very much for real, and that the top price for a film property seemed to be $500,000, then a princely sum, I wrote to him and stipulated that amount. Josephson replied that the offer was $350,000, and it was absolutely firm and put in writing. The matter was dropped until I saw Beckett again on St. Patrick's Day for dinner at the Ile des Marquises. Anxious to secure some money for Sam, I told him of the offer for the proposed film, playing up Steve McQueen and, for some reason, Brando. Beckett asked what this McQueen looked like and I, grasping at straws, summoned up an image of James Garner. "He's a tall, husky, good-looking guy," I winged it. And Marlon Brando? "Even bigger, a huge, heavy-set fellow." Sam thought for a while and then said, "No. It will never work. My characters are shadows."

Near the end, Beckett refused to go to his old haunts, and it all narrowed down to an ersatz bistro called Le Petit Café in a monstrosity of a new hotel near his apartment. Originally the hotel was called the PLM, later changed to Pullman St. Jacques. It had a garish, undersized, Vegas-like marquee, and I thought of its lobby as resembling a souped-up railway station at rush hour with busloads of German and Japanese tourists swarming up and down its long escalators. All it needed was a bank of slot machines. Visiting athletes were also a specialty, and I remember the Scottish rugby team, brawny men in tams and kilts, all drunk as lords, horsing around in the lobby to the astonishment of a tour group of early-teenage Japanese girls. I also recall a boxing ring being set up in the lobby, and a loudspeaker announcing: "Will the Australian trampoline team please report to the fourth floor." Beckett stayed oblivious to it, totally out of place and impassive in the midst of all this international action.

I, after intricate maneuvering, brought Beckett and photographer Richard Avedon together in April 1979 at Le Petit Café, in one of the most awkward and enigmatic encounters of my life. The celebrated photographer said his technique of using a white sheet as a backdrop was philosophically derived from Beckett. He also said to me that he'd shot everybody he wanted to with the exception of Greta Garbo and Beckett. I made arrangements for Avedon and Beckett to meet, stressing to Avedon that there was no guarantee Beckett would actually agree to pose and it would not be an easy task to convince him.

Avedon came from Tokyo and I from New York with my fourth wife, Lisa, Tansey, and my son, Beckett, now ten years old. Sam Beckett was his usual self, silent but listening. Lisa and my kids did the same, while Avedon, who seemed nervous, talked nonstop for about an hour until finally he said: "OK, let's take the pictures." He asked Samuel Beckett and my Beckett to go with him, and the three of them crossed the street and, for about half an hour, disappeared into a passageway through the Metro overpass. When they returned, nobody described what had happened, but I assumed the pictures had been taken.

I heard nothing further for a couple of months until one day I received two superb, very moving photos of my son with Samuel Beckett, beautifully mounted and framed and signed by Avedon. About a month later Sam himself, who had never before shown the slightest interest in such matters, asked what had happened to the photos. I wrote Avedon and received what I thought was a very peculiar response to the effect that Avedon had not taken any pictures of Samuel Beckett alone that day because the writer had seemed "unhappy," but that, because I had gone to so much trouble, he had taken a few shots of the two Becketts together.

My son, Beckett, said that after crossing under the Metro overpass they'd come to a wall where a white sheet had been tacked up and an assistant waited for them in a car. There was a large camera fastened to a tripod. He described Avedon setting up the shot, then focusing his camera with a black cloth over his head, then stepping out and squeezing the bulb a few times for the two Becketts and then for Sam Beckett alone. The missing Beckett photos supposedly appeared in the French magazine *Egoiste.* I have never seen them, but a portrait of Sam alone was in Avedon's retrospective at the Metropolitan Museum of Art in New York in 2005.

* * *

A later, thornier encounter at Le Petit Café involved Beckett and Peter Getty, son of the famously wealthy Ann Getty, who, with Lord Weidenfeld, had bought Grove from me in 1985. After Getty and Weidenfeld promised to keep me as CEO, they ousted me without ceremony the following year. Smart and young, Peter Getty, who often borrowed subway fare from Grove employees to get uptown to his Fifth Avenue apartment, had learned I was meeting Beckett in Paris soon after my ouster, and asked to be introduced. I agreed, and Getty flew over, checked into a suite at the Ritz, and taxied out to Beckett's unlikely hangout, Le Petit Café, with a book he wanted autographed.

This was the only time Sam was not friendly to someone I introduced him to. It was a short, tense meeting. After autographing the book, he glared at Peter and asked: "How could you do this to Barney, and what do you plan to do about it?" Peter was very embarrassed, and mumbled something about consulting with his mother. Later, I heard that Beckett had told another suppliant from Grove, "You will get no more blood out of this stone," and he never allowed them to publish anything new of his again.

To me and a group of others assembled in his honor at La Coupole he said, "There is only one thing an author can do for his publisher and that is write something for him." And he did exactly that. It was the little book called *Stirrings Still*. It was to be his last prose work, and he dedicated it to me.

Stirrings Still is the meditations of an old man contemplating death. It brought back to me an ether dream I had had as a little boy. I had an out-of-body experience, seeing myself as an object rocketing into space, zooming through a black void until I was transformed into a "knob of blackness." I knew I was experiencing the terror of my own death. Still, now, unable to sleep in a totally darkened room, I am hounded by that dream. When he wrote *Stirrings Still*, I don't know how much Sam was actually thinking of me, but I think I know why he wrote it. He was facing his own dream of death, which was fast approaching, and which, possibly, he finally made bearable by acceptance of that approaching darkness.

> Such and much more such the hubbub in his mind so-called till nothing left from deep within but only ever fainter oh to end. No matter how no matter where. Time and grief and self so-called. Oh all to end.

* * *

Beckett's health was clearly failing, although I couldn't admit this to myself. We now met exclusively at Le Petit Café, which had become his "club," and where he was totally ignored by outsiders. I took to actually staying at the Pullman St. Jacques, the hotel where the café was located, in order to be near him, and sometimes I ate meals alone in the fast-food café off the hotel's lobby. At breakfast they gave you a set of plastic-coated photographs, not unlike a deck of cards. One card had an egg on it, another card two eggs, another card a strip of bacon, and so on. To order, you went to the cashier and handed her the cards you'd selected. In a funny way, it was pure Beckett. They'd done away with the menu entirely, eliminating the need for words or translations of words; you could choose a meal in total silence. In the same vein, Beckett had made increasing use of the stage directions "pause" and "silence" in his work, and had pared down his vocabulary to fewer and fewer words.

At some point, Sam began having dizzy spells and falling in his apartment; apparently not enough blood was circulating to his brain. After brief stays in several hospitals he was moved to a nursing home only a few blocks from where he lived. The desire to go on had lessened even more. He was unsteady on his feet and even thinner, if that were possible, and therefore seemed taller and more and more like a figure done by his friend Alberto Giacometti, who had given Sam a drawing of a thin, striding man. Sam gave it to Cristina and me as a wedding present, and we later used it on the cover of a reprint of Sam's novel *Molloy*. Now he was just a ghost of even that drawing.

The nursing home was on a side street, and looked like the other small buildings on the block with only a discreet plaque announcing its institutional function. You entered a sparsely furnished sitting room in which a number of old women, some with walkers, watched a couple of ancient TV sets. Then you went through a little dining room out into a tiny courtyard with a walkway and some grass. There were a few rooms looking out onto it. Beckett was in the first room, a cubicle with space enough only for a bed, a table, and two wooden chairs, with a small bath off it.

I visited Sam there a number of times. I found it cell-like and depressing and, along with his British publisher, John Calder, tried to devise ways to move him to more comfortable quarters. But it wasn't easy to do Beckett a favor.

He also seemed to resist attempts to make his life more pleasant, in his perverse fashion managing to get a phone on which he could not make overseas calls, declining to have a TV set or stereo equipment (although he loved music) or a bookcase or even a typewriter. He wrote things down in a little notebook in his small, intricate handwriting, kept his engagement records meticulously, and he did always seem to have a bottle of Irish whiskey handy.

With Beckett it was a mistake to suppose that problems readily lent themselves to solutions, or that one thing necessarily led to another. Sam had started to go for walks, and sort of boasted to me—if you could ever say that about Beckett—that he could walk farther than where his own apartment was, five blocks away. One day he had told me he needed some papers from his apartment, so I asked why he didn't go home and pick them up and I would go with him. Beckett threw up his hands. First roadblock: There was too much traffic on his boulevard; it made him dizzy. Well, let's go in a car, I said, pressing on. Beckett replied that he didn't have a car. Not to worry, I said, I'll get the car. Let's drive there. I was greeted with stony silence, and that was the end of that.

Perhaps a major factor was that Suzanne was still at the apartment and Beckett was ambivalent about the idea of seeing her. It was such an archetypical Beckett situation. It was *Endgame* again. Now they were Nagg and Nell in their garbage cans, unable to reach each other. She was ill, dying actually, although I didn't know that, and he was ill. They were separated by only five blocks, yet they couldn't see each other. He needed papers from his apartment, yet he couldn't go there—all the entrances and exits were blocked.

The last time I visited Beckett I brought along an American TV set I had kept in Paris just for possible use with Sam, and a videotape of *Godot* being performed by the inmates of San Quentin Prison. I had previously carted all this heavy equipment—the set, a transformer, and a VCR—in a huge shopping bag through customs to the Pullman St. Jacques, where Beckett used to actually come to my room. Now I lugged it all to the nursing home.

Sam was visibly moved by the tape; the inmates had understood his play. So I thought, now I've got something going that he can enjoy in this arid place—we can have a correspondence utilizing video-tapes. As I left, I casually asked Beckett if he would store the set for future viewings. "Oh no, no, no," Sam answered, "I have no use for it." And the subject was closed.

As I struggled out with my shopping bag, he said: "Oh, Barney, that's too heavy for you. You shouldn't carry that." Then he walked over, lifted it, turned to me, and said, "No, it's all right. You can." Again: You can't go on, you'll go on.

It was clear that the prospect of the introduction of ease or entertainment into his life distracted Beckett from the larger endgame already embarked on in his mind. A few months later he was *Not I*, as in the title of one of his plays. There was, at last, an *Act Without Words*.

Sam died on December 22, 1989. He was buried next to Suzanne, who had died six months earlier, in the famous Cimetière du Montparnasse.

I was told that Barbara Bray was one of the few mourners at the secretive funeral. I received a letter from her that began:

Dear Barney,
What can I say? We are all huddled together in our loss.

Ave Virgil
Thomas Bernhard

—*Translated from German by James Reidel*

> *I sat upon the shore*
> *Fishing, with the arid plain behind me*
> *Shall I at least set my lands in order?*
>
> —T. S. Eliot, *The Waste Land*

I.

WEDDING PARTY

Where did you hear me in this cold . . .
    Where did I bring names and contra-names
into the story, into this account
    out of poverty, my specter . . . My Word picked
sheep, pigs, whipped oxen in calf,
    drank from the back of the cow . . .
in thousand-year-old books
    my father's plow scarred the stars back and forth . . .

Octobers mowed down the truth,
    the wild wheat, the black cities,
to the very edges and into the darkness
    in a gull's cry, in a donkey's bray . . .

I spoke for many, but to speak
    I had to fly up
like one of these birds,

flailing through the earth,
    converging with millennia,
boring through the firmament . . .

October, my old chum, my humble father,
    prodigious alcohol

who scrawls "hell, hell, hell, hell"
    on my intestinal walls,
beer drinker for the poor,
    frostbite carrier for the mediocrity,

Me in the forest,
me in the cold,
me in the rivers,
me in the thick books,
me on the hillsides . . .

The autumn commingled with its triumph
the language of the thrush,
caned the serpent undergrowth, made Raftery[1]
    rise
        ". . . and death will never come
near us, never ever in the sweet wood . . ."

I fought the idiot winters
down in the valley,
I came up the autumn slopes,
above me
flocks of hopeless birds,
the dying of gill-less fish
below me . . .
                a priest paralytic
in the pulpit of the Milky Way . . .

Bride:

Nothing but dead faces
and then
nothing but dead trades
dead time and dead dying
dead pastures, dead fields
dead farms, dead cows
dead pigs, dead streams
and in the streams
dead fish

---

[1]The blind Irish bardic poet Anthony Raftery (1779–1835).

dead prayers, dead women
dead cities, dead winters
and then

dead knowing and dead crying
dead autumn and dead spring
the dead madness of my dead soul . . .

Bridegroom:

What kind of dead are they without a sea,
what kind of questions are they, what kind of answers,
what kind of people are they . . .

What kind of children are they without spring,
what kind of conversations are they without substance,
what kind of dead ends are they, tell
what kind of desperate dogs are they . . .

What kind of snowflakes are they without eyes,
what kind of surrenders are they,
what kind of words are they that don't comfort,
what kind of a cold is this . . .

What kind of mornings are without skies,
what kind of men are without women,
what kind of women are without men,
what kind of cows are without milk,
what kind of churches are without priests . . .

What kind of dreams come without the dead,
what kind of winters are without white,
what kind of graves are these, what kind of . . .
what kind of screams are without crying . . .

You wake up at three in the morning . . .
                              to harness horses,
     to roll barrels,
that wrecked piano gets swept away . . .
     to pigs grunting . . .
sleep, sleep, sleep,

laughing, coughing, puking, laughing,
    a sentence you have already heard before
or read in a book . . . The closing of the cellar door,
    two horses, seven or eight people,
the voices from another shore . . .
    Zell am See . . . Caliban, the barkeep . . . bursts of laughter . . .
crammed in, shrieking, galloping . . .
    soon the sleigh is on the frozen lake,
    soon there is only a line on the lake,
    soon there is only a black line in the white night . . .

II.

WINTER MORNING

Not that I am incapable
of pronouncing Your Name . . .

and they lynched me in the village square,
    tossed me in a dark pit
and spat upon my skull
    and even fought over my dick,

reverend Father,
    please accept my stammer,
give me a pronoun

that called none of my fatherly hosts
    for a cask,
no pig for its oink . . .

Legends, winters, overpopulations . . .
those wild leaves in the rainy autumn during sleep,
    that early stupidity of nights drunk dry,
    a ratio of black snow
to newlyweds . . .
    Wind and pain and truth
above the shadows of the world . . .
    the unmade bed,
the cry of the dark bird . . .

Thomas Bernhard

In the wheat field:

Had I not paid the price for my life
    before I told the dark apart from darkness . . .
praised the evening's cool glory too soon . . .

Ships, my brothers of the horizon,
    tell me about my mother . . .
. . . where my brother stood on the shore,
    where my sister slept off her falseness,

I spoke of the green of apples and the winter bran,
    I searched through my coat pockets . . .
I spread nonsense psalms from the pulpit,
    cast down bird cries in this utter *wheatness* . . .

Two thousand years after you,
    I discovered the cities,
I perished on the hill,
    a charred skull from the north I . . .

The heat lightning of every star hits me,
    it gave me the tongue of foreign people,
the alphabet of Virgil, the diction of my country folk . . .[2]

Two thousand years after you,
    I am in the countryside, sick,
freezing in December's beds . . .

FREUMBICHLER INN[3]

Through the window:

Who slept together with *my* chin,
    bore *my* leg in the war and *my* arm?

---

[2]An allusion to the *Bucolics* and *Georgics*, the epic poems of rural life and social commentary by Virgil, on which Bernhard has modeled *Ave Virgil*.
[3]An ironical reference to Bernhard's mother's family name and the household in which he was raised, that of the minor Austrian poet Johannes Freumbichler (1881–1949).

Thomas Bernhard

Not that I lived do I want to protest,
  not that I died and died *deeper*,
not that I was *once* and *no one*
in a word remembered . . .

  Not that I outlasted their jaws
and overwhelmed their stupid nonsense,
not that I talked like a madman:

          apostles of ham,
          depraved parishioners,
          choking you,

            those ushers in the forests,
          those evil twins
            of impotent rivers . . .

        inside the confessional booth
            the virus crawls between your testicles,
        the sour psalm

        rained down on you
            with the dropped apples
          of your children's children . . .

and then:

What of this necrosis is *Yours*
and what in this necrosis is *mine?*
    I couldn't suffer You without knowing,
You or I
or anyone sleeping with my name,
You, who confuses me with someone else,
who wakes me up for someone else,
You, who proscribed me from their self-importance,
You, who discovered me, You my only poetry . . .

In the village below:

BREWMASTER, LORD UNWORTHY
   in archbishop's purple,
shadow colonel in exile,

my voice is the voice
   of last rite's oil,
my voice is the voice of sorrow . . .

Priests with your watered-down wine,
   pawning you,
a horde of parish clerks,

   . . . the night is long before God,
immoral is the evening star . . .

you who pursued
   and whipped me
in the twilight of the blackbird,

you who abandoned me,
   me, a head of cattle,
pissed away like beer . . .

No stanza have I borne for the amusement
   this stupid province,
I sleep through my poetry unwashed.

        . . . and you knowing nothing
        about the rustle of the rowanberry,
        about other lives
        that were my life
        and were never my life,

        many lives' life
        and unheard of
        and nothing
        and without question . . .

Thomas Bernhard

At the crossroads I read
    the small minds of peasants,
the lonely dying of the birds,
    in the streams I find
April gnawed,
    the ulcer,
the carcasses of winter deer . . .

My poetry on a foundation
    of prose,
my betrayal,
here,
there.

Four times, five times, ever sharper:

    In these houses my beer
                drinking
    in conversations of air,
      in the cold of thinking . . .

Not one of my grave diggers
    dug me up
    my early despair . . .

    With the stick of cheese making, with the
          clatter of wood shoes,
    am I, for no reason,
      the bone dust of my
        debt-ridden neighbors . . .

    Going forth, worthless, moving on,
     you turn away from their
           funerals . . .
  that exhaustion without feeling,

   the long evenings in the grist mill
          of accusation . . .
  sail away, sail away,
    you need no judge . . .
    sail away . . .

Away

Where did I put my ship's ticket . . .
    black fellow,
do you have my ticket . . .

who as I stand alone
    in Piccadilly Circus
cannot say YES to the world

and can't say NO either,
    and my ship's ticket . . .
where is my ship's ticket . . .

ask the woman with the blue
    umbrella, with the blue heart,
with the blue compass,

ask the man who has folded up
    The Sunday Times
and where is he now . . .

ask at Trafalgar Square . . .
    O you in your parable
amid nothing but strange men and women,

happily dead and gone
    with the birds,
and where is my ship's ticket . . .

on Lambeth Bridge and down below . . .
    and who cries down below . . .
and who remembers me . . .

and the skulls . . . the women
    with their carbon necks,
the elegant all-lookalike,

nothing but philosophy
    and black walls and like a song
that tree with black fingers

leading it into the night . . .
  the day before yesterday, yesterday . . .
Two lay in their own blood,

spraying it into the air,
  they got seasick on the upper deck,
sucking in their cheeks . . .

you must go for a walk every day
  in Hyde Park for an hour,
down Oxford Street,

don't forget Charing Cross,
  those black girls
with those black hearts,

or that white heart
  under their black skin,
who knows that . . .

III.

GRIEF

Every day wakes up to some abuse,
  in my narrative
the legend of my grief is embedded,
  with a thousand years of grief
I prevailed over my filthy life,
  but not over the common sense of winter cold . . .

In barrooms you tear at
  this little shred of your tragedy,
no woods, no reward, no archangel . . .

Above birds swarm, mowing down your poetry,
  mowing and mowing life insistent . . .
nothing for anyone
  in the proximity of this dream,
nothing for lovers in this life . . .

Fruit of rottenness,
    a miserable sun . . .
Temple ruins, broken pieces pile up
    on the rediscovered shore . . .
in dark courtyards opened books . . .
    Verses on abandoned walls . . .

          . . . *not* the perfect,
not the dead who drove you into the cities . . .
          Trust in your song.
You plow the earth with your fragments,
cold produced you . . .
You, left behind by your makers . . .

First Song:

It is about the purging of all our feelings
from the newspapers and from the narrow streets,
from the concerts
and from evening prayers,

it is about the purging of our waking up,
it is about every good intention
and against all despair,
it is about the coexistence of twin absurdities . . .

it is not about this city and not about another city,
it is not about this earth and not about another earth,
it is not about tomorrow and not about the day after tomorrow,
it is not about all that is and what is not,
it is about nothing but us both . . .

Second Song:

Where in the world are you, if not
    in these ears of grain, in this degradation,
    if not in my nearness, then nowhere,

didn't you hear *why* I said NO,
didn't you hear my eulogy
that had nothing to do with pity,
only with our dead parents . . .

Where in the world are you, so that I can
go and find you there. . .
But my death is as final as your death,
I want to tell you that . . .

Third Song:

Winter, I was ashamed of my speech,
calling, calling,
lacking an echo I was a withered tree
without roots . . .
                      I asked the woods,
foul and head deep
with rotting soldiers, no longer living
a life even *close* to life . . .

I did not mention the word of God,
                      waking the toad and the partridge,
the fat pheasant and the hungry crows
with my plaint . . .

Fourth Song:

Words seek words, going
from one mouth to the other . . .
. . . and into your cities
and into your darkness
and into your silent word . . . nothing . . .
bearing grief, leading
conversation of different words
into open wordless books . . .

Fifth Song:

Lacking every skill I looked at this sea,
possessed by the idea of destruction,
by the soundless relapse into the ode of youth . . .

Wherever you cry
I am . . .
a thousand years
to this day
and a thousand years later
with you
always
when you cry,
and many
are killing you
and many
you cry to
and always . . .
wherever you cry
I am . . .

Scenes in Verona

Frozen solid in my country, I have
   gone ahead of the truth,
patrons, my upholders,
   twice through the winter of poetry
into the faltering light of the Milky Way . . .

I.

In the century of cows,
Catullus, "gens Valeria . . ."[4]
In the drought-stricken valley
you led the dialogue with the dead,
   upon dark names you have
established your silence:
   Two bird shadows
   Two nevers
   Two without end

---

[4]The Roman poet Catullus (84 BCE–54 BCE) was born in Verona.

II.

Great suffering was not their strong point,
they invoked the future
and called on you to explain . . .
  Two thousand years too little lived,
this destroyed you . . . once they
were devoid of time, were
without end . . .
  He wept, withdrawing into her dream,
awaited the undulant wordings
  of her beauty . . .
she felt nothing,
  he entered this NOTHING . . .

III.

With what
  right to these places,
with *what* right . . . ?

IV.

Whispering shapes drew the darkness
  over you,
broken chains, where you existed,
  whipping yourself with the scourge of birds . . .
a monument to boredom on the hills of frost,
  the days stay black
and you in your hunger.

V.

At the foot of the grave I heard
  your voice
in the crows rising up,
  with cheap lies I tried to hold you
on the river's banks . . .

VI.

Who wrote before me,
  that no one lived before you
  and no one died
and no one existed in me,

who wrote before me,
that spring was winter
and winter spring,

who wrote before me:
that our names were:
a *black* green,
a *dull* red,

who wrote before me
that the cold wind came and cold death
entered those cold graves?

VII.

you in your shadows,
you in your waking up,
you in your time,
you in your glory,
you in your word,
you!

VIII.

On the hillsides along the Adige,
I learned days and nights.

IX.

With my finely sharpened knife
I scratched your beauty
into the skin of heaven,

I dressed your wound with snow,
and dried your blood like the wind . . .

X.

For a long time I did not know
who they were,
I trusted their cries for help,

told them about the cry
of our crying,
because *my* country betrayed me.

XI.

I tore the noble faces
of ancient races from paintings.

XII.

The orders of the night
last on.
    you spend it in books,
me the earth holding back
    its thoughts.

IV.

YOUR DEATH IS NOT MY DEATH

i.

. . . watch how the mole digs . . .

II.

Hymn to Mercury, hymn to Aldebaran,[5]

III.

before the rose the thorn,
    before the light the shadow,
before the old death . . .

IV.

the dusty chronicles,
the eight-hundred-year-old names
have betrayed you . . .

V.

Then I came before you in your suffering
    as though you were filth
and could suffer me . . .

VI.

that ludicrous phrase of your death
    never fails for me on high feast days . . .

---

[5]One of the Orphic hymns and the star of fortune and fame in astrology.

VII.

with a number of dirty cows,
   am I their shadow of killing time . . .

VIII.

My shoe just proves how sad these songs are
   and how few sing along with me, today no one,
      I don't know anymore *why* they're all silent . . .

IX.

My prayer leader, for you I press
   out my worthless eyes,
with an honest tongue I speak to day laborers,
   in your name
I bandage the inner strife
   with sleep . . . with the treetops . . .

X.

Until I got down, my knees hurt,
the thought of my grave made me shake,
my grave, far greater than the grave of the longest funeral,
yet higher than who survived me,
who died alone in someone else's grave.

XI.

In the end Death descended into life,
   slaying many while waking up,
   going to work, tired, insensible.

V.

OCTOBER

The mother crying on that pile of rubble
   means nothing,
nor the drunken father's intercession,
   nor the death report of the lieutenant,
nor the cardinals rising up,
   nor the blame of the future,
nor entire peoples weeping,

51

nor the killing air,
    the end of the oceans . . .

I dig up the buried beetles,
   the humiliation,
I raise my impotence

to my rotten mouth,
   to my shriveled brain
during my morning's wretchedness . . .

At night
   you make up for the world's conflagrations
with my brotherly idiocy . . .

CHORAL:

What does the day want from me,
asking me questions, a hundred thousand questions,
showing me names,
stirring up my mindlessness with its crying . . .

What does the day want from me,
nailing me to a thick tree,
wiping its blood into the corners of my eyes,
so that I see no land anymore, nothing . . .

What does the day want from me,
pounding stakes into my flesh and making me sing . . .

Song of the Butcher's Boy

You skillfully cut this white
   body in two,
you misuse the tools
   of my tears,
with both knives you cut
   into October's skull . . .
my death, my dispatched bird,
   the one who convinced me . . .

I am, Father,
    an evangelist of the deformed,
above
    and below,
mightily herding
    the lambs in my head
together,
    I, the butcher's boy,
sitting with my PASCAL in the slaughterhouse . . .
on the doorpost hangs my brain;
    for as long as I can remember
it rots . . .

When my morning, the morning of the world mix together,
when the sea emerges from the forest
and the houses take on the color of the afternoon,
    the pestilent face of the dull summer,
when ninety thousand awake and a hundred thousand,

I pose to the ninety thousand
    the hundred-thousandfold question following the lies of this world.

Dried Out

Rome ruined
my awe
with the sick feeling
of its antiquity,

Catania, a bitch
at the foot of Etna,
Syracuse, a monument
to boredom . . .

                    In Sapri I slept through
                    that ugly sea
                    on a scaffold . . .
                    bitten by pines . . .

the festering beach
on the west coast
produced my tears
from the swimmers' pores,

I created the waves
over them,
I murdered them,
vipers from the north,

their appearance
on the sand
made the tragedy
all the more laughable . . .

Reggio, Calabria,
dull thuds,
clockwork . . . the deadly
knife sharpening of the trains . . .

that woman from England
pursued me
all the way to the cactuses . . .
my heart broke hers . . .

Taormina, tropical February.
From Calabria
I posted
deadly letters.

VI.

WHO IN THIS CITY

Who is the morning in this city,
with what right
to other men with open minds,
not the soldiers' story,
not my concoction . . .

Who lived because of me in this city,
merely made an echo
incapable of one jot of truth,
furthered nothing but the sobbing of the dog souled
in the afternoon heat . . .

Who can't bear the beating in this city,
the fourteen-hour-long tribunal,
the unceasing interrogations of the night . . .
Who wouldn't die in this city
relegated to the margins of great sentences,
outside great books
down, like the pigs
down into oblivion . . . ?

You on the avenue of thought . . .
　　　　　　cow-brained fields steam
in perfection.
Conquerors of the world:
　　　　　　Dante, Virgil, Pascal

Karakorum/Mönchsberg[6]

Where is your pact with the fatherland,
that dirty piece of paper?

When you ask, no one knows where you are,
no one has ever seen you, still less heard,
the tree doesn't know your name, the city doesn't,
in not one street have they sought you out . . .

When you ask, will the winter answer,
it knows nothing, nor the mayor,
nor the governor in the *Residenz,*[7]
not once among the dogs are you the talk of the town . . .

[6]Mönchsberg is a hill and fortress that overlooks Salzburg, the city in this poem. Bernhard has ironically juxtaposed it with the ruined Mongol capital of Karakorum in Mongolia.
[7]I.e., the Salzburg Residenz, a baroque palace and seat of the regional government.

When you ask, they shake their heads . . .
When you ask, all are dead, dying
for nothing and for this alone, that no one would know . . .
         no one weeps for him
because he was no more or no less like everyone else . . .

Decades sacrificed
    for some rained-out procession,
for some ridiculous poor man's sermon,
for the character of the butcher,
    for the gnawed laurel
of crude fantasies . . .

Decades sacrificed . . .
    embroiled in the discussions
of an infinite November,

I gave order to the disorder,
    I buried the rotting limbs
in the shadows of tall trees . . .

VII.

WITH ME AND MY COUNTRY

Where I lived is
    hearing your obscene voice,
not a single verdict
    did I dream up in your shadow . . .

My relationship to its rivers
    is between you and me,
I have but one thought:
    to sell this stupid country
                down the river,
these hopeless tributaries with all
the children and children's children . . .

I get my wisdom
    from potato diggers,
from the darkness of pigsties

Thomas Bernhard

I have studied heaven and earth,
I am my endless psalm
    in the stone till of October apples . . .

Without you to see, I listen
    to what you say, I am always
in your houses,
    in the darkness of *your* house
I know *my* father
    as the inventor of my death,
as the bringer of my sorrow,
    as its prime author,
as the father of my crime . . .

Who speaks from the bush?
. . . the evening is silent.
They found me dazed . . .
    I knew no stanza, no verse,
still everyone rose up against everything . . .
as if I had not appeared in their cities:
    like cold wind, like a curse of the elements . . .

With this pathetic country alone
    don't think . . .
    neither open windows, nor open doors,
    just legible inscriptions on the gravestones.

                              1959/60

NOTE. *Ave Virgil* originated in England during 1959 and '60, from everything
in Oxford, and in Sicily, from everything in Taormina. For twenty years I had
forgotten about it. Then I rediscovered it among other poems from that
period, of which about thirty could be destroyed, and the reason to publish
it now is the state of mind in which I found myself at the end of the fifties—
the beginning of the sixties—recreated and concentrated into this poem as
in no other. During this time, after graduating from the Mozarteum, my
theater studies occupied me as did everything written by Eliot (*The Waste
Land*), Pound, Eluard, and César Vallejo as well, and the Spaniards Rafael
Alberti and Jorge Guillén.   *—Th. B. 1981*

From Antwerp
Roberto Bolaño

—Translated from Spanish by Natasha Wimmer

TOTAL ANARCHY: TWENTY-TWO YEARS LATER

I WROTE THIS FOR MYSELF, but even that I can't be sure of. For a long time these were just loose pages that I reread and maybe tinkered with, convinced I had no *time*. But time for what? I couldn't say exactly. I wrote this for the ghosts, who, because they're outside of time, are the only ones with time. After the last rereading (just now), I realize that time isn't the only thing that matters, time isn't the only source of terror. Pleasure can be terrifying too, and so can courage. In those days, if memory serves, I lived exposed to the elements, without my papers, the way other people live in castles. I never brought this novel to any publishing house, of course. They would've slammed the door in my face and I'd have lost the copy. I didn't even make what's technically termed a clean copy. The original manuscript has more pages: The text tended to multiply itself, spreading like a sickness. My sickness, back then, was pride, rage, and violence. Those things (rage, violence) are exhausting and I spent my days uselessly tired. I worked at night. During the day I wrote and read. I never slept. To keep awake, I drank coffee and smoked. Naturally, I met interesting people, some of them the product of my own hallucinations. I think it was my last year in Barcelona. The scorn I felt for so-called official literature was great, though only a little greater than my scorn for marginal literature. But I believed in literature: Or rather, I didn't believe in arrivisme or opportunism or the whispering of sycophants. I did believe in vain gestures, I did believe in fate. I didn't have children yet. I was still reading more poetry than prose. In those years (or months), I was drawn to certain science fiction writers and certain pornographers, sometimes antithetical authors, as if the cave and the electric light were mutually exclusive. I read Norman Spinrad, James Tiptree Jr. (whose real name was Alice B. Sheldon), Restif de la Bretonne, and de Sade. I also read Cervantes and the archaic Greek poets. When I got sick I reread

Manrique. One night I came up with a scheme to make money outside the law. A small criminal enterprise. The basic idea was not to get rich too fast. My first accomplice or attempt at an accomplice, a terribly sad Argentinian friend, responded to my scheme with a saying that went something like this: If you have to be in prison or in the hospital, then the best place to be is your own country, for the visitors, I guess. His response didn't have the slightest effect on me, because I felt equally distant from all the countries in the world. Later I gave up my plan when I discovered that it was worse than working in a brick factory. Tacked up over my bed was a piece of paper on which I'd asked a friend from Poland to write, in Polish, Total Anarchy. I didn't think I was going to live past thirty-five. I was happy. Then came 1981, and before I knew it, everything had changed.

—Blanes, 2002

When I consider the brief span of my life absorbed into the eternity which comes before and after—memoria hospitis unius diei praetereuntis—the small space I occupy and which I see swallowed up in the infinite immensity of spaces of which I know nothing and which know nothing of me, I take fright and am amazed to see myself here rather than there: There is no reason for me to be here rather than there, now rather than then. Who put me here? By whose command and act were this place and time allotted to me?

—Pascal

GREEN, RED, AND WHITE CHECKS

Now he, or half of him, rises up on a tide. The tide is white. He has taken a train going in the wrong direction. He's the only one in the compartment, the curtains are open, and the dusk clings to the dirty glass. Swift, dark, intense colors unfurl across the black leather of the seats. We've created a silent space so that he can work somehow. He lights a cigarette. The box of matches is sepia colored. On the lid is a drawing of a hexagon made of twelve matches. It's labeled "Playing with Matches," and, as indicated by a 2 in the upper lefthand corner, it's the second game in a series. This game is called the Great Triangle Escape. Now his attention comes to rest on a pale object. After a while he realizes that it's a square that's beginning to disintegrate. What he at first imagined was a screen becomes a white tide, white words, panes whose transparency is replaced by a blind and permanent whiteness. Suddenly a shout focuses his attention. The brief sound is like a color swallowed by a crack. But what color? The phrase "The train stopped in a northern town" distracts him from a shifting of shadows in the next seat. He covers his face with his fingers, spread wide enough so that he can spot any object coming at him. He searches for cigarettes in the pockets of his jacket. With the first puff, it occurs to him that monogamy moves with the same rigidity as the train. A cloud of opaline smoke covers his face. It occurs to him that the word "face" creates its own blue eyes. Someone shouts. He looks at his feet planted on the floor. The word "shoes" will never levitate. He sighs, turning his face to the window. A darker light seems to have settled over the land. Like the light in my head, he thinks. The train is running along the edge of a forest. In some spots, traces of recent fires are visible. He isn't surprised not to see anyone on the edge of the forest. But this is where the little hunchback lives, down a bicycle path, a few miles deeper in. I told him I'd heard enough. There are rabbits and rats here that look like squirrels. The forest is bordered by the highway to the west and the railroad tracks to the east. Nearby there are gardens and tilled fields, and, closer to the city, a polluted river lined with junkyards and Gypsy camps. Beyond that is the sea. The hunchback opens a can of food, resting his hump against a small rotted pine. Someone shouted at the other end of the car, possibly a woman, he said to himself as he stubbed the cigarette out against the sole of his shoe. His shirt is long sleeved, cotton, with green, red, and white checks. The hunchback holds a can of sardines in tomato sauce in his left hand. He's eating. His eyes scan the foliage. He hears the train go by.

I'M MY OWN BEWITCHMENT

The ghosts of the Plaza Real are on the stairs. Blankets pulled up to my ears, motionless in bed, sweating and repeating meaningless words to myself, I hear them moving around, turning the lights on and off, climbing up toward the roof with unbearable slowness. I'm the moon, someone proposes. But I used to be in a gang and I had the Arab in my sights and I pulled the trigger at the most inopportune moment. Narrow streets in the heart of Distrito V, and no way to escape or alter the fate that slid like a djellaba over my greasy hair. Words that drift away from one another. Urban games played from time immemorial . . . "Frankfurt" . . . "A blonde girl at the biggest window of the boarding house" . . . "There's nothing I can do now" . . . I'm my own bewitchment. My hands move over a mural in which someone, eight inches taller than me, stands in the shadows, hands in the pockets of his jacket, preparing for death and his subsequent transparency. The language of others is unintelligible to me. "Tired after being up for days" . . . "A blonde girl came down the stairs" . . . "My name is Roberto Bolaño" . . . "I opened my arms" . . .

CLEANING UTENSILS

All praise to the highways and to these moments. Umbrellas abandoned by bums in shopping plazas with white supermarkets rising at the far ends. It's summer and the policemen are drinking at the back of the bar. Next to the jukebox a girl listens to the latest hits. Around the same time, someone is walking, far from here, away from here, with no plans of coming back. A naked boy sitting outside his tent in the woods? The girl stumbled into the bathroom and began to vomit. When you think about it, we're not allotted much time here on earth to make lives for ourselves: I mean, to scrape something together, get married, wait for death. Her eyes in the mirror like letters fanned out in a dark room; the huddled breathing shape burrowed into bed with her. The men talk about dead small-time crooks, the price of houses on the coast, extra paychecks. One day I'll die of cancer. Cleaning utensils begin to levitate in her head. She says: I could go on and on. The kid came into the room and grabbed her by the shoulders. The two of them wept like characters from different movies projected on the same screen. Red scene of bodies and turning on the gas. The bony beautiful hand turned the knob. Choose just one of these phrases: "I escaped torture" . . . "An unknown hotel" . . . "No more roads" . . .

Roberto Bolaño

AMONG THE HORSES

I dreamed of a woman with no mouth, says the man in bed. I couldn't help smiling. The piston forces the images up again. Look, he tells her, I know another story that's just as sad. He's a writer who lives on the edge of town. He makes a living working at a riding school. He's never asked for much; all he needs is a room and time to read. But one day he meets a girl who lives in another city and he falls in love. They decide to get married. The girl will come to live with him. The first problem arises: finding a place big enough for the two of them. The second problem is where to get the money to pay for it. Then one thing leads to another: a job with a steady income (at the stables he works on commission, plus room, board, and a small monthly stipend), getting his papers in order, social security, etc. But for now, he needs money to get to the city where his fiancée lives. A friend suggests the possibility of writing articles for a magazine. He calculates that the first four would pay for the bus trip there and back and maybe a few days at a cheap hotel. He writes his girlfriend to tell her he's coming. But he can't finish a single article. He spends the evenings sitting outdoors at the bar of the riding school where he works, trying to write, but he can't. Nothing comes out, as they say in common parlance. The man realizes that he's finished. All he writes are short crime stories. The trip recedes from his future, is lost, and he remains listless, inert, going automatically about his work among the horses.

MY ONE TRUE LOVE

On the wall someone has written *my one true love.* She put the cigarette between her lips and waited for the man to light it for her. She was pale skinned and freckled and had mahogany-colored hair. Someone opened the back door of the car and she got in silently. They glided along the deserted streets of a residential neighborhood. It was the time of year when most of the houses were empty. The man parked on a narrow street of single-story houses with identical yards. She went into the bathroom and he made coffee. The kitchen had brown tiles patterned with arabesques, and looked like a gym. She opened the curtains; there were no lights in any of the houses across the street. She took off her satin dress and the man lit another cigarette for her. Before she pulled down her underpants the man arranged her on all fours on the soft white rug. She heard him look for something in the wardrobe. A wardrobe built into the wall, a red wardrobe. She watched him upside down, through her legs. The man smiled at her. Now someone is walking down a street where cars are parked only next to their respective lairs. Above the street, like a hanged man, swings the spotlit sign of the neighborhood's best res-taurant, closed a long time ago. Footsteps vanish down the street, headlights are visible in the distance. She said no. She listens. There's someone outside. The man went over to the window, then came back naked toward the bed. She was freckled and sometimes she pre-tended to be asleep. He looked at her from the door with a kind of detached sweetness. There are silences made just for us. He pressed his face against hers until it hurt and pushed himself into her with a single thrust. Maybe she screamed a little. From the street, however, nothing could be heard. They fell asleep without moving apart. Someone walks away. We see his back, his dirty pants and his down-at-the-heel boots. He goes into a bar and settles himself at the coun-ter as if he felt a prickling all over his body. His movements produce a vague, disturbing sensation in the other drinkers. Is this Barcelona? he asked. At night the yards look alike, by day the impression is dif-ferent, as if desires were channeled through the plants and flower beds and climbing vines. "They take good care of their cars and yards" . . . "Someone has made a silence especially for us" . . . "First he moved in and out and then in a circular motion" . . . "Her but-tocks were covered in scratches" . . . "The moon hides behind the only tall building in the neighborhood" . . . "Is this Barcelona?" . . .

THEY TALK BUT THEIR WORDS DON'T REGISTER

It's absurd to see an enchanted princess in every girl who walks by. What do you think you are, a troubadour? The skinny adolescent whistled in admiration. We were on the edge of the reservoir and the sky was very blue. A few fishermen were visible in the distance and smoke from a chimney rose over the trees. Green wood, for burning witches, said the old man, his lips hardly moving. The point is, there are all kinds of pretty girls in bed at this very moment with tech-nocrats and executives. Five yards from me, a trout leaped. I put out my cigarette and closed my eyes. Close-up of a Mexican girl reading.

She's blonde, with a long nose and narrow lips. She looks up, turns toward the camera, smiles: streets damp after the rains of August, September, in a Mexico City that doesn't exist anymore. She walks down a residential street in a white coat and boots. With her index finger she presses the button for the elevator. The elevator arrives, she opens the door, selects the floor, and glances at herself in the mirror. Just for an instant. A man, thirty, sitting in a red armchair, watches her come in. He's dark haired and he smiles at her. They talk but their words don't register on the soundtrack. Anyway, they must be saying things like how was your day, I'm tired, there's an avocado sandwich in the kitchen, thanks, thanks, a beer in the refrigerator. Outside it's raining. The room is cozy, with Mexican furniture and Mexican rugs. The two of them are lying in bed. Small white flashes of lightning. Entwined and still, they look like exhausted children. Though they have no reason to be tired. The camera zooms out. Give me all the information in the world. A blue stripe splits the window in two halves. Like a blue hunchback? He's a bastard but he knows how to feign tenderness. He's a bastard but the hand on her side is gentle. Her face is buried between the pillow and her lover's neck. The camera zooms in: impassive faces that somehow, without intending to, shut you out. The author stares for a long time at the plaster masks, then covers his face. Fade to black. It's absurd to think that this is where all the pretty girls come from. Empty images follow one after the other: the reservoir and the woods, the cabin with a fire in the hearth, the lover in a red robe, the girl who turns and smiles at you. There's nothing diabolic about any of it. The wind tosses the neighborhood trees. A blue hunchback on the other side of the mirror? I don't know. A girl heads away, walking her motorcycle toward the end of the boulevard. If she keeps on in the same direction, she'll reach the sea. Soon she'll reach the sea.

TWENTY-SEVEN

The only possible scene is the one with the man running on the path through the woods. Someone blinks a blue bedroom. Now he's twenty-seven and he gets on a bus. He's smoking a cigarette, has short hair, is wearing jeans, a dark shirt, a hooded jacket, boots, the dark glasses of a political commissar. He's sitting next to the window; beside him a workman on his way back from Andalucía. He gets on a train at the station in Zaragoza, he looks back, the mist has risen to the knees of a track worker. He smokes, coughs, rests his forehead on the bus window. Now he's walking around a strange city, a blue bag in his hand, his hood pulled up, it's cold, with each breath he expels a puff of smoke. The workman sleeps with his head resting on his shoulder. He lights a cigarette, glances at the plains, closes his eyes. The next scene is yellow and cold and on the soundtrack birds beat their wings. (He says: I'm a cage—it's a private joke—then he buys cigarettes and walks away from the camera.) He's sitting in a train station at dusk, he does a crossword puzzle, he reads the international news, he tracks the flight of a plane, he moistens his lips with his tongue. Someone coughs in the darkness, a cold clear morning from the window of a hotel; he coughs. He goes out to the street, pulls up the hood of his blue jacket, buttons all the buttons except the top one. He buys a pack of cigarettes, takes one, stops on the sidewalk by the window of a jewelry shop, lights a cigarette. He has short hair. He walks with his hands in the pockets of his jacket, the cigarette dangles from his lips. The scene is a close-up of the man with his forehead resting on the window. The rest is tiny passageways that hardly ever lead anywhere. The glass is foggy. Now he's twenty-seven and he gets off the bus. He heads down a deserted street.

A WHITE HANDKERCHIEF

I'm walking in the park, it's fall, looks like somebody got killed. Until yesterday I thought my life could be different, I was in love, etc. I stop by the fountain, it's dark, the surface shiny, but when I brush it with the palm of my hand I feel how rough it really is. From here I watch an old cop approach the body with hesitant steps. A cold breeze is blowing, raising goose bumps. The policeman kneels by the body: With a dejected expression, he covers his eyes with his left hand. A flock of starlings rise. They circle over the policeman's head and then disappear. The cop goes through the dead man's pockets and piles what he finds on a white handkerchief that he's spread out on the grass. Dark green grass that seems to want to swallow up the white square. Maybe it's the dark old papers that the cop sets on the handkerchief that make me think this way. I decide to sit down for a while. The park benches are white with black wrought-iron legs.

A police car comes down the street. It stops. Two cops get out. One of them heads toward where the old cop is crouched, the other waits by the car and lights a cigarette. A while later an ambulance silently appears and parks behind the police car. "I didn't see anything" . . . "A dead man in the park" . . . "An old cop" . . .

BIG SILVER WAVES

The foreigner stayed here. That tent you see there was his tent. Go on in. He spent a long time under that tree, thinking, though it looked like he was dead. From where we're standing you could see his face covered in sweat. Big drops formed on his chin and dripped onto the grass. Here, feel, he slept for hours in the weeds here, like a dead man. The guy came into the bar and had a beer. He paid with French money and put the change in his pocket, not counting it. He spoke perfect Spanish. He had a camera, but it's in a police evidence locker now. He walked on the beach in the evening. The beach looks pale, pale yellow, with fading golden splotches in that scene. He dropped onto the sand, like a dead man. The only soundtrack was the dry obsessive cough of someone we could never see. Big silver waves, the guy standing on the beach, barefoot, and the cough. A long time ago were you happy in a tent too? In some corner of his memory there's a scene where he's on top of a thin brown girl. It's nighttime in a deserted campground, somewhere in Portugal. The girl is on her stomach and he moves in and out of her, biting her neck. Then he turns her over. He lifts her legs onto his shoulders and both of them come. An hour later he's on top of her again. (Or as a Conde del Asalto pimp says: "Wham bam wham bam times infinity.") I don't know whether I'm talking about the same person. His camera's with the police now and maybe no one's thought to develop the film. Endless hallways, nightmarish, along which strides a fat tech from the Homicide Squad. The red light is off now, you can come in. The policeman's face relaxes into a smile. From the end of the hallway the silhouette of another policeman approaches. He crosses the stretch that separates him from his colleague and then both of them disappear. *Empty* now, the gray of the hallway quivers or maybe it swells. Then the silhouette of a policeman appears at the other end. He advances until he's in the foreground, pauses. In the background another cop appears. The shadow moves toward the shadow of the cop in the foreground. Both disappear. The smile of a tech from the Homicide Squad keeps watch over these scenes. Fat cheeks drenched in sweat. There's nothing in the photographs. (A stifled attempt at applause.) Nothing we can see. "Call someone, do something" . . . "A fucking cough echoing across the beach" . . . "The tent full of spiderwebs" . . . "Everything is wrecked" . . . "Faces, stray scenes, kaput" . . .

THE MOTORCYCLISTS

Imagine the situation: the nameless girl hiding on the landing—it's an old building, poorly lit, with an open-grille elevator. Behind the door a man of about forty whispers, in a confessional tone, that he too is being chased by Colan Yar. The brown-and-black opening shot fades instantly, giving way to a deep panorama—stores with multi-colored roofs. Then: dark green trees. Then: red sky with clouds. Was a kid asleep in the tent just then? Dreaming of Colan Yar, police cars parked in front of a smoldering building, twenty-year-old criminals? "All the shit in the world" or: "A campground should be the closest thing to Purgatory," etc. With dry, trembling hands he pushed back the curtains. Below, the motorcyclists revved their engines and took off. He whispered "very far away" and clenched his teeth. Fat blondes—young women from Andalucía confident of their appeal— and among them the nameless girl with her guillotine mouth, strolling by the past and the future like a movie face. I imagined my body tossed away in the countryside, just a few yards from the town's first houses. A camper out for a walk found me, he was the one who alerted the police. Now, under the cloudy sky, I'm surrounded by men in blue and white uniforms. The *guardia civil* and the tabloid photographers, or maybe just tourists whose hobby is taking pictures of dead bodies. Gawkers and children. It isn't Paradise, but it's close. The girl goes slowly down the stairs. I opened the office door and ran downstairs. On the walls I saw furious whales, an incomprehensible alphabet. The street noise woke me up. On the opposite sidewalk a man yelled and then wept until the police came. "A body just out-side town" . . . "The motorcyclists are lost on the highway" . . . "No one will ever close this window again" . . .

LIKE A WALTZ

In the train compartment a girl on her own. She looks out the window. Outside everything splits in two: tilled fields, woods, white houses, towns, suburbs, dumps, factories, dogs, and children waving goodbye. Lola Muriel appears. August 1980. I dream of faces that open their mouths and can't speak. They try but they can't. Their blue eyes stare at me but they can't speak. Then I walk along the corridor of a hotel. I wake up sweating. Lola has blue eyes and she reads Poe stories by the pool, while the other girls talk about pyramids and jungles. I dream that I'm watching it rain in neighborhoods that I recognize but have never been in. I walk along an empty passageway. I see faces with eyes that close and mouths that open, though they can't speak. I wake up sweating. August 1980? A girl, eighteen, from Andalucía? The night watchman, madly in love?

LA PAVA ROADSIDE BAR OF CASTELLDEFELS (EVERYONE'S EATEN MORE THAN ONE DISH OR ONE DISH WORTH MORE THAN 200 PESETAS, EXCEPT FOR ME!)

Dear Lisa, once I talked to you on the phone for more than an hour without realizing that you had hung up. I was at a public phone on Calle Bucareli, at the Reloj Chino corner. Now I'm in a bar on the Catalan coast, my throat hurts, and I'm close to broke. The Italian girl said she was going back to Milan to work, even if it made her sick. I don't know whether she was quoting Pavese or she really didn't feel like going back. I think I'll go to the campground nurse for some antibiotics. The scene breaks up geometrically. We see a deserted beach at eight o'clock, tall orange clouds; in the distance a group of five people walk away from the observer in Indian file. The wind lifts a curtain of sand and covers them.

ANTWERP

In Antwerp a man died when his car was run over by a truck full of pigs. Lots of the pigs died too when the truck overturned, others had to be put out of their misery by the side of the road, and others took off as fast as they could . . . "That's right, honey, he's dead and pigs are running over his car" . . . "At night, on the dark highways of Belgium or Catalonia" . . . "We talked for hours in a bar on Las Ramblas; it was summer and she talked as if she hadn't talked for a long time" . . . "When she was done she felt my face like a blind woman" . . . "The pigs squealed" . . . "She said I want to be alone and even though I was drunk I understood" . . . "I don't know, it's something like the full moon, girls who are really like flies, though that's not what I mean" . . . "Pigs howling in the middle of the highway, wounded or rushing away from the smashed-up truck" . . . "Every word is useless, every sentence, every phone conversation" . . . "She said she wanted to be alone" . . . I wanted to be alone too. In Antwerp or Barcelona. The moon. Animals fleeing. Highway accident. Fear.

POSTSCRIPT

Of what is lost, irretrievably lost, all I wish to recover is the daily availability of my writing, lines capable of grasping me by the hair and lifting me up when I'm at the end of my strength. (Significant, said the foreigner.) Odes to the human and the divine. Let my writing be like the verses by Leopardi that Daniel Biga recited on a Nordic bridge to gird himself with courage.

—For Alexandra Bolaño and Lautaro Bolaño
Barcelona 1980

A Simple Question

Francine Prose

As soon as Vogel realized he could end the interrogation simply by staring unblinkingly back into the light, he awoke with the full moon shining in his eyes. He pulled the sheet, scented with lavender water, over his head, but still the moonlight soaked through, pooling on his sleeping wife's chest, which shuddered like a baby's. Even now there were nights when Vogel woke from yet another failure to answer the question that had upended his future as a philosopher and dumped him into his actual life in the family jewelry business. A man can do what he wants but not *want* what he wants. Identify source, and explain. It was Vogel's luck that the examining professor was the one man on the planet immune to the lure of cuff links or perhaps a brooch for the lady.

Exiled from academia, Vogel was still a philosopher. There was no way they could stop him from being a practicing metaphysician with a special interest in how the mind stepped away from itself and watched its own responses. Wasn't everyone like that? Even at a rally, with thousands of people shouting with one voice. Weren't those people conscious of thinking their thousands of separate thoughts? Vogel, for example, was thinking, You can scream all you want about the spilling of precious German blood and our homeland stabbed in the back, but what I am hearing is that the most desirable and formerly elusive clients will now quit shopping in Paris and stay in Berlin, where they belong. How many in the thunderous crowd were contemplating, as was Vogel, all the Jewish-owned jewelry about to come on the market?

He himself had nothing against the Jews. He had met many in his business and had concluded that the proportion of honesty and dishonesty was the same in every population. In fact he despised the smashed windows and his own need to make sure that the ignorant thugs knew he wasn't Jewish. He'd refused to become a party member, and a few sparkly trinkets distributed here and there had worked wonders to lift the pressure on him to join. He didn't believe the Communists would have done any better. And the Republic, bless its naive heart, had had everything stacked against it.

Still, it was insulting to imagine that he or any sentient human would confuse the hook-nosed, slobbering Shylocks in the pamphlets and films with the exquisite Frau Rubinstein, who contacted Vogel and Sons (there were no sons, he'd been the son, and his father was dead) to inquire about selling her earrings. Vogel understood that this would be a very special sort of transaction, requiring a particular set of attitudes and manners. He reached this conclusion not because Frau Rubinstein was beautiful, nor because her earrings, tiny dewdrops of opal and pearl beading up on a pair of golden spiderwebs, made him gasp when she unwrapped their velvet bunting, but because it was a transaction in which so much had to be communicated: regret, nostalgia, helpfulness, respect, collective but not personal shame, mutual awareness of an unfortunate necessity. In other words, civilization.

Vogel paid Frau Rubinstein fairly and managed to leave her feeling as if she had not sold her beloved earrings so much as entrusted them to a kindly uncle who would safeguard them until her circumstances improved. The jeweler longed to ask her to try on the earrings one last time. In his mind he rehearsed a joke about wanting to see them in their natural habitat, twin constellations in the glossy black firmament of her hair. But at the last moment he realized it would have been tasteless and cruel. Sensing hesitation, she asked, "Is there something else?" Vogel shook his head.

Later, this conversation would join the regrets that woke him at night, disguised as the full moon. Sorrow at not having seen the earrings on a woman so radiant with gratitude and terror distracted him momentarily from his grief at having forgotten that the quote, a man can do what he wants, et cetera, was from Schopenhauer.

Predictably, circumstances did not improve for Frau Rubinstein, though she and her family were able to emigrate, partly thanks to the money she received from Vogel. But circumstances did improve for Vogel, who became known among buyers and sellers alike for his fairness and tact. As time went on, the government became interested in Vogel's business. He was required to hand over the diamonds, but it was understood that he was free to set aside the most handsome or unusual pieces for the discriminating buyer. Each time Vogel looked over his stock, deciding which gorgeous bauble might best suit which client, he found himself passing over the opal earrings, which gradually migrated to the back of his safe.

Late one summer afternoon, Vogel received a phone call from a secretary who identified himself as working for a man so powerful that Vogel trembled when he heard the name and could not stop trembling until he decided to think of him not by name but only as Commandant H.G., though he could not have said why this should be any less disturbing. Vogel had imagined this phone call so often that when it finally came, it was as if it had happened so often as to have become tedious. In fact, he'd thought about getting the call less than about *not* getting one. So many others had. Frequently the Commandant summoned the highest-level artisans and purveyors, dealers in furs and antiques, to parties at his villa in the suburbs of Berlin. It was traditional for the guests to lavish their host with gifts, in return for which the Commandant sent the best customers their way.

At one such party, the Commandant arranged for his guests to meet him in a meadow. He drove up in sports car wearing goggles, a leather cap, and a floor-length ermine coat. Shouting through a megaphone, he lectured the group on animal husbandry, then tried to get a bull to mate with a cow as a demonstration, then gave up and ordered the guests to meet him back at the house, where he greeted them dressed as one of the Three Wise Men, in a mink-trimmed turban and a brocade caftan.

Vogel was especially sorry to have missed something like that. Vogel's wife had repeatedly asked him why they weren't invited to the Commandant's, like this or that girlfriend who wasn't any prettier than she was and whose husband wasn't any richer than Vogel.

The car that picked him up was driven by two junior officers in the Luftwaffe. Vogel had hoped to find out from their conversation to what sort of party he'd been asked, but neither of the handsome young men spoke as they headed toward the edge of the city. For a moment Vogel had the ridiculous notion that his companions were uniformed store-window mannequins or ingenious automatons. As the houses grew sparse, and the headlights became the only light beside the moon, he thought, Surely we will be there soon. But they kept on driving. Eventually his uneasiness was replaced by the pleasant sensation that he had waited exactly the right amount of time and was being rewarded for his patience by the fact that the warm air streaming in the windows was scented with orange blossoms, literally inebriating, so that when they turned off the road and a gate swung open, Vogel felt he had already enjoyed a glass or two of expensive champagne.

For another party, the Commandant had managed to find actual Nubians, or anyway black people, whom he costumed in loincloths and gave torches to hold along the path to his front door. But tonight there were no torches—or other cars in the gravel courtyard. The officers ushered Vogel up the steps to a building that looked like the Pergamon Altar. Flanked by the lieutenants, he was escorted along a corridor lined with ancient maps, then through a succession of parlors decorated in silver and gold in the style of the French kings. Had those fleshy pink goddesses been painted by Rubens or Fragonard? Vogel couldn't enjoy, or even marvel at, all this luxury and beauty, so busy was he adjusting to the growing conviction he had been summoned to a small or even a private meeting. What could the Commandant want? Vogel fantasized a little play in which he was asked to assume a high government position or undertake a secret mission for which he was uniquely suited and which, after protesting his unworthiness, he modestly accepted. How proud his wife would be to accompany him here when the borders of their lives expanded to include the Commandant's villa!

Vogel found himself at the door to a huge room, its high ceiling supported by massive rough-hewn beams. Candles burned in candelabras made from braces of antlers, the hides of exotic animals lay about on the floor. At the far end was a fireplace, and in front of it a long couch. On the couch sat a woman with her back to the door. How strange, a roaring fire in July, when one would expect stifling air trapped among the heraldic flags and beneath the fur of the safari trophies. But in fact the room exuded a glacial chill, as if frozen forever in the endless winter of some Teutonic chieftain.

Here the lieutenants left him, and Vogel approached the woman, who continued gazing into the fire, without turning, which was lucky, because more readjustment was required as Vogel understood that he had not been called to see the Commandant but rather his wife, suggesting that his secret mission had something to do with jewelry. Fortunately, he had brought along a pocket watch on an aviation theme for the Commandant, and a pretty bangle for his wife, platinum studded with ruby chips.

That is, for the Commandant's second wife, famously unhappy because her husband was still grieving for the first wife, after whom he named everything: his yachts, his stables, this villa. Every year, on the anniversary of her death, the Commandant held a gathering at which black-robed guests listened to the solemn chanting of monks imported from Greece. Vogel had heard all this from his own wife, who loved this sort of gossip.

As he approached the woman, Vogel noted that the angle of her head and the slope of her shoulders—both bare white arms were outstretched along the top of the couch—expressed some deep mysterious melancholy. She remained so still that Vogel felt as if he were looking at a painting, a painting he'd seen and knew by name: A Woman Sunk in Sorrow. A curl of smoke twisted up from a cigarette she held in an ivory holder. Vogel supposed he should make a warning noise, but the soles of his good leather shoes brushed silently against the marble, and everything else—a cough, a cleared throat—seemed rude and artificial. It occurred to him that the woman knew he was there, and that not acknowledging him was something only a woman would do.

Vogel liked women, whom he found not only charming but usually smarter and wittier than their husbands. And women intuited that, which surprisingly was all it took to be what was called "lucky" with women. They liked it if a man had thoughts that were flowery but not too flowery, and if he told them some of those thoughts, in a slightly ironic tone that created a kind of privacy, just the two of them together.

Also it was amazing what happened to a woman between the moment she admired a piece of jewelry in the window of his store and the moment she walked in and found him alone there. Vogel prided himself on never having taken advantage of the desperate Jewish women, though some of them, like Frau Rubinstein, had been extremely pretty. His standards were more relaxed with the casual shoppers. Vogel's wife had been one of those, and though he didn't believe she had married him for a hat pin, their married joke was that an amethyst had arranged the introduction. Since his wedding, there had been other girls, not many, but enough so that Vogel felt he was still in practice and could deal with whatever the evening ahead might bring. How accommodatingly his fantasies had shifted from power to sex. Obviously, it would be suicide to flirt with the Commandant's wife, but, in Vogel's experience, one could have a lot of fun before it qualified as flirtation.

Energized by the prospect of bringing a smile to the lips of the grieving woman, he walked around in front of her. Of course she knew he was there. She was wearing a sleeveless green velvet gown, Grecian or medieval. She rearranged the skirt, uncrossing and recrossing her legs, as she waved him into the chair at her right. Sighing deeply, she threw back her head and shut her eyes. Then she roused herself and offered Vogel a cigarette from a silver tray, probably Venetian. As he leaned forward to take it, he saw, by the flickering light, what he had known from across the room but had refused to to admit.

It was not the Commandant's wife, but the Commandant. That too was gossip one heard. That the Commander's fondness for extravagant costumes sometimes led him to borrow his wife's gowns. Some said this had started after the death of the first wife, others said he had been like that as a child and as a bold aviator flying bombing missions with blond ringlet wigs stuffed under his helmet. So Vogel was less startled than he might have been to find himself alone with the former President of the Reichstag and the Chief Commandant of the Luftwaffe, in a pair of high-heeled sandals with pom-poms on the straps.

Even so, it was unsettling. Vogel could understand the Commandant indulging this eccentric whim in the company of his wife and trusted friends, but Vogel was a stranger, a jeweler from Berlin. He concentrated on keeping control of his face so that when the Commandant looked at him, he would see . . . what, exactly? No surprise, no surprise in the least. Admiration. Appreciation. Perhaps even that was excessive. A purely relaxed neutral friendliness. Mixed, of course, with respect. But the most important thing was not to show or think that this was in any way abnormal.

The impression of normality was reinforced by the lieutenants, who reappeared with two glasses and a bottle of champagne. One of them filled a glass and gave it to the Commandant, or rather, wrapped the Commandant's free hand around it. Not trusting his voice, Vogel nodded to the officer, who poured him a glass and put the bottle in its cooler on a low table beside Vogel, along with a silver bell. It seemed peculiar that he, the guest, was being given charge of the champagne and the servants' bell until he noticed that the Commandant was drinking with his eyes closed.

Vogel was careful not to look at the officers as they left. He took advantage of the Commandant's somnolence to drain his own glass and refill it. The bubbles popped against his brain like snowflakes hitting a window. How powerful the champagne was, and how little it took to make it seem as if the fire suddenly blazed more brightly, revealing a world infinitely more interesting and less alarming than it had seemed just minutes ago.

The Commandant raised his chin, as if in greeting, then burrowed his head into the crook of his arm, so that he looked like a cross between a sleeping bird and a Romantic painting of a sleeping woman. Vogel had got it right before. A Woman Sunk in Sorrow. The other bit of gossip one heard was that the Commandant was fond of morphine, a habit dating back to a near-fatal wound sustained in the early, violent days of the party. Vogel's eyes brimmed with shocking tears, sympathetic, but someone else's, and he felt a churning inside his chest, as if his heart were being squeezed and prodded to see if it was ready.

The Commandant wore a caplike auburn wig, and his lips were painted a candy heart that matched his rouged cheeks and gave his face an eerily doll-like perfection. His gown was gathered at the breast with a large enamel clasp in the Chinese style that Vogel recognized as having passed through his hands in '38 or '39. In each ear was a large diamond stud. Vulgar, but somehow touching.

Neither male nor female, the Commandant was like a mythological figure who had been both male and female and therefore understood how hard it was to be either. Had Vogel tried to picture this scene, he might have visualized something grotesque, but in person—in the flesh, as it were—the Commandant was lovely. Not lovely like Frau Rubinstein, or like Vogel's wife, or like the two wives of the Commandant, whose photos Vogel had seen, but lovely in his woundedness, in his raw awareness of how painful and lonely it is to live and die in your body. How helpless the Commandant looked as he dozed against the couch, but also how heroic, not like the young aviator he had been, but heroic in his insistence on finding something transcendent and brave amid the grief and suffering everywhere around him. The grief and suffering he has caused *others*, said a voice inside Vogel's head.

Vogel grabbed the lit cigarette from the Commandant's drooping hand. The Commandant's knees slipped apart. Vogel glimpsed a scallop of pale lace and was astonished and embarrassed by a faint tug of arousal. Not sexual arousal, he told himself, but *spiritual* arousal, something he'd felt only twice in his life, both times when he'd gone to hear Bach played in a cathedral. Was it possible to live so long and be homosexual and not know it? But Vogel didn't want to have sex with the Commandant. He wanted to cradle him in his arms and talk to him and tell him secrets and jokes and put his head against his head and never leave his side. He felt a familiar longing, the hollow draining chill he'd felt as a young man, worshipping girls from afar.

Perhaps it would be helpful to frame this as a philosophical question. How reliable is the past as a guide to the future? And couldn't it be said that every anomaly is a bandit lurking in ambush by the side of the road? A man can do what he wants but not *want* what he wants. Maybe this was like Vogel's dream of the philosophy exam, or like any of those dreams in which you can choose to fall to earth by weighing yourself down with reality: your bed, your name, your city, the sleeping woman beside you. In this case the ballast would be what the Commandant had done—the murders, the forced labor. The burning of the Reichstag! But what did the man who had masterminded all that have in common with this fragile, elegant creature who lay, so trusting and vulnerable, half conscious on the couch? And why should he be so unhappy? The war was going well.

Patiently Vogel waited until the Commandant opened his eyes and said, "Good evening" in a voice like someone blowing smoke through a flute.

"Good evening," Vogel replied.

The Commandant clutched his pale throat. "Excuse me. Laryngitis."

"Summer colds are the worst," Vogel said. How banal he sounded! "My mother always said . . ." He paused. Why was he talking about his *mother?*

"So you had a mother?" the Commandant asked. What kind of question was that?

"I did," said Vogel. "Not anymore. Doesn't everybody?" He heard himself rattling nervously on, like a hysterical girl. He didn't even sound like himself. Vogel knew how to talk to women.

"Oh, please," the Commandant said. "Let's not fool each other." He laughed, and Vogel laughed as well, then stopped when the Commandant stopped, or a moment after.

"When I was growing up," the Commandant said, "my mother's lover went hunting every Sunday afternoon. We—the boys—went along, of course. We were living in the man's house. His idea of sport was to wheel a cannon to the edge of a field and blast away at tiny birds and send us to gather the feathers! From which he had fans made for my sisters' dolls. Let me ask you, why would a little girl need fifteen *thousand* feather doll fans?"

"I don't know," said Vogel.

"Well, of course, you don't," said the Commandant, "because there *is* no reason a little girl's doll needs fifteen thousand fans! No, wait! It was only ten thousand fans and five thousand doll feather dusters." He waved at the room behind him. "All this taxidermy was his."

Firelight sparkled in the tears trickling down the Commandant's cheeks, and it seemed to Vogel that these tears were washing away not only powder and age but the sins committed in his daylight life lived among uniformed men. For example, the new law, a product of the Commandant's interest in animal rights and game protection. Convicted poachers were sentenced to join the mobile units assigned to track down partisan units. The theory was: You like hunting so much, we'll give you something to hunt.

Vogel fought an urge to get up and run from the room, an impulse rapidly muscled down by a stronger desire to reassure the Commandant that everything could be forgiven. Odd, because not for a moment did Vogel believe this. How had they gotten to this point in such a brief time? Two grown men, one in a dress, both of them in tears.

Vogel said, "How can I help you, Commandant?"

The Commandant peered at him and after a while said, "I remember now. You're the jeweler."

"That I am," Vogel said. "Though, to tell you the truth, my ambition was to be a philosopher. . . ."

"As you can see," the Commandant said, "I love beauty above all things. If beauty were an actress, I would sit in the theater and watch her hour after hour, year after year, until I died in my seat. Died of happiness, I mean. . . ."

Vogel fingered the case containing the pocket watch and the bracelet, which now seemed like cheap toys one might find baked into a holiday cake. He said, "I brought you a little . . . token. But now, having met you, I realize I have a piece in my safe that would be perfect. Perfect."

"What is it?" The Commandant looked almost pleased, or anyway as close to pleased as Vogel expected to see.

"Earrings," said Vogel. "Opal and pearl."

The Commandant frowned. "Opals are bad luck. Opals mean tears."

"Life is tears," said Vogel flirtatiously. "And in my career as a jeweler, I've observed that luck pays no attention to what stones a person wears."

"When will you bring them?" the Commandant said, leaning yearningly toward Vogel.

Vogel stared back into the Commandant's dark eyes until the

room, the fire, the couch, and finally the Commandant's face vanished from the edges of his vision. Maintaining this steady gaze was a challenge, but it was easier than answering the Commandant's deceptively straightforward question. Had it been a woman who'd asked, had Vogel been in his glory days, he would have said, For you, for you, my darling, I will go home and get them now, I won't be able to sleep a wink until I've seen them on you. But this wasn't a woman. This was the head of the air force.

Finally he decided to say, "Whenever you wish."

Disappointment pushed the Commandant back against the couch. Hastily, Vogel corrected himself. "I mean I can get them now."

The Commandant said, "I will have my secretary telephone you in the morning." And with an airy but imperious gesture, he sent Vogel from the room.

The two lieutenants waited outside the door to walk him back to the car. On the long ride into town Vogel felt queasy with shame and regret at having given the wrong answer. Should he have sounded more impulsive? More devoted? More generous? What had the Commandant wanted?

He told his wife that he had eaten a bad oyster at his club. He fell asleep, exhausted. In the morning, he asked her to bring him tea in bed, then retreated under the blankets, where he replayed every instant of the evening before, all the time asking himself what else he should have done at the end.

Just after eleven, his wife told him that a man was on the phone, claiming it was urgent. When Vogel hung up the phone after hearing that a car would come for him at the same time and place, his wife said, "*You* look happy." Vogel told her that he was about to conclude a lucrative transaction with an important client.

He had been granted a reprieve. Or maybe he'd been mistaken. Maybe the Commandant had grown tired, maybe it was the morphine. But the sense of having been pardoned and saved stayed with him through the day, as he went to his shop and opened his safe and found the earrings, which were at once more delicate and dazzling than he remembered. The Commandant loved beauty. Vogel felt no regret at giving up the earrings, but rather the wild surrender he imagined affecting the beneficiaries of miracles who hand over their whole fortunes to the interceding saint. He felt as if he'd been reading a fascinating book and dropped it by accident into the ocean. And now, against all odds, the book had washed up, whole and dry, so he could read the next chapter.

Once again, the car arrived with the two lieutenants in front. The one in the passenger seat got out, as he had the night before, and Vogel—joyous now, he had to admit—waited for him to open the door. But this time the young man's mouth emitted a scatter of words that Vogel slowly assembled into the information that the Commandant had an important meeting and regretted that he could not make time for Herr Vogel but would appreciate it if Herr Vogel would entrust his officers with the item they had discussed.

"So you can talk, after all!" was Vogel's first response. Then, even more shamingly, "I'm afraid I'll need to ask for a receipt."

The lieutenant laughed and held out his hand. Vogel gave him the earrings. He watched the car drive away, even as he watched himself thinking bitterly that it was only fitting that the earrings should go to the man who stole them in the first place. Then he hurried back into his shop, possessed by the irrational idea that anyone who saw him would be able to read on his face everything that had happened.

But of course no one did, and Vogel never told anyone. Not his wife, who left him when he refused to sell what remained of his jewels to escape Berlin at the last possible instant, nor his second wife, who was drawn to him because what remained of his jewels seemed to offer some security at the end of the war and who divorced him because there was almost a child, which starved before it was born. By then Vogel's philosophical musings focused on the subject of how the mind apprehended the concepts of forgiveness and retribution.

Eventually, there was an inquiry, during which Vogel's attorney solicited letters from Jews, living safely abroad and all attesting to the fact that Vogel had behaved with consummate professionalism. He was cleared of any wrongdoing in return for the promise that he would do his best to see that the looted jewelry was found and returned to its rightful owners.

Some years later he received a letter from Geneva. After thanking him profusely, Frau Rubinstein asked if by chance he had any idea what had happened to her earrings.

It was the closest he would ever come to telling someone the truth. And perhaps he would have, had he known what it was. By then, the Commandant was dead, a suicide in his prison cell, after having performed brilliantly, with unassailable logic and eloquence, in response to the prosecutors' searching and frequently harsh interrogations.

Vogel wrote back and told Frau Rubinstein that he was sorry, but many precious objects had passed from hand to hand to hand until someone carelessly opened his hand and dropped them and lost them forever. He wanted to, and didn't, add a philosophical postcript. Had he formulated and sent such a message, it might not have become the lodestar to which he gravitated, night after sleepless night, re-writing, rephrasing it in his mind whenever the moonlight woke him.

He and Frau Rubinstein were veterans of an extraordinary history, and, as a fellow veteran, he wanted to ask her something. He had lived his life, which, he had always known, would be his only life. He had experienced a fairly standard proportion of satisfaction and regret, remakable in light of the era through which they had lived. But what he wanted to ask was how, given all those days and years, all those minutes and seconds he had somehow managed to fill, after witnessing such a long parade of dramatic and ordinary events, how could it possibly happen that the only occasions he remembered with any clarity or feeling were the times when he had tried and failed to answer a simple question.

The History of the *History of Death*

Paul La Farge

From "Postmortem of the Printed Word," a symposium held at the University of Melbourne, July 7–10, 2——

AROUND 490 BCE, HERMODORUS, an Ephesian, undertook to refute Heraclitus's claim that "everything changes and nothing remains still" by writing a *History of Death,* in which "only those things that have ceased to change" would be recorded. Neanthes of Cyzicus says that Hermodorus had written the first book of his *History* when he died of a seizure. And Neanthes, says Athenaeus in his *Deipnosophistae,* had just managed to record the fact of Hermodorus's death in his *Annals* when he himself fell ill and died. Georg Kaibel, who prepared the Teubner edition of the *Deipnosophistae,* makes the joking suggestion that the *History* might have done Athenaeus in also, inasmuch as he (Athenaeus) was trampled by a horse not long after the fifteenth and final volume of his great work was completed. As for Kaibel, the *Neue Deutsche Biographie* says that he died of stomach cancer, but Schulze, in his *B. G. Teubner,* remarks, "Teubner was much moved by the death of Kaibel, who fell to the floor one day in his office, still holding the last pages of a manuscript he had come to deliver." It is possible, likely even, that the manuscript in question was his commentary on Athenaeus.

Kaibel's *Deipnosophistae* was the standard edition for half a century, and scholars were drawn to his mention of the *History of Death* like moths to a flame. So great was the number of late-nineteenth-century classicists who perished after running afoul of Hermodorus that, in the preface to his *Ammianus Marcellinus,* C. D. Yonge refers to the *History* as a "trap for bookworms," a trap that he seems to have escaped—although it's interesting to note that the 1911 edition of Yonge's *Marcellinus* calls the work "The History of *Neath,*" and presumably the earlier edition, from which it was stereotyped, had the same misprint. W. Yorke was less fortunate: His *Athenaeus* was only half completed when he died, apparently of surprise at a bird that had flown through the window of his study and was found

82

fluttering in the rafters, still unable to leave the room. Yorke's friend and biographer, F. B. Stern, wrote in his *Memories of Yorke* that "he [Yorke] had just mentioned a work by Hermodorus, the name of which I shall not repeat here, as it is believed to bring ill-luck." Stern lived into the twentieth century. Why Yorke had brought up the *History of Death* in the middle of his commentary, rather than at the end, is not known. Wyzantsky, who finished Yorke's *Athenaeus*, is believed to have deleted the reference to Hermodorus, although the manuscript was lost in a fire that destroyed Wyzantsky's Cambridge rooms while the scholar was out to dinner at the house of an unnamed friend.

C. B. Gulick, who prepared the Loeb *Deipnosophistae*, does not mention Hermodorus, or Neanthes of Cyzicus. This omission—which was so striking that E. Harrison rebuked Gulick for it in *The Classical Review*—can perhaps be explained by the fact that Gulick and Wyzantsky had roomed together at Cambridge. Some say that they were lovers, although it is by no means necessary to suppose so; even as a friend Wyzantsky would have warned Gulick against writing about the *History of Death*. E. Harrison died shortly after his review article was published. He was struck by a falling weight.

The Loeb *Athenaeus* likely saved many scholars from becoming aware of Hermodorus's work; of the ones who nevertheless stumbled upon it, I will mention only two. Godfrey Sizer couldn't avoid mentioning Hermodorus in his article on Neanthes for the *Biographical Dictionary of Classical Historians*, but he tried to protect himself with the remark "It has become an article of faith among classicists that even to mention the *History of Death* is to court misfortune; a risk that cannot be avoided here, although perhaps frank acknowledgment of the superstition will serve to dispel it." Unfortunately for Sizer, this attempt at countermagic was in vain: A year after Volume 7 (Marcellinus–Pictor) of the *Dictionary* appeared, he was eaten by his own dog. Meanwhile, Miroslav Marcovich denied that Hermodorus wrote the *History of Death* at all; the work, he asserted, was most likely a scholar's joke, invented by Kaibel or possibly by Athenaeus. Marcovich, whose edition of *Heraclitus* was a touchstone for scholars until recently, disappeared while hiking in the Peruvian Andes; it is believed that he ran afoul of the Sendero Luminoso, the Shining Path. Curiously, a tract entitled *Historia de la Muerte* was distributed to villages in the province of Cangallo, illustrating, with photographs, the various ways in which opponents of that organization had been murdered.

Does a curse really hang over the *History of Death*? The question was taken up by Dick Gordon, the paranormalist and deep-sea diver, who wrote about it for the *Fortean Times*. Gordon was the first person to figure out that only *writing* about the *History* bears ill consequences; his energetic if not exhaustive search turned up no one who was harmed by reading the works mentioned above, a fact that you will doubtless be pleased to learn. Gordon's article promised a sequel that was never written. His son Dale told me that Gordon had found Hermodorus's manuscript in the Egyptian National Library in Cairo, just a few months before he died. (Gordon was asphyxiated while trapped in the hulk of a ship he believed to be the *Alcoa Puritan*, sunk by a German U-boat in the Gulf of Mexico, but which was later discovered to be the salvage ship *Texaco Lost Cause*.) But neither I nor anyone else was able to locate the supposed manuscript before the Egyptian National Library was itself destroyed, along with everything it contained, by a fire, the cause of which has not yet been determined, and probably never will be.

Gordon's explanation of the curse is woefully unsatisfying. He connects the *History of Death* to the continent of Atlantis, which—this was one of the many bees in Dick Gordon's bonnet—according to him never sank at all but was dismantled, he doesn't say how, by its own inhabitants, who took their secret knowledge to the Atlantic Ocean's various shores, and kept it safe there, so says Gordon, indefinitely. Hermodorus, Gordon suggests, must have become aware of these facts, and mentioned them in his *History* as a case of truly noteworthy survival. The Atlanteans slew him to protect their secret, and presumably they slew Neanthes to be sure that Hermodorus hadn't passed it along. Why they should have slain Athenaeus and Kaibel and E. Harrison and so on is a question for which Gordon has no answer.

J. Peach gave a more somber interpretation of the curse in his *Material History of the Written Support*. (Was Peach afraid to write the word *book*, which had already acquired negative connotations?) He proposed that the *History of Death* partakes of a fatality that is diffusely present in all books and documents, a will to eliminate the reader, by violent means if necessary. Books, Peach wrote, before his appalling death in an Algiers hotel room, want a world without people, just as people yearn for a world without books. This led him to the dictum "Documents, far from being the record of history, are its motor; all historical events are brought about by the ineradicable enmity between human beings and the written word." Peach's disturbing hypothesis was read only by his editors: The entire print run of *Material History of the Written Support* was lost at sea on its way from the printer (in Singapore) to the distributor (in San Diego), a fact that Dick Gordon would doubtless have made much of, if only he had lived to see it.

Since Peach, there has been no serious writing on the *History of Death*. The history of the *History* would not be complete, however, without some mention of the people who have tried to commit suicide by mentioning Hermodorus's work: the graphic novelists, the punk rock bands, the teenagers who, in the last years of our old civilization, wrote *History of Death* on their jackets, their knapsacks, their blue and black jeans. None of them were successful, from which I conclude that the curse, if there is one, can be activated only by a work of scholarship. (As for the suicide of George Oshima, author of *The Death of History*, which won the last Pulitzer Prize to be awarded for nonfiction, it was probably a coincidence. Oshima doesn't mention Hermodorus, nor is there any reason he should.)

Even the memory of books is passing out of the public consciousness now, and scholars are becoming scarce, to the point where symposia like this one remind me a little of Nevil Shute's book *On the Beach*, which was, if I remember correctly, set in the city where we are now assembled. No one is likely to write again about the *History of Death*. How many of you are familiar with the Loeb *Deipnosophistae*, or with Kaibel's Teubner? Who here has read Neanthes' *Treatises on Rhetoric*? As for the modern commentators on Hermodorus, their names will be unfamiliar to almost everyone, except Godfrey Sizer's daughter Erin, who is now a graduate student in philology at Brown, and Dale Gordon, who is serving a fifteen-to-twenty-year sentence in the Dade County Correctional Center, after the Coast Guard seized ten kilograms of cocaine from his fishing boat; and Mme Hélène Marcovich, who still stands outside the headquarters of the Policía Investigativa in Lima, holding a candle and a sign with no words on it, only a photograph of her husband's face.

I met Mme Marcovich there one night, and told her that I had met her husband at various conventions in Europe and America. We had never been friends, but we had been out to dinner on several occasions, each time as part of a large group. Miroslav is part of a very large group now, Mme Marcovich said, and she told me about his disappearance, the months she had spent trying to find out what had happened to him, the likelihood that he had been murdered. All I want, she said, is for someone to find his body, so that I can know his story is truly over. I expressed my sorrow at the news, and we agreed to meet the next day in a café by the square, a place she often ate when the police office closed for lunch. We talked about her husband over *patatas bravas*. I said that I admired his work, which was true, although I found his annotations a little impatient and pedantic. She told me about the years Miroslav had spent on his *Heraclitus*, and how, during that time, she had felt like a widow, only to discover, when he disappeared in the Andes, that actual widowhood was something else entirely. Then she began to speak about Hermodorus and the *History of Death*, which at that point I had barely heard of. Apparently her husband, after dismissing the *History* as a joke, had turned up some evidence that the work really existed. Disbelief shaded quickly into obsession, as it often did with him, she said, and when he disappeared he was planning a history of the *History* from Neanthes' *Treatises* to the present day. The book had an almost mystical importance for him, said Mme Marcovich. It stood for everything changeless in the world, and in particular it stood for books themselves, which, as Marcovich liked to say, look like rivers, in the sense that your eye flows across the page, but in fact are fixed and unchanging, like rivers of glass. The very existence of the *History* would in some sense have refuted Heraclitus's claim that you can't step in the same river twice—which was not, Mme Marcovich observed, something Heraclitus had ever said, but never mind. But of course what happened was that Miroslav disappeared, Mme Marcovich went on, leaving behind only a handful of notes for his unwritten project. Which leads me to think, she concluded, that Heraclitus was right after all, and that the only certainty is the certainty of loss. Then she excused herself: The detectives would be returning from their lunch break, and she wanted to be there when they went into the building.

I think that is as good a place to stop as any. I love you, Peter; I love you all. Don't forget me.

The Automatic Garden
Adam McOmber

AT A LATE AGE, Thomas Francini, the engineer responsible for many of the grand fountains at Versailles and infamous for his will to control, married the sixteen-year-old daughter of the Compte de Frontenac, a pristine child whom he dressed in taffy-colored velvets and ribbons and paraded through the Villa di Pratolino near Florence. Francini bought his young wife what she pleased from torch-lit shops, and what she could not find, he invented for her, producing a variety of curious windups. She possessed a clock in the shape of an oversized parakeet with pearl eyes and jade plumage, set to trill at the lunch and dinner hour. There was also a small silver man that cried like a newborn until held, at which point he would grow intensely warm to the touch. Finally, the pinnacle of her collection, a miniature Madonna that swung open to reveal a trinity—the fierce and stoic God and fiery dove of the Holy Ghost ready to be birthed alongside the infant Christ.

When asked about her husband, the child bride, called Florette, said it was as if the Lord had sent his kindest angel to care for her and keep her heart in a treasury box, safe from all those who would harm it. She could never be bruised or pierced with the great inventor at her side. But soon she learned that even Francini could not stop time and disease. Plague blossoms spread on the skin of her throat, and he was reduced to sitting at her bedside, wiping sores with swabs until the organic machinery of Florette's heart and lungs had stilled. He declared he would not marry again and wore a musical locket around his neck that held the child's portrait and played strains of "Come, Heavy Sleep" at intervals timed to match those that sounded inside Florette's own mechanical coffin. Soon after the girl's funeral, Francini purchased a portion of land and announced he would construct his final great invention there, a monument to sorrow for everyone to see—the automatic garden at Saint-Germaine-en-Laye.

The writings of Clodio Sévat, vicar emeritus and servant to the dauphin, give us a brief glimpse of Francini's garden and echo the general anxiety of seventeenth-century French and Italian aristocracy concerning that place: "Though it has been nearly a month since my pilgrimage to Saint-Germaine-en-Laye, I still cannot wipe the yellow-stained eyes of Thomas Francini's metal men and beasts from my memory, nor can I forget the sight of Francini himself stalking through his field of glass flowers like some devil, dragging what appeared to be a common garden hoe behind. Does Francini believe that God's good works should be made again, and that *he*, however noble an engineer, can improve upon them? And what soul motivates these new creatures? He assures us it is mere water and steam, but, dear reader, I tell you it is more than that."

Gladly, not all travelers were as brief as the vicar emeritus, or the automatic garden, which burned to the ground nearly a year after its opening, might have been lost entirely to time. "Maestro Francini's water-and-steam-powered automata," wrote the Duchess of Langres in her private journal after a trip to the garden, "are of a new and unexpected breed. I was warned by my companion that these false creatures might disturb me with their preternatural resemblances to life, but I instead found myself intrigued. Their ability to exude what appeared as emotion was startling, yes, but not frightening. Never in my life did I think I would see a tiger ravaged by *sadness* crouching in the underbrush and looking at me with amber glass eyes, or Poseidon himself, crying tears into the very ocean that he rules—tears that were then swallowed by a thick and toothy monster who lives in the ocean's depths. I was moved to call for an interview with Maestro Francini, wishing to inquire about the labyrinthine secrets of his inventions. And yet despite my status and the fact that I had attended the funeral of his bride, Florette, I was rebuked by what appeared to be a page in a red tunic who told me that the master was frail and no longer tolerated audiences. It was only after the page's retreat into a forest of metallic pines that my companion, characteristically droll, asked whether or not I'd caught the sun glinting oddly off the young man's skin or whether I'd seen the glassiness in his eyes.

"I drew my wrap closer and begged my friend to assure me he was not implying that the page had been some advanced version of Francini's moving statuary. He replied with a laugh, saying he'd only been trying to give me chills, but by the time I'd reached the garden's third terrace, I did not need such humor to provide tremors. It was there that I saw what I can only describe as a 'dragon' rising from a stone basin, only to be slain by a lifelike knight in white armor who descended from the columned ceiling on a golden rope. The dragon's blood was as red and real as my own, yet it spread across the flag-stones in delicate calligraphy as if sketched by an artist's hand. I was forced to ask my friend to find a bench on which I could gather my wits. 'We shouldn't have come here, Duchess,' he said, but I replied that I was glad we'd come, despite the effect. Francini's automatic garden showed me that a certain sickness—a questioning of one's world—could serve as an enlightenment."

Like the automatic garden, the answer to whether the death of Francini's wife, Florette, had truly given rise to his monument of sorrow is largely lost to history. Francini's motivation for his final invention was a topic of debate in fashionable circles, and many argued that there was more to the inventor's grief than the death of poor simple Florette. Gossip about such details was often named as the cause of the inventor's self-imposed exile to Saint-Germaine-en-Laye and his distancing himself from the aristocracy. It was not Florette who'd shamed him after all but the prior object of his passions who had made for a near public embarrassment and perhaps even venial sin.

Antonio Cornazzano had been a danseur and general actor of the Florentine stage who'd met the great engineer during the period when Francini was commissioned to build a revolving set for *La Ballet de la Délivrance de Renaud*. Francini, who could then still be called a young man, adored the danseur, and that affection was apparently reciprocated. The two were often seen huddled in the dimly lit taverns of Florence over a candle and a serving of black ale, discussing topics in such hushed voices that no one else could hear. Despite the apparent gravity of these discussions, Francini and Cornazzano sometimes burst into hearty laughter, and tavern patrons reported an unnatural magnetism between the two men. There were even rumors of sorcery, though André Félibien, court historian to Louis XIV, dismisses such conjecture as peasant talk. "Simply stated," he writes, "Thomas Francini and Antonio Cornazzano behaved as artists will, and though such behavior seems, at times, against nature, we must learn to accept and make do if the theater is to persist."

Francini's stage set for the ballet was said to be a marvel—a replica of the city of Florence itself. And the ninety-two dancers and singers employed to move through the mock streets, bedrooms, and common houses did so in an exhaustive display of "city life" that also encompassed a *spiritual dimension,* as the upper parts of the central stage contained sets for the unmovable empyrean of the Heavens.

89

Masked angels and demons pulled silken ropes connected to doorways that affected the lives of the human dancers. Cornazzano acted as choreographer for the production and worked closely with Francini to create what many called a "threatening sense of fantasy."

The emotion between dark-featured Francini and agile Cornazzano developed a volatile irrepressibility. They could not contain themselves even when they worked with the dancers, and were often seen erupting into laughter and pulling each other out into the alley behind the theater to calm themselves with sobering talk. It was only when they lurched back to Francini's rented villa one night after drinking and were set upon by a band of Florentine locals and dashed to the flagstones that the two men became more cautious.

When precisely they decided to begin living inside of Francini's revolving set for the ballet we do not know, but a number of sources document that Francini, who'd already made his fortune at Versailles, started stocking the taverns and shops of the set with actual goods and even hired out-of-work ballerinas to act as barmaids and shopkeepers. He and Cornazzano lived privately on the stage, setting up house each night after the performance ended, enjoying that false city as they had previously enjoyed the actual streets of Florence. There were taverns in which the two could drink black ale by candlelight without the interruption of noisy patrons, and there was a library filled with fake books. Actual texts proved unnecessary because Francini could recite portions of *Le Morte d'Arthur* as well as *Gargantua and Pantagruel* by heart. At times, the two men climbed into the heavenly domain, lit the wicks of the stars, and floated through the empyrean on Francini's cleverly concealed wooden pallets.

A ballerina managed to steal a letter that Francini had left for Cornazzano on a pillow in one of the small apartments. The letter ended with a line that became popular in Florence as fashionable blasphemy: "I do not love God, my darling 'Tonio. For what is God when there is you?" Cornazzano's response to those words remains in ellipsis. The content of the young man's heart is largely unknown. It is only years later that we hear from him in his own words. By then, he had married and seen the birth of three children with his wife, Marie, and together they owned a small theater in Charleville. Cornazzano wrote his thoughts in a sturdy leather diary that he then concealed in one of the walls of his home. In recent times, the diary has surfaced, and while it provides an uncomfortable end to the story of the two men, it gives evocative details of the automatic garden itself, which Cornazzano was invited to visit by the great inventor a month before fire consumed it.

Cornazzano begins the journal with intimations of the falling-out between himself and Francini years before. They'd apparently abandoned their home in the revolving set long before the *Ballet de Renaud* had closed. "It has been years," he writes in his careful yet unschooled hand, "and I wonder if I am being overly cautious or cruel by suggesting that we meet at the garden itself rather than at Francini's home. I do not want to recall our *privacies* or the invented world we shared. It wasn't merely the stage—our fake city. We invented places in our minds as well that we could slip off to even in a crowd. I remember what Thomas said to me—that two men living together is in itself a kind of invention, a household of dream furniture and shadow servants. Is it wrong that I do not want to even come close to this dream again? How would I explain such a thing to my dear Marie or to my children, the eldest of whom is almost the age of Thomas's own bizarre deceased bride. By coming to the automatic garden, I hope to appease him, so that his letters will stop. I admit I am nervous to see what he calls his 'great defiance,' his palace against the day."

Cornazzano writes that he was greeted at the garden's columned gate by a page draped in a cloak dyed the color of saffron and told that Master Francini was unwell and sent his apologies for not being able to join Cornazzano on the tour. This came as quite a surprise to Cornazzano, who'd believed the entire reason for this trip was so that Francini could see him again and perhaps persuade him that this place was like the other fantasy in which they'd lived—a new set for a fresh and dangerous ballet.

He attempted to beg off, saying that he was a busy man with a theater to run and did not have time to walk the garden if Francini could not be bothered to escort him, but the page became insistent, grabbing Cornazzano's arm and pulling him into the garden toward the forest of the gods. "Please, Monsieur. Master will be miserable if you don't at least give me some word of praise for his inventions." Finally Cornazzano conceded to take a short walk through the place, writing, "The page's hand was cold—not like a dead man, but like one who has never lived. I feared disagreement, so I allowed myself to be led." The walk turned into a game of mad circling through the garden's multiple levels, and in the dim light of a forest path the page disappeared and Cornazzano was left alone with Francini's glowering mechanicals.

He became intrigued by a bed of glass chrysanthemums—a flower of the Orient, rarely seen in France. The stem of the mechanical chrysanthemum was made of green copper with sharp-edged leaves protruding, and the petals of the flower itself were crafted from thin pieces of stained glass. Inside the stem was what appeared to be a small flame of the sort one finds in lanterns, which was given oxygen at regular intervals, causing the chrysanthemum to pulse with a light that suggested the process of blooming. The brightening of the flower was subtle, nearly imperceptible, and Cornazzano writes that even after studying the chrysanthemum for a few minutes, he was hard-pressed to say whether it was growing brighter or dimmer. The light seemed to exist somewhere inside his own body, in fact, a warmth in his core. "The mechanical chrysanthemum causes a momentary dizziness with its warmth," he adds, "a sensation that is not altogether unpleasant."

So entranced, Cornazzano did not recognize the approach of the figure in black, and when he caught his first glimpse of it standing at the stony edge of the garden path, he did not fully comprehend what he saw. He attests instead to being startled as one can be startled by an unexpected mirror hanging at the end of a gallery. The figure that stood in the grass and watched him was not an obvious automaton. Unlike the moving statue of Poseidon who wept into his miniature ocean, or the huntress, Diana, who drew her bowstring in the dark forest, this figure had a versatile range of movement. It was able to crouch, then stand, and then to caper there at the edge of the path, as if begging for Cornazzano's approach.

Our chronicler likens the figure to one of the dancing fauns in the garden's Doric gallery, but man sized and wearing a garment that looked like a merchant's robe with a wide lace ruff around its neck. The collar was crenulated and gave the appearance that the automaton's head, bearing its pale and almost luminous face, was displayed on a black plate. Its mouth was open in what could not be called a smile, and so surprising was the creature that Cornazzano did not at first recognize it as a replica of himself. "Would any man know himself clothed in such odd garments," he writes, "and set to caper and leer like a demon?"

The automaton turned from the path, and its fluidity of movement made Cornazzano momentarily believe the thing must be an actor in heavy makeup or mask, merely pretending to be a machine. But there were subtle inhumanities to its gestures that soon convinced him otherwise. Just as one could never mistake the mechanical chrysanthemum for a real flower, neither could one think this object was a man.

The creature fled across the garden, black boots flickering over the grass, and was it any wonder that Cornazzano left the safety of the path to chase his double, hungry for a better look? The automaton darted playfully beneath an evening sky as dark as iron. It ran through a swamp of reeds that hummed sad flute song, and then across a plain of grass that rippled, though there was no breeze in the air.

Cornazzano watched as his replica slipped into one of the many grottoes that were too smooth for nature. No longer the agile danseur he'd once been, he found himself winded at the entrance to the cave and stopped, considering whether he should continue following the creature. His blond hair lay wet against his forehead. His gut heaved. He knew he should walk away—leave Francini to his madness. But still some part of him wanted to doubt what his eyes had recorded. It was not possible that Francini had built his own Cornazzano to live in his garden of gods.

Cornazzano writes, "I crept into the cave and found the creature no longer dancing but crouched near one wall, huddled in its tunic as if for warmth. Seeing the details of my own face—or rather the details of how I had once been, a young and foolish boy—gave rise to an intense and surprising anger. I wondered if Francini was making a mockery of me, or worse, if perhaps he used this metal man for some type of pleasure. And I found myself gripping the thing's pallid face, feeling the contours of its chin and cheeks. I pulled at its nose, which was made of soft metal, pushed at its eyes until the bulbs of glass cracked beneath my thumbs. The automaton did not struggle. It allowed its destruction. Perhaps that is even why it led me to the cave. And when I reached into the creature's mouth, trying to find some tongue to pull out, I heard behind me the scuff of a leather boot on the sandy cave floor.

"I turned to see Francini himself—hair shot through with silver, eyes set deep in his skull, standing and watching in the fading light. This was not my laughing friend from Florence with bright eyes and wine-stained lips. This was a poor copy—an old man—ruined and sad.

"'What have you done?' he asked in a soft voice.

"By then, I had managed to rip the automaton's lower jaw from its head, and I tossed it at Francini's feet. 'That question,' I said, 'would be better put to you, Maestro.'

"'I thought you would *like* him, 'Tonio,' Francini whispered. He bent to pick up the jaw from the cave floor, and as I formulated some rebuke, feeling the old dangers and passions rushing back into the causeways of my heart, I realized something was wrong. Francini's fingers were around the jawbone, but he did not grasp it, nor did he attempt to straighten himself. He had grown intensely still in his awkward, bent position, and it was only then that I realized—this was not Francini. It was not even alive.

"Such horror I felt. I could not move my arms or legs, could not look at this false Francini with limp gray hair hanging against its brow. I wondered if my old friend even still existed. I wanted to cry out for him. I wanted Francini to reveal himself in flesh and blood, but I held my tongue. How I escaped the automatic garden, I do not know. It seems that the gods called to me as I ran—begged me not to leave at first and then mocked me for my foolishness. And even as I sit composing these lines at my own wooden table in my home where I can hear the sound of my good wife speaking to my children in the upper rooms, I wonder if I am still there in that garden, lying on the cave floor, broken into my separate parts."

Professor Skizzen Gets the Word
William H. *Gass*

SOME STRANGE-LOOKING MEN left this on our doorstep.

In our mailbox, you mean, Mother?

Rolled in our door handle. Does it matter?

How the message is received? I think so.

I guess. I thought this was meant for you.

It was meant for me. I saw them from an attic window.

I saw them from the garden.

Two men, their skins dressed for a funeral.

Yes, one large, the other larger. In dark suits too. They must be from out of town.

Yes. No one in Woodbine looks like that.

Risky.

Risqué.

What does it say?

I don't know yet.

Professor Skizzen slid inside the screen, taking the small pamphlet with him. He was registering every detail as he took it up the stairs, rather reverently, he would later remember. Across a cover that aspired to represent deep and dwindling space, a light blue grid retreated toward infinity. Upon this checkerboard a silhouette, like those fixed to the doors of johns, stood outlined by a thin halo of steam, while behind the figure, who had been placed there as an icon for mankind, mooned a swirly half round of world with a few seas and continents showing like bits of underwear. At the bottom of the cover one question was put to its handler:

Will This World Survive?

Flimsy little announcement for a show so spectacular, Skizzen tried to complain, though his hand shook with another feeling. In the light of a dormer window, he took a closer look. This piece of paper was important to him. Could there be others of the same mind? walking strange streets in protective pairs? waiting for the removal of man?

The pamphlet unfolded to form five small pages, though it counted the cover as a sixth. And there, on number two, the question was put again in print that shouted, as if at someone deaf. **Some say the world will be destroyed by an atomic bomb; others suggest that it will poison itself with its own waste; still more are sure that famine and poverty will cause the masses to take up arms.** What, Professor Skizzen wondered, no epidemics of disease? no alien invasions, or meteors, or calamities of climate?

Don't be impatient, Joey, Skizzen said to his attic audience, adopting the pamphlet's point of view. Plagues and other calamities are on their way. Radiation running enraged and loose as a wild hog! Every paragraph appealed to scripture as the final truth, of course, so citations outnumbered commas. The text reminded him of how the world had ended once before. Its Maker, as quietly as an eraser, could have rubbed out each and every dishonest one of us, and with a single swipe returned his creation to a day before Light. Instead he chose a painful and dramatic alternative. To no reader's surprise, along came Noah with orders about his little boat. Build an ark in your backyard. Wait a while. As I said to Joey, don't be impatient. The sky will open and the seas rise. Then the flood will come to lift your vessel, as if blown like paper, safely onto the oncoming surge. The pamph didn't quite say that Adam's progeny were a rascally sort, but it did insist that God had drowned the world and almost everything in it—flying things were given a mizzenmast to perch upon—because human beings were ungodly. Noah was presumably the only righteous man. That embarrassing drunk. What an admission!

First mistake, Skizzen said aloud, pointing a pedagogical finger at the text. We are to assume there are gods and that we know their intentions. Were there any deities, they would devour us for dinner. The professorial voice was sterner than the classroom had ever heard, and, of course, he would never actually speak that way to the bearers of the pamph. Our religious inventions are as mean and whimsical as we are—and we are pretty whimsical, pretty mean, aren't we?—in truth, these gods are merely agents, emblems, and instruments of human hypocrisy and wickedness. Skizzen paused to let that evaluation sink in. He hoped he had struck a tone appropriate to the pulpit.

After all, this was his personal church. He understood his role as an audience too: attentive to a fault, generous with its amens, patient about his longueurs. But this time his enactments were anxious, as if there really were a world of ears out there, beyond the fruit box he sat on, or the rafters hung with clippings from the newspapers. It very likely would be intimidating to find at your front door these two big black men bearing messages from the Lord. He supposed they were intended to overwhelm. Skizzen was determined to meet the challenge.

Ask Noah if his instructions were clear and unambiguous. Was he told to repair to his nearby ark shop where a boat was waiting for him, or was he ordered to build his own ship according to God's specifications? Was he to invite a married pair of every creature who lives in air or dwells on earth, or was he told to put on seven pairs of clean creatures but only two of the unclean kind? If the whole shebang, how big a boat would that require? Flora and fauna as far as the eye could squint. Or, in those days, were there only a few plants and fewer animals flourishing on the earth? By the way, was the Flood to last 40 days and 40 nights or were the waters to take 150 days flowing in and another 150 draining out? The text is double tongued on these points as it is on so many others. Ask Noah did he board a pair of rabbis or did they all drown.

Professor Skizzen put down the pamphlet and got to his feet. His right hand caressed his throat while he cleared it. He then stood to the music stand that served as his attic podium and said in a resolute voice:

They all drowned.

Mistake two: Who had the fig tree offended that it should perish with its figs? Perhaps it was the fig and not the apple that was the ultimate instrument of our destruction. Your good book just says—vaguely—fruit. He began to wave his hand as if it held the handout but immediately realized he had left it in the sunlight by the window where it could be more easily read. Perhaps it was a fig the temptress offered Adam and not the apple. The fig, he had been told, possessed a more appropriate configuration.

Was slyness the trait that proved ruinous for the foxglove? Now he had the flimsy and could flourish it. Long columns of newsprint, which he had fastened to flypaper thumbtacked to the rafters, swayed as if dancing in the draft.

What say you, peddlers of disaster? OK . . . how about vines. Why drown vines? Is it because they crawl along like the tempter? while holding figs in the hands they had before they became snakes?

Professor Skizzen began to show some impatience with the mute stupidity of his audience, waddling across his imagined range of vision like two crows. OK, how about every fragrant meadow? those glorious golden waves of grain? He perceived a few signs of response.

97

Yes, at last your sympathies have been stirred. And not one fruited plain was saved. They lay calm and unmoved as land usually lies—what harm in that?—wishing merely to grow and watch bloom their indigenous weeds.

While we stand here talking, what is that fellow Noah going to be up to? In every class, there'll be a Mr. Win to be brought aboard first, with Mrs. Place in reluctant tow. But "no!" will be the response to brother Show, because no third thing will be permitted to live. You pair of black birds in the last row: I hope you appreciated my low-culture joke. Students admire such stuff. Yet, as we chosen few check tickets, those who have been refused the opportunity to board are being overwhelmed by their own tears. Drowned in sorrow, don't we say? Well, stand up to it: The devout perished as surely as pheasants or flowers. Streams and rivers were engulfed by lakes. Oceans drowned in other oceans. Debris would be all that you could see. Corpses of men and animals, as soft and brown as bananas, would float hip to hip aimlessly about wearing nothing but bracelets. Both little hills, and a thousand times a thousand trees, will sink beneath the new sea to become sticks with mud stumps. Kill 'um, kill 'um all! But is that the way for a God to behave? God so loved the earth he murdered every living thing he'd put upon it. Or was he—who parted the Red Sea, remember?—was he unable to pick us out like flies in a pudding? So he threw away the whole bowl.

Mistake the Third: So God had to start all over again with the children of Noah, but this bunch was to fare no better than the first, and God was on the job in both cases, wasn't he? How many days in that workweek? Was God defter, more efficient, the second go-round? Don't tell me men were at fault for cyclones or tidal waves, eruptions or earthquakes. Why didn't he at least fix those failures on the second try? In the mind's eye of Professor Skizzen, the seats were now full of hand-clapping black people. They were the only folks left who cared about God. Jesus freaks were plentiful among whites but unforeseen like mushrooms in the woods. Where oh where has our little god gone? Where oh where can he be? You . . . you, on the other hand, have Jehovah on your masthead. Ten . . . I see twenty nods. Nevertheless, it is Jesus who is wearing the sandwich board and proclaiming your news.

This Noah was a Darwinian all right; he only intended to rescue each species, individuals never had a vote. Did Noah remember to coax some bishop's weed to board? Two flies and two mosquitoes—mind—for every type, a pair like gloves—or do viruses come in couples? Neither God nor Noah could get it right, confess it, they couldn't get it right. The Garden of Eden had thrips. So the third time is supposed to be a charm? What are our chances for improvement? We got a promise—remember?—pried out of God like a bent nail from a board—a board from the bargaining table—no more bloody floods, we insisted, even if we do screw up again as expected. Fire, then, next time? Next time is it to be a dirigible that will save our sperm?

The audience is shocked by the professor's daring use of the word dirigible.

The first time was bad enough. Imagine a million children, sinners somehow, drowning in their mothers' arms? Just picture it, you guys in your best funeral suits. No one wants to think things through, come close enough to death to smell its breath. For instance: Primroses, my well-informed mother informs me, don't need to board in pairs like new socks. One such flower should suffice. And why favor fish? They already have so many seas. Whales also get a break. Cuz one coughed up Jonah? Unless the water boils, they will get another pass. Now picture cute kittens with their skins aflame if it's to be fire this time. All the Madonnas that have been painted—the sainted mother in her blue cloak—and pieces of his history pledged to the glory of his name—burnt to a cinder along with baby Jesus. Should the church consent to be consumed first? or last as a lesson? Lesson for whom, with everybody dead but that dumbbell Noah and his klutzy kids? you know what happened to him, sirs?

Where did all the water go when it receded last time? Or did God with his big mouth just slosh some saliva about from place to place? Did he suck up the Caspian Sea and spit it out in the Mediterranean? Ah, sir, you don't understand. Skizzen imagined their reply. The water came from huge windows in the sky that someone left open to air the bedding, and from wells deep in the earth. You have perhaps—sir—heard the expression "The rain came down in buckets"? Those were the buckets. Wooden buckets from the wells of sorrow. This final line was sung: wood-en buck-ets from the wells of sor-oh.

Professor Skizzen made one entire turn about his music stand. Add up the pain that existed then in all God's conscious creatures. And you want me to believe in and to worship such a callous savage creature?

The professor went on in his own head although his enthusiasm was on the wane. When Noah found himself and his ark stuck on the peak of Mount Ararat, he dispatched one of his two ravens (smart choice) and one of his two doves (not as smart) to find out what was going on. But his listeners were also fading.

Why?

Because Professor Skizzen was himself rather unhinged by the very existence of this threatening message, wrong as it might be in texture, if not in tenor. The end of the world should be at hand, deserves to be at hand, ought to be at hand; but suppose . . . suppose God is not the stern no-nonsense guy he's been said to be. Maybe he'll make it seem as though the fire of life is everywhere extinguished when it actually still flickers a bit and consequently continues bravely on in pain and boredom . . . like a foreign movie . . . or the so-called eternal flame featured for the Olympic Games—a fake constantly relit when no one is looking. Was the lamp of life restarted just to amuse the arsonist? For the fun of it? There is no fun in Forever even if it's fun you begin with. No . . . no . . . no . . . fun at all.

Skizzen was suddenly delighted by a thought that was dismaying. It was a pilot light—life—and always waiting, in a boiling cloud, gas log, deep cave, or fever victim, ready to ignite.

What Professor Skizzen was required to understand, the paper said, was that these human malfeasances, reports of which he had so carefully collected in the attic where he was sitting now, were signs, omens, portents. Our habitual bad behavior was an indication—and this was clever—that Jesus—no—Christ had returned and was nearby, ready to punish his enemies with water, sword, and fire. And that included you and me; it included almost everybody.

We had entered "the last days." The signs were up—wars, famines, quakes, plagues, pogroms, anarchies—it was time to repent, believe, obey—then this catastrophic ending would be revised as a prologue to the New Eden—depicted here by smiling farmers and their happy families sharing sheaves of grain, baskets of produce, and movie smiles. Hmmm . . . were they all white? Well, only white folks were shown. One, pictured near a paragraph on pestilence, was on a respirator.

These prophets of God were nuts, of course: Was Skizzen a nut too? He had a number of questions he'd love to put to any one of them, should they come this way again. It would be fun to wrestle over old Noah too, though his first rehearsal now seemed to him confused. He had heard that they were prepared—even eager—to enter your house, accept your lemonade, and dispute with the larger one while persuading with the smaller. He had heard they remained calm and polite no matter how heated you became; that they took one cookie like a ration, and appeared ready to pull on the drapes that presently darkened your soul until they drew apart and you saw the light. He had heard they had a book they would sell you, and slick brochures they would fan across a coffee table like dealt cards. *Seven Days and Nights in Paradise.* They carried this material in twin valises the way doctors carried their instruments in the early Ford and buggy days when they would come to see your sickness if your call seemed to merit it. Skizzen couldn't remember: Were these guys accompanying any kind of case?

It would surprise them, wouldn't it? to receive the lecture rather than give it; to be pinioned in midmuffin, unable to speak, apt to choke while trying to reply. Beg your pardon, Brothers of the Great Truth, but when a species of grass or any small animal—say—becomes extinct, it threatens with death all those who used to feed on them. Oaks die, acorns disappear, squirrels follow. Had you considered that? If voles go out of stock, hawks must seek for other food; add themselves to the list that favor quail. Soon the quail have gone too. When human cities suck every drop of water from the sky, the soil blows away, and so do they. Had you taken your thought any distance in that direction? The threats in your pamphlet are not numerous or scary or concrete enough. The professor would be happy to help them with that. Skizzen's pulse raced. He had foolishly believed he was alone in his research, with his persistent sentence, and here was his worry being peddled door to door like books or brushes. By African strangers.

Suddenly he saw the pair on the street, on the street that used to be named Elm for its elms, now named Elm for its diseased trees. Three blocks away by footstep. Although his wind wasn't what it once was, Skizzen cast his dignity behind him like a shadow to scoot pell-mell down the narrow staircase, sweep as a breeze would the wider one, and burst onto his own lawn, yelling, HEY THERE with the bass part of his lungs.

Joey ran for half a block before they heard him—one man heard him—and that man sent his head swiveling to see what he had heard, and whether it was what he had heard, or whether there was nothing to be heard. Sir, Joey cried, sirs. I have received it—your missive—could I have a minute? They turned all the way round—the men did—and stood motionless in some surprise since what appeared to be enthusiasm was not an emotion they were used to eliciting. This enthusiasm was approaching like an excited dog so it was difficult to know whether to stand or bolt but at the moment they were standing, not bolting. The man holding a handful of handouts—the same large man who had first turned at the reception of the shout—said—he did not shout—he said, "Yes, sir" in the sort of voice that transports questions.

It happens . . . as luck would have it . . . I am myself . . . I am engaged in something resembling something in the neighborhood of your project . . . your whatchamacallit here . . . Skizzen said, waving his piece of their paper like a flag. Easy . . . they tear easy . . . the shorter of the two men said. Yes . . . well . . . Skizzen was running now only to catch his own breath. For some years . . . I have been collecting—what do you call them?—signs . . . signs of . . . sort of . . . the end of things, and the wickedness of the world, oh yes, the wickedness of the . . . a world of wickedness—you seem to agree. We're just handing these things out, the smaller of the large men said nervously. The bigger large man was slow and ponderous but there was no mistaking his confidence: We need to learn God's will and do it, so we can survive this world's end—But that is just the problem, Skizzen interrupted, now more in control of himself. That is just the problem. You shouldn't want to survive. No nono. You should strive to end with the ending, you see, otherwise there will be others like you—you know, of the same species—left to start over and do dreadful things again—over and over. The big man was clearly puzzled. No, he said, you misunderstand us, I am afraid, sir. We will enjoy the blessings of God's new world. We want you friends here in—where are we, George?

Woodbine, Ohio.

In Woodbine, Ohio, to enjoy them too. God will wipe the weeping eyes of those who do his will. Woodbine's eyes will be wiped. And death will be defeated.

I suppose you want everybody here to be saved.

Yes, sir, indeed sir, the smaller of the two men said. We've got no problems with anyone.

I suppose you want every living soul to do the same. . . . Obey, I mean.

God. Yes, sir. Surely. So no one will mourn anymore and no one will weep anymore, or cry to the sky, or suffer pain.

But then, don't you see, there would be no need to bring pestilences among men, or suffer men to starve, or for men to engage in war with one another—all your signs would be lies if everybody escaped their just deserts, if everybody all of a sudden saw the light

102

and did as they were told. We have to be punished. We deserve the deaths we end with.

No no. George was energized. You guys . . . persons . . . may be that guilty, who's to say? Not I, sir, certainly. God decides that. But if you turn your back on the Great Blessing . . . well . . . you take your chances, don't you? Because you haven't been walking the rounds, giving out the handouts, distributing the message among the masses—

George.

Every front porch gives us the funny face. As if it were bad news we bore.

It is bad news. It's bad news for all the people who don't know that the end is at hand though you are telling them it is . . . at hand. And it's bad news for people like me (there may be only one of me) because you are excluding your precious selves . . . from the inevitable end. . . . That's always how it is, isn't it?

We are warning people to change their ways before it is too late, George said. That's good news.

If the doctor says you have cancer, but if you let him remove most of you—gizzard, kidneys, and liver—you may survive . . . that's good news? . . . you call that good news?

The virtuous don't have cancer, George said triumphantly. Only the wicked have cancer. It's a small punishment before the big one.

You gentlemen, Skizzen said firmly, would be out of a job if you succeeded in doing your job. You'd be all dressed up with no bells to ring and no message to take to the masses because everybody would be blessed—what an awful bore—everybody blessed. And everybody would live forever begetting more and more of everybody in every place until everybody would be standing as close to one another as we are. With nothing to do and no nose to breathe with.

There'd be no more begetting? Why? There was enough surprise in the big man's voice when he drew this inference to give Skizzen hope for future consternations.

George, don't argue with the man.

Skizzen pursued him. Mothers would be barren. He thought—it brought on his own surprise—these guys speak tolerable English, not a mumble.

Mothers can't be barren and be mothers.

A technicality, Skizzen said several times quite rapidly, noticing his own annoyance.

George was trying to catch up with his own train of thought. We

103

would have different bodies, he insisted—new—improved bodies—well, not bodies exactly—something our souls would wear like a skimpy swimsuit—

God needs you to have bodies that are guaranteed, after years of riotous living, to wear out; so you can be crippled by those diseases that cripple, go blind and live in the dark, or grow deaf and sit in silence, possessing only a nose that runs and a tongue to be bitten; that is, barely enough to boast bone, flesh, and function, so you can roast in a hell that will burn that body to a crisp without consuming a hair of it.   That swimsuit was a marvelous comparison.

The men stared at him.

Don't misunderstand me. Don't . . . I'm in favor of it. Hell. Damnation. I just don't have the hope. Perhaps you might furnish me the hope. Perhaps you might give me reason to . . .

Come on, George. Are you coming? I'm going. Sorry, sir, we can't conversate, we've got pamphlets to distribute.

They began to move away.

The ground where Abel was killed became barren, Skizzen reminded them.

They were moving away.

That barren patch grew like a scratched rash.

They were off.

Don't forget, Skizzen shouted, during the next flood, make sure everybody drowns. We've had quite enough of us.

Surely, sir, the big man over his shoulder said. We'll try.

Break on Through to the Other Side:
The War Crimes Trial of General Nelson Miles
Held by the Dead

Bernard Pomerance

He's whipped out rebs and redskins and he's made some dagoes dance
And he's good for lots more fightin if he ever gets the chance
And here's the moral to this talk—I'll ask no price but thanks:
Miles may not have a stand-in, but he's solid with the ranks!

> —A tribute to General Nelson Miles, 1910,
> quoted by Brian C. Pohanka in *Nelson A. Miles:*
> *A Documentary Biography of his Military Career*
> *1861–1903*

AN ACCOUNT OF THE FIRST *session of the trial, convened by the dead, of General Nelson Appleton Miles, died 1925. Presiding officer for the proceedings: Major General George Crook, died 1890. Plaintiffs in attendance included deceased from the tribes and nations of the Lakota, Apache, Nez Perce, and others directly affected by General Miles's military career.*

The trial had been prepared for many years before Nelson Miles passed on, and commenced upon his death. Many of the plaintiffs, as well as the presiding officer, had been waiting decades for an occasion they considered necessary to rest in peace. Sitting Bull had died in 1890. Chief Joseph in 1904. Geronimo in 1909. Crazy Horse way back in 1877. By 1925, there had been plenty of post-mortem time—if "time" is the right word for an afterlife—to examine and analyze the evidence as well as to sharpen the language skills needed for the occasion.

CROOK AND MILES: THE TRIAL

We begin the first session of this trial, General Crook said, with the complaint of some Indian leaders, that to have surrendered to you was a virtual death sentence. That you ordered the murders of prisoners of war. As a soldier, you recognize the gravity of this charge.

105

Liars, all of 'em, General Miles said.

You'll find it is impossible to lie here, Crook said.

Crook held out a slip of paper. This is a note you sent to a subordinate, Lieutenant Gatewood, in 1886. Geronimo was his prisoner. He was in the lieutenant's custody on the way back from Mexico. Care to refresh your memory?

Miles glanced at it, then glanced away quickly. No, he said.

Crook said, Does it say bring him back dead or alive?

General Miles was now dead less than an hour. He was feeling dislocated by these strange and unforeseen circumstances.

Geronimo was already a prisoner, Crook pressed. What does "bring him back dead or alive" mean?

Miles cried with exasperation, How did you get that?!

It's an invitation to subordinates to murder a prisoner of war, but without the direct order that would make you accountable, Crook said. Isn't it?

Miles conceded, When I wrote it, I hadn't met him. I thought we'd all be better off without Geronimo. After I met him, I was impressed.

This note's the smoking gun, Crook said. I will show that Indian leaders surrendering to you were indeed under a virtual death sentence. We will examine why.

Miles nodded to Geronimo. Glad you survived, he muttered.

GENERAL GEORGE CROOK, PORTMORTEM

Even while they were both alive, some Indians had figured out the antagonism between Generals Crook and Miles. They'd become shrewd observers of the differences in American officers, if stoically unamazed by the uniformity that coated them in the end. To summon George Crook from his limbo—if you wanted to prosecute Nelson Miles, Crook might have seemed the prime choice. They'd both battled tribes in the Northern Plains, they'd both struggled with Apaches in Arizona, they despised each other with much the same intensity, but turned inside out, with which they served the United States Army.

Who'd summoned George Crook's spirit to full-fledged ghosthood remained obscure. No one among the ghost Indians was telling how it had happened. As he realized there were many ways a ghost might be summoned, he stopped inquiring; he wasn't sure they knew any more than he did. One moment he'd been stone dead, staring outward, trying urgently to communicate by telepathy with his newly dead wife, Mary. He was excited to be near her again. Finally Mary came "awake," and screamed, Oh *God*, George, cut that out! You know I'm ticklish.

Next thing, he was standing in his major general's uniform in front of a mass of too-familiar Indian ghosts. Lame Deer, Crazy Horse, Sitting Bull, for starters. Sitting Bull walked around him neutrally, almost dreamlike, like a man of horses checking a horse he might or might not purchase.

He said nothing. He glanced at Crazy Horse, and shook his head no.

Crazy Horse examined Crook briefly, and then nodded yes to Lame Deer.

Mary, he called softly. I'm dreaming. I'm seeing Indians.

Well, the newly deceased Mary murmured, You always had a certain je ne sais quoi with Indians. Ask what they want.

We need to speak with you, Lame Deer finally said.

Aw . . . shit-for-Christmas, Crook said, craning his head around.

He wasn't dreaming, just a full-fledged ghost standing there in a pack of other ghosts. Mary was gone.

The ghost of the Lakota chief Lame Deer reassured him. You join her again when you finish this work. If you can do it.

Crook was incensed: *Work?!* What goddamned work? I'm dead, for heaven's sakes.

Lame Deer: We want you to make a trial of General Miles.

Crook: Well, now. That sure got my attention.

He was a contentious choice to deal with a trial for Nelson Miles. That didn't take long to realize. Not everyone had wanted him summoned to help. Worse, Miles wasn't dead yet and no one knew when he'd die. Being disturbed prematurely by dead Indians can be irritating as all get-out, he thought. He cranked up the crankiness on the George Crook crankometer, to 99.9, and trudged around the afterlife like a homeless phantom from an unimaginable future, say an emaciated grizzly ransacking garbage containers at a national park. He resented being separated from Mary, his wife and soul mate with whom he'd only just been reunited. He'd died in 1890; she'd missed him and followed in '95.

*

Crook came to understand their choice slowly as he heard their complaints. They had an intuitive understanding that he would know about Miles and the ways of the Army and government in ways that they didn't; and they knew Miles was no friend of his. Also, he had become a two-star, a major general, years before Nelson Miles. Seniority. He could give Miles orders again. That would be useful to keep the notorious blusterer in check. He began to be intrigued by the possibilities of a trial for Miles: It was apparently impossible to lie in the afterworld. My dear, dear Lord, Crook cheered up. No lying here. Nelson sure won't like that. That's certainly gonna be a change from the Army.

Miles's and Crook's fifteen-year-long antagonism had begun when General Crook was posted as commander of the Platte District in the northern plains in 1875, where Miles also had been posted from the southern plains. Sioux, Cheyenne, and Arapaho nations were fighting off American encroachment on lands guaranteed to them by treaties.

Miles had heard Crook praised earlier, from the highest of authorities. He resented that his uncle-in-law, the General of the Armies Sherman, thought so highly of George Crook as the greatest Indian fighter of their times—the greatest Indian fighter!?—Why, that judgment about Crook was premature! Miles avowed to his wife, Mary— Miles hadn't yet had a chance to prove his own mettle.

Crook wasn't sure what to make of this officer who'd married General Sherman's niece, Mary Hoyt Sherman. To help his advancement? You mean an Army social climber? his own wife, also named Mary, asked. She told him later, No, dear, Miles loved the Sherman girl. The girl herself swore to it. And girls, you know, know.

Girls know what? Crook asked. He had no idea what she was talking about.

She thinks Nelson will rise quickly, once the Army realizes what a treasure it has.

You are saying . . . ? Crook asked, puffing his pipe. The marriage was for *her* advancement?

Let us say, Mary said, they agreed to believe in Nelson's prospects with General Sherman behind him, and sealed it with a marriage.

Jesus Christ, Crook muttered.

Hon, Mary ruffled his hair. That's just marriage.

Crook thought the young women, both named Mary, wanted to believe each other for the purely female reason that they had the same first name, Mary, and bullet-scarred officer husbands who did the same romantic and noble American thing. They fought and preserved the Union during the Civil War. Then they took on the Army's new task, the pacification of the western Indians.

When Crook and Miles met that year, the praise they'd heard about each other seemed to guarantee a mutual dislike. They didn't even like how the other man looked. They were equal in height, at just over six feet. Crook was a decade older, leaner, forked bearded in a style from the Civil War, and was more at ease with authority. He was sparing in public speech, self-possessed, and carried an aura of absorbed command he'd taken from years around generals like Sherman and Grant, and formidable tribal chiefs like the Apache Cochise and the Cheyenne Dull Knife. He'd subdued the Paiutes by force, dealt with Cheyennes, brutally broken the Tonto Apaches' resistance, and had relations of uneasy respect with Cochise's Chiricahuas. He was not competitive-but-clubbable, as officers in the West were expected to be. General Sherman's praise of Crook as the greatest of Indian fighters seemed to exempt him from ordinary fellowship. Young officers attached to him thought of him as a loner, an anomaly in a military hierarchy, but were devoted to him. Given a few days' free time, he'd pack provisions, slip his rifle into its scabbard, and head off alone to the mountains, to relax, hunting and smoking his pipe by fast-rushing streams. He found his fellowship in wilderness, but never discussed it. He never took anyone along.

Nelson Miles was a natural-born intimidator. He grasped it as a sign that he was meant to be a leader of men. He believed in his destiny, but acknowledged that he'd been born with no advantages. He knew he'd have to beat his path through life with his forehead as a club. A stiffness and defensive effrontery leaned forward from him everywhere he walked, an aggression waiting for challenges. He chafed that his record for bravery in the war hadn't made him the equal of the West Point graduates.

His wife, the other Mary of the two rivals, soothingly noted George Custer had been a brevet general in the war too; he'd been a West Pointer but he too was just a colonel now, and disappointed to a turn. Nelson had an ally.

A fine, brave ally, Miles nodded. We will rise together, just you watch.

Miles had been a Civil War volunteer who'd risen to high field rank on exceptional battle courage. But he wasn't a West Pointer, a pedigreed member of the officer class. He made sure they understood his battle record made him an equal; he intended to get the same promotions.

A visiting retired officer at a Nebraska mess recounted that he'd met Napoleon's brother Joseph, exiled in Philadelphia before the war. He'd heard amazing tales of the conquering little emperor.

Uh-huh. Europeans . . . *empires*, General Crook pondered it, fixing the well-known Crook glare rays on the old soldier. *My Ohio butt.*

No, sir, Miles rose to say, pleased to set Crook straight. Buonaparte was a self-made man. Opportunity offered him something; he took. That is the best thing for a man. I think we all agree on that.

No, Colonel, Crook said. Some of us do not.

I spoke only of Buonaparte's character, Miles glossed over Crook's opposition. His seizing of the opportune moment. In a republic, naturally, we do not take emperors for our models. Sir, he added.

Indeed, Colonel, Crook eyed him steadily. Indeed not.

Crook understood which opportunist Miles meant; Miles's wife being General Sherman's niece made other officers wary of standing up to him. He'd mistakenly assumed, because of Crook's laconic style, that even General Crook was wary.

That forked beard! My God, it's preposterous! Miles thought of Crook. It's an age problem. Old-fashioned. Out of date. He's got too old for this Indian warfare. A good goatee and mustache, like Colonel Custer has, is virile and up to date, however. I will grow one.

The preposterous vanity of that man, Crook thought. Miles's presence perturbed him. Miles reminded him of the roadrunners in Arizona. A ridiculous thing for a man. They'd preen, strut, puff out their chests, adjust their wings and tails, and look around to see if a mate was paying attention. Miles always appeared to be puffed up and posing for an invisible photographer. Miles's lack of West Point training shows up in his pomposity. But marriage to the mighty Shermans or not—*that's* sure putting your dick in the wringer—they say he was wounded four times, and was exceptionally brave in the war. His troopers love his bravado, and that he rose from the volunteer ranks—gives 'em hope for themselves—and they fear his temper. He'll be a useful officer, maybe.

They say Crook was brave in the war, Miles squinted across the Nebraska parade ground at his imagined rival, but, hell, I missed Gettysburg because of my gut wound or I'da been even more than I am. I'd be brigadier general too. I just need a good Indian victory under my belt and I will take him on.

When Chief Joseph and the Nez Perce surrendered to Miles in 1877, Miles claimed his first Indian victory.

Crook acknowledged that the Army still direly needed Colonel Miles to lead raw, frightened troops against experienced Indian warriors, but he made his opinion plain: Awarding him the victory was an offense against Army protocol.

It had been General O. O. Howard's weeks and thousand-plus miles of pursuit and battles with Joseph and the Nez Perce, in their attempted exodus from the United States to Canada, which had compelled Joseph's surrender. Howard ran the Nez Perce into exhaustion and despair, at great cost to his own troops. Miles apparently shouldered himself into the surrender at Bear Paw, and scooped up the credit that was rolling around loose between two exhausted adversaries, as they tended to their dead and wounded. By Army rules, Howard should have received the victory. Some wondered if getting credit for the Nez Perce surrender had something to do with Miles's wife being the niece of General of the Armies Sherman. Crook discovered from a former aide that it did not have anything to do with Sherman, although he approved it. It seemed already known at War that Sherman could barely tolerate the nephew-in-law Miles. That made it all the more a puzzle. Miles's seizure of another officer's credit caused consternation in the officer quarters.

West Pointers' jealousy! Miles claimed. Stew in it, fellas. I got

Chief Joseph. It's official and that's that.

He was exasperated that no promotion came immediately. But he smiled now, and nodded as an equal, when he rode past General Crook on the parade ground. Crook failed to notice him.

George Crook had a one-timer fondness for the notoriously Jesus-crazed General Howard. Howard was a Civil War hero who'd lost an arm in combat and gained an intense, all-embracing Christian belief, embracing Negroes and women and Indians as his equals in Christ, to the appalled scorn of most fellow officers. Life for General O. O. Howard was a righteous battle for the Lord, and when Otis got going on the Holy Word, Crook noted, stand back, the spittle's gonna be flying. Crook's fondness for Howard, Mary, his wife, later noted, was love from a man, George Crook, who excluded nearly everyone, for one who included nearly everyone, even the laconic, unclubbable George Crook.

Generals Crook and Howard had both been sent to Arizona in 1872 as emissaries of President Grant's new peace policy toward the Indian nations. They carried orders from Washington to establish a peace between Chief Cochise of the Chiricahua Apaches, other Apaches, and the citizens of Arizona.

Geronimo, a war medicine man, or *diyyin*, allied to Cochise, was present. He would remind Crook years later that it was General Howard who sweetened the treaty offer to Cochise with a gift of a dozen fat cattle. General Howard simply turned up at Cochise's stronghold, optimistic as an apostle, and herding twelve fat cattle for the tribe, hard pushed by a decade's war. The hard-to-budge Apache chief was warmly pleased with the gift, and the new goodwill it signified. A treaty was grandfathered into being with a few tons of beef. Cochise sent messengers to all his allied southern Apache bands: He was content to have peace with the Americans; they would fight no more. Cochise's word was law.

Crook's temporary commission as a brigadier general was made permanent for overseeing Howard's treaty with the Chiricahua Apaches, and his own victory with the Tonto Apaches. Ten years of war, initiated by American soldiers but dominated by Cochise, were suspended. Apache fighting had secured Crook's reputation. Crook never forgot what he owed to Otis Howard. Miles had some neck to steal Howard's victory over the Nez Perce. Keep an eye on this son-ofabitch, he scrawled a mental note to himself.

Crook had counseled the Arizonan territorial authorities to forget the past. Cochise would control his "bad Indians" in return for his guaranteed homeland, traditional lands south of Tucson, and a United States treaty: The conflict would stop now. In their somewhat hesitant gratitude, he noted later to his wife, the Arizonans wanted to know, uh, when was the Army going to stop shilly-shallying, and exterminate the savages.

Treaties mean nothing to these people, Crook wrote home. Keeping the peace will not be an easy road. But it is my road.

The idea that making war makes the man, a lesson gained as a provincial Ohio boy at West Point, had lost its crazy grandeur after too many Civil War battles, and the effects of modern weapons at their play with his troops. Fighting for and enforcing treaties is what makes this man, he thought. It is the work of the future of the country. It is the honor of the officer doing it, it preserves the honor of the Indian tribes reciprocating, and it is the honor of the American nation that counts on him to represent them at their best. General Sherman, a man of sorrows stingy with praise, often said General Crook was the perfect officer to carry out a peace policy: the best of Indian fighters because, simply, he not only had the balls for it, he respected the enemy as worthy of good American fairness in defeat; a democratic spirit bound in an imperturbable will—add the physical endurance of a bronze statue—it all made Crook an officer whom all Indians understood quickly as a warrior.

Posted to command the Platte District in the northern plains, Crook quickly saw the problems a peace policy would confront.

*

113

Crook wrote Mary late in '75: You would think all the glorious space in the Dakotas and Montana would keep a fellow from feeling squeezed. On the contrary, my dear, he was being squeezed on all sides. On one side, the Sioux and Cheyenne who had roamed too long and too far to accept being confined to reservations, even if it was for their own protection—as the Army believed—against a tide of white settlers pounding up the dust to the West. On the other side, bloody-minded hurrah-for-the-Union Civil War throwbacks, like Colonels Custer and Miles, who wanted to relive Civil War glory, despised the peace policy as unmanly, and planned to be promoted to generals again by fighting and killing Indians—in Custer's case, Crook noted sardonically to an aide, hopefully when they were asleep.

It was national news when Custer attacked his last sleeping Indian village, pop. ten thousand or so, June 25, 1876, and was appalled, as the sun reached its zenith in the Montana blue, to find himself getting slaughtered by Crazy Horse, Gall, Two Moons of the Tsistsistas, and hundreds of angry local Sioux and Cheyenne home owners.

A dismayed Crook saw the soldier-splattered Little Bighorn battlefield a day later. There was something poignant, foolish, and small about the dead Custer, and his brother Tom, sprawled on the slope of their catastrophic misjudgment. Like thrown-away, shot-up children's dolls with bared teeth, empty, pale eyes.

Some among the Lakota ghosts present, such as Lame Deer, still remembered Starchief George Crook generously, as a fair, truthful soldier, who never lied to them. Others in the afterlife had doubts.

Tatanka Iyotanka, Sitting Bull, never liked Crook, or any U.S. officer who led armies to force the Sioux onto reservations.

He made it plain with characteristic directness: See for yourself—he gestured around him—no United States. No government. No Army. No generals. No America. Washington is not in charge here. You died and forgot to bring Washington with you. I don't believe you understand where you are yet. I didn't want you brought here. I didn't trust you; dying hasn't changed my opinion.

114

*

Hats off to him, Crook thought. That's why he walked around me like a man who might or might not purchase this horse: reminding himself I was just who he thought I was, and he didn't want me here doing anything for him.

Tatanka Iyotanka had been killed only months after George Crook's heart popped apart in 1890, but he hadn't changed much since life. The medicine man hadn't lost his usual clarity. Crook was more than a bit lost, he had to admit. Despite the major general's uniform he had been buried in, there was no authority after death that he represented. It was not a country he was in now, it did not have a postmortem army, he was not one of its generals. It was not a geographical location that he might find poring over maps.

Equally, he found it was hard to abandon all of his earned self, just like that. To take off the uniform and the identity that went with being a major general might reveal a damned void, a skeletal insignificance with nothingness showing through the bones. Even as a ghost, he continually wanted to tell someone that he still soldiered loyally as a major general of the Army of the Republic of the United States of America. Well, Crook admitted, that surely sounded shit brained now. But—but he didn't know what he could think about himself in its place. It's not like death was a demotion or a decommission, he rationalized. Why shouldn't he remain Major General George Crook? He rationalized it over and over. It did not strike him until later that it was a plain and simple lie. As the unease and dislocation of being raised from dead, but not in any manner anticipated by his stern-eyed, hopeful mother, faded—raised in fact by Indians, of all the god-damned things—Crook could imagine his late mother, hands folded in front of her apron, glancing around with some scandal in her eyes at the Indians and asking: George, are you *sure* you said your prayers? *All* of them?—that it was a lie became plain as the nose on his face. If there was no country, if there was no American Army, claiming to still be a major general made no sense. He had always hated lying. He would not lie to others. He hated especially lying to himself because that was always a prelude to lying to others. Lying to yourself made you a lie entire, down to the bones. Lying to yourself was the fatal flaw, the last of all flaws to leave the spirit.

*

George Crook realized he couldn't articulate the place where his ghost had been summoned to, because it wasn't a place. Some kind of state of being perhaps, but not a physical place. A memory place? No. You could to some degree control memories, and summon memories, and dismiss memories. No such control existed here. He sometimes had memory flashes, almost dreamlike, of the rolling hills, rivers, and battlegrounds of eastern Montana, or a tree-lined cliff above a meadow with horses in South Dakota, or a bare red-rock Arizona valley with dust devils dancing across, and a horseman with a red headband, an Apache scout, moving in his direction, holding up a Sharps carbine, signaling he'd found the track of Geronimo's fugitives. The flashes lit him up like forked lightning bolts and then faded away, as he gazed in wonder, like an immigrant in a new land. Which I am, I reckon, he thought.

Over time, of which he was hardly aware, he guessed the place might be something else: an echoing canyon for the actions of his life. As he passed through, his presence called out himself and his life. The things he was and he did ricocheted back and forth. A place where the unfinished business gets heard again as an echo of itself, and finally has to be done right. Where the cries and echoes of the done and the lamentations of the undone can finally die out. There was always the business not finished. Not necessarily the business you'd thought was unfinished but the business you'd be surprised to find out was your business at all, much less that you'd left it unfinished.

Unfinished business and Nelson Miles, Crook thought. Two names for the same thing, maybe. Same as "chicken bone" and "stuck in the craw." "The Apaches" was a simpler name for it.

Crook had been posted back to 1880s Arizona immediately after the northern plains campaigns. "Apaches—out of control again," he was told by War Department authorities, quoting local reports; Crook was the veteran Apache-fighting general the Arizonans were counting on to help them. Geronimo and Chief Naiche's band were wreaking havoc. Geronimo wanted the late Cochise's treaty lands south of Tucson for his Apaches; he wanted American settlers driven

116

away, and the freedom it would restore to Apache raiding and trading southward into Mexico. It was their old life. Crook didn't like or trust Geronimo, as he'd liked and trusted other Apaches, but he gave credit where it was due. Geronimo must have figured it out for himself. If the free Apache life ended this time, Apacheria would be ending for good north of the Rio Grande. It was going to be harder fighting with his people's finality at stake. Geronimo would not have to hear the dialogue in Washington to know George Crook was coming. *It's a reservation now—of our choosing and say-so, not his. He doesn't get a goddamned vote.*

It'll be a surprise, you returning, his wife, Mary, said.

Doubt it, Crook said, packing his case. Geronimo's probably expecting me.

How could that be? Mary said. He's two thousand miles from here.

Beats me all to hell, Crook thought. But he will.

He decided not to alarm Mary. You're right, he said. It couldn't.

They'd proceeded to skirmish and fight for nearly four years, and hundreds of miles around the compass, and hundreds of miles back again. When Geronimo's band tired of being harried, and reduced by attrition, by the relentless Crook, they accepted periodic breathers— as Crook thought of them—on a reservation with other Apaches— Apaches whom Geronimo scorned as beholden to the white man— and American authorities' rules, which he liked even less. Periodic breathers were followed by prolonged escapes, and another yearlong pursuit through the mountains by Crook's forces. After four years, Nelson Miles arrived to take command. The frustrated Arizonans conveyed to Washington that they did not find Crook an adequate exterminator. Confinement does no damn good; they need wiping out. Miles was to capture the hostiles and send them to Tucson for criminal trials and prompt hangings. Crook saw Miles, and exhaled an unadmitted sigh. He understood his effort was over, and submitted his resignation.

Miles tricked everyone, Crook learned later. He tricked the Arizonans by refusing to forward the hostile Apaches into their custody. He tricked the president who'd ordered him to. He tricked Geronimo into surrender with promises of a homeland reservation, and deported the Chiricahuas and allies to a prison fort, Fort Marion, Florida. Here is where the chicken bone became the craw sticker, Crook reflected later. The unfinished business began exactly here.

117

*

The Apaches had been moved out of Fort Marion, Florida, when tuberculosis flared up in the fort and ravaged the prisoners of war. Crook had heard of their plight, and in 1890 had taken the trouble to visit his old adversaries in their second prisoner-of-war camp, across the Florida state line in Alabama.

Some had been surprisingly touched to see the old enemy visiting. Old combatants have a mighty peculiar bond, Crook thought, as he traded grim smiles and shook hands with the mellowed once-nemesis Geronimo. Miles promised us two years in Florida, no more, Geronimo said.

Crook shook his head. Miles was lying. You would have done better taking my terms and waiting it out.

I could not do what you offered, Geronimo said. San Carlos reservation was Apaches like indeh—dead men. I didn't like it.

My surrender terms kept you in Arizona, Crook said. It was the best you could expect.

Apaches cannot live that way, Geronimo said. You know us.

No, Crook said. I understand.

We die here, Geronimo said simply. Arizona was made for Apaches by our Creator. This place was made for others. We don't want to die here, he said. We want to go home.

Arizona won't ever permit you back, Crook said. You know that.

I hear it, Geronimo said, nodding. But we want our home.

Crook sought out the Apache scouts he'd enlisted to track Geronimo; it was one of his successful innovations, brought from the northern campaigns, for this hit-and-run warfare: Only Apaches could track other Apaches successfully. Despite their loyalty to Crook, or, Crook suspected, because of it, Miles had deported Crook's scouts to Florida along with the hostile Apaches. He was happy to see the ones still alive again, but the sight of his scouts in the same barracks as the men they'd helped track, and who hated them as traitors, was desolating.

As he shook hands with familiar former enemies, and former friends, and looked into their eyes, the desolation that had accompanied his approach to the prisoner barracks pressed in again on Crook's chest. He forced himself to breathe deeply and unbuttoned his collar. He found himself sweating profusely in the Alabama humidity, and his lunch kept trying to lurch back up his gorge. He kept it down and breathed deeply.

Lozen, sister of the long-dead Chief Victorio, spoke to Crook quietly about the difficulties their families had had at the Florida prison. Crook could see she was dying. Like her people's old life, he couldn't help thinking when he saw her. The fire in her eyes had receded into a tired calm. She was in the last stages of her tuberculosis ordeal. She seemed determined to remain upright in bed to the end. An Apache woman was brushing her hair as Crook entered. Lozen smiled faintly at her, and the woman withdrew. She looked at Crook and nodded. She had asked to see him.

He'd heard about Lozen from his scouts. Fearless, devoted to her dead brother's example, a favorite of Victorio's war chief Old Nana, and apparently a crack shot at a quarter of a mile. He'd seen her at parleys with Apache leadership; she'd always lingered in the background. They hadn't spoken. She radiated a powerful presence, even with her shoulders hunched by illness. The Chi'inde Apache women around her were still, unreadable, wary of Crook. Undaunted by her raspy, disappearing voice, and a hesitant interpreter, she stared beyond Crook as she spoke.

At the former prison fort in Florida, children would die of the coughing disease. No Apache knew this disease before, she shook her head. Their children also were being taken to Indian schools, to be made into white eyes. Apaches were alarmed by what they heard. Children beaten with sticks for speaking Apache instead of American. The Dene do not beat children, she said, continuing to stare beyond him. She'd heard Nantan Lupan—as she'd heard Crook called by her people—was here to see them as a friend now, not an enemy. That is good, she half glanced at him. The war was hard for everyone. He knew them. He knew their children. She had seen him, their worst enemy, kneeling to speak with their children at truce meetings. He must be a good man. Could he do something for the children? Bring them back from the schools?

A good man? Crook thought. His lunch made a halfhearted jump up his throat and fell back exhausted. He hesitated, then nodded. I'll have to see what I can do. The government feels Indian children are better off getting an American education. He could see from her dismayed reaction that she knew he was fibbing: He believed the Indian schools would do great good. The schools would teach a new generation of Apaches how to live in the new American world. To read, write, to speak English like white men. She glanced at him finally, too fragile now to confront him, intent on conserving her energies, but her sharp glance told him everything. I'll see what I can do, he repeated.

The women were quietly dismayed, Crook saw. They'd hoped for better; their missing children showed in their faces like a tragic illness, for which no medicine was known.

Finally Lozen tried to speak again. For an instant she'd summoned all the Dene ancestry she had left. Her intense black eyes looked beyond him again, powerfully accentuated by her high cheekbones. Already talking to the next world, he thought, not to me. She hesitated, then looked away quickly, hunched over. She was clearly pain ridden and holding back the coughing. Crook waited, then leaned in closer to hear her, nodding encouragement to speak. Go on, he murmured. I'm listening. Before the interpreter could translate, Lozen was seized by uncontrollable, detonating bouts of coughing up blood. Suddenly gouts and strings of blood and sputum spewed out everywhere and he and the interpreter had to jump back from the gasping, hemorrhaging woman. She was choking on blood and had to stop. Then, as Lozen sprayed gobbets of lung blood all over herself, over the bedclothes, and sucked hoarsely for air, any air, the women around her hurried to shield her from the American. They shrieked, and wildly waved Crook out of the way, to go away, go away!

One time, he thought, this woman had taken out two of his scouts at four hundred–plus yards with a single-shot Sharps carbine. Their only woman warrior. Dying like this.

When Crook tried to look in on her before leaving, he saw all the aging, notable warriors standing outside the barracks. They waited, in their brand-new midnight blue Army tunics. They looked smart in the neatly pressed uniforms and curl-brimmed straw hats, given them to tell them something about the American prisoner/soldiers they'd been enlisted as now. They were all silent, looking down. Chief Chihuahua, who was usually genial with Crook, looked up at him impassively and shook his head no once. Lozen was dead.

*

Crook had been left so enraged he could feel his heart beat in his body all the way back home. His stomach continued its mutiny. He had to lean off the hurtling train platform, grasping his beard out of the path, to vomit his guts up. I have just thrown up at a speed greater than my father ever traveled, or dreamed of, Crook thought. Progress abounds.

Miles had used the Apaches' '86 surrender to advance his career without insuring their welfare afterward. Grab the credit and run. Clamor for the promotion. Bang on the table until they give it to you just to make you go away. He'd heard from a former aide how Miles had "Jack Russelled their ankles at War" for Crook's major general's two stars when he retired. Nag and bite and growl and bite and bark and nag and growl and bite. Just like with the surrender of Chief Joseph and the Nez Perce in '77. Send 'em to Leavenworth Prison for years, watch the Nez Perce lands and horse herds given to grateful ranchers who praise your wisdom to congressmen, forget the Nez Perce who'd fought bravely, howl to the moon for promotion. Because it was Miles, Crook felt an old fever flowing through his stringy muscles all over again. My unfinished business, he thought later, before I ever understood it was my business at all.

Before departing, he'd told Kayeteneh to tell Chief Naiche and Geronimo that he'd help now. It was a plan he'd been figuring out for a while. An association, the Indian Rights Association he had formed, with some other retired officers and some reform-minded civilians, to benefit Indians like them, to help them to a new life. They knew him from the old wars; his personal word was his honor. They had been enemies, but he had never lied to them.

Enju, Kayeteneh said. Agreed.

It upset you, Mary said. The woman dying.

Crook shook his head no. Lying upset me.

The woman dying upset you, Mary put it out there again.

Nothing like lying badly to a dying woman, Crook said. Beats drowning puppies by a mile.

You did your best, she soothed him.

No, I didn't, Crook shook his head again. But I intend to.

I don't suppose you ever foresaw a day, Mary mused, when you would be redeeming a man you loathe, Geronimo, from another you despise, meaning Nelson. Now if that is not being between a rock and a hard place, the words have no meaning at all.

Crook stared at her a moment. Mary—, he said. He gave up. He started to laugh and stopped himself. Mary, he smiled. My dearest Mary.

It gave him enormous pleasure, he described to Mary, to see them with their hopes slightly raised. He had to explain to her something uncomfortable and hardly acknowledged before in himself: He felt a proprietary interest in Apaches. They were a depletion on his life and career, but he couldn't help himself: They were *his* Apaches. He was not certain she could understand, because he was not certain even he understood.

I *do* understand, Mary nodded. My father, who, being a Southerner, of course would know, used to say, We are a deluded and tragic race. We need to kill what we love best, or die trying. I do not know to this day if he was referring to the Union, or to Negroes, whom he was unable to help himself from spending an inordinate amount of time with. He couldn't help himself; they were *his* Negroes, and hon, I don't mean he owned them as slaves. I mean he couldn't let go of them, as if they had something he had to have, but couldn't have. There was that same "proprietary" interest upon him, like some kind of hunger. Lord, in town, the black folks'd be trying to do their work, or shoeing his horse, and Daddy just couldn't stop talking with them, and trying in earnest to get their opinions, so he could talk their ears off even more. He scared them to hell and never knew it. They must have known somewhere in their hearts that this is the man who kills what he loves best, or dies trying. He had *the need*, you see, and that's all it's about.

Leave me apart from this, Crook instructed her. I do not love Apaches. It would help if you remembered that.

Yes, you do, Mary said. You just do not know it. You also have the need.

What need? Crook said. For God's sakes.

To know what it is on the other side, of course, she smiled.

No, he insisted. There may be such a place as the other side, but he was no longer sure, after years of fighting them, that he was not half on that other side already. Not after years. It was what the Arizonan authorities accused him of, not in so many words, but in the vague attribution of his final lack of success with Geronimo to a disloyalty to his own race. Which he balked at, which he rejected. Count on stupid people to think of stupid things to say, like apple trees are prone to produce apples. It was not love, as she thought, and it was not a disloyalty of any kind, racial or otherwise. It is hard to explain what you find in yourself to become over a prolonged period; you can take on half the nature, if not the skin and appearance, of those you fight. Apaches were a tough band; he respected them for that. Stay months on a mule for its surefootedness, tracking them through mountains, beneath an Arizona sun as big as the capitol dome on fire; do not neglect to notice the scents of pine forests or the silver creeks tumbling along, or the beauty they passed through where you had to follow, or the blazing emptiness of the desert expanses they traversed leaving hardly a sign; do not forget you yourself have said they were very dangerous enemies on horseback, but, uniquely, far more dangerous on foot in their mountains; try living hourly with the long-distance .45–70 caliber rifle shot that might remove you from the saddle and your own life at any moment: He promised by the end you would respect them for it too. They would do this for a freedom necessary for them to know who they were, a form of honor he understood, since he could not be who he was either if he did not force himself to the extreme measure that tracking them demanded of him; but he served, and was loyal beyond the extreme to the United States and they were impossible for the United States to afford any more. Why was simple. They killed anyone who intruded on their need to be as they'd always been. Their bad reputation was based only on that. Given the cruelties done to them first by Mexico for two centuries, including slave taking of Apache women and children, random slaughters, and the seldom-mentioned rapes, and later by the U.S., which did not pay good Yankee dollars for the Gadsden Purchase of borderland Arizona only to cede the best lands of it to a residual Apache dominance, always known in polite circles as savagery—to accuse them of cruelty was true enough, no frivolous complaint. They were cruel beyond polite description to an enemy; but it was pointless to make a meal of home-fried outrage out of it. They had reached a peace with the simplest of modes of survival. No quarter asked, no quarter given. If stolen from, they stole back. If hurt, they punished multiple times with ferocity, until something in them was satisfied with the balance only they determined and understood. It was a boxing match with ten angry bears in their own forest. It was a fight by bears' rules, and it ended when bears had enough or were dead. When treated fairly and in peace, the ten angry bears magically turned into ten pretty good men and women, calm and courteous in comportment, good to their word, with their own meals, their own dances, their own stories, and so forth. They were enduring as the mountains they came out of and returned to. He knew them by name, by the peculiarities of individuals, he knew them to shake hands with, which God knows makes a difference. They'd been subjected by Miles's decision to deport them to Florida to degradation, disease, and squalor; that was not in his opinion what surrender to the United States Army was supposed to be about. After the Civil War, they'd tried that German fella who ran Andersonville Prison Camp for the Confederates. He'd been found guilty of forcing surrendered Union prisoners to die of wasting and disease, and he'd been hung.

But they were white men, Mary said.

White men, Crook nodded. Not Apaches, you mean.

There is a difference, she said.

Not in my rules of war, he said.

An excuse to criticize Nelson, she said.

No, he shook his head. There are rules, Mary. They are real.

Smile for me, will you?! she cried. You are so serious!

He laughed, held her, and gave up his soul to her gratefully.

Anyway, a waste of time hoping to punish Miles. But he'd try and redo the bad deal the Apaches'd got from the government he'd represented in subduing them. Find them a western home maybe. Possibilities existed. He wasn't about to let what Nelson Miles had done be the last word.

Miles was up north in Chicago now, he'd received word, appointed in 1890 as Army commander of the Department of the Missouri. He was overseeing the Sioux Reservations and others.

Where we just were? Mary asked. Your old command?

Exactly, Crook said.

Is Nelson following you? she asked.

I think they just send him to mangle up whatever I managed not to, Crook grumbled.

For heaven's sakes, why? Mary asked.

Welcome to the United States Army, Crook said. Don't ask why.

He belched. His stomach was troubling the waters again. It had started in Alabama, looking at all the despair, tuberculosis, and suicide direct in the eyes, and become more frequent, and made his chest feel tight sometimes. She'd tell him to see a doctor if he said anything about it, and he lacked her fondness for the medicos. He'd been through worse, he figured.

Gas, darling, he said. Excuse my manners.

Miles was following Crook's path again. The Department of the Missouri, headquartered in Chicago, had been a command Crook had occupied just before he retired. The Ghost Dance had begun on Sioux reservations while Crook was there. Harmless if backward, he'd observed—although the church denominations, having succeeded in getting the Sun Dance banned, were mightily alarmed by the backsliding of the Ghost Dance and the dancers' claim to speak to dead relatives in a trance—*Christ. God help the Sioux and Cheyenne if Miles was there.* But Crook's business was now the perishing Apaches. A quarter of them dead from tuberculosis or suicide already. His unfinished business, he reckoned. He was still Major General George Crook, even retired. He was only sixty-two, and raring to get his teeth into something good he could do something about. He still had friends in the government. He still had admirers in the Army. They'd help.

George? Mary began before stopping to think what she wanted to say. He reflected often that she was the loveliest woman, Virginia born, comfortable, and amused with Army folk. Lucky man? As all get-out.

You are clearly one of nature's curmudgeons, dear, Mary finally said. You really do need an enemy. Poor Nelson.

There is no such critter, Crook said, puffing his pipe. There are skunks and snakes; there are coyotes and javelinas. No one has ever seen a Poor Nelson. Trust me.

The way he always seems to follow you—Mary said and stopped to think again. I wonder if all this time he really wanted to be you. Y'think?

He wanted to be Custer, Crook said. But without the failure.

I was always taught that failure is the part of life you learn most from, Mary said.

Oh, Mary, Crook groaned, that is the kind of lie they teach young ladies to prepare them for the excuses their men are gonna make all the day long. You ought to know better. If failure is such a great teacher, George Custer's an encyclopedia moldering in his grave, or whatever was left of him when the Sioux ladies, who are not taught that failure is such a great teacher, got finished with him. I doubt that. However, he nodded to give credit where it was due, you are correct with respect to the need to know about failure if you are in the Army. We lose limbs, Crook began to count on his fingers. We lose fingers and eyes and noses. We lose men. We lose battles. Some lose their minds. We fail all the doo-dah day. And hope to learn. Or at least until we get too old to use learning as an excuse for going through obvious nonsense and mischief. And you are half right with respect to Nelson. Failure was not something he ever thought he'd need to learn about. Failure is the nightmare for Nelson. That means the higher he rises in the Army, the more he will do anything to avoid failing, and that is, plain and simple, not a good commander. *That*, Crook leaned toward her, is why he wouldn't go to war with Geronimo. He had to trick them. He couldn't fight Apaches in a thousand years. He'd have failed.

So he betrayed them, Mary said.

Crook leaned back again, and said, Nelson just figured out what was best for his career. He wouldn't recognize betraying another human being if it bit his keister.

Had George Crook been in a theater play, exchanging conversation with Mary on a well-upholstered couch in the set of a comfortable home, wearing a tweed suit and puffing his pipe, an audience waiting and following it in the darkened theater, he would have been interrupted now by a surprising knock on the door. Who can that be? the audience would wonder. Another officer? A famous Indian warrior? A messenger of some kind? Mary's left hand unconsciously inspects the bun at the back of her head to make sure all is right.

Yes? she calls. Come on in. We're home.

George Crook felt the wrongful pounding at his chest, like the knock at the door he realized too late he'd always known would come, the bad messenger sent in the middle of unfinished things, and he was suddenly rising from the couch, pipe tumbling to the floor, struggling to draw breath, and he was clutching his breast, as Mary rose to her feet in alarm, just as he caved downward, his knees failing him sideways, in the chest-crushing grip of the invisible enemy, the one who

could not be beaten, gasping, Mary, aw God—MARY, my heart!—
and Mary dropping down, kneeling beside him, calling, George, oh
George, don't leave me, no no no!

I'm sorry, Mary, he whispered. I'm so sorry, dear.

Unfinished business, he thought at the end.

NOTES. In 1855, Chief Seattle signed a treaty and made a speech yielding tribal lands
in Washington State to the United States. In the 1970s, a poetic version of Seattle's
speech began to circulate. It proclaimed that Indian ghosts would always roam the
lands they had been dispossessed from, because their love of the lands would never
die. That version of the speech was revealed to be a 1970s counterfeit. Its expression
of certain tragic realities, however, had served to give it a wide currency in the world.

This is a story of many roaming ghosts. It is not merely fictional, but absolutely,
unqualifiedly counterfeit. It is also based in certain tragic realities about the love of
American lands.

For information and documents on the career of General Nelson Miles, I relied on
Nelson A. Miles: A Documentary Biography of his Military Career 1861–1903,
edited by Brian C. Pohanka, in collaboration with John M. Carroll (Glendale, California: the Arthur H. Clark Company, 1985).

For the career of General George Crook, I used Peter Aleshire's *The Fox and the
Whirlwind: General George Crook and Geronimo, A Paired Biography* (New York:
John Wiley and Sons Inc., 2000).

The Light of Two Million Stars
Andrew Ervin

EVEN WITH THE SMOKE and the grime scrubbed from the pores of his face and drained down into the belly of the city, sleep remains an impossibility. He lies down nevertheless to welcome the voices he knows to expect. He does not fear them now, in the gentle twilight of his unconsciousness. In a matter of hours he will loosen on the world his new opera, *The Golden Lotus*. Again, Lajos Harkályi will take the songs of his family, of his people, his fellow prisoners at Terezín, and share them with the fickle-minded public, who will purchase copies but, he knows, never *hear* them.

He can already picture before him hundreds of thousands of shiny DVDs, and hear the corresponding number of dead souls calling, admonishing him, encouraging him. So much music has been lost, more notes than he could draw in this lifetime or in a hundred of them. The faces want Harkályi to speak for them, and it is a responsibility that weighs heavily, much too heavily, upon him. He must answer to them first, and only then to himself.

These half a million compact discs are perfect reproductions of each other, but in the hands of his public they will reflect half a million different realities. Each is unique, every spin through the home high-fidelity system a new event, a new experience for the listener. The recorded music changes over time, and there exists no thing that can exhume the spectral presence of a living performance. The concert hall has become a sacred place, as sacred in some ways as where he learned to compose music.

It is impossible now to comprehend such a thing, yet the hideous truth remains that it was Zoltán Kodály himself who suggested that Lajos, a thirteen-year-old violin prodigy, should wait out the remainder of the war at the Terezín ghetto. Better there, he thought, than fending for scraps in the subbasements of Budapest.

Almost two hundred fifty years ago, Joseph II ordered the construction of an outpost at the confluence of the Ohře and Labe rivers, the first line of defense protecting the Austria-Hungary Empire from the savage Germanic hordes. Across the Ohře from the small fortress, in which, more recently, the regicide Gavrilo Princip perished, stood the spa town of Terezín. The Nazis offered that village, Kodály told him, to the Jewish population of Central Europe as a safe haven, sequestered from the general population. A former Liszt Academy colleague, immediately upon his arrival, had sent Kodály a postcard boasting of the vast and vibrant musical life that flourished under the protection of the administrative Council of Jewish Elders. Karel Ančerl himself conducted a resident orchestra. Wealthy Jews from all over Central Europe, denied their civil rights and freedom of movement at home, funneled toward Czechoslovakia.

Budapest was no longer safe. Lajos's father had not been heard from since his departure for forced labor at a brick factory someplace beyond the city limits. With the blessings of their mother, Kodály made arrangements, at tremendous personal expense, to have Lajos and his brother, Tibor, smuggled safely to Vienna. One June evening, at dusk, they emerged from the cellar beneath Andrássy Boulevard in which they hid from the Arrow Cross. His mother did not cry as they were hoisted into the bed of a horse-drawn wagon. She handed Lajos a sack of walnuts and a smooth, round stone he could use to break them open. He would not see her again, though her voice still rings in his ears. It is her song that the world will hear later, in the afternoon. "Do not be afraid," she said. As they pulled away, she sang to them, and to herself, a gentle lullaby.

The boys hid for hours beneath a bed of straw and manure, stopping finally, before dawn, in Vienna. They had already eaten all of the nuts, three days' worth, yet Lajos held fast to the stone and would continue to do so for more than half a century. In Vienna, or near it, they waited in lines that extended to the very horizon, until a small pack of bored German officers chose which among them to herd aboard two vacant boxcars. A soldier pulled the paperwork from his hands, and Lajos and his brother were permitted to join a hundred and fifty others on Transport No. IV/14i from Vienna; a far greater number, most of them elderly and infirm, remained behind. The endless clip-clop syncopation of the locomotive disgorged from the passengers a stench, more animal than human, that can on occasion still make Harkályi's eyes water. The hideous music of moaning and sobbing, of death itself, cannot be notated by human hands. It was hours or days—perhaps a month, or ten years, or a thousand—before they reached Terezín, a town that he and Tibor and so many others would come to regard as the anteroom to hell itself.

Harkályi rises from his soft bed, entirely unrested, and closes the bathroom door behind him. The joints of his elbows and knees ache; there is pain in his lower back. The steam of the shower warms his naked body, the skin that hangs loosely from his arms and belly, while he rubs the debris from one eye and then the other. His woolly, normally wild hair is shorn close and tame for the events of the day about to unfold before him.

The faint daylight oozing through the ceiling of clouds makes the temperature even more jarring. It feels colder now than it did in the middle of the night, when he was drenched in sweat. Harkályi avoids making eye contact with his own face, which stares out at him from an advertisement poster in the window of the record shop, which is not yet open for business. Perhaps it will remain closed in honor of Independence Day; it is difficult to say—everything is different now in Hungary. It feels like snow could fall.

The sidewalks of the *körút* are full of people, many of them seemingly already intoxicated. He has left his wristwatch in the room. Over at the National Museum, they are already reenacting Petőfi's speech of March 15, 1848, when the poet spoke out against the empire and instigated a revolt that failed to gain from Austria the independence that Hungary so desperately desired and would not earn until the end of the Soviet regime. If even then. There are speeches, nationalistic hymns, a brass band. Children wave flags while men pass bottles of *pálinka* through the smoking crowd. Harkályi has watched the ceremonies on satellite television and has no desire to witness it in the flesh.

The underpass beneath the Nyugati Train Station has awoken, or remained awake, as he has, all night long. A band of South Americans in colorful attire is performing primitive music in a circle, to the delight of passersby. Waves of people spill from the metro's escalators. Women sell onions and roasted pumpkin seeds. A freshly shaven youth attempts to hand Harkályi a religious pamphlet, but he recoils from the boy's reach.

He has time to waste before meeting Magda and wants to take a stroll, to clear his head before the concert, an event lingering ominously at the furthermost poles of his thoughts; he knows it is there, yet refuses, still, to bring it into focus. It is embarrassing—the pageantry and applause, the idolatry that conflates him, this tired old man, with his compositions. He cannot wait to see his niece; she alone will relieve the tedium of public appearance.

Above the clapping and pan fluting of the South Americans, he is able to discern some kind of commotion emanating from a hallway leading to the rear of the train station: the prolonged, rapid-fire clinking of a slot machine. There is cheering, a crowd forming. A shabby man, older in appearance than his age would dictate, with the gray pallor of lifelong drunkenness, has won a small fortune in coins. His excitement infects all of those within the glass-enclosed pub, as well as those outside, noses pressed against the filthy windows. The man buys three liters of wine, which the scantily clad server ladles from vats built into the surface of the bar. She hands unstemmed drinking glasses to all present, and more people cram their way inside to partake of the free alcohol. It is a minor stampede of the borderline homeless. It is the greatest day in the entire life of the winning man; he will tell stories of this morning for the short remainder of his dull life. The scene sickens Harkályi, but fascinates him also. He envies the men's easy camaraderie, so utterly free of pretense.

Farther down the hall, he happens upon a scene so foreign that he questions if he has fallen asleep after all, if it is but a dream shaken loose from the recesses of his memory. It is real. A band of skinheads—true skinheads, in the flesh, six or seven of them—is attacking a Negro man without stop, without mercy. Blood drools from the young man's eyelids, from his lips. They kick at him from all sides.

"Stop that!" Harkályi orders them, before he has the opportunity to think better of it.

The smallest of the assailants, no more than sixteen years old, approaches with the silver blade of a serrated knife drawn. He says something in Hungarian, his voice cracking, which Harkályi cannot fathom. His armband does not feature a swastika but, instead, a green machinery cog. They stand toe-to-toe, but this boy is half a foot shorter. Harkályi must crane his neck to look into the dusty-glass color of the child's eyes. He cannot find it in himself to be afraid. The noise of the gamblers behind him swells, draws closer. The skinheads drop their prey, shout at the child, whose vodka breath pollutes his own; the boy lifts Harkályi's necktie and runs his knife through it, dragging it downward to split the silk into ribbons. "*Zsidó disznó*," he says. The boy then backs away, and steps on the fallen Negro as the skinheads retreat to the rear of the station.

The drunken revelry spills from the pub and into the hallway. The bums laugh and cheer and ignore the unconscious black man. Harkályi kneels next to him, dirtying his pants. The man's jacket reads U.S. ARMY and GIBSON over the left breast. There is not as much blood as he thought, though the man's face has already started to mutate into some hideous mask: One eye has sealed entirely closed under the weight of a large lump on his brow, his nose appears broken, a safety pin affixed to a tiny Hungarian flag juts out of his bottom lip. When Harkályi removes it, the man gains consciousness.

"The fuck happened?"

"You were attacked—by skinheads," Harkályi tells him. "Wait here and I will summon a doctor."

"I don't need no doctor. Help me up."

Harkályi attempts to lift the man from under his arms, but he is surprisingly heavy for his diminutive stature. He is solid muscle, but now his neck cannot fully support the weight of his own head. It is only with significant struggle that he is able at last to climb to his feet.

"I understand that you are an American?" Harkályi asks.

The man does not respond, except by way of a deep-bellied groan. Saliva and blood drip freely from his mouth.

"You require medical help. Please."

"I said I don't want a doctor, old man. Did you say skinheads?"

"Yes. Today, apparently, is their big occasion to go wild, or even wilder than usual."

"I guess so," the man says. The pain must be excruciating. It is a wonder that he has the strength to stand. "I need to go. Thanks for your help."

"Of course. Are you certain you would not prefer for me to find a doctor?"

"No, I'm good."

The man draws himself to the crowded underpass. Harkályi watches his slow, ambling progress. He can still smell the alcoholic stench of that murderous child; his was the very face of his own parents' murderers, whom he has loathed since he hid in those underground passages so similar to this one. Only now Harkályi is not angry—his lifetime's worth of fury has dried up, and he can muster only some sensation approaching pity for the boy. It is ignorance, as much as it is evil, that makes him dangerous. And it is the joy in his own heart, and the forgiveness, that distinguishes them. He removes his ruined tie and leaves it on the ground, in the small pool of spilt blood.

*

With an hour yet before he must depart for Buda, he sits on the plush sofa to watch the television. There is no news, only reenactments of previous events, the cyclical return of war and famine and genocide, interrupted by equally crude commercial advertisements. Only the longitudes change, and now it is the Americans who put men in concentration camps. Harkályi, to his regret, will not live long enough to hear the music composed in Guantánamo, in these secretive black sites speckled like cancerous moles on Europe's backside.

Miraculously, the stories concerning the tremendous musical life of Terezín proved to be true, yet every other storied detail about the concentration camp—and it was most certainly a concentration camp—proved to be willfully exaggerated if not criminally false. The Schutzstaffel used the site as a model facility, as the set of an elaborate staged drama demonstrating to the world their kindly treatment of Europe's Jews who, in reality, were upon arrival stripped of their possessions, shaved and deloused, and forced to live in prisonlike dormitories.

When Lajos and his brother arrived, in June of 1943, preparations had already begun for an inspection of the facilities by the Red Cross. To prevent the appearance of overcrowding, additional labor engagement transports were loaded and dispatched at all hours of the night and day, carrying up to a thousand people at a time to Poland and places unknown. Rumors filtered back, even among the children, and presumably to the entire world, about the nature of those steady departures. He and Tibor too could have been condemned at any time. The kapo of their dormitory provided them with a postcard on which they were to inform their family about the comfortable conditions in which they found themselves. They did not use Kodály's address, for fear of raising suspicion among the authorities about his activities, and instead they had the card sent to their former neighbors, the ones who had alerted the Nazis to their whereabouts and had had their father sent away; the boys hoped that the Arrow Cross would deliver it personally and arrest them as Jewish sympathizers. Only years later, during his previous visit to Hungary, would Harkályi learn that Kodály and his wife had by that time already abandoned their home for the dank basement of a Budapest church, where he completed his *Missa brevis*.

The Red Cross arrived, and then departed again, and tens of thousands more souls continued to Poland.

There existed in Terezín any number of ensembles, tolerated by the Nazis and consisting of rotating rosters of musicians, which performed everything from complete operas—almost exclusively German and Italian—to decadent, American-style jazz. A small town square contained a wooden riser, upon which public concerts were performed on weekends. There was even a baby grand piano, albeit a crippled one, its legs shorn off as if it had stepped upon a land mine. Most of the serious musical activities occurred in secret, however. As a "millionaire," camp slang for a new prisoner, and at his age, Lajos was not at first provided access to one of the many violins circulating through the town, some of them carried to Czechoslovakia unassembled and glued roughly back together. He and Tibor were assigned to the Halfsdienst, a work detail for young people, but were also permitted to participate in a children's chorus. The boys learned to speak Czech despite the proclamation that all public utterances were to be in German. In his precious free time, late in the night, Lajos transcribed for violin, from memory, Bartók's *Fourteen Bagatelles* and performed them on a borrowed instrument for a small but enthusiastic audience in the attic of the dormitory in which he lived.

When word of his musical prowess spread, as it was bound to do in such a setting, he was given the regular use of a too-small, half-sized violin, on which he was able to practice for the occasional private violin lesson. He also found himself relieved of his work duties and, to the consternation of his jealous brother, assigned to the exclusive group of Notenschreiber, who reproduced by hand the rare, precious scores that arrived at Terezín, or were composed there amidst the chaos and horror. Every so often, Lajos would change a note or two, such as those at the very center of the violin part of Gideon Klein's *Trio*, and await with great joy his surreptitious contribution to the public performances. Many of those scores have since been lost, and little by little Harkályi has in the intervening years attempted to resurrect them in his own compositions.

His mother sits alone, a porcelain cup of weak tea held on a saucer in her lap. The room is strangely bright, as if bleached by a sun that has drawn closer. He approaches her, as if dreaming, finally asleep, and as she stands her smile grows bountiful enough to rid Lajos of all that plagues him. "You made it," she says. The porcelain makes no sound as she returns it to the table.

"Yes. Yes—I have made it."

"Let me look at you."

She takes his shoulders in her hands and can feel that he has grown thin, that the meat has atrophied and shriveled from his bones. But her arms around him—this is why he has come. The tears swell in his eyes. "I am so happy. So happy to see you." He holds on to her so she can absorb all of his suffering and sleeplessness, through her youthfulness and beauty make it dissipate like smoke.

"You are so thin," Magda says, "but you look healthy."

Neatly attired strangers murmur around them in countless languages about the current state of Europe, about these awful, dreadful times, about what new travesties today will bring. They stir cubes of refined sugar into their teacups and stab tiny forks at their plates. A young girl, not yet a teenager, winds her way through the labyrinth of tables, collecting soiled plates.

"It is unbelievable. Have I told you that you look exactly like your grandmother?"

"Only every time I see you."

"She was—"

"'—the most beautiful woman in Budapest.'"

"Are you mocking me, Magda?"

"Only a little, *bácsi.*" She is his same height, if not slightly taller, and she kisses him on both cheeks. "How is your room?"

"Fine, fine. Very comfortable."

"*Két* cappuccino," she tells a passing and disinterested waitress, and they sit. "The coffee here's great, ten times better than what we get down at the base. Are you hungry?"

"No, I had room service deliver some things. You should eat, however."

The resemblance is impossible to fathom. She is the same age, or very close to the same age, that his mother was when he and Tibor saw her for the last time. Even her voice rings with distinct and soothing similarity.

The *cukrászda* doubles in the morning as a dining room for guests of the hotel, and the odors of baking sugar and of stale coffee linger in the atmosphere. The pastry chefs arrive with regularity behind the counter to load the glass display cases with decorative cakes and tortes and every manner of creamy, rich dessert. The array of treats simultaneously fascinates and repels him; that people would consume such junk is an outrage, but that such an ocean of options exists, and in Budapest, is cause for celebration.

The difference between communism and democracy, he has come to believe in the course of his travels, can be witnessed in this very display case full of cakes. On his last visit, he spent an afternoon at

Gerbeaud, the famous coffeehouse on Vörösmarty Square. At that time, they had one variety of cake available, which was extremely dry and not very delicious, but which cost him only ten forints. That was communism. Now, he can choose from a hundred varieties of cake, but each costs a thousand forints. This is democracy. Europe has chosen to choose, but Harkályi fears that they have accepted only the illusion of choice. This display case is a mirage, a distraction. They are deciding from among different combinations of the very same ingredients used to make that flavorless cake in 1967.

"What would you say to a serving of *Somlói galuska?*" he asks.

"*Bácsi,* it's not even noon yet."

"What better time." He, with some difficulty, gets the attention of a waitress. "*Somlói galuska.*"

She appears to be surprised. "*Igen?*"

"*Igen. Két.*"

"*Kettő?*"

"*Igen, kettő.*"

"Your Hungarian is returning."

"Maybe one could say that I am returning to it. Perhaps that is why I am so nervous."

"Nervous? You've been through this a million times."

"Yes, and a million times I have been nervous. I cannot tolerate the pageantry involved with these events, yet I cannot avoid them because—"

"Because you are the 'world's greatest living composer.'"

"I have told you to stop that, Magdalene."

"I'm only teasing. You're not really the world's greatest living composer."

"Thank you."

"But a new opera! I'm so excited. It must be strange for you being home."

"The opera is not so new for me, Magda. And I must admit that I have not thought of this city as 'home,' as you call it, but it *is* a joy to see you." She leans forward to kiss him on the side of his face. "I am afraid that I'm not very good company this morning."

"Are you still having trouble sleeping?"

"Yes, sadly, but it's always worst before a concert, much less before a premiere. But I am very deeply moved to see you. Before I get too sentimental, however, let us try this *galuska.*"

Magda has been rendered speechless. She taps at her eyes with a white napkin.

The cake—if that is the word for this bowl of unruly slop—looks awful; it is a mess of undercooked dough and runny chocolate sauce buried under whipped cream. The sight alone makes his stomach turn. He will soon need to find a toilet.

"Perhaps this was not such a good idea after all. I think it is time that I got dressed. There will be a car to meet us at one o'clock. I will feel fortunate to have a personal translator with me today. We will go to Buda for the concert, and then have some photographs taken with the prime minister. Now, however, please excuse me." He pushes the bowl of sugary goo away from his body and stands, with some effort. His knees can no longer function as they once did. "I will meet you downstairs. We will continue this conversation shortly. Seeing you, yes—it does almost feel as if I have come home. You are the last of the Harkályis, Magda."

"It's great to see you too. Just remember, you've been through this a million times before. Don't be afraid."

Luck, a phenomenon that at age fourteen Lajos already discerned as the afterthought of an indifferent God, one eclipsed from view in Bohemia, kept him and Tibor off those cattle cars bound for Poland and beyond the notice of the Council of Elders, whose unfortunate responsibility it became to condemn their fellow Jews to that passage across Mitteleuropa. While lethargy and apathy and incomprehension demagnetized the globe's moral compass, bodies continued to burn in the distance, the smoke rising to obscure the light of two million stars, still twinkling bright yellow, though already dead.

In the spring, a film crew arrived from Berlin to shoot a documentary that would be shown to the world. Karel Ančerl was ordered to prepare a special concert, with only a few days' notice, to take place on the main grandstand in the town center. It would include the *Study for Strings* by Pavel Haas and the children's opera *Brundibár* by Hans Krása, both residents of Terezín, and both major influences on Harkályi's earliest compositions.

Lajos copied the music feverishly, with the promise that he would be granted the honor of performing amid the second violins. The orchestra rehearsed around the clock, confident that their very lives depended upon a perfect performance. Haas and Krása attended every rehearsal to assist with certain questions of interpretation that arose, ecstatic that their music would gain a worldwide audience. Lajos's hands ached from the constant scribbling of notes, yet, as he was frequently reminded, his suffering did not match that of his brother, whose tireless physical servitude to the kapo made him invaluable. Lajos's own hard work and dedication, rare for a musician of any age, endeared him to Ančerl.

In preparation for the film, and apart from a small circle of musicians, every able-bodied woman and man—which is to say every woman and man, as those who were not of able body did not remain for long in Terezín—dedicated their labors to the beautification of the town. They added fresh coats of paint to the buildings, planted vast flower and vegetable gardens, though few among them would live to see them bloom again.

For days, the filmmakers shot images of children playing soccer, of families sitting around large, food-laden tables, of citizens in line to deposit fake money at the town's newly built bank. The world would see the glorious gift that the Kaiser had given to the Jews—their own Edenic village, far from the devastation of the war. The concert would be equally farcical, with a row of plotted plants placed in an orderly line along the front of the stage to hide from the camera's view the shabby shoes that failed to match the dark, hastily tailored suits, each with a bright and prominent Star of David emblazoned on the chest.

On the morning of the performance, at the instruction of Ančerl, the concertmaster approached Lajos while he practiced his scales, a chore he relished for its distraction. The maestro had decided that he would not allow Lajos to perform in the concert. His cinematic debut would have to wait for another day, and for different circumstances. When asked why, he was told that he did not appear sufficiently Jewish to make the proper impression for the camera and, in addition, that his playing was simply not up to par with the adults in the string orchestra. If he wanted to become a concert violinist, he would have to dedicate himself to practicing more, without the distraction of copying music or notating the melodies that even then had started to ferment in his imagination. The disappointment stung; anger surged through his sunken frame, but he was powerless. The memory of that rage embarrasses Harkályi to this day. He said some things out of his youthful indiscretion that he will always regret.

He refused to attend the concert, and instead hid in the barracks. Tibor would later describe the event in detail, movement by movement, and in particular the immediate aftermath: Once the camera stopped rolling, Ančerl with a wave raised all of the musicians to their feet and asked them to place their instruments on their chairs. He led the procession, baton still in hand, as they lined off the riser in single file, laughing at the joy of a successful performance. Men shook hands, grabbed proudly at their fashionable lapels. Smiling the entire way, they followed Ančerl's slow, funereal pace straight into the cars of the transport train, which already contained the families of every participant of the concert. Word quickly spread that they were being freed in recognition of their gift to the Reich, and they cheered and shouted to each other, despite the crowded conditions. At Auschwitz, so Harkályi learned many years later, only Ančerl among the hundreds of them would survive the day.

The maestro had rehearsed and conducted the concert, under the gaze of the cameras and of the entire world, with the full understanding that immediately afterward he would lead the men in his charge to their deaths. In dismissing Lajos from the performance, Ančerl knowingly and deliberately saved his young life.

Twenty years later, Ančerl toured the United States, and Harkályi, by then a professor of music in Philadelphia, though not yet internationally recognized, attempted to arrange a reunion. His letter to Ančerl was returned unopened by the management of the Czech Philharmonic, and he never spoke with the maestro again, not even after he emigrated to Canada.

"Goddamn Karel Ančerl," he had said back then, at Terezín. It was the first instance in his life that his prayers would be answered.

Lajos was left behind to rot at that time while, so he believed, all of the other musicians and composers gained their freedom in Western Europe and elsewhere. He grew embittered, but also productive. With the sudden shortage of competent performers, the homesick guards began to approach him with commissioned work. They had grown tired of hearing the same few marches, so they sent to Leipzig and Berlin and even Paris for new music—tangos and *csárdás*, airs from the latest operettas—that Lajos had to transcribe for a rotating cast of musicians and whatever instruments were on hand. The living could fill out the chords of the dead. He assigned all of the parts to all or almost all of the musicians simultaneously, with only slight variations in form or timbre, so it didn't matter if he only had three violins or if his oboist had been shot, or even if there were no cello strings to be found within fifty miles. His inner ear grew accustomed to awkward variations in pitch, which he learned to incorporate into the music he composed based upon the *volkslieder* the weeping officers sang drunkenly to him. The rapid turnover of musicians made it difficult to orchestrate precise melodies, so Harkályi taught himself a unique compositional style, a style that eventually gained him a vast, international following and has brought him back here to Budapest.

For all of these years he has kept private, for now, only one final element of his being, but come the last measures of his opera, even his mother's departing lullaby will become another morsel for public consumption.

Geraldo
Peter Orner

HE WARNS US THAT what's inside might not be appropriate for children and other sensitive viewers. It's 1986, Chicago. A forgettable year. Al Capone's missing vault. Who knew he lost one? But now that we know it, the city is awash in hysterical anticipation. They're tearing down the Lexington Hotel, once the Big Tuna's headquarters, and have discovered a vault that's been sealed for decades. Decades. And Geraldo Rivera's got the exclusive. *Live.* I'm alone in front of the TV with a bag of Doritos. There's a team of hard-hatted workmen with jackhammers and high explosives. There are wafts of dust and lots of noise and Geraldo half shouts, half whispers into the microphone about Capone's infamous murderous ways. *We're making history here,* he says. It goes on for more than an hour and a half with frequent commercial breaks.

Geraldo talks and talks and talks and talks. At one point he says, "I feel like Jeremiah walking among the ruins." Huh? Just open the vault already. Finally—finally—they blast the door off. Geraldo coughs and gasps, says something inaudible. There's an enormous crashing noise, shouting. The camera jumbles and the screen goes blank. Cut to commercial. Geraldo's dead and they're selling antacid. Then Buicks and Mountain Dew and Kodak.

And then he's back, still breathing, brave, undaunted. Geraldo knows no daunted. Wait, he's holding something. A wine bottle. Ladies and gentlemen, citizens of Chicago, interested parties around the world, we've made a discovery. Pause. Swallow. Alphonsus Capone—alias Scarface alias Big Tuna alias Big Fellow alias Snorky—may have once drunk from this very bottle before carrying out yet another infamous dastardly act the likes of which have made this city infamous around the globe. Go to the deepest Amazon, as I have, Geraldo Rivera says, and there you might meet, as I did, a little Indian boy, naked, nothing but a loincloth barely covering his burgeoning private parts and tell him, as I did, that you are from Chicago, and he'll say, Chicago! Chicago! Capone! Pow! Pow! Kill! Kill! Kill! Yes, the lips of such a man may have once touched the phallic spout of this very bottle—

But the camera zooms in on the label. Maybe the producer was thinking now at last we'll get rid of this clown. *Ernest and Julio Gallo, 1981.* Pans back to Geraldo's stricken face. He looks like he wants to eat the microphone's afro. Not much can leave Geraldo wordless. But I keep watching. We all keep watching. The wonder of live television. Even after nothing's happened it keeps happening. Plus, there is always the chance that Geraldo might spontaneously combust.

Soldier on, Geraldo, we're still with you.

Friends, he says, his voice rising to a kind of squeal. Friends, how on earth did this bottle find its way through the impregnable walls of a sealed vault? Only in a city as diseased as this one, where vice still flows like milk down an innocent child's throat, like blood in the veins, like sewage in the sewage and drainage canal, could one of the greatest robbers in the history of the known world be himself robbed, the thief thieved, the boodler boodled. Oh, my friends, how did this bottle get into a sealed vault? Mystery begets mystery begets mystery, it's the very fornication of existence in this modern Gomorrah we call Chicago.

What were we expecting? Loot, diamonds, the skeletal remains of enemies? This empty vault was supposed to be our King Tut's tomb? Our lost Atlantis? Our Pompeii? Even here, something survives, something remains. In a city where all is knocked down and all is replaced—didn't we just want to find something that was there all along?

A solitary man holds a bottle amid plumes of old dust. And we watch it like a miracle.

Maybe the truth is we really don't give a damn what's in the vault. Maybe it's only you. You, Geraldo. I'm seventeen. In the afternoons, I bag groceries at the Dominick's on Skokie Highway. I'm trying to move up from bagging to produce. Free fruit. Better hours. Customers are friendlier when they're picking out their lettuce than when they're paying. They're surly when they pay. Who likes to pay? Mostly, though, I'm just lonely, a kind of lonely I'd never known and have never known since. You know what I mean? Do you remember? When all you had was your own sweaty needs, your own endless furious needs. I come home to an empty house and think about all the eyes that will never look my way. Times like these all you want is to hear a voice, a voice that won't quit you. So prattle on, my journalistic desperado. Next year in Jerusalem, my fake Mexican Jewish brother. You spew, I exist. All I want right now is someone to keep talking.

Modernist Poems
Elizabeth Robinson

MADAME BLAVATSKY TO ROBERT McALMON

I prefer you skeptics to the credulous ones. You

have a more fulfilled sense of silence. Those who

claim that my chamber was equipped with trap

doors amuse, even excite

me. That's your mode of gift, is it

not? Gossip? The aggregate of your disbelief

mutes the generosity behind it. You've heard

the term "clairaudience"? The ability to

receive messages through the ear? The voices

arrive with their own suggestions. They teach

by the Socratic method, plying questions which,

like you, I decline to answer. The lengthy pause

is what they are after, their medium, so that

long after you and I are banished inside that intermission

we'll still be geniuses together.

PAMELA COLMAN SMITH AND HAVELOCK ELLIS

She dreams that there is a blister of dried skin on her forearm, and when she tries to rub it off, it opens as a flower, still soft and dry, layer after layer opening up.

Each layer she tries to scratch away and

so forth.

She hums: "I am speaking of course of myself."

He arranges her bare limbs, bending the knees and angling them away from her pelvis, then steps back to look. From the horizon, her legs form an M. So he tells her.

"But I am not an M."

"At the crux of the M," he explains, cupping her vulva, "this is your mandorla. Do you know this word?"

"I'll investigate it."

"Yes," he says.

"Temperance," she comments.

His gaze lowers.

"Not abstinence," she clarifies, "but what is poured between two vessels, all tempered by their conjoining."

> She has had a dream in which "biting one's tongue" means to remove it as a parcel from one's mouth and to stuff it with its own content.

Elizabeth Robinson

ROMAINE BROOKS EVADING NATALIE BARNEY

Does a painting have a protagonist or only a subject?

                                    She knows too well about being subject.

There's a little, purpling deity being rubbed as sand
into the muscle of the breast.

There's a sibling rivalry sans sibling.

                            She knows that haunted houses are banal.

An auto-portrait, where the subject is the doctor of the protagonist.

                        A sibling rivalry where the sibling has been effaced.

One is an only child and the other is not.

                        The painting suffers its own apparitions, but only just.
                        As with all runaways, they are forced back to the fold.

The physician claims that death reversed is inertia, petrifaction,
somnambulism.

This was death footnoted, in which two sisters become lovers.

Their intimacy is the measure of the protagonist, in whose beloved is begun an

                    absence that exceeds conception, also known as the self-same.

In other words, the ghost was bottom heavy, a sleepwalker after all.

Elizabeth Robinson

THE BARONESS ELSA HARANGUING W. B. YEATS

As for myself, I am a patriot of the body, but we each speak with an accent.

Brevity has not been my strong suit, nor yours,

but let our prolixity make us to fly as the crow

flies, transceptual, over each our allegiance

to impulse, vision, the carnal insight that makes a citizen.

I restate citizenship as

an ultimate penury,

as you must know, and as

the anatomy of

the absurd:

my skull lacquered and your male parts

sewn together with monkey glands,

though perhaps these are traitorous forms,

these bodies who breed us in countries, who

sign us to pacts, we,

in our ludicrous uniforms.

Elizabeth Robinson

AMY LOWELL DROWSING WHILE ANTONIN ARTAUD
PICKS HER POCKET

I love you perhaps enough

not to caricature you, as I love

your sodden pockets, planted, a mess, with the detritus of wealth, wriggling

with blooms. Your American garden, I hear,

is extraordinary enough that the posies cry from across the ocean

when I take

my leave of you. A magic cane that crooks into

your possession to break my body and put it back together like stems who

decapitate their blooms.

Your fattened body is its own locket, and I rub my gaze across its interior

leaving my death portrait enclosed for you to discover.

It is not the image of me, but a "pattern"—all right,

a joke at your expense. An asylum in which I am safe to

offend your proprieties, as sleeping, you are the actress

I covet most. A genteel lump made of knuckles.

MINA LOY AND OSCAR WILDE

I'm running quite late, harried by my own exile.

I suspect

you'll expect me

to say so prettily, or

at least smartly, but the quip will no longer do. When

the boat sailed round the bend, it was

inevitable that onlookers

would foresee it reaching

its destination. And now we know

that destination is the quip, the

brilliant element, the horizon that

can be folded handily,

crowning the daylight like a lampshade—

Glare.

Lost jest on

the rough

wave we thought would return

our wits to us.

SIGMUND FREUD THINKING ABOUT BRYHER

I think of islands.

Here is a place that is not a place,

and a refugee adopts a name, a code,

a symptom, just as an island

is a symptom

of the landmass that once attached to it.

Far beneath the horizon, the water suggests,

the island extends like a trauma

through the sea.

At its base: We do not know.

It is not a science, this passage to neutrality.

The island is not a surety, it is a symptom, a beneficent symptom.

The Little Death
Gabriel Blackwell

> *In its essence, the crime story is simple. It consists of two stories. One is known only to the criminal and to the author himself . . . consisting chiefly of the commission of a murder and the criminal's attempt to cover up after it. . . .*
>
> *The other story is the story which is told. It is capable of great elaboration and should, when finished, be complete in itself. It is necessary, however, to connect the two stories throughout the book. This is done by allowing a bit, here and there, of the hidden story to appear. It may be a clue, it may be another crime. In any case, you may be certain that the author is having a pretty difficult time.*
>
> —Mary Roberts Rinehart, "On the Crime Novel,"
> *The Saturday Evening Post,* March 11, 1939

I.

THE PROBLEM WITH THE Greene case was that it didn't have a center. Or maybe that there was a hole where the center was supposed to be. Or maybe it was that there was more than one center, more than one hole.

Even when General Greene first explained the case to Raymond Chandler's barely disguised fictional dick, Philip Marlowe—in real life, Stanley "Doghouse" Reilly—he threw at least three cases into Reilly's lap—the disappearance of Sean Regan, the legitimate but mysterious debts of his daughter to a gee named Joe Brody, and the blackmailing of that same daughter by another man, Arthur Gwynn Geiger.[1] Chandler had reason to throw a little dirt on Brody, sure, but he wasn't far off even for that—he was right about the other two.

The Greene case was first given the go-by by a private dick named Joe Brody, the same Brody Chandler names in his book. This pee-eye,

---

[1] Raymond Chandler, early (1937?) manuscript version of the book that would become *The Big Sleep.* The manuscript is not paginated and is entitled "The Little Death."

a "slender fellow with a high forehead,"[2] kept a desk at L. D. "Puss" Walgreen's outfit in the Fulwider Building on Santa Monica, but he spent most of his time away from it. In those days, there was very little money in the detective business—that is, if the detective was honest. Brody wasn't. Few were.

Brody's money sideline was making titty books that pervs like Googy Geiger put out on the street. Geiger operated a front on Sunset, Arthur Gwynn Geiger, Rare Books and De Luxe Editions, with the help of Reilly, who was also playing the private detective game and not winning. When Brody passed on Greene's green, Reilly took on the case and tried to use it as an in for the Brody book business. Armed with that jimmy, Reilly managed to get Brody whacked, a chauffeur knocked off, a girl knocked up, and a sweet little blonde powder puff put into restraints at the county sanitarium.[3]

Truth be told, though, that sweet little blonde looked pretty good in restraints. She looked pretty good out of them too. She was the peek in the book Brody was working on when Reilly creased Brody's business and sent him to the farm.

II.

The Greene case was just a missing persons case that had got out of hand when Brody was first called in. Lots of things got out of hand at the Greenes'—mostly the two daughters. A man by the name of Sean "Rusty" Regan had married one of those daughters, Helga Greene, in 1934, only to disappear like a showgirl's chastity less than two years later. Helga, the oldest daughter of General Lloyd Greene, oilman, had a reputation in town as a black widow, the kind that eat their husbands. After consummating the marriage, that is. She was a bottle blonde with a taste for the bottle and a taste for the kind of men who could help her to find it. Regan was a rum runner, Tijuana to the Canadian border, who had settled down a little to life in Los Angeles, tailor-made for Helga, even if Helga wasn't tailor-made for him.

Even for a castle like the one the Greenes kept in San Pedro, just over the hill from the oil wells that pumped green into the Greenes, Helga and Regan, Carmen, the staff, and the General himself would have made a crowded house. By all accounts, though, life at the

---

[2]Agnes Lozelle, interview for *Life* magazine, conducted February 8, 1965, and February 13, 1965, never published. These are the tape transcripts from that interview.
[3]Chandler, op. cit.

Greene mansion was pacific if not entirely hunky-dory for those two years, with Helga trying her damnedest to keep it in her pants and Regan and the General getting along like a house on fire. On his days off, Regan ran a small gaming operation near Venice Beach, and Greene sat on his friends in high places for Regan from his wheelchair at the house at the top of the hill.[4] Unfortunately for both of them, Helga was a lush and an inveterate shooter, and couldn't play the nice girl forever. Ray Chandler had her pegged as a roulette player, but one of the boxmen, Harry Jones, says that Greene, as she was still known then, spent most of her time in the pit, "rattling the bones so beautiful it would make you feel warm all over." Jones writes:

> She was trouble. She would lose her shirt and then roll over Rusty for a few bucks. If she won, she walked, but if she lost, she won then too—she was playing with Rusty's money anyway. Rusty was sick over the dame. Had to marry her just to keep the money in the family.[5]

That was before the marriage. Things got worse after.

Even more unfortunate for the Greenes, though, was that the sweet little blonde powder puff due to appear in Joe Brody's girlie book was Helga's younger sister, Carmen. Daughter of a wildcat oilman, Carmen had inherited all of the wildcat and none of the oil. At least, none of the money that went along with the oil, not yet. Carmen had problems, almost as many as her sister, not all of them as easy to get out of as big sis's marriage. Gambling, at least, wasn't one of them— not for money, anyway. Heroin was.

III.

The Regan operation at Venice went out of commission before Helga reported Regan missing. In any other family, this would pass for news. After almost a week of no news from Venice, a man named Theodore "Eddie" Mars reopened Regan's joint as the Cypress Club. Concerned, General Greene tried to call in Brody as pee-eye, with Helga still not saying a word. Brody took his retainer to keep the old man quiet before eventually passing on the case, telling the General there wasn't enough to go on. Seemed Brody had enough on his hands with the other Greene daughter and his current "business

---

[4]Chandler, op. cit.
[5]Harry Jones, *A Year in the Pit*. (Los Angeles: Lap Steel Press, 1963), 53.

associates." While there were certainly debts to be paid Brody by Carmen Greene, he didn't stake the General for them, no matter what Chandler says. Brody had his own idea of a payoff.

Eddie Mars, whom Brody hoped would back him in the smut business, had been small-time muscle with a big-time chip on his shoulder until the takeover at the Cypress Club. Mars came over the hill from the town of Pasadena, making his big move in the big city. It was a clumsy one, like most first moves, but sometimes you get lucky. Mars went all the way. He had muscle behind him and a head of steam. Another thing Mars had going for him was a knack for timing, and timing, in his business, was everything.

With Regan gone, Mars got the Cypress Club up and running after a long weekend. The closing brought some complaints, but only among the clientele, not out on the street—the Cypress Club wasn't exactly a member of the Chamber of Commerce—and business was as brisk as before, putting Mars in a good position to invest his money elsewhere. One old customer who didn't raise a fuss even in the club was Helga Regan, which raised everyone's eyebrows.[6] All in all, it looked like a pretty smooth job of work for "a guy with a face like a flatiron steak, and just about as many brains too."[7]

The General, out of luck with Brody, turned to his old friend District Attorney Buron Fitts for help. Reilly, always busy looking for his angle, got a bent captain of detectives named Gregory "Lash" Canino to put his name in the district attorney's ear. Fitts, a politician who was born with a silver spoon in his mouth, turned to Canino, who at least had an ear to the street, for help in filling the spot left open by Brody's duck out. Canino, a bloodhound in a policeman's uniform, and beholden to Reilly for the odd slice of peach, wasted no time plugging Reilly in.[8]

The General wasn't really ready to face up to exactly what his pride and joy were up to nights, no matter what he might have told Chandler—"I guess they both have their vices, but I'm too old to think I can change that. I have my own vices. I'm sure everyone does."[9] Maybe so, but his daughters didn't have the usual vices—

---

[6]Jones, op. cit., 62.

[7]Ibid., 97.

[8]Chandler, op. cit. Chandler creates the character Bernie Ohls to fill both these positions in *The Big Sleep*, and puts Canino in as a gangster, which is only fair. Canino was not a friend to Chandler, whom he apparently once described as "a broad in a man's body, or maybe just a really ugly broad."

[9]Ibid. In the finished version of *The Big Sleep*, Chandler puts more high-flown language in the General's mouth. In life, Greene was an uneducated man, not one for a

at least, they didn't *only* have the usual ones. The younger one, Carmen Greene, was getting paid in skag for cheesecake photos taken by Brody. When Brody showed up at General Greene's:

> Carmen just about fainted. I guess she knew him from before, because she kept asking me why that man was here, why that man was here. . . . The General wanted me to keep it from them. . . . I didn't say nothing, but she kept after me. She had her back up against my front like she'd do. . . . I spilled the beans, and that wasn't all I spilled.[10]

This from Greene's butler and chauffeur, Owen Taylor.

IV.

Arthur Gwynn "Googy" Geiger and Stanley "Doghouse" Reilly were an unnatural-looking pair, a Laurel and Hardy couple of gees if ever there was one. Geiger was a full head taller and a good sixty pounds lighter than Reilly, bald, and with a glass eye. He would have stuck out in a circus sideshow. Reilly was a squat joe, vain and sullen, with wild hair plastered back in a modified Valentino and big thick lips, who stuck his nose in so many pies it came away bent. Geiger was the brains behind the operation, with Reilly providing the muscle, but reports from their contemporaries had it going the other way—Reilly as the puppetmaster, with Geiger dancing at the end of the line. Reilly was, by all accounts, a half-smart guy with a head for angles. But it was Geiger who wound up with the money, leaving Reilly holding the bag, a fact passed over in Chandler's book.

At the time of Mars's takeover at the Cypress Club, Reilly was working on roping some of Brody's girls, "models," including Carmen Greene, into posing for Geiger, who figured to cut Brody out completely and deal with his potential backer, Mars. Geiger had had the good sense to get in on the ground floor with Eddie Mars, and looked to be playing both sides against each other when he bought the farm. Geiger didn't have the good sense, however, to keep all this from his "partner" in the books biz, Reilly. What Geiger told Reilly and Reilly relayed to Mars really crossed Mars up, so that he had to

---

clever turn of phrase. He was also cruel, incredibly lucky in business dealings, and incredibly unlucky in his private life, as the cruel so often are. He had cause to hire a string of detectives over the course of his life, none of them retained more than once, and more than one "disappeared" afterward.

[10]Taylor murder file, Los Angeles Police Department, October 1935.

give Reilly a piece of the action, which made Geiger about as useful as a milk bucket under a bull, what with Reilly already pulling all the skirts.

Geiger looked too desperate and goggle eyed to approach dames, the kind of guy who walks home carrying a plain brown wrapper. That's the reason he brought Reilly in on his business in the first place, pulling him up out of the phone directory like a genie who won't fit back down the neck of the bottle. Reilly was better than Geiger with the girls, but still not half as smooth as Brody. Unlike Brody, Reilly was useless at the soft touch. He used the gow to bring in the pin jabbers, what little capital Geiger had managed to pull together for the rest, and leaned on his friend Canino for the strong arm on Agnes Lozelle, who would be the peek in Geiger's first book. Lozelle was a B-girl with a B-face at the Cypress Club until Reilly saw her body and liked it.

V.

Lozelle was one of about three B-girls regularly working Mars's new joint at the time. She had come over from Riverside the previous year to "make it big in the movies."[11] Her parents didn't know how quickly that dream went out the window. She said her problem in the pictures was childhood acne that left her with a face that was pure wide shot. She was told she would never star because the camera couldn't get far enough away to hide the fact that she had to wear about a pound of makeup to keep the lens from cracking. The rest of her was more than halfway to all right, though. She had legs like two grown women stuffed into pantyhose, a waist as thin as a wasp's, and a couple of the Grand Tetons crammed into the space between the buttons of her shirt.

Reilly saw her working the barflies and approached her. In the dark of the Cypress Club, men couldn't see her makeup, just her figure, and those flashing green lamps. Her standard ploy was to push the bubbly for a ten-cent-on-the-dollar commission, netting her about fifty cents a bottle. Not much, but enough to live on, if all you needed was cigarettes and gin on weekends. Reilly wouldn't bite on the bubbly, but he offered to pay her twice what she made in a week to do a naughty teacher layout, the only set Geiger had ready to go. "This Reilly was persistent, I'll give him that. He kept after me for

---

[11] Lozelle, op. cit.

a solid week. Meanwhile, he's giving the stink eye to every likely customer comes on to me, so I'm not even making what little I was making before."[12] Lozelle wasn't biting.

The Cypress Club was "little better than a clip joint, really. Back when it was Regan's joint, it had class—a band to liven it up every night, just a little, not enough to scare people away from the tables, and a bar well stocked enough for that time,"[13] says Harry Jones. "When Mars moved in, B-girls set up shop in the lobby and the bar. Don't get me wrong, most of them were nice girls, but the types they brought in, the types they *had* [emphasis in original] to bring in to make a living . . . Fatty Arbuckle wouldn'ta been seen with 'em."[14]

Jones remembers seeing Canino at the Cypress Club pretty often in those early days. "Lash" Canino was known to be on the take, with a finger in several county pies. One of those pies happened to be a little shop on Sunset Boulevard, Arthur Gwynn Geiger, Rare Books and De Luxe Editions, where he met Doghouse Reilly. Canino fancied himself a lady's man—"Canino was in and out of the joint as soon as it was out of Rusty's hands . . . he was always with a different blonde. Liked them leggy, though—not much to some of their faces."[15] Jones, at least, thought they were real 'walkers, maybe rung up on charges and pressed into service, a quick nod in return for Canino's wink.

Canino agreed to bring Lozelle over on a doping charge for a cut of Geiger's take on the new book. Lozelle's peek comes on page thirty-three of the only copy of the Blue Stripe Edition of Geiger's *Talking out off School* (sic) that has survived. Sonia Darrin describes seeing the book while "researching" her role in Howard Hawks's 1946 movie version of *The Big Sleep*:

> Oh God! You could see everything in that book. I don't know why you would want to, but there it was, page thirty-three, black and white, for all the world to see. I knew what kind of a girl would do that for a living and I had my Agnes.[16]

Lozelle herself claims that she was coerced into the shoot, and didn't know they took that particular picture until she first saw the book at Reilly's office.

---

[12]Ibid.

[13]Jones, op. cit., 63. "That time" was Prohibition.

[14]Ibid., 83.

[15]Ibid., 101.

[16]Sonia Darrin, *It's a Living.* (New York: Scribner and Sons, 1972), 101–102.

He brought it out from under his desk like it was some kind of present. Those books didn't have dust jackets or what have you, just a kind of blue striped leather, front and back. No title, not a word on the spine. He flips through it, and I see what he's got. Of course, I go all red, but he keeps on flipping, and he's getting closer. Well, when I saw "the peek," I stopped him right there. I couldn't believe it. It was like my whole life was over the minute I saw that picture. . . . Reilly wasn't hardly finished, though. The look gave him courage, the little man. . . . He had me boxed in. What was I supposed to do?[17]

Lozelle was blackmailed into working for Geiger at his store. In those days, a peek like that pegged you forever as a particular kind of girl. Not the marrying kind, you might say. With Lozelle in the front and Reilly in the back of the shop, Geiger had his hands free to pick whichever pocket held the most green, Brody's or Mars's.

VI.

Lozelle's shoot for *Talking out off School* was done in Geiger's "home studio," entered into evidence by police as the scene of Geiger's murder, on or about the night of October 26, 1935. Police photos show Geiger's house at 7244 Laverne Terrace as a two-bedroom Craftsman. Laverne Terrace was a bedroom community used to sleepy crimes like vandalism and cat burglary, and the sound of gunshots woke every neighbor not already awake, and all the cats besides.

The large den of Geiger's house had been converted into a temporary studio, with the schoolhouse set used in Lozelle's sitting partially hidden behind what Ray Chandler describes as "strips of Chinese embroidery . . . [and] bits of odd silk tossed around."[18] Geiger had set up the den as a kind of Egyptian tomb or Temple of Isis—it's unclear from the photographs. Then again nobody ever called Geiger a historian; maybe he just didn't know the difference. Carmen Greene was, again, according to Chandler, "rescued" from the scene by Reilly. Police reports indicate the presence of illegal narcotics in Geiger's liquor cabinet, in particular an "unspecified opiate alkaloid, probably codeine or morphine,"[19] which Chandler misidentifies as

---

[17]Lozelle, op. cit.
[18]Chandler, op. cit. This passage passed muster and appeared in the finished *The Big Sleep,* as published by Alfred A. Knopf, in 1939.
[19]Taylor murder file, Los Angeles Police Department, October 1935.

"ether."[20] Given Reilly's close relationship with Geiger, Chandler's little scenario is about as likely as a hungry fox in a full henhouse.

Chandler has Reilly charging in from his waiting chariot like Sir Lancelot to save Guinevere. But Carmen (whom Chandler calls Carmen Sternwood in his finished book) was more Morgan le Fay or Lady Godiva than Guinevere, and Reilly was hardly Lancelot. Forensic evidence proves that Reilly probably didn't have a hand in Geiger's death, but as for the girl's condition, Reilly's attempted cover-up makes it even odds that he provided the hop to the girl, as he had been doing for some time. Reilly must have been somewhere on the premises when Geiger was shot, even if his wasn't the gat to put Geiger under glass. Chandler makes the triggerman Owen Taylor, which, for Chandler, explains Taylor's murder later that night by Brody. According to this scenario, Brody was after Taylor for the prints of Carmen that Taylor lifted from Geiger's house while Reilly was tending to Carmen. But if that was the motive for Taylor's murder, Brody probably wasn't in on the Geiger business, because he wouldn't have needed Geiger's prints of Carmen when he had his own, soon to be published in his own book, *Greek Goddesses.* Probably Geiger caught wind of Brody's peek before Brody had the smut inked, and tried to go him one better with his own book with the same frail in a similar situation, trying to hop on Brody's book's back in the event that *Greek Goddesses* did well at the shop. New ideas in the entertainment business are like virgins in Hollywood: hard to find, and even harder to keep to yourself.

There still isn't much in the way of a solution to the mystery of Taylor's death. Chandler famously told Hawks that he didn't know who killed Taylor when the director called him in to settle a rowdy-dow on the set between stars Humphrey Bogart and Lauren Bacall. Taylor was found off Lido Pier the morning following Geiger's greasing, October 27. Police reports indicate that Taylor had been sapped before he hit the water, and then, in an "incapacitated state, drove the vehicle into the water, possibly in order to evade an assailant."[21] One scenario has Taylor driving Carmen Greene to the Geiger house, then getting sapped and finally pushed into the water when Reilly caught Taylor trying to beat feet with the camera and prints while Reilly was cleaning up Carmen. Reilly's fingerprints were found on the dash of the car Taylor was driving, on the license holder, and a

---

[20]Chandler, op. cit.
[21]Taylor murder file, Los Angeles Police Department, October 1935.

smudged print that was likely Reilly's on the back of Taylor's seat. Reilly rolled him into the ocean to cover up the murder, and Captain Canino tried to bury the evidence when it came to light the following day by falsely claiming that Taylor had been conscious when he went over the edge, walking away from any sapping alive if not unharmed.[22]

VII.

All of which helps clear up Geiger's murder about as much as a bar of dirt soap. If the theft of the prints of Carmen in the buff was what triggered the murder, then Brody would lose his motive for the rub out. Brody didn't know yet that Geiger was skimming off the top, so that's a dead end too. In Carl Lundgren's memoir, *Twenty Years on the Force: Working the Los Angeles Homicide Beat*, Lundgren gives that explanation—Brody putting Geiger into a bag after all, Geiger having ripped Brody off on profits on the titty book trade for months in order to get the scratch to start his own book-binding business to sell to Mars—but there are problems with Lundgren's theory.

According to that theory, Brody killed Geiger and Reilly sapped Taylor and made off with the prints, which once again has Taylor nabbing the prints from Geiger's house. But Reilly tried to bring out another book before Canino nixed the Sunset Boulevard trade for good, and Carmen's pics weren't in it. There was no reason, including his "work" for the Greenes, that Reilly wouldn't have included her photos in his book. He would have had to spring for another session to get enough material for the binders to get the full sixty-nine pages of that book, which Reilly called *While the City Sleeps*, after the Lon Chaney movie. Even the material doesn't match; the book was about a bent dick turned straight by a 'walker with a heart of gold. Carmen was a proven seller, star of Brody's *Greek Goddesses* book, which, in the event, probably would have rented well. The girl in Reilly's book looked like she needed a face transplant, and maybe a bath and a hot meal.

Besides, it was Mars, not Brody, who fronted the money for *While the City Sleeps*. Mars too doesn't play in the whole business, even when Chandler tries to put him there. He didn't yet have a stake in any of Geiger's business, either as wholesaler or retailer.

---

[22]Chandler, op. cit.

The small possibility that it was Carmen herself who snatched the peek pics is nixed by her condition at the time: "Miss Greene gave off a smell of ether so strong that it nearly put me [Reilly, not Chandler, in this case] down. Her naked body was the only thing that was holding me up. I slapped her to bring her out of it, and then I slapped her a little more, because she deserved it."[23]

Police files do not show any pics recovered at the scene. Canino himself might have fixed this after the fact, but in light of later events, it looks like he didn't have to.

VIII.

The one character who doesn't seem to play much in Chandler's accounting of things is Chandler himself, and it's not just coincidence. Ray Chandler, jowly and sporting a spare tire approaching middle age, was beginning a second career at General Greene's oil company, South Basin Oil, when things started to heat up around the Greenes'. Chandler liked to paint himself a family man, but all the family he had was a wife eighteen years older than he was who had never "treated him like a man should be treated."[24] He was mesmerized by every skirt within reach, but he would have needed a crowbar to get into a can of peaches, and he was stuck in a whiskey bottle half the time. The other half he spent helpless and speechless like a teenager about to spend prom night at home with his mother.

Chandler climbed the ladder at General Greene's company from bookkeeper to vice president in just about two years, by framing his superiors for big falls and putting himself up for promotion. It was a swell tactic to get yourself from the basement to the boardroom, but didn't leave you with too many friends, as Chandler was soon to find out. He had decided to take out a little insurance policy on his time in the vice president's chair, and went looking in the General's garbage for gold. He found some in the form of Carmen Greene, whom he had dead to rights as a hophead.

Figuring to get himself some snaps of the pin jabbing to use against the General, Chandler followed Reilly and Greene to Geiger's house on Laverne Terrace the night Geiger was murdered. It was Chandler who came away that night with the pics of Carmen in the chair—not the pics he was looking for, but pics that would do the job just the

[23]Ibid.
[24]Frank MacShane, ed., *Complete Letters of Raymond Chandler.* (New York: Columbia University Press, 1979), 569.

same.[25] In *The Big Sleep*, Chandler puts the pics in the hands of Joe Brody, and not by accident. But it was Chandler who took them from Geiger's house.

IX.

Geiger's plan for that night had been simple: By shooting Carmen, he would get a couple of peeks to tease a little money out of her father, enough money to start his own book business and shed Brody for Mars; failing that, he would still have material for a second book with a girl who had been popular in the rental business already, if he could turn up enough scratch to get it printed. Reilly showed up at the Greenes' through Canino's ploy with the DA, and scored with Carmen almost instantly; Carmen was a pushover for aggressive men. Reilly arranged for her to go to a little Chinese chicken party with Geiger and Lozelle. But while birds of a feather flock together, kittens only play together until they grow up. Then the claws come out. Carmen didn't like Lozelle, and the feeling was mutual: "She was an animal, really, just a dumb brute with a pretty face and a body to match. Men crawled all over themselves to get to her, but she would have been with any swinging dick, or all of them," says Lozelle.[26] Geiger decided to handle Carmen himself, and Lozelle took a hike, with Reilly waiting in the wings, and Taylor and Chandler waiting outside.[27]

X.

Geiger's house got out of control, and Reilly was left in the dark, without a hole to crawl into. He lammed with the girl and laid low until he could square the whole thing with Canino, his only hope of rehabbing his name in LA. Taylor got axed probably, given the physical evidence, by Reilly himself, and Chandler wandered in to snatch the prints while everyone was busy covering themselves. It wasn't until later, as Chandler tells it, that Reilly realized the prints were missing.[28]

---

[25]Lozelle, op. cit.

[26]Ibid.

[27]Ibid. This leaves open the question of how Lozelle got where she was going. She didn't know Taylor, didn't have a car, and Geiger, Reilly, and Carmen all stayed in the house. She would have been on her own in any case. While Reilly was cleaning up Carmen and busing her back home, it seems that he had left Lozelle high and dry.

[28]Chandler, op. cit.

Reilly didn't have a line on the missing pics, and Mars wasn't putting out his hand to Reilly until Reilly came in out of the cold with Mars's original pocket money, spent on *While the City Sleeps*, a book without a future if Geiger's shop couldn't be opened. Canino and his coppers had the lid clamped down tight to cover Canino's tampering with the Taylor case. Reilly knew he was caught out, and without some business to get the ball rolling again, his name would be mud no matter what the city PD thought.

Lozelle was lying low too. "I thought with Googy out of the picture, I could maybe go back to Mars, to the club, but Mars wouldn't have it, the creep."[29] Lozelle wasn't welcome until Reilly returned Mars's money. "Reilly had really saddled me with one. . . . That double-dealing son of a bitch [Mars] wouldn't even let me work on the side. No place would," because of Mars's reputation—being on Mars's blacklist in the Los Angeles club circuit was as good as being worm food in those days.[30] Lozelle didn't want to be flat out at the end of the month, so she went to the next most likely tap—Reilly, who then passed her off to Chandler.

XI.

While Ray Chandler's wife, Cissy Pascal, wasn't meeting his needs, Chandler was out looking for women who would, with the help of Reilly. He makes several mentions of indiscretions and infidelities in his letters of the time, but either had the good sense not to name names or places, or had no names or places to name. Lozelle described Chandler's relationship with women: "Ray spent more time talking about [sex] than he ever spent in the company of women, as far as I could tell. He liked . . . [to] pretend to himself that he was saving me from something. . . . He was like a child walking in on his mother and father, coming to Mother's rescue."[31] "Ray—we all knew him as Ray—came into the shop with Reilly," according to Lozelle.

> He was a desperate sort, with a lot of money to spend. He said he loved his wife, but she was "frail." That's what he told me. That she wasn't well. . . . When I got down on my luck, he put me up for a few nights. . . . He couldn't get it up anyway. He was drunk most of the time. Reilly thought he was a fruit,

---

[29]Lozelle, op. cit.
[30]Ibid.
[31]Ibid.

but I think he was just lonely, didn't really understand women. . . . Reilly met him through Greene. They both worked
for Greene, and Reilly said he knew where he could get
girls—I guess that meant me, even though I wasn't for sale—
I just went with Ray because he seemed so sad. I felt sorry for
him, more than anything else. And I didn't have anywhere
else to go.[32]

She posted a speed limit, and Chandler was such a sucker he didn't
get pulled over once, or else he was too drunk to even start the car.

Chandler knew Reilly by sight—his office was just at the bottom of
the General's hill—and may have even had occasion to talk to him
before the events of that October. In any case, Chandler was an easy
mark for Reilly, a desperate joe hungry for jollies—Geiger's meat and
potatoes—and a willing one, sniffing for something he knew Greene
was hiding. He didn't know whose house he had been in when he
swiped the pics, and had no thought of squeezing Reilly for the
dough. He made enough at South Basin that he wasn't greedy for
more—he just wanted to make sure he didn't lose it. But he was reckless, and drunk. Chandler was so drunk, he showed Lozelle the pics
he had swiped from her boss's place, and explained his plan to stay
on at South Basin Oil. Lozelle was hip to the business, and knew it
was only a matter of time before someone like Mars got his hands on
Chandler and the pics. It wouldn't have been quite so pretty a picture
as Chandler was holding, that's for sure. Lozelle urged him to give up
the business before he got in too far. When it's sink or swim, you
have to get wet either way, but Lozelle had pity on the sad sack and
didn't want him getting wet if she could help it. She slipped the pics
from Chandler—easy enough to do while he was passed out on top
of her—and passed them off to Brody, whom she thought she could
tap next when time ran out on Chandler. Lozelle knew Brody would
have no angle on the pics, other than their fair use in a new book.

XII.

Brody lived in the left-hand apartment on the fourth floor of a building on Randall Place. Brody had moved the books from Geiger's store
to his apartment to a storage unit in Pomona the day after Geiger
went underground, according to the logs of the two moving compa-
nies he hired to shepherd his books from Hollywood to the Inland

---

[32]Ibid.

Empire. Brody wasn't around when either company came calling at his apartment, and he didn't make any of the arrangements himself. The only thing he did wrong was to use his own apartment as the staging area. That brought Lozelle in, following the books to Brody.

> Lozelle: Brody wasn't in that day or the next, but he showed on the third day, Thursday.
> Interviewer: [unintelligible]
> Lozelle: I didn't really have a choice, did I? Geiger wasn't exactly keeping me in furs, you know, Reilly went missing, and Ray was blotto all the time. I had nowhere to go, and not too much time to get there.
> Interviewer: So how did you approach him?
> Lozelle: He knew me already. I didn't have to approach him at all. He invited me up.[33]

At the time, she says, she hadn't wanted to get anything out of Brody, just to turn over the pics and ask him to help her figure out her next move.

XIII.

Brody offered her work in a future book in return for the prints, and said there might be a living in it, if she played her cards right and was willing to go the extra mile. He said her body was good enough to make up for her face, and anyway, johns weren't renting the books for the faces. Those they could see on the street. This was not exactly what Lozelle was looking for, but

> A girl's got to make a living. I said I'd give it some thought. Brody said he had somebody coming up from a big syndicate just then, that maybe he could get me in on the ground floor with these guys if I played ball, but I didn't have all day to decide.[34]

"Brody explained that he had two pairs of curtains on the window on the street . . . It was a system, see? The ones that were on the window side were kind of tan-brown colored, and the ones that were on the room side were pink."[35] Brody's system let callers know whether

---

[33]Ibid.
[34]Ibid.
[35]Jones, op. cit., 235.

to expect heat or to come on up. On that night, "Brody had just the brown-colored curtains open a little bit, just showing a little bit of the pink curtains. Maybe that meant something more than just open or closed—I don't know, it wasn't like he went into too much detail about it."[36]

The door buzzer sounded and Brody, leery of letting the frail out of his sight, sent Lozelle behind the pink curtain. "Brody was sweating he was so nervous. His forehead was practically spraying, it looked so wet. He just kept rubbing it with this handkerchief he had in his hand."[37] Brody had reason to be nervous—the new syndicate was Eddie Mars's syndicate, and Mars wasn't known for being a great negotiator. Mars was someone who broke arms and legs and took what he wanted. Lozelle too had reason to hide, after she heard who was in charge of Brody's big new syndicate. Mars had turned her down once. To be seen trying to sneak in through the back door could mean winding up in the backyard, taking a dirt nap.

The visitor announced himself as Peter Mann, but Lozelle recognized the voice as belonging to Doghouse Reilly. Brody cracked the door, and Lozelle heard bits of their conversation, but couldn't piece it together. Chandler's account is as follows:

> Reilly: Hey . . . Geiger.
> Brody: What was that?
> Reilly: I said Geiger. Arthur Gwynn Geiger. The guy that has the books. My partner. Seen him lately?
> Brody: I don't know anybody by that name, and I don't know you, Joe. Does he live around here? Maybe you got the wrong place.
> Reilly: You're the Joe, Brody.
> Brody: Yeah? What's it got to do with you? You selling something, or just playing games?
> Reilly: So you don't know anybody named Geiger? That's very funny. Geiger sure knew you.
> Brody: Yeah? Maybe we don't have the same sense of humor, partner. Beat feet, before I get really angry.
> Reilly: I know you got the books, Joe. You know I got the front. We ought to have a little chat, don't you think?[38]

This jibes with what Lozelle remembers of the conversation.

Reilly wanted the books, or failing that, an agreement that Brody would supply him with the books when he reopened Geiger's store,

---

[36] Ibid., 235.
[37] Lozelle, op. cit.
[38] Chandler, op. cit.

but what he was missing was the strong-arm that could twist Brody. Reilly had not been in touch with Canino, who by this time had a detail on the shop, and Reilly had not even been to the shop in several days, ducking the goon squad. Brody, on the other hand, saw the writing on the wall. A man, Geiger or not, doesn't get plugged without the heat coming down hard on his front. Brody figured that Geiger's business, anyway, was done for, no matter who was running it. The books were safely in storage, and in circulation in Pomona, and it would stay that way until Brody could find a new front with a new face—that's where Mars came in.

> "Look, Joe, I got Canino in my pocket. He can be bought for a dollar or two and a pat on the head. He'll let me open up the shop if I ask."
> "You look, Reilly. Canino and you might be joined at the hip for all I care, but it ain't gonna do you no good here. Maybe you got Geiger's store open and maybe you don't. But maybe Geiger isn't such a good friend to you right now."[39]

Brody tapped the blue-striped book on the table next to the sofa Reilly was sitting on.

> "Seems to me that Geiger had it coming, one way or the other. You don't double-cross your only friend. Biting the hand that feeds you ain't smart business. I don't think I got any books like what you want. Seems like maybe I got some locked away, but then again, my memory's bad."[40]

Lozelle recalls that the conversation was just getting heated when the buzzer rang again. This time, it was a woman's voice, another one that Lozelle recognized. The woman was Carmen Greene, come for the pics she thought Brody had laid hands on in Geiger's house that night. She was hopped up and mad as hell. Lozelle:

> I know a crazy broad when I see one. Brody didn't like her barging in when she wasn't welcome, but he must have known what she was up to, because he didn't raise too much of a fuss. Pretty soon, she's got Brody and Reilly on the couch with their feet up. . . . Reilly was naked too, pretty stupid for a guy coming to run a shakedown, but he said he never carried and wasn't going to start just for the night.[41]

---

[39]Lozelle, op. cit.
[40]Ibid.
[41]Ibid.

Chandler also says Reilly walked softly without a big stick, but it seems unlikely that Reilly didn't carry a piece regularly—maybe he had found it more prudent to leave his heater at home with the heat on, in case of a dragnet.

And then Brody's buzzer sounded again.

XIV.

At the door was Ray Chandler, drunk as usual and tired of being left out in the cold. He had followed Lozelle there, and hid out in the hallway while first Agnes, then Reilly, and finally Carmen entered the apartment. He figured it was a party and walked right into the lion's mouth like a babe in the wilderness. Carmen turned the gun on him and sat him down next to the rest. Chandler started bawling about Agnes, and that's when she got the bum's rush from the curtain gig. Carmen saw Agnes and hit the roof—Brody and Reilly and now Agnes all in the same room! And her father's bookkeeper there too! She was beside herself, ready to start slinging lead at the next surprise. The buzzer sounded again, and turned the apartment upside down.

At the door was Harry Jones, on an errand for Mars to meet with Brody. This was the meeting that Brody had been waiting for, with tan curtain open, but if two is company and three is a crowd, Brody had a full-blown church service going on in his apartment, and with him a nonbeliever. Brody started for the door, but Carmen shot first and would skip the questions later. Brody took a hot one and lay down. "Such a lot of guns . . . and so few brains,"[42] as Chandler put it. Jones broke down the door when the shot rang out, with gat in hand.

Reilly slapped the gun from Carmen's hand and saved the day, but he also managed to pocket Carmen's pics while no one was looking. No one, except Ray Chandler.

Reilly tried to clean up the mess, telling Jones that, with Brody out of commission, Mars'd have to deal with him from now on for his little racket, but Reilly was never anything more than a small-time hood in over his head. He didn't know Mars's angle, and he didn't know where the books were being stored. He didn't even know about Brody's connection in Pomona. When Jones relayed the scuttlebutt

---

[42]Chandler, op. cit. This one was another keeper. Chandler liked a nice turn of phrase, and kept a record of every zinger he came upon in his little notebook, even before he tried writing. He liked to read them out loud when he got tight.

to his boss, Mars laughed in his face, and called Reilly a little man pissing in his own bathwater. Reilly was washed up.

Lozelle went home to her parents, but they put her back on the street when she came up pregnant a few months later. Her boy, Stanley Jr., was born in July of 1936. She briefly made a stir a decade later when she was revealed as the "inspiration" behind the Agnes "character" in Chandler's book, before being sent back to the minors when she said more than she was supposed to and the General caught wind of it—he still had friends in high places.

In the month after Brody's murder, Chandler's colleagues at South Basin jumped all over themselves to add to the list of things Chandler was screwing up around the office, and he found himself washed up on the same beach as Reilly, who had Chandler's "insurance policy" in hand. Reilly convinced him to go in on the last chance racket he had come up with, a blackmail job on the General involving Carmen's pics and the IOUs that Geiger had already delivered to the old man, but the General countered the pair by committing his daughter to the county sanitarium to head off rumors that she had been involved in the murder of two known pornographers—first Geiger and now Brody. Chandler later said he never felt right about the scheme, but he was desperate for money at a time when money was as hard to find as an egg in a rooster's roost.

Reilly used Chandler's guilt about trying to pull weight on the girl and her father to his advantage. He got Chandler to write him in as a white knight, and to erase some of his bad behavior in the story that Chandler was working on. The gambit worked, and "Philip Marlowe," alias Doghouse Reilly, was seen as a modern-day knight of the Round Table. Chandler couldn't complain; he made his living on the same horse as his knight.

Captain Canino, to head off any embarrassment, tried to come down hard on Reilly, but Reilly slipped through his fingers, leaving behind his office and everything in it to try his hand in Chicago. Canino followed up on some phone numbers found there, which led to Chandler's time on the hot plate downtown, which then explains his harsh treatment of the captain in his "novel."[43] Chandler was not one to let old grudges die easy. Jones got his own cover, as did Mars, mainly because Chandler didn't know what their real angle was.

---

[43] And of Carl Lundgren, who probably had a hand in Chandler's interrogation. Lundgren he makes a demented homicidal homosexual lover of Geiger's—could be Lundgren was even harder on Chandler than Canino; Chandler was certainly harder on Lundgren. It's a good thing for Chandler that Lundgren was close to retirement.

In the end, though, Chandler's part in the whole drama haunted him like spooks in the attic. The man simply could not leave well enough alone, as Reilly was doing in Chicago. Chandler's book, *The Big Sleep*, was written in desperation following his firing and the failure of Reilly's plan, but did well, and with the General and his family coming out more or less clean in it, it was let pass. After shoring up the long green with seven novels in fourteen years, Chandler looked to have it easy, but once the sucker, always the sucker. Chandler's only friend, his wife, Cissy, passed, and he tried to fill his time drinking in seedy bars and at la-di-da ladies' luncheons, crying into his beer about his past sins. Trying to atone for those sins, he would write: "Marlowe is a fraud. A guy like him wouldn't make a cent in the private eye business. The kind that make it are hacks with crooked noses and more guts than brains . . . the kind with no more fellow-feeling than a sack of potatoes and a permanent crease in their pants."[44] If Reilly had read this, he would have put Chandler to bed earlier.

Chandler retraced his steps along with his sins, and wound up at South Basin Oil, and the house at the top of the hill. Carmen had long since passed away, victim of the gow, but Helga took some strange sort of pity on the sap, and the two shared a bottle now and then, reliving old times and past lives. For his part, Chandler at least had never left them behind. Helga had mellowed some with age, and with always having her hand out to her father, who was still clinging desperately to life. She was eager to get out from under his roof before it fell in, but by this time was too attached to him to leave without his blessing. Chandler felt he owed the man something, maybe many somethings, and, as his novels show, had an affection for the way things used to be done. He went to the General on bended knee to ask for his daughter's hand in marriage, after a lengthy courtship. The General, still clinging absurdly to the hope of a return of the flown Regan, saw a flabby, weak, ailing man in front of him, scarcely healthier than he himself was, a photo negative of the young Regan he still saw sitting beside him. He told Chandler, "Under no circumstances."

Thinking about *The Big Sleep* years later, Chandler wrote, "The mystery is in the story behind the story . . . [Agatha] Christie [went about it] all wrong: you're out to fool the reader into trying to solve

---

[44]MacShane, op.cit., 115.

the wrong problem, not in setting them an impossible task."[45] Chandler had set himself an impossible task. He died in 1959, in the La Jolla Convalescent Home, where he was being treated for a case of pneumonia he had contracted in a drinking bout following his embarrassment, just two weeks after the old man had turned him down.

---

[45]MacShane, op. cit., 237. Chandler wrote extensively about the "rules" of the detective genre—unlike Christie, he thought that the mystery writer shouldn't try to hide the necessary clues until the very end and then wrap everything up in a neat little package. He said he wanted the reader to be able to solve the mystery right along with the detective. Really, though, he wanted the reader to be as confused as he himself was.

La Pu

Stephen Marche

THE RUMOR THAT RAN through the Drake Hotel after Theo Godechaux left Toronto was that he had fled the city to avoid charges of
desecrating a corpse. In the summer of 2006, he allegedly organized
a funeral for a musician couple who were burying their stillborn
baby girl, and the ceremony involved eating small portions of the
girl's thumbs. The police hadn't yet charged him, so the rumors
went, due to the legal complications of the victim's prebirth death
and the fact that no one has ever been charged with cannibalism in
the province of Ontario. Theo has never discussed the matter. He left
the city, I later learned, to bury his father in Paris and to run the family perfume business.

I met him for the first time a few days before his flight, at the fifth
anniversary party for the Drake. I'm anosmic and he was fascinated
with the details of my condition. "Is it a reduction of your capacity
to smell or are the necessary parts broken?" he asked.

"No, I have all the parts. They just don't work."

"Not one percent?" he asked.

"I was born with the condition. I can't smell anything."

The information delighted him. "I must prepare a ceremony for
you then."

It started immediately. We just went up to his room, the one the
hotel's owner had built for him with a centralized chimney to allow
open fires on the floor. Theo made a living designing and arranging
small private ceremonies then. Like almost all Europeans who move
to Toronto rather than New York, Theo had come from Berlin, but
he had taken an undergraduate degree in "ritualism"—a program of
his own design—at Indiana University. A Godechaux ritual invari-
ably accompanied the reception at a hipster wedding in Toronto. He
would set up a small enclosure with elaborate screens that the couple entered. I've heard that these cached acts can be as simple as eating a dish of stewed beans or as complicated as recreating the elaborate sexual performances of primitive fertility rituals.

The ceremony he created for me that night in the Drake was

171

simple. He lit a small fire and we sat across from one another. He allowed the pyre to smolder until it burned at an even heat. Fifteen minutes later, three women entered and walked around the fire. They threw flowers at their feet—carnations, I think—stomped them, and threw the crushed stems and petals into the embers. After the women left, Theo took out a small bottle shaped like an orange (a bottle of Cachette, his family's perfume) and scattered a few drops on the fire. He seemed to be gauging my reactions minutely. We waited until the embers were completely covered in white ashes before returning to the bar.

It may have been the last ceremony he performed before returning to the family business. He was his father's only child, and none of his cousins "had the nose," as parfumists say. L'Orangerie had belonged to a Godechaux since the eighteenth century. It produced only a single scent: Cachette. The reports of the odor are nearly as meaningless to me as the perfume itself. The scent is pleasant but not remarkable, the critics say, with notes of citrus, bergamot, gaiac, and myrtle. What makes Cachette worth thousands of dollars a milliliter is the pheromone TnGH-885, the effective agent that was known as diacetyltreffaline in the nineteenth century, and that has never been successfully synthesized in laboratory conditions.

At different times and at different places, the scent has been described as "the emotional combination of a day of horse riding, examining a large butterfly collection, and a breakfast of clover honey on toast"; "the right smell for a Kentucky heiress who has become a German artist and was once the girl stuck at the bottom of the well"; "the smell of green tea, money, and life after death." Charles de Gaulle described it as "a spell in a bottle," and when he heard about the planned invasion of Normandy, declared "a bottle of Cachette is worth five thousand ships." Georges Clemenceau gushed, "The dew of dark sprites gathered at midnight from only the most fragrant lilies."

In Massenet's opera *Le Parfum*, which he based on Theo Godechaux's great-great-great-great-great-grandfather Florent Halevy and his discovery of Cachette, the young Florent is an obsessive parfumist, akin to a medieval alchemist. The plot is typically operatic: The young Florent falls in love with a count's young daughter, Marie de Trefailleur, who has escaped from a convent and is hiding from the officers of the Great Terror. At the end of the second act, Marie dies from tuberculosis and, during a magnificent duet in which the soprano interrupts the tenor from beneath the stage, her lover Florent creates Cachette in order to capture her essence.

The plot of *Le Parfum* omits some key details, as operas will. Florent Halevy had been apprenticed to L'Orangerie since 1776, and proved a gifted enough nose that, by the 1790s, he had married the owner's daughter and ran the store after his father-in-law suffered a stroke, so he was nearly fifty when he met Marie de Trefailleur. Marie, however, did lose her family to the Terror and was hiding at L'Orangerie as a shopgirl under the protection of an old maidservant of her family's. She fell in love too, just not with Halevy; she began an affair with the neighborhood smith, became pregnant, and died before giving birth of an unknown ailment, probably tuberculosis. So there is a tragic love story at the origin of L'Orangerie but it was not Florent Halevy's. He was obsessed with Marie's smell and started purchasing her used underwear from the shopgirl who was protecting her. When Marie died, he washed her used clothes and added the residue of the evaporated slops into bottles of the shop's best perfume to preserve the essence of his obsession.

L'Orangerie would be no more than a small footnote in the history of smell if a young woman named Marie-Josephe-Rose Tascher had not happened to be in Paris in 1795 and happened to stop in at L'Orangerie and happened to buy a bottle of the essence of Madame de Trefailleur. Josephine married Napoleon later that year, and the original anomaly of feminine mysticality was born. Nobody, not even a generation of French men familiar with every nuance of womanly loveliness could explain how Josephine managed to be a great beauty whose every feature was plain. She left men racking their language. Napoleon's final summary was "She's a real woman." Others spoke of her languid walk or large eyes or her voice. She bought up every bottle of Cachette, and when Florent refused to sell the final bottle—his sole memento of Mademoiselle de Trefailleur's dirty underthings—she kept raising the price until it reached the outrageous sum of ten thousand francs. Florent appears to have had a touch of the Romantic. He refused to sell the last bottle at any price.

His third son, Gustave Halevy, watched this scene and took a businessman's lesson. The hard head in a family of Romantics, he more than anyone else was responsible for setting up L'Orangerie as the business it continued to be into the modern era. For over a decade, on the strength of Josephine's money, he experimented with different ways of replicating his father's accidental plunge into the wonderful. He bought the undergarments of prostitutes, which didn't work. He bought the undergarments of noblemen's mistresses, which were difficult and expensive to acquire; these too did not provide the desired effect. Eventually he tried to recreate the original scenario—hiring distressed noblewomen for his shop and surrounding them with good-looking working men. This model, while expensive, worked—Cachette as a going concern was born.

Gustave's relentless experimentation sought endlessly to refine and isolate what he called *"la pu,"* the ineffable appeal at the base of the perfume. Within a few months, he realized that the active ingredient was produced by women who desired men they should not desire. His first attempts to capture this essence were clumsy. He developed a paper suit of fine crepe that he asked the women to wear sitting in a bakery, surrounded by good-looking bakers, until they were sloppy with sweat. The quantity of liquid did not affect the potency, however. After nearly a decade of trial and error he figured out that *"la pu"* was produced in the vaginal secretions of ovulating women who desired men they shouldn't desire. He abandoned the paper armor for a kind of cotton diaper that he then pressed in a small olive press in the store's back room. (This machine was only replaced in 1973 despite the undesirable trace odors of olive oil in Cachette's nose.)

The only question the family had to answer after then was what price to set on the appearance of being a "real woman." Throughout the nineteenth and twentieth centuries, L'Orangerie generated vast sums of money for the Halevys and the Godechaux. The family has unfortunately had a taste for financial adventure—there is hardly a bubble market in history during which they have not lost a fortune. It didn't matter. Not only did they make money from the sale of Cachette; they made money from the restriction of sale. The House of Saud paid a premium of twenty-five million dollars so that theirs would be the only family on the Arabian peninsula with access to Cachette. Quantities have always been limited. After the Dreyfus Affair, in an attempt to display their patriotism, the Godechaux announced that they would sell Cachette only to French women, and did so until World War II. Until the eighties, L'Orangerie and the Godechaux family never produced more than five liters of the perfume, which they sold for rates exorbitant enough to maintain a lifestyle of Norman country homes and investments in Paris real estate.

The sources for *la pu* required maximum tact and discretion to acquire but there was never a lack of destitute noblewomen who desired men they should not desire. The Godechaux paid the women enough to stay in their ancestral homes, and even sent gardeners—extremely attractive gardeners—free of charge. All the women had to do for their fee was wear the slightly uncomfortable diapers for two weeks a month. In the late nineteenth century, L'Orangerie extended its reach to England, where there was a whole new country full of aristocrats living beyond their means. Thousands of diaper shipments crossed the channel but the boutique did not move or expand—it sold its product to the women who knew that they needed it. They briefly closed shop during the Nazi occupation of Paris—moving the whole family to Los Angeles—but they returned within months of the liberation, and resumed operations as if nothing had happened.

And so the company might have continued indefinitely, if Theo's grandfather Emanuel hadn't had a taste for Cohiba cigars. "In those days," Theo told me when I visited the store in Paris in the fall of 2007, "Cohibas were just for the Castro elite, the inner circle. You could not just buy them. You had to know Communist powers."

Through various Eastern European connections, Cachette was introduced to post-Cultural Revolution China, where its popularity was instantly immense. Even though there were less than five milliliters in Asia, they were the most important dibs and dabs since Josephine walked into the shop. With glasnost, Russian gangsters bought it for their wives and mistresses without the slightest worry about the cost. And Cachette, established as the ultimate symbol of luxury, was there at the beginning of the liberalization of the Chinese economy.

"We have always been exclusive," Theo smiles, "but when they come to you offering ten or fifteen times the price, which was already a high price . . ." His voice trails off. "I don't blame my father."

The improving economy and changing social reality meant that there were fewer destitute nobles to generate *la pu*. The family invested heavily in research, trying to find a viable way to synthesize the pheromone. Several attempts were made but they never resulted in anything concrete.

Then, in 1997, a Chinese company called Lintech came to Philippe Godechaux with a proposal. They could produce TnGH-885 for five hundred dollars a centiliter. L'Orangerie had expanded its business before, buying from foreign suppliers, but never on such a scale. The new markets opening in the East seemed to require a new approach. The exploding demand from China required an exploding supply, which could only come from China. "Life was simple for my father. He met two people, each twice a year. To the first he would give a small packet of money. To the second, he would give *la pu* for an immense sum of money. The rest of the time he bought art."

Without the knowledge of the Godechaux family, a chasm of horror had opened under L'Orangerie. Lintech operated out of the Shenzhen Free Trade Zone. As Jujie Ng, one of the first workers to be hired by Lintech, explained in her letter to the Global Action Network—the activist group that brought L'Orangerie's business in Asia to world attention—the workers at first were not even required to stay at the offices for most of the workday. They needed to arrive early in the morning to put on the company's special diaper, but then they were instructed to go out into the streets and "look at inappropriate boys." The women hired were either from good families in Shenzhen or a part of the wave of village girls moving to the city whose innocence could be turned into a commodity.

Quickly, however, Lintech discovered that better results could be had under "hothouse conditions." The GAN reports are damning:

> At the main factory in Shenzhen, separated rooms projected different pornography depending on the level of the victims' acclimatization. New recruits would be sent to the park for "dirty thought treatment." After a month or so they would be constrained in a small chamber to watch hardcore gay pornography. As the effect of that wore off, they would have to endure more and more grotesque images, up to and including incest, bestiality, and rape. All this in swelteringly hot rooms that give new meaning to the term "sweatshop."

Women could not endure such conditions for longer than a year. The Lintech technicians soon discovered, in a further refinement of their production methods, that younger girls produced more potent quantities of *la pu*. When Chinese authorities broke down the doors of the factory in 2007, they discovered a room full of fifteen-year-old girls, all fresh from the Chinese hinterland, sweating in ninety-degree heat, drinking huge glasses of purified water, and watching African frozen-food gang-rape scenes.

The arrests made the front page of every newspaper in France, the scandal threatening to bring down the two-centuries-old company. *La pu* is still the subject of complex international legal battles. "I am being sued in Delaware," Theo says with a shrug. "I never even heard of Delaware. I have since learned it has the lowest highest point in the United States." Proceedings against Godechaux are also under way in China, France, and Britain. And then there are the protesters, a loose affiliation of fair trade groups, spearheaded by the Global Action Network. The press release they circulated on the day of their protest ended with the statement: "The products of L'Orangerie, in particular the organic compound diacetyltreffaline, have been harvested by some of the cruelest, most barbaric and misogynistic industrial practices on the planet or in history."

Godechaux sighs when I show him the quote. "I received many more orders the day they printed that. I think you could just sell cruelty and there would be a queue beyond the block."

When protesters arrived to picket L'Orangerie, they couldn't find the storefront. The store's marker is a miniature bronze orange hanging from the lintel of a clean, plain glass door, easy to miss on Rue Villon, maybe the most decrepit and obscure street in the Eleventh Arrondissement. Carla Bruni-Sarkozy, however, had no trouble finding it the day after the protest. She's been a regular customer since the nineteen eighties.

"You cannot have women friends in this business," Theo says. "But Carla is close."

Theo shrugs when confronted with his Asian associates' practices. "How could my father have any idea? He had a terrible fear of flying and did not leave Paris for seventeen years before his death."

The protesters do not impress Theo though he regrets the company's involvement with Lintech. "This is a mature product for a mature clientele. Do they have any idea what goes into a pair of sneakers? You cannot buy anything anymore that has its innocence intact." The GAN does not protest the manufacturers of the pornography the girls were watching, Godechaux complains, or the offices of his Chinese supplier. (The last option is no longer available since the CEO has been sentenced to death by a Chinese court.) "They are opposed only to beauty. All the ugly materials of beauty they do not bother with."

Theo is far more troubled by the economic collapse. He has lost his main source of *la pu*, and the orders from China quickly dried up during the trial. His father, Philippe, invested the boom-time money mainly in American banks—ironically hoping to avoid the wild speculations of his ancestors. At the moment, Theo is selling to only the limited number of women who come into his store in Paris.

Theo's physical appearance has changed since I knew him in Toronto. The scandal has slumped him. His eyes are particularly ravaged, their new deadness bringing a surprised and suppressed O to his bland, suspicious face. There are two Theo Godechaux, though: As we are talking, a small bell rings as the second customer of the day enters L'Orangerie, and he appears magically to shed thirty pounds. His back straightens and his suit snaps to perfection, like a ship catching the wind with its sails and ropes tucked and angled just so.

She is a short woman, thin, midthirties, with chestnut-colored shoulder-length hair. Even to me, she radiates an aura of suppressed power, her kindness more like mercy than kindness. Her smile is effortlessly gracious—a combination of Saint Teresa of Avila and a nineteen thirties piano singer.

"Mr. Godechaux," she says in English, exquisitely charming, as if speaking English were a private joke between herself and Philippe.

"Madame Kovalov," Godechaux replies.

"I don't suppose you have any of your marvelous perfume today?"

"We do."

When the woman leaves the store with her purchase, Godechaux slouches again. "I suppose she will have to find another way soon."

L'Orangerie finally closed its doors on November 12, 2008. Theo moved back to Berlin, where he began organizing controversial ceremonies again. The last few bottles of Cachette were sold at private auction at Sotheby's, with the purchase price suppressed, maintaining until the end L'Orangerie's tradition of never revealing the cost of a bottle. The closure occupied a register in my mind of rust and slime and bends and damp stains and the decline of all that is fragile and beautiful, and so, when I was passing through Paris in Christmas of that year, I had to visit Rue Villon again.

A Popeyes had already moved into the space opened up by L'Orangerie's closure. It was France's first, and the novelty had sparked a minimania for the chain's fried chicken and biscuits. At lunch the queue filed out the door, lining the sidewalk with the reverberations of an excited, happy crowd. The whole street seemed brighter and wider with the hungry people filling it, brighter and newer, as if a thick layer of warm scum had been wiped from the window of the sky.

From The Face of Lincoln
Peter Gizzi

FROM NOWHERE WITH NO ONE WHO KNEW ME

Imagine a pair of cordovan ankle-high boots with silver
    buckles.
Worsted slacks charcoal with a large blue grid stitched in.
The shirt a paler shade of blue, almost white, and the
    polyester tie about the boy.
The jacket was a deep maroon, double breasted with fake
    brass buttons, many of them, and wide lapels.
It was 1972. If you were there I don't need to tell you.
The constant backdrop of coffins and flags on the wavy TV
    screen after dinner,
the death count in bloodred over the newscaster's head
    in our den.
They had dens then. We had one. Denning and empty.
    Nothing "out of sight."
Trust me, I would rather be anywhere else than 1972
    at my father's wake. Tell you about it?
All I can say is years later, getting stoned, some kid
    told me, I guess in a moment of intimacy,
he worked at that funeral home—turns out half my
    father's body was faked with cardboard.
I don't remember now who told me, it's long ago.
No one gets it, how we feel. It's not personal.
They really don't. And that's where I live.
                         Nowhere

with no one who knew me.
I'm sure I'm not the only one here or rather there.

Chances are if you are reading this you might come
        from there too. Most likely
you got an urge, like they used to say, an urge
        to write I mean, you know,
to quote make a better situation for yourself
like you moved in next door for life
and got the eyes you walk around in like a piece
        of inherited real estate.
You got it free or so you think. And so you'll expand,
build up, renovate, generally improve the property.
And maybe it's that word "free,"
prompts me to sit here and peck these keys like I, like you,
        got something to say that matters.
Maybe free. Or maybe "property,"
the endless boring war of ownership that starts as a dream, a
        national dream, and moves on to a militia, tax cuts, etc.
Where are we and how did we get here?

                                            "Improve?"
That's it, it must be improve, what? And just as someone
        mouths this particular chestnut
there is already the enabling narrative in place
        of the pronoun we
when more often than not historically it winds up we
        singular,
no surprise, me myself and I. So that's not it. Okay.

The phrase that hovers near and might reveal the true
        purpose of this is "next door."
As in "to move in next door," to be adjacent to oneself,
to occupy the space just out the frame forever and always

and to live in such a way as to accept the borderless nature
  of seeing and feeling.
I have always felt far from myself, so I mention my father's
  mutilation as a clear marker
to when I can say I actually died in this life
and have learned to go with it, empty and present,
a state of being
and remaining, to see, unencumbered (hence "free"?)
without property and with no aim to improve anything
other than to be here. And to be here with you
  in all your opened-up agony and strife
with all your asymmetries intact, everything possible
  in your hopescape,
to be strong and open, open and vulnerable, to be real,
  alive and breathing just next to you.

RUINATION DAY

A touching relic with provenance
from the Lincoln cortege in New York City.
Black mourning crepe worn in mourning
by a Guard of Honor at City Hall
where Lincoln lay in state.

Spectacular Victorian gold mourning brooch.
This oblong, gold-filled brooch contains
an albumen portrait of Lincoln by Brady.
Beautiful condition and perhaps the finest
known example.

A most unusual mourning medal, white metal
with original luster, suspended from an eagle pin

and affixed black ribbon, with legend "Martyr President."
This is a scarce tribute piece in excellent shape.

1865 Mourning Medal. An oval gilt brass medal
with the words "Martyr to Liberty" and the date
of death, April 15, on verso. Uncirculated.

Quite rare "American Protestant Association" mourning silk
"We Mourn Our Loss Abraham Lincoln."
Wonderful cemetery scene in center,
an excellent ribbon in lovely condition.

A simple, elegant memorial ribbon,
tiny pinhole at top from being pinned
to the chest of a mourner, a silk that says it all.

Spectacular mourning ribbon on heavy fabric,
gold on white with black mourning border.
As good as it gets, and in pristine condition.

A fine silk, proclaiming "The Nation Mourns
His Loss He Still Lives in the Hearts of the People."
Bold design, some staining at bottom does not detract.

Perhaps the smallest tribute . . . but still
an evocative mourning piece! Paper mourning
ribbon printed in red, blue, and black,
"We Mourn Our Martyred President."
A lovely period item from the grief of 1865.

Among the more desirable Victorian-era
memorial displays. A bold white metal high-relief
mourning bust of Lincoln against black velvet
set into a deep frame.

A gilt high-relief bust of Lincoln in a shadow box. Lovely.

A good high-relief mourning bust in a simple shadow box.
Likely cast in brass or copper. A pretty piece.

Isaac Goldstein "The Levite." Autograph Manuscript
Signed in Hebrew, an acrostic poem in which each line
begins with a different letter of Abraham Lincoln's name.

On the morning of 15 April 1865, after Lincoln's body
had been removed and visitors had left, Henry set up
his camera and took an eerie, haunting photograph
of the deathbed, with its bloody pillow and rumpled coverlet.
This clandestine image was not published until 1965.

Lincoln's Tomb. A set of three pieces, including
a slab of marble from the Lincoln burial vault
where he lay from May 4 to December 19, 1865.

The Chair that President Lincoln occupied
at the time of his assassination at Ford's Theatre.

A great stereo view, "Place where President Lincoln
was assassinated." On flat orange mount,
exceptionally rich with great detail and contrast,
only a hint of foxing that detracts little.

Funeral stereo view, "Passing Out of the State House
after Seeing the Corpse."

A poignant stereo view of Lincoln's home, draped
in mourning bunting, horse standing in front of the house.
Light wear, else very good.

Rare 1892 stereo view, "In this Room the Great Emancipator,
Lincoln, breathed his last."

"The Assassin's Vision." Booth, on horseback, drops his dagger
as he sees little heads of Lincoln popping out on trees
and a standing figure appearing between tree trunks.
A fine example; an odd souvenir of a tragic event.

"Lincoln Funeral Procession, New York City."
A magic lantern slide, circa turn of the century.
The cortege was in front of a building advertising
"Imported Saddlery" and "Dr. Palmer's Arms & Legs."
Excellent.

A very clean silk mourning ribbon, with an excellent
portrait festooned with patriotic imagery. One of the best
designed tributes on silk; truly mint condition.

An excellent silk mourning ribbon: "Rest! Statesman!
Rest! Await the Almighty's will; Then rise unchanged,
And be a statesman still." A bold design.

Lincoln Mourning Handkerchief. Quite rare mourning silk.
Embroidered in one corner "Lincoln the good 1865."
In overall fine condition with some light scattered age.
It is actually quite remarkable that this delicate silk piece
has survived in this nice state of preservation.

Tremendously rare mourning broadside.
"HE BEING DEAD YET SPEAKETH."
A wonderful tribute, the only example we have seen.

"We Mourn our Loved and Martyred Guide!"
A simple yet poignant mourning broadside.
Partial fold separations with minor loss, light toning,
several minor marginal chips and tears, else very good.

A fine pair of mourning song sheets with excellent imagery.
One bears an image of Lincoln's funeral cortege
passing in front of City Hall in New York. Both very clean.

The only extant example. A fabulous mourning vase,
with photographic-like presentation of the martyred Lincoln,
1865. One minor restoration to tip of one leaf at top of cluster,
etched on bottom.

Special Pass to Lincoln's official funeral held in the East Room
of the White House.

Black-bordered Lincoln funeral broadside, detailing the
"Obsequies of President Lincoln/Order of Funeral Procession."
A scarce paper mourning ribbon from the "National Day
of Mourning," June 1, 1865.

A small, quite touching paper mourning ribbon, bright red
and blue elements to flag make this an attractive piece
of ephemera. The first example we have encountered.

One of the classic "tombstone cards," this is a rather different
embossed design with black mourning rule and appropriate ode.

A lovely—and scarce—tribute by the great Reverend
Henry Ward Beecher. Presentation Memorial to Working Men.
"Oration at the Raising of 'The Old Flag' at Sumter; and Sermon
on the Death of Abraham Lincoln, President of the United States."

MELVILLE LOG: AUGUST 2000

You spoke with the native authority of a child adrift,
could voice the nervy ambiguity of a child with a serious
     question forming on your lips.
Last week was your birthday, I didn't forget nor did I miss
     the frightened child of your rhetoric.
The longing to repair a world of penury, ruin.
This summer they are advertising *The Perfect Storm.*
They report the Confederate submarine *H. L. Hunley*
     was lifted from the ocean floor.
They report 40 million acres are burning to the west,
that the famed tigers of India have almost gone out,
     emblem of the poet,
their roar heard for miles and neighboring villages.
I wonder if Hart Crane loved you for singing of his coffin
     outside the lifesaver's neat masquerade.
Hard to forget your descriptions of the heartbroken boy—
more durable than that of the man. There is adventure in despair.
You held fast insisting on pilgrimage, could draft a chill
from summer pavement and conjure the present
to a clinging stone to lighthouse waters and their sideshow
     attractions
to the action of wheeling stars. A tale to rouse all fallen craft.
Hold fast, Pierre, with this prose I thee wed. They are hopeful
118 sailors can be rescued from a Russian sub stuck in mud
at the bottom of a wintergreen northern sea. Yes, there is hope.

Yalta

Maureen Howard

HYDE PARK

"OUR CARD TABLE EXACTLY."

His head in a book always.

"A wedding present, Uncle Dan gave it to my mother. The Queen Anne mirror, that too."

Let him pursue Roosevelt's fourth-term election, a landslide when we were at war: That's where he'd got to flipping the pages.

His bewildered question, brushing off another shard: "Our card table?"

They were drinking green tea, so good for you, from dangerous plastic bottles. Had it never occurred to him, that the table leaf, propped against the wall, had a purpose? "Swing out the back legs, flip it down, and deal."

You'd have to scout the apartment to find a deck of cards. They did not play gin, canasta, tell fortunes—that's for sure.

"It's not old," she said. Till this moment, she'd forgotten the provenance of the table that came with her uptown, along with the mirror at the end of the hall. She'd come to him with baggage unpacked over thirty years ago, and her boys not yet grown. They sat on a bench in Hyde Park watching children file past to a bus, quiet kids in camp shirts, perhaps subdued by mighty legends just learned. She had seen them in the burial ground, obediently silent at the simple memorial the president had designed for his family. Watching the film in the Visitors' Center, they were solemn, too good to be true. Now a boy broke from the line, ran toward the counselors, his fingers flying, signing his joy of release. So, in the cocoon of their silence, they had not heard the aristocratic timbre of Roosevelt's voice in a fireside chat comforting the American people or his wife's high chirps of hope, irritating and consoling at once.

187

> 1941. May 21st a German U-Boat sank the US merchant ship
> Robert Moore. I felt strangely detached, as though I were
> outside, a part of the general public. I represented no nation,
> I carried no responsibility. . . .
>   Then the President began to speak. . . .
>   As our guests had departed, we went to the Monroe room
> to listen to Mr. Irving Berlin sing two new songs. . . .
>   —"My Day," Eleanor Roosevelt

What a flop, this end-of-summer outing. She had come here in college. *In college,* a phrase that rearranged boundaries, diminished grievances, enlarged good times. Hyde Park had been a misadventure with a popular girl, a senior who had an interest in a history major at Yale, not FDR. She remembered the fieldstone barns, that's all, and the Roosevelt big house that could not be viewed that day. No café or bookshop back then; the library—a different building entirely? As for the fledgling historian, he had nothing to request, not a letter or document essential to his project. Touchy, feely—the lovers whispered to each other plotting their need, then ferried her to the bus station in Poughkeepsie. By some ruse she was dismissed; a story of broken rules and regulations so dated she remembered only the humiliation of her role as a cover. They married, the history major and the smart senior far ahead of the pack. Last she heard, he wrote copy for the Esso account; she sang in a suburban chorus, Gilbert and Sullivan operettas.

At the first splat of rain, he closed the book. "I've got as far as Yalta."
  "Speed-reading?"
  They ran back to the Visitors' Center, where a plump guide in a Smokey Bear hat was explaining that Eleanor had her house, Val-Kill, and Franklin his stone cottage still under construction when he died. Of course the guide had little to say of the Roosevelts' separate lives that were totally entangled. Eleanor's broken heart, not a simple love story: He stayed with the fieldstone appropriate to the Dutch, who first settled up the Hudson. Of course her husband was not speed-reading, that craze long gone, a fad of the late sixties, gobbling printed pages in a pathetic predigital race that reduced history, sonnets, novels, and definitive biographies to mere information. He had turned to the inset photos, thus the quick trip to Yalta: the famous shot: Stalin—smug; Churchill stuffed into a khaki overcoat—all

smiles; Roosevelt—wasted yet handsome with the black cape so often thrown over a wheelchair to conceal his infirmity. On this bright, cold day in the Crimea, had they divvied up Europe, or must they still confront the sticky wicket of Poland? Let Joe pack it home under his military cap?

> Yalta was only a step towards the ultimate solution Franklin had in mind. He knew it was not the final step.
> —*This I Remember*

The tourists, mostly Asian, sailed forth under black umbrellas. A sporty grandma in sandals and sari made a run for the jitney that would take her to the big house, Sara Roosevelt's manse, and to Franklin's cottage, but not to Val-Kill, another tour entirely. The bookshop closed; a waitress was clearing up the last paper plates of the day. When the rain turned to mist, they found their car with slickers carelessly left behind. On Route 9 a rainbow graced the sky, the whole arc of it distinct, from Home Depot to the parkway. Stunning, nature imitating the supernatural. The day rescued, faint sun at last and no traffic to speak of. Given the long drive back to the city, they tolerated the Awful Restaurant on the corner—limp pasta, leather scallopini, complimentary grappa from the maître d'. Home at last, she had a sense of purpose, final lap of the day, taking the lamp and a Moroccan bowl off the card table, swinging the fourth leg free.

"Too small for poker," he said.

"Could take a Scrabble board. It's not old, not Colonial."

"Old enough, if a wedding present for your mother." He was, in fact, a speedy reader, just now finishing off Franklin Delano Roosevelt as a cutup at Groton, not much of a student at Harvard. He left her with a swift kiss, did not, as was his custom, take the book he was reading off to bed. She turned to a photo of Eleanor in a wedding dress fit for a queen, not a politician's wife: propped by a gilded chair, not a studio photograph. The Roosevelts, her side of the family and his, provided their own elegant surround. ER, as she signed herself in over three hundred thousand personal and official letters, looked just splendid, hair piled high as she would always wear it. Yes, lovely for this moment, might be a poster girl by James Montgomery Flagg, though she would call herself an ugly duckling, easy to say when she was well along in years. *My mother was troubled by my lack of beauty.* This from the last autobiography: She wrote four as though to see her reflection splintered in a fun-house mirror. The collapse of the chin, the overbite, matronly bosom, but the toothy smile as she bent over a wounded soldier in the South Pacific, that was beauty indeed.

In the morning the card table would be upended, examined for questionable joints, braced by the honest wood of reproduction Colonial, a mere eighty years old, but now, now she must close the book, turn off the light that displayed the water ring left by her husband's Scotch on the rocks. She had scolded him, when she didn't give a damn about antiques, not really.

As she undressed in the gleam of the night-light, he turned to her. "Uncle Dan?"

"He ran a shop."

Which left it till morning: why this fellow, never mentioned, gave wedding presents of questionable value to her mother.

VAL-KILL

If mapped out, the journey was long, from New Brunswick (Campobello) for family fun to Albany as governor's wife to the White House to a garden on the Black Sea where she taped her meeting with Khrushchev.

> As I was leaving, Mr. Khrushchev wished me a pleasant trip and asked, "Can I tell our papers that we have had a friendly conversation?"
>
> "You can say that we had a friendly conversation, but that we differ."
> —*The Autobiography of Eleanor Roosevelt*

Hyde Park would always be central. Val-Kill Cottage was finally her home, two miles from the big house, her place on the creek with the Dutch name. Oh, the big house was dark, plunged in shadows by her mother-in-law's heavy drapes; by armchairs and sofas stuffed to bursting, though burst they dare not in accord with the rules of Sara Roosevelt's tight grip on her country place, on her son and his family. Franklin loved it—the trails, the boating. When afflicted by polio, he took up residence, installed the hydraulic elevator, never again to climb the stairs. The birds he shot and stuffed as a boy are

190

still there preserved in a glass case, no longer molting.

At long last, the tourist enters the big house, a scene denied her in college. She dislikes every carpet and bronze lamp, the dark wood paneling, the high-backed chairs in the dining room where Sara presided, head of the table. Eleanor hated this gloomy place. Their guide, on the day of the outing, was the lanky one, laconic, bored with his recitation. Someone asked about the sketches of boats on the wall.

"The president," he said, nothing more, not a clue as to Franklin's hobby. "We now split into two groups to view upstairs."

She did not want to see the bedrooms, how the family was deployed after FDR's love affair with Lucy Mercer, after the crippling disease took over his body. There would be flowery wallpaper and perhaps a clear view of hills sloping to the Hudson that could not be denied, even by a president's mother.

"I'm happy to leave," he said, though not delighted when she said we must take the last tour of the day to Val-Kill, Eleanor's furniture factory. She could see the clouds of his discord gathering, but was firm in her purpose. It was the height of the Great Depression when ER, with two lady friends, devoted their generosity to craft, to handwork by which men and women might earn a decent wage. Rather noblesse oblige, wasn't it? Eleanor put up the money from a recent inheritance and they were in business, hiring distinguished cabinet makers and weavers to train workers. It was not a fresh notion—Arts and Crafts; Colonial Revival was, in fact, a vogue, this desire for pre-industrial furniture made of native wood—no mahogany, please. Honest, direct, sincere, a ladder-back chair or a settle with rush seat hand woven; the oak of a cupboard quartersawn to reveal the grain, ornaments pegged in, never glued, never. Val-Kill was successful for a while. Shuttles of the hand looms beat their soft rhythms.

We must go back to pick up that thread: It had been known to her: that her husband had an affair with Lucy, once her social secretary, now his pretty aide. It was a time of healing for Eleanor. Business was good, then down: The lady friends quarreled. ER survived. Val-Kill became her cottage—bright and cheery. She was writing, earning money from her writing. In time she would write her syndicated column, "My Day," three hundred words six days of the week: wise thoughts on family life and pleasant chatter; clever though often deeply felt political observation. How, during all the years of her marriage, had she gulped back her pride, written sticky phrases to her

191

mother-in-law most every day: *Much love always, dearest Mummy?*

Val-Kill is a touch dowdy, pine paneling on the walls, white muslin curtains. A low bench, Colonial if you will, sits in front of the fireplace to the left of her wing chair. On the mantel, a clutter of photos. Sara, Franklin, and their five children.

> I was so hidebound by duty that I became too critical, too much of a disciplinarian. I was so concerned with bringing up my children properly that I was not wise enough to just love them. Now, looking back, I think I would rather spoil a child and have more fun out of it.
> —*The Autobiography of Eleanor Roosevelt*

Her husband left his wife (his fifth cousin) more than property, a legacy of service, but she had already signed on. ER did not need his name to be appointed to the American Delegation to the United Nations. Her post, U.S. Representative to the Humanitarian and Cultural Committee drafting the Universal Declaration of Human Rights.

> *Whereas* recognition of the inherent dignity and of the equal and inalienable rights of all members of the human family is the foundation of freedom, justice and peace in the world,
> *Whereas* disregard ... for human rights [has] resulted in barbarous acts which have outraged the conscience of mankind ...
> *Whereas* a common understanding of these rights and freedoms ...
> Now, Therefore, *THE GENERAL ASSEMBLY proclaims THIS UNIVERSAL DECLARATION OF HUMAN RIGHTS* ...
> —Adopted by the General Assembly
> of the United Nations, 1948

In the morning, her husband is off to the law office where he will work ahead on a matter of federal jurisdiction, an area that FDR had enormously expanded. Yesterday he reminded her, Franklin went to Columbia Law School, not Harvard, to be near to Eleanor. She finds the card table in the middle of the living room where she left it. For a moment she feels the slick surface where she attempted to wax out the water stain, then steels herself to pull the knob on the drawer. Dry glue joining mortise and tenon turns to dust. Under cocktail napkins, coasters, the wood on the bottom of the drawer displays the even swirl of an electric saw.

192

Uncle Dan's Antiques and/or junk shop. Her mother dropped in for a vase or a candlestick often, perhaps too often before she married, before she had a house of her own. Nobody's uncle, the man with the tousled red hair, bib overalls, black boots, not brogans like her father's. His truck in the driveway when she came home from school, once or twice. Stalled in the kitchen, she heard only their laughter. The family came into the house by the back door always. The card table stood lifeless in a narrow front hall, an artifact not used for games, never used at all. The mirror hung over it. She had hoped, unreasonably, it might be a Val-Kill treasure, Depression Colonial—the pretty fake, the fraud.

The Lights of Kadhimaya Hospital
Mark Edmund Doten

FOR YEARS MY CITY lived within the language of sleep. Then the Americans came, and we awoke—this, the worst sort of illusion. Every month a knock at the door, and Othman, my husband, disappeared into the night. Before he disappeared, I would stop him at the door, knife in hand.

I unbuttoned his shirt, and though he struggled, even beat me with his fists, I held him fast, until tremors ceased. Then I dipped the blade into his chest, between two ribs, and cut away a strip of his heart. While he was gone I salted it, and squeezed it together with the other strips of his heart.

There are five neurosurgeons in Iraq. One was kidnapped and ransomed and fled. Two fled without being kidnapped. Two refuse to practice out of fear of being kidnapped—and yet they don't flee. Our patient needed a special stent—we couldn't secure a neurosurgeon, but there was a second potential surgery. No longer a life-saving surgery, but an ameliorative stent procedure. Othman was able to secure this stent—was able to speak with the chief of the branch in charge of stent importation. He knew a man who worked for the chief of this branch; such was our luck, many others had been waiting for months or years.

In Kadhimaya Hospital, after the lights went out, I couldn't pull the mask from her face. My hands half wrecked from the care of the heart—I was clumsy, I couldn't remove the mask. The lights of Kadhimaya Hospital went out, and if I could no longer see our patient, our family member, I could hear her scream and feel the strange wind of it, my fingers caught up in the mask.

When the lights went out, Othman and Father were speaking of their drives. Othman said that the checkpoints had changed, why had they changed? Father and I had crossed the A'ema Bridge—such was

194

our decision. I'd listed the Adhimaya checkpoints for Othman when we first arrived. Father had told it all too, but here he was, telling it again. He kept on and on, as though preparing for some future when the telling might decide everything.

I wasn't thinking about the drive—I was thinking about the injection. How I would need to bribe them with one thousand dinars for the next injection, as I had for the previous injection, and the one before that. To get her blood pressure—that would be another one thousand dinars. I was seeing all of our dinars in stacks of one thousand, winking out.

Until the lights went out, I was thinking of dinars and stents, thinking, *Perhaps I'll be next, I'll soon take our patient's place.*

Sometimes I feel the filth building inside.

I am young, but my future is destroyed, just as Othman's future is destroyed, and Father's too—I could surrender, give voice to the scream inside, release my bowels—this is my fantasy. But where would the money come from—the money for my stents, my injections?

The lights went out and Father rested a hand on her forehead. I tried to force her mouth open with the spoon. I wanted to get it over, get the ice chips in—I wished I hadn't started. Her mouth so dry— our patient parched—I wanted her to be comfortable. She choked on the ice, screaming and hacking, as it slid down her throat. Father and Othman looked on. There was nothing they could do, it was only an ice chip, it wouldn't kill her. I snapped the oxygen mask back in place.

Just then the claw at my back fell away. Perhaps the deranged woman, the lunatic in the next bed, had finally croaked, would no longer clutch at me, as she had been clutching at me since our arrival.

There is nothing here but filth, I thought, *and I have locked it in place.* I thought: *I have failed to succor the dying.*

Othman and I live apart now, as we must. Yesterday, Othman, on the phone: *Live your life, go away, our future is destroyed.* Go where? I wanted to ask. He knows I cannot leave, the necessary papers out of reach, infinitely so, still he pretends I can escape—first I will escape, then he will escape. He pretends love is keeping me here, or loyalty, or foolishness, or hope. *You must end this foolishness, stop traveling to Kadhimaya Hospital, it makes no difference,* Othman said. He said, *And they'll kill you.*

Fine, I said, *let them.*

He cursed me. And I knew this without seeing—his eyes rolled up.

The victims of the latest bomb lay torn on rude cots or slumped against the wall when we rushed into the hospital, and it seemed to me, as Father wrenched my arm to propel me forward, that I passed nothing but the legs of children, legs peppered and flayed and seeping, and though I knew that these legs were attached to bodies, to faces crying out in pain, all I saw as Father dragged me to the stairs was children's legs—so many dark bloody legs, the trousers cut away.

I see these legs now, in this foul little room. Two smeared windows, eight beds, the three of us the only visitors, all other patients abandoned, ours—our patient before us—the fortunate one, I suppose, if visitors bring fortune and not mere darkness.

But I am evading the main point.

My lesson for today—today's *new truth.*

The filth—how I forgot it; how could I have?

When we entered the hospital this morning we gaped at the stench. But then, as if we were victims of some spell, the stench vanished— or, rather, *it vanished from our minds.*

Though we speak on the phone most nights, it had been months since I'd seen Othman. Our patient had been here eleven days, this was Othman's first visit, the drive too risky in the face of those Adhimaya checkpoints, we didn't embrace.

And why didn't we? Was it the filth? Othman stood and sat back down quite smoothly, as though our touching—ever touching again— was perfectly out of the question.

Othman's cheekbones have grown sharper and his beard has thinned; when I first saw him I wanted to ask him to finish pasting on this new stage beard of his. There was as well a swelling and discoloration under his left eye, which neither Father nor I have asked about.

Meanwhile in the past weeks—it struck me only now, as I took inventory of my husband's altered countenance—Father's face too had changed, losing all definition, flesh swelling beneath a shiny skin.

A cramped space, a fetid space. Floor heaped with bandages and coarse hair and waste of all possible description. I would never again touch my husband—that much did I know. Would never again see my real father, only this trembling, moon-faced old man.

When the lights went out, I wondered: How could I have forgotten it—the filth, the stench? How could this have happened?

Perhaps that's why I tried to give her the ice chips: I was ashamed of myself for forgetting. And ashamed of the lights of Kadhimaya Hospital. Ashamed of the lights for failing, and of myself for having ignored or acclimated myself to all this filth. And so I said, *Shall I give her some ice chips? Yes, I think I shall.* I must have said something of the sort, I wouldn't have taken such a wild chance unannounced.

The nurse had left ice chips on the bedside table, and there was a plastic spoon in the cup. The lights went out, and all at once I tasted the filth. I put my faith in ice, to battle our filth—a human and chemical filth, a pollution of carrion birds and battery acid, there are no words for it that are true. Lights had kept the stench of Kadhi-maya Hospital at bay, and lights were gone. Light staggered down the filthy hallway, first darkness staggered down the hallway, then light, and I choked on the noxious waste, the corruption of everything we should have kept inside. I thought: *Until today I never knew the taste of true filth. I thought I knew the taste of filth in this, my beautiful city, but I did not.*

She screamed as I tried to loosen the elastic straps.

She'd been screaming all day, screaming for months now, involuntarily, a scream that began faintly, as you scream in your sleep—a barely audible exhalation, then an increasing outflow of air. Then the piercing shriek of a little girl. Before Kadhimaya Hospital, she'd screamed every twenty minutes or half hour. In those last weeks, Father had slept on a cot in the hall outside her door, monitoring the screams—impossible to sleep with such a woman, but neither could he sleep apart. So all night he would lie supine, arms crossed at chest, eyes fixed on ceiling, and when she was removed to Kadhimaya Hospital, he returned to the bedroom only reluctantly, surveying the empty bed, the end table with so many pill bottles in disordered ranks. Early the morning after they took her I found him back in the hall, where he'd again made his bed.

Today the screams came twice a minute. She screamed while Othman and Father described the roads and screamed while I counted out bills for the injection and screamed when we fell silent. She

197

couldn't move, except her head, she was paralyzed now, but you'd see the scream building—to be wrenched out and swept with the lamentations deeper within the ward; then this dolorous noise would pour down the stairs and crash into the fury of the emergency room (during our own passage through those flayed legs, I heard all of this: the sound that was, that will always be), where the echoed shrieks of men and girls, the barking of doctors and the perpetual sobs of the wives and mothers of the martyred held sway.

Meanwhile the woman in the next bed hissed at us.

She'd been hissing for hours, the deranged one.

Eight beds, all occupied, only two bearing bodies in possession of a voice, only two patients manufacturing noise, all the rest dying silently, too deaf or apathetic or weak to respond to the plaints that assailed them from all directions, but especially from our patient, all dying silently but the deranged old woman lying behind me, clawing at my back, she just hissed and hissed: *Praise God*, she hissed, *can't you let me die in silence, go to God in peace, at least give me that?*

And:

Dear, give us some water—thus the voice behind me, the deranged woman.

She saw me going for the ice, the deranged woman; she must have seen my gambit when the lights went up. Those were her last words—she couldn't speak any longer, her vocal apparatus had at last given out—perhaps she was dead, I thought, the claw still knotted in the fabric of my dress, and in truth I had no way of knowing if those were or would be—if those were and are forever her last words, the end of her hissing. I did not turn to look, she had no family here—no, none of the other women jammed in this stained and window-less chamber, little better than a closet, had family here. But the deranged one must have had visitors, I thought—it was her family who swaddled her head in pink towels, so that the blood leaking from her skull was less striking—such were my thoughts, which I knew to be nonsensical.

The deranged one had croaked at last, I thought, not turning to face her, not reaching and slapping at my own back to disentangle the claw, because I refused to slap at my own back, and I thought, *She has finally departed this, our ruined city.* Then a hiss, so I knew I was wrong. What she needed was water—water so she could continue to excoriate us. But I wouldn't give her water, I didn't want to hear her excoriations, not in all this filth.

Over the past months we'd grown accustomed to the accusers and attackers ranged round our patient—accustomed long before Kadhimaya Hospital to the voices mumbling and hissing or reproaching us with mute and burning condemnation—every soul in this our city hating us more and more; everywhere hate-crazed heads rotating in our direction, a whirring and clicking in each of these skulls. We ourselves despised the screams, even as we loved our patient—but we were the only ones who loved her.

The screams provoked a fury in Father's neighbors. They couldn't take the screaming, they said. Each time Othman and I visited Father's Kadhimaya apartment (the apartment of my childhood, which is now again my apartment, in this, my second and inward-burning childhood—yes, since abandoning Othman to Adhimaya and his night missions, smuggling away the salted heart, I have watched myself become again a helpless and quite stupid child, incapable of spooning ice into a parched mouth), a neighbor—a crone, without exception—would accost us in his lobby.

On this day (I'm speaking here of the past, of that time when Othman and I lived as husband and wife!) a widow—another crone, another of the *deranged ones*—laid her lobby trap in the stairwell and sprang it—without hesitation. She seized my arm, and shook my whole body, through the upper bones of my arm, on account of the screaming. It *annoyed her so much! so much!* All neighbors in accord, said the widow creature. Oh, yes, she said.

This creature told us that we had to put our patient away *this week! today! It's a danger! We'll take steps!*

Othman raised a hand. I can take steps too, he said—and grinned.

An awful sight. Teeth so sharp, his threat expanding and gathering force above the cracked tiles of the lobby, blowing the deranged one back on her heels, then literally whirling her up the stairs.

This was not my Othman, but it was. The men have new eyes and new teeth, we are all becoming something else. We are growing in the filth and in the filth we are purified, the eyes and teeth of the men gleam white, but they're jagged, there are too many teeth in their mouths, too much white in their eyes.

Men came to our door on five nights to ask Othman for a favor— he went with them on the night missions, there is no choice, he goes or he dies. He has not told me a word about these night missions. Only once did I ask; he stared with his vast white eyes, then turned away—but not before I saw the grin playing at his lips, Othman identical now with all of the men in this, our city, I look at them in the streets, the vendors and cabbies and beggars, and I don't see mouths, I see an explosion of jagged white teeth. I look into eyes and see whites and nothing else, rolling up and up. These men with their night missions are by daylight enervated, shuffling things—after the night missions began, silence reigned in the streets and alleys, and not only in Kadhimaya, but also in al Kesayah Street, while in al Mustaburg not a sound was to be heard. In the whole city, day and night, hours would pass in which only our patient, her screams, sounded (and the hissing of those around her)—but watch closely and you will see the men tilt back their heads and soundlessly howl, thrilling in that anguish that converts them all to a single wild religion of eyes and teeth.

All this to say: a knock at the door, then Othman would be gone until morning (and before he went, I cut a strip of his heart).

This and no more can I tell you about the night missions.

Thus the men; but what of the women?

We have a secret from the men, oh yes.

The widow whore perched on the landing two flights up, she eyed us as we backed out of the lobby, and I saw a spider inside her heart, the same size as her heart.

In my own heart too there is a spider the size of my heart—do you understand our spiders? our secrets? In all women's hearts in this city there is now a spider, the size of a heart. The men live without these spiders, the men just die and die, their teeth and eyes a blinding white. At last the ambulance took our patient to Kadhimaya Hospital. She was dying, would soon die, any hour now she'd be dead—for days, though, she has stared up into the corner of her room. Her birdlike eyes watch and her mouth screams—her eyes lock in terror on the dark shapes she sees there and that cracked mouth emits one scream after another—she has no spider in her heart, thus the screams. A woman without a spider must go mad in this city, screaming without end.

When the lights went out, the sun burned through the filth of the high window until clouds or smoke rolled across the sky, and the room—all of us—tipped once again into oblivion.

*

The surgery itself was the wildest sort of chance, the operating theater run off generators—machines for breathing and light, machines monitoring her vitals, the power to these machines flooded and ebbed, you couldn't trust them. I was thinking of this—of stents and dinars and our misplaced trust in machinery—when the deranged woman twisted the fabric of my dress, clawed at my back, and again I tasted the filth—the lights off, then on.

Father pressed his hand to our patient's forehead, and for a moment I forgot all about the night missions, the stents, the duplicity of machines; at his gentle touch the wretched twisting of her face seemed for a moment to ease, and a look of repose crossed both their faces. But then the lights went off, and the filth was borne down on us. When the power came back, Father had withdrawn his hand; he leaned back in his chair, eyes registering nothing as she screamed; he started up again about the drive, the checkpoints—how I hated him then for his timidity! Othman too, as though infected by Father, cast a single glance at our patient, at the place where Father's hand had rested, and at my own hands struggling with the elastic straps, then he too looked away, he sank back and spoke of his drive in precise imitation of Father.

And what about our patient: Did she understand any of this, any of this filth? *She is part of the filth now*, I thought. *She is now filth, that's all, pure filth.*

Our patient couldn't look away from the stains in the corner, there was a fascination in her eyes—such fascination goes, I now understood, hand in glove with *such filth, such terror.*

Her screams weren't screams of *recognition*, they were screams of *becoming*, I thought—*becoming pure filth.*

I am with child, and I don't know whether to pray that it is not a boy or that it is not a girl. For a spider in the heart or a heart to be salted and clutched to the spider heart of the loved one. Better a boy, I think, not a girl who will one day be forced to take on both hearts, the salt heart and the spider heart, and weep, that is too much. No longer a natural weeping woman but a tear-production machine winding and thumping out of control, and shrieks that never end. Our men's hearts are meat and blood, and before they leave on their night mission we remove their hearts, we salt them so they don't rot, so they don't become a part of the filth. We wait at the window for their return, squeezing shriveled bits of dried meat in our fists. I carry Othman's heart and I think that I will die before I give birth, I hope for that.

There will be no money for the birth—only more filth. Our patient has swallowed our money and excreted it as filth. Surgery, basic care, one hundred thousand dinars cash—money torn from our mouths and pockets. One hundred stacks of one thousand dinars, winking out in those first twenty-four critical hours. The doctor made notes on the chart, indicating that instructions had been left to medical assistants—this was all rhetorical. The doctor would leave us a phone number, but never once answered—he'd be asleep, or in another ward, or a different building. The medical assistants as well were asleep, or in another ward, or a different building, and the nurses too, sleeping, other wards, different buildings, now and then these sham assistants and nurses would show their faces to flip through the chart and scribble down some procedure that had never been administered before vanishing for good.

I held her hand in my own—I had been holding it for hours. (My story is almost over.)

Father and Othman sat across from me, near the door. Father was telling about the drive. *Will they change the checkpoints again on the way back? Will there be a false checkpoint? Will I be kidnapped?* Father had long ago decided that he would be kidnapped, even before his brother was kidnapped. *I just hope they kidnap me before the money runs out*—he said this often, as though kidnappers, like lightning, strike only once, as though he couldn't be kidnapped again and again, till the day our last dinar was gone, till they slit his throat.

Othman started, and his eyes wheeled to a space behind me—the space of the arm again clutching me, the deranged hand—but he said nothing.

It's so new to us, we're reduced to eyes and teeth, we see everything and nothing, we tear into flesh we should have buried.

I reached for the ice chips. *I must succor the dying*, I thought. *I must—now, immediately. And without fail.*

Our patient's face had withered, shrunk, she was a famished baby bird, I thought. This wasn't quite right. But I knew one thing: What came out of that wasted body was filth. Her voice expressed nothing but filth, and it had to be stopped. You have to put a stop to such a process, you have to do your best. You cannot let your patient, your family, *turn to filth*. You must not let the process complete itself, I thought wildly, you have to salvage what you can, nurture it, bring it back to the light. I tried to unbind the mask, she screamed, and her arms trembled. I was holding her hand—I'd been holding it for hours, but now I went for the mask.

Dead muscle, pus, bitter, vomited olives—the filth commingled with our patient's breath, I didn't know one from the other.

The deranged woman clawed at me from behind, tugging me back, with a strength that surprised me—but her strength was not greater than my own.

I worked my fingers free of the elastic straps, and the mask snapped back in place—I would not touch it again. It pulled at the lines of her face, fixing them. And I again took up her hand.

And now for the first time our patient's eyes rolled away from the stains in the corner. They drifted at Father, abstracted, glazed, empty now behind a terror they'd let go, or almost let go—a terror floating between Father and our patient, touching neither, irrelevant. Her eyes drifted and may have touched his own—I'd like to think their gazes met.

Othman looked away; his own eyes could have tipped the balance somehow—sent our patient away for good. He looked away but kept watching—we all held our breath. Father's eyes burning from outside in, lids wide, straining to see. The lights flicked off, then on, but his gaze didn't flick off—only burned. And I remembered something— you see, just then I remembered *past* the filth, *past* the screams, *beyond* this rime of salt that withers my hands—years ago Father had shouted at her, at our patient. And how his eyes were burning then—and with what a different fire. A cool, dark evening before the invasion, when our patient, our dear one, our dearest family member, was just beginning to forget, just losing control of her bowels— screaming still months away.

Steadily at first, twisting a rag between his fists with increasing agitation, Father tried to get her to understand—understand about laxatives and pink bismuth. She'd been taking one when she was supposed to be taking the other, or taking both at once, pink bismuth, laxatives. That evening his voice went wild: "We've been over this," he shrieked—like a bird, I thought, a broken bird.

He turned away, face leaping uncertainly between disgust, weariness, and fear, and saw me watching.

"I shouldn't raise my voice," he said. He tossed the rag to the floor, eyes racing, nowhere his eyes could light.

And I wonder: Did he think that was filth—*real filth?*

He didn't know any better. None of us did. Now he is in Kadhimaya Hospital, and everything is all new. He's whispering, but it's not just that. "Oh I know," he says. He strokes her forehead like she's a child. "I know," he says. He says, "I'm so sorry."

Drafts for Shelley

Andrew Mossin

What dream ye? Your own hands have built an home.

—Shelley, *The Revolt of Islam*

Faced with the danger of seeing the crypt crumble, the whole of the ego becomes one with the crypt, showing the concealed object of love in its own guise. Threatened with the imminent loss of its internal support—the kernel of its being—the ego will fuse with the included object, imagining that the object is bereft of its partner. Consequently, the ego begins the public display of an interminable process of mourning. The subject heralds the love-object's sadness, his gaping wound, his universal guilt—without ever revealing, of course, the unspeakable secret, well worth the entire universe.

—Nicolas Abraham and Maria Torok,
The Shell and the Kernel

Andrew Mossin

> *'In heart's temple*
> *suspended this votive*
> *of memory'*

COULD HE COLDLY

instruct visions ethic   veiled glory

When all light was

Supernal   Captivating 'antique symmetries'

Of sound & color

As one night he said   'Even as you descend

A figure of uneven marking

Even while you sink

Beneath the sea

Falling like a dizzy moth

Whose flight is

An image of departing

Oversoaring   F l a m e s

In which You & I are

Captive   Transitory

Elements of loss'

'For the bodily returns—woman and man—agonized—maneuvering against the exigencies of available form—and devours long-lost spirit—in a vituperative dispensation of psyche's drama.'

Andrew Mossin

The hand is s o l v e n t

As it fits a line to this

S e a l of whorls

As one zigs

Out from underneath

    A dead
   Light set
      Free on the page

      This human heart

   Dreaming   inside
          its fiery recluse

          Up from the EARTH

          Our face all turned

          To meet a stranger

3091 'We live in our own world—'

'Fleshless bones' 'spotted with nameless scars' . . . One left off unsaid, as if he and
I were gathered by the same power, like 'all things hidden' a face posed to meet mine,
'the loaded weary wind' that enters and moves behind.

A voice melded in place of another

    Grafted into place

    The fierce omnipotence

    Of an invisible power

    Of one moving at break of day

    Earmarked

    'around each quiver'

    'cheeks and fingers glowing'

    This vying for control

    These flowing outlines mingling

Breaking apart in my hands

    'The words are awed   like careless revelers'

    And they have bound me loose

    And they have folded me among their dwellings

    'In the same manner as gravitation is a power

    according to whose name we find ourselves

    at large in the world'

'Words

Are quick and vain . . . Grief

Is blind as if each embrace

in such calm / in such silence were infinite

And the lagging a fall through boundless

Passages of art'

For to inquire what death is . . . to see what is supposed and measured

Is to risk again incipience of the illumined sea

      And to hover at evening

      The brightness of white light

      Scattered into line

      As the image returns of woman & man-child

      Radiance of their formed likeness

      A force of symmetrical keeping

        As light shines onto the path

  A L L that is i n s u p p o r t a b l e

Betokens this ground of living romance

This transit of aethereal pearl

A phantom   from the dream

Of the
     of its wan   waning
   Long-lost beginning   as if childless

As you and I questioned every tongue
         to give it form again

'Our happiness & all that we have been—I visited but saw you
sadly changed—homeless—you had become—on the path lit by
moon & stars & sun—after long years—already changed—
from many beatings & in many thoughts—wandering out—
a sense of words—delivered not received'

And the isles blue in the wind

And the City below dissolved in stars

'How every pause is filled with under notes

And pierces the skin—'

An age has passed since then

How will our eyes hide and our breath

Return

'wandering beneath the beam'

'beautiful as a ghost'   out of memory
                                    and all the while   afraid

    When we have seen

        When we are seen

  By one returning
        Ascending stair by stair

    A woman gray & white & brown

    Stair by stair

    Ascending stairs the pilot has hidden.

And he took to his side

One whose guilt
Was greater

A tomb of e c s t a s y   extinguished & desolate

O

'Nuptials
From which this veil
Of illusion
Springs up against
Their haunting—'

And flowers
C u t their face

And cut their hand in two

And rocks

Gave them shelter

T H O U   T E R R O R   &   B E A U T I

'sky wet with ocean & the birds

red & white along the border'

Of Nature's hand

In whom all forms are

Infinite   'these winged
               injured hours'

Andrew Mossin

As one stands apart
And gazes out

       at f a I r g r e e n s h o o t s

       in may or june the green

       which are gentle summons

       of divided grief

All who can pity come toward

As feeling is made through line

And each pause is the limit of what went before it

'There lay one

leaved lemon bud

and winter unremembered

to which these

additions of red are'

       'As notes are

       of music a scale

       formed from the other

       half & insist on difference

       blessed in continuous air'

Andrew Mossin

A COURSE OF POESY

For Wisdom comes through movement

And is read as motion in time: *She passeth*

And goeth through   all things by reason

Of purity

Light is beginning

Without words A shape of
                    Insistent indwelling

There is a

There was a being

A beginning of *Thee—*

'And there was silence accompanying

My journey and the Broad Heaven

Shone unimpeded'

Thou in the beginnings of wander

            Brought from woe [wood]

As what is dared l i f t s   incarnate

These suppressed dreams of everafter

215

I know
I have heard)
My Sister is G o n e

And all my Spirit transformed

Wresting these words in place

Of worship

As all I know of words

Is in line

Bending toward
God

Crossing to which shore?

Level with what ground unseen?

I came upon its
Hull

Cracked in two—

And saw the boat with one sail

The helmsman pilot

And pale light o'er the sea

And from the beams
  Awkward a g e l e s s
    sphere

     I drew

From what was   scan of such light

And from the singing made a course

Breathing into depths

And from the rain & beams

I sank & from the wind

Which came westward

Through amatory movement

I drew passing change

And moved through Earths upturning

And lay dimly down a surface of motion

A shape of Light

          'as on a line

    suspended between two heavens'

Andrew Mossin

W H A T have I lifted where am I

_____

Mesmerized & half bewildered by new forms

If I could find one form resembling

And every voice

And every mouth

Lifted to receive

'Among the dead we traveled alone, with language set free . . .'

Paths of sonic e t e r n a l rock

>   Each vowel

>   A shade of antique song

>   'Moon among the clouds'

>   As if sound were

>   A crypt

>   And our lives mirrored

>   Within

Privileged lights wild shore

From every beam I

K n e w

Its snow bright marge

Its radiant isle

    A trail of matter

A root of rime

And I s a w

    where he   under roof of blue

Ionian weather

Was again

A form of himself

And bright sun

Spread Across

The Spheres

The winds are soft   in autumn
& a luster in the sky

And every form containing thee.

—*For Ronald Johnson*

His Last Great Gift
Matt Bell

SPEAR HAS ALREADY BEEN living in the cabin overlooking High Rock
for two weeks when the Electricizers speak of the New Motor for
the first time. Awakened by their voices, Spear feels his way down the
hallway from the dark and still unfamiliar bedroom to his small
office. He lights a lamp and sits down at the desk. Scanning the press
of ghastly faces around him, he sees they're all here tonight: Jefferson
and Rush and Franklin, plus his own namesake, John Murray. They
wait impatiently for him to prepare his papers, to dip a pen in ink and
shake it free of the excess. When he's ready, they begin speaking,
stopping occasionally to listen to other spirits that Spear can't quite
see, that he doesn't yet have the skills to hear. These hidden spirits
are far more ancient, and Spear intuits that they guide the Electricizers in the same way that the Electricizers guide him.

What the Electricizers show Spear how to draw they call the New
Motor, a machine unlike anything he's ever seen before. He concen-
trates on every word, every detail of their revealment: how this cog
fits against that one, how this wire fits into this channel. In cramped,
precise letters, he details which pieces should be copper, which zinc
or wood or iron. The machine detailed in this first diagram is a mere
miniature, no bigger than a pocket watch but twice as intricate.

It's too small, Spear says. He puts down the pen, picks up the crude
blueprint with his ink-stained fingers. He holds it up to the specters.
He says, How can this possibly be the messiah you promised?

Jefferson shakes his head, turns to the others. He says, It was a
mistake to give this to him. Already he doubts.

Franklin and Rush mutter assent, but Murray comes to Spear's
defense. Give him time, the spirit says. At first we had doubts too.

Murray touches Spear on the face, leaving a streak of frost where
his fingers graze the reverend's stubbled skin. He says, Have faith. It
is big enough.

He says, Even Christ was the size of a pea once.

*

221

THE FIRST REVEALMENT

First, that there is a UNIVERSAL ELECTRICITY.

Second, that this electricity has never been naturally incorporated into minerals or other forms of matter.

Third, that the HUMAN ORGANISM is the most superior, natural, efficient type of mechanism known on the earth.

Fourth, that all merely scientific developments of electricity as a MOTIVE POWER are superficial, and therefore useless or impracticable.

Fifth, that the construction of a mechanism built on the laws of man's material physiology, and fed by ATMOSPHERIC ELECTRICITY, obtained by absorption and condensation, and not by friction or galvanic action, will constitute a new revelation of scientific and spiritual truths, because the plan is dissimilar to every previous human use of electricity.

This mechanism is to be called the NEW MOTOR, and it is wholly original, a mechanism the likes of which has never before existed on the earth, or in the waters under the earth, or in the air above it.

In the morning, Spear descends the hill into the village below, the several pages of diagrams rolled tight in the crook of his arm. On the way to the meeting hall, he waves hello to friends, to members of his congregation, to strangers he hopes will come and hear him speak sooner or later. He is confident, full of the revealed glory, yet when he reaches the meeting hall, he does not go in.

Spear's friends and advisers—the fellow reverends and spiritualist newspapermen meeting now inside the hall—have followed him here to Massachusetts because he claimed there was a revelation waiting for them here, and already he knows they will not be disappointed. It is too soon to tell them about the blueprints, to allow them to doubt what the Electricizers have given him. He leaves the meeting hall without entering, wanders the town's narrow streets instead, waiting to be told what to do next.

It takes all morning, but eventually Rush appears to tell him which men to pick, which men to trust with the knowledge of what will be built in the tiny shed beside the cabin atop the hill.

He chooses two Russian immigrants, Tsesler and Voichenko, who speak no English but understand it well enough. He has seen the big bearded heads of these devoted followers of spiritualism nodding in the back row at fellowship meetings, and he knows they will be able to follow the instructions he has to give them.

After the Russians, he selects a handsome teenager named Randall, known to be hardworking and good with his hands, and James the metalworker, a man who has followed Spear since the split with the church.

He chooses two immigrants, an orphan, and a widower: men in need of a living wage, capable of doing the work, and, most important, with no one close enough to obligate them to share the secrets he plans to show them.

Spear selects no women on the first day, but he knows he will soon. One of the women in his congregation will become his New Mary, and into her will be put this revealed god.

THE FOURTH REVEALMENT

Each WIRE is precious, as sacred as a spiritual verse. Each PLATE of ZINC and COPPER is clothed with symbolized meaning, so that the NEW MOTOR might correspond throughout with the principles and parts involved in the living human organism, in the joining of the MALE and FEMALE. Both the woodwork and the metallic must be extremely accurate and crafted correctly at every level from the very beginning, as any error will destroy the chance for its fruition. Only then shall it become a MATHEMATICALLY ACCURATE BODY, a MESSIAH made of singular, scientific precision instead of biological iterations and guesswork.

Before they begin, Spear gathers his chosen men together around the table in the shed, lays out the scant revealments he's received so far. He says, This is holy work, and we must endeavor at every step to do exactly what is asked of us, to ensure that we do not waste this one opportunity that is given to us, because it will not come again in our lifetimes.

He says, When God created the world, did he try over and over again until he got it right? Are there castaway worlds littering the cosmos, retarded with fire and ice and failed life thrashing away in the clay?

No, there are not.

When God came to save this world, did he impregnate all of

Galilee, hoping that one of those seeds would grow up to be a messiah?

No. What God needs, God makes, and it only takes once.

Come closer. Look at what I have drawn. This is what the Electricizers have shown me.

They have revealed to us what he needs, and we must not fail in its construction.

As soon as the work begins, Spear sees the Russians have the talent necessary for the craft at hand. They work together to translate the blueprints into their own language before beginning construction, their brusque natures disguising an admirable attention to detail. At the other end of the shed, James shows Randall how to transform sheets of copper into tiny tubes and wires, teaching him as a master teaches an apprentice.

Spear looks at the tubes the two have produced so far, and he shakes his head. Smaller, he says.

Smaller is impossible, says James.

Have faith, says Spear, and faith will make it so.

James shakes his head but with Randall's help he creates what Spear has asked for. It takes mere days to build this first machine, and when they are finished, Spear throws everyone out of the shed and padlocks the door. He does not start the machine, nor does he know how to.

He cannot, no matter how hard he tries, even see what it might do.

He thinks, Perhaps this is only the beginning, and he is right. The Electricizers return after midnight, and by morning he's ready to resume work. He calls back Tsesler and Voichenko and Randall and James and shows them the next blueprint. The new machine will be the size of a grapefruit, and their first machine will be its heart.

Franklin stands beside Spear on the hill, while in the shed behind them the work continues. Spear has the next two stages detailed on paper, locked in the box beneath his desk, and he is no longer concerned about their specifics. Instead, he asks Franklin about this other person, the opposite of himself. He asks Franklin, Who is the New Mary? How am I supposed to know who she will be?

Franklin waves his hand over the whole of High Rock, says, She has already been delivered unto us. You need only to claim her, to take her into your protection.

He says, When the time is right, you will know who to choose.

But the time is now, Spear says. If her pregnancy is to coincide with the creation of the motor, it must start soon.

Franklin nods. Then you must choose, and choose wisely.

On the Sabbath, Franklin stands beside Spear at the pulpit, whispering into Spear's ears, sending his words out Spear's mouth. There are tears in Spear's eyes, brought on by the great hope the Electricizers have given him. The reborn America the New Motor will bring is the most beautiful thing Spear has ever imagined. The abolition of slavery, the suffrage of women and Negroes, the institution of free love and free sex and free everything, the destruction of capitalism, of war and greed—Spear tells his congregation that, with their support, the New Motor will make all these things possible.

Franklin whispers something else, something meant just for Spear. The medium nods, looks out at the congregation. One of these women must be the New Mary, and so Spear waits for Franklin to say a name, hesitating too long when the specter fails to reveal the correct choice. He looks out at all of the women in the audience, searches his heart for their qualifications. He thinks of the first Mary, of what he understands as her beauty, her innocence, her virginity. The girl he selects to replace her must be young, and she must be unmarried.

Spear does not know the women of his congregation well.

He can recognize them by sight, but remembers their names only when he sees them beside their husbands or fathers or brothers.

There is only one he has known for a long time, who he has watched grow from a child into a young woman, all under the tutelage of the spiritualist movement. He has always felt discomfited by the attention he paid her, but now, at last, he sees the reasons for his lingering gazes, his wanting thoughts. From the pulpit, he says her name: Abigail Dermot.

He says, Abigail Dermot, please step forward.

He doesn't watch her stand, confused, and walk up the aisle. He averts his eyes, both from her and from the front pew, where his wife and children sit.

The thoughts that are in his head he does not want to share with his wife.

He turns to Franklin, but the specter is gone. What he does next, he does on his own.

THE SEVENTEENTH REVEALMENT

Among you there will be a NEW MARY, one who has inherited at the outset an unusually sensitive nature, refined by suffering. To her will be revealed the true meaning of the CROSS, as the intersection of heaven and earth, as positive and negative, as both male and female. She will become a MOTHER, but in a new sense: the MARY OF A NEW DISPENSATION. She will feel a maternal feeling toward not just the NEW MOTOR but also to all individuals, who, through her instrumentality, will one day be instructed in the truth of the new philosophy.

After the services are over, he takes Abigail into his office in the meetinghouse and motions for her to sit down before taking his own seat behind the desk. He believes she is sixteen or seventeen, but when he asks, she says, Fifteen, Reverend. She has not looked at him once since he called her up to the front of the congregation, since he told the others that she was the chosen one who would give birth to the revelation they all awaited.

Spear says, Abigail, you are marked now, by God and by his agents and by me. You are special, set apart from the others.

He says, Abigail. Look at me.

She raises her eyes, and he can see how scared she is of what she's been called to do. He stands and walks around the desk to kneel before her. She smells like lavender, jasmine, the first dust off a fresh blossom. His hands clasped in front of himself, he says, Can you accept what's being offered to you?

He rises, touches her shoulder, then lifts her chin so that their faces are aligned, so that her blonde hair falls away from her eyes.

He says, It is God who calls you, not me, and it is he you must answer.

But Spear wonders. It is just he and she, alone, and without the Electricizers he can only trust what he himself feels in the hollows of his own imperfect heart.

THE THIRTY-SECOND REVEALMENT

The MEDIUM is rough, coarse, lacking culture and hospitality, but with the elements deemed essential for the engineering of the NEW MOTOR, for this important branch of labor. At times he must be in the objective position [not in a TRANCE] while at other times he must be erratic, must ignore his family and friends so that he might hear our many voices. Acting upon impulse, this person will be made to say and do things of an extraordinary character. He will not be held accountable for his actions during the MONTHS OF CREATION. Treading on ground so delicate, he cannot be expected to comprehend the purposes aimed at. Do not hold him as a sinner during this time, for all will be forgiven, every secret action necessarily enjoined.

The services of many persons must be secured to the carrying forth of a work so novel, so important. The NEW MOTOR will be the BEACON FIRE, the BLOODRED CROSS, the GENERAL ORDER OF THE NEW DAY. Whatever must be sacrificed must be sacrificed, whatever must be cast aside must be cast aside. Trust the MEDIUM, for through him we speak great speech.

That night, Rush shows Spear the next stages of the New Motor, detailing the flywheel that will have to be cast at great cost. Spear is given ideas, designs, structures, scientific laws and principles, all of which he writes as quickly as he can, his hand moving faster than his mind can follow. When he reads over what he has written, he recognizes that the blueprint he has been given is something that could not have originated from within him. He can barely comprehend it as it is now, fully formed upon the paper, much less conceive how he would have arrived at this grand design without the help of the Electricizers.

Rush says, The motor will cause great floods of spiritual light to descend from the heavens. It will reveal the earth to be a limitless treasure trove of motion, life, and freedom.

Spear dutifully inks the diagram and annotates each of its intricacies, then asks, Did I choose the right girl?

Rush points to the diagram and says, That should be copper, not zinc.

Spear makes the correction, but presses his own issue. She's only fifteen, from a good family. Surely she's a virgin.

He says, I have seen her pray, and I believe she is as pure of heart as any in the congregation.

Rush says, We want to reveal more, but only if you can concentrate. It isn't easy for us to be here. Don't waste our time.

Spear apologizes, swallows his doubts. He silences his heart and

227

opens his ears. He writes what he needs to write, draws what he needs to draw.

A week later, Spear sends Randall down into the village to fetch Abigail. When the boy returns with the girl, her mother and father also walk beside her. Spear tries to ignore the parents as he takes the girl by the arm, but her father steps around him, blocking the path to the shed.

The father says, Reverend, if God needs my daughter, then so be it. But I want to see where you're taking her.

Spear shakes his head, keeps his hand on the girl. Says, Mr. Dermot, I assure you that your daughter is safe with me. We go with God.

What is in there that a child would need to see that a man cannot?

You will see it, Mr. Dermot. Everyone will, when the time comes. When my task—your daughter's task—is complete, then you will see it. But not before.

Spear holds the father's gaze for a long time. He wants to look at Abigail, to assure her that there is nothing to be afraid of, but he knows it is the father he must convince. Behind them, her mother is crying quietly, her sobs barely louder than the slight wind blowing across the hill. Spear waits with a prayer on his lips, with a call for help reserved farther down his throat. Randall is nearby, and the Russians and the metalworker will come if he calls.

Spear waits, and eventually the father steps aside. Spear breaks his gaze but says nothing, just moves forward with the girl in tow. Out of the corner of his eye, he sees the curtain of his cabin parted, sees his wife's face obscured by the cheap glass of the window. He does not look more closely, does not acknowledge the expression he knows is there.

Inside the work shed, construction continues as Spear shows Abigail what has been done, what the New Motor is becoming. He explains her role as the New Mary, that she has been chosen to give life to the machine.

He says, I am the architect, but I am no more the father than Joseph was.

He tells her, From this point forward, this is your child, and God's child.

He says, Do you understand what I am telling you?

The Electricizers are all in the shed, watching him. He looks to

228

them for approval, but their focus is on the machine itself. Inside the shed, the words he says to them never have any effect, never move them to response or reaction.

Work stalls while they wait for supplies to come by train to Randolph, and then overland to High Rock by wagon. For two weeks, Spear has nothing to do but return to the ordinary business of running his congregation, which includes acting as a medium for congregation members who wish to contact their deceased or to seek advice from the spirit world. A woman crosses his palm with coin and he offers her comforting words from her passed husband, then he helps a businessman get advice from an old partner. Normally, Spear has no trouble crossing the veil and coming back with the words the spirits offer him, but something has changed since the arrival of the Electricizers, a condition aggravated since the beginning of construction on the motor. He hears the other spirits as if his ears are filled with cotton or wax, as if there is something in the way of true communication, and the real world seems just as distant, just as difficult to navigate.

By the time the spinster Maud Trenton comes to see him, he can barely see her, can barely hear her when she says, I'm hearing voices, Reverend. Receiving visitations.

She says, Angels have come to me in the night.

Spear shakes his head, sure he's misunderstood the woman. He feels like a child, trapped in a curtain, unable to jerk himself free. He hasn't crossed the veil, merely caught himself up in it.

He says, What did you say?

Maud Trenton, in her fifties, with a face pocked by acne scars and a mouth full of the mere memories of teeth, says, I told the angels I was afraid, and the angels told me to come see you.

Jefferson appears behind her, with his sleeves rolled up, wig set aside. His glow is so bright it's hard for Spear to look directly at the specter, who says, Just tell her that God loves her.

Spear's eyes roll and blink and try to right themselves. He can feel his pupils dilating, letting more light come streaking in as wide bands of colors splay across his field of vision. He's firmly on the other side now, closer to what comes next than what is.

Jefferson says, Tell her we're thankful. Tell her we venerate her and protect her and watch over her. Tell her the whole host is at her service.

Spear is so confused that when he opens his mouth to say Jefferson's words, nothing comes out. And then the specter is gone, and Spear is freed from his vision, returned to the more substantial world, where Maud sits across from him, her eyes cast downward into her lap, her hands busy worrying a handkerchief to tatters. Suddenly Spear feels tired, too tired to talk to this woman anymore, or to concern himself with her problems.

Spear opens his mouth to say Jefferson's words, but they won't come out, and although he knows why, he blames her instead. He says, Woman, I have nothing to say to you. If you feel what you're doing is wrong—if you've come to me for absolution—then go home and pray for yourself, for I have not been granted it to give you.

At dinner that night, Spear's forehead throbs while his wife and daughters chatter around him, desperate for his attention after his day spent down in the village. He continues to nod and smile, hoping his reaction is appropriate but unable to tell for sure. He can't hear their words, can't comprehend their facial expressions, no matter how hard he tries.

He does not try that hard.

What's in the way is the New Motor. The revealments are coming faster now, and Spear understands that there are many more to come. It will take eight more months to finish the machine, an interminable time to wait, but there is so much to do that Spear is grateful for every remaining second.

The New Motor is ready to be mounted on a special table commissioned specifically for the project, and so Spear brings two carpenters into his expanding crew, each once again hand selected from the men of High Rock. The table is sturdy oak, its thick top carved with several deep, concentric circles designed to surround the growing machine. When the carpenters ask him what the grooves mean, or what they do, Spear shakes his head. Their purpose hasn't been revealed yet, only their need.

Abigail is now a fixture in the shed, spending every day with the men and the motor. Spear spends part of every morning talking to her, relating scriptures he finds applicable. The girl is an attentive student, listening carefully and asking insightful questions. Spear finds himself wishing his own children were so good at absorbing instruction, and more than once he finds the slow linger of a smile burnt across his cheeks long after he and Abigail have finished speaking.

In the afternoons, he joins the others in the day-to-day work of constructing the machine, but even then he continues to watch her, to notice her. This is how he observes the way she sees Randall, the talented young worker who will have his pick of trades when the time comes. Metalworking, carpentry, even the doing of figures and interpretation of the diagrams come easy to Randall, the boy's aptitudes speaking well of his deeper, better qualities. Spear has often been impressed with the boy, but now, watching the quick glances and quicker smiles that pass between Randall and Abigail, he knows he'll have to study him even closer.

He tells himself that it's not the girl he cares about, but the motor. After she gives birth to his machine, Randall can have her. But not before. Spear is sure that, like Mary, Abigail must be a virgin to bring the motor to life, and he cannot risk Randall ruining that. He decides that he will take the girl home to live with him, just until summer. She will become part of his household, and he himself will keep her safe. Although he trusts all those he surrounds himself with, it is only himself who he can vouch is above reproach.

Spear is no engineer, but he knows enough to understand that the New Motor is different. Where most machines are built in pieces, one component at a time, the motor is being built from the inside out. It is being grown, with the sweat and effort of these great Spiritualist men, all excellent workers, excellent minds. Tsesler and Voichenko especially seem given to the task; their ability to translate the complexities of the diagrams and explanations into their own language is almost uncanny. The others work nearly as hard, including Randall. Despite Spear's misgivings about the boy, he knows the young man is as dedicated as any other to the completion of their work. Six days a week, for ten or twelve or fourteen hours, they slave together in the forge-heated shed to fulfill the task handed down to them by the Electricizers. By the time the first snowfall covers the hill, the machine has enough moving parts that a once-useless flywheel becomes predictive, turning cogs that foretell the other cogs and gears and pulleys not yet known to Spear. The first gliding panel is set in the innermost groove of the table's concentric circles, moved all the way around the motor once to ensure that it works the way it is intended to. The panel's copper face is inscribed with words that Spear does not know, but which he believes are the hidden names of God, revealed now in glory and in grace.

On the day of the fall equinox, the men work and work. When they finish after dark, Spear gathers them all around himself. He is covered in sweat and dirt and grease and grime. They all are, and Spear smiles, prouder than he has ever allowed himself to be.

He looks over his men, and he says, It took a quarter of a million years for God to design our last messiah, and even then, he could only come in our form, created in our image, a fallen man. Our new messiah will take only nine months to build, and when it is done it will show us who our own children will be, what they will become in the new kingdom.

This New Motor, it will be the first of a new race, unfallen and perfect, characterized by a steamwork perfection our world is only now capable of creating. God has shown the Electricizers and they have shown me and I have shown you, and now you are making it so.

The New Motor is his task, but Spear knows that there are others working too, all of them assigned their own tasks somewhere out in America. He knows this because, even on the nights when the others fail to materialize, Franklin comes and takes Spear from his bed and out into the night. The two men walk the empty streets, Spear shivering in his long wool coat and hat and boots, Franklin unaffected by the cold. The specter tells him of other groups sent to help, of other spirits in need of a medium. These other groups are called the Healthfulizers, the Educationalizers, the Agriculturalizers, the Elementizers, the Governmentizers, perhaps others that even Franklin hasn't yet heard of.

Franklin says, I can't know everything.

Like you, he says, I am just a vessel.

He puts a cold hand on Spear's shoulder, causing the medium's teeth to chatter together hard, too hard. If the specter doesn't release him soon, Spear worries that he'll break his molars.

A new age is coming, Franklin says. The garden restored.

He says, Fear not.

He says, Through God, even one such as you might be made ready.

*

As the motor grows in complexity, Spear begins to lose his temper more and more often, always at home, always behind closed doors. He tells his wife again and again that Abigail is not to work, that she is not to lift a finger, but more than once he comes home to find the girl helping his wife with her own chores.

To his wife, he says, Why is it that you can't listen to even the simplest of my instructions?

Pointing to Abigail, he says, She's pregnant, with the growing king of our new world. Why can't you do what I say, and treat her accordingly?

His wife begins to weep, but her fury is uncooled by the tears streaming down her face. She says, sounding as tired as he's ever heard, She's not pregnant, John. The only reason she's here is that you want her instead of me.

To Abigail, Spear says, Child, return to your room. Then he waits until Abigail has left the room before he strikes his wife across the face with the back of his hand.

He says, Christ forgive me, but you watch your tongue. You either recognize the glory of God or you do not. Only you can choose which it will be, and in the end, you must choose.

By December, there have been sixty-five revealments, and by the end of January there are thirty more. The New Motor is growing larger, taking up the entire table with its array of sliding panels and connecting tubes and gears. Loose bundles of wires dangle from the construct's innards, waiting for the places where they will connect and give life to extremities that only Spear has seen so far, to other appendages even he can't yet imagine.

This machine, it does not resemble a man, as Spear once thought it would. What's worse, it doesn't resemble anything anyone has seen before, causing the other workers to question him. He does his best to quell their worries, but as the team grows they ask their questions louder and louder, until their concerns leak out of the shed and into the congregation below. The collections that once went to feeding the poor or funding abolitionist trips into the South have for months gone to the motor, and now the congregation's patience grows thin, especially among those who haven't seen the motor, who cannot conceive of what it is, what it will be.

Spear counsels patience, counsels faith. From the pulpit, he says, We have been given a great gift, and we must not question it.

But he does. He questions, he doubts. His resolve wavers. He opens his mouth to speak again, but cannot. He hasn't eaten or changed his clothes in days, and has taken to sleeping in the shed, beneath the copper reflection of the motor. He doesn't go home to the cabin except to fetch Abigail in the mornings and to take her back home at night.

On the Sabbath, he stumbles at the pulpit, but the Electricizers at his side catch him with their frosty hands and return him to his station.

Spear shivers, wipes the drool off his lip with the back of a shaky hand. He waves his hand, motions for the ushers to pass the collection plate. They hesitate, look to the deacons for confirmation, a gesture that is not lost on Spear, who knows his authority has been questioned, his future dependent on the successful outcome of his great project.

Spear closes his eyes against his congregation's wavering faith, then says, God blesses you, in this kingdom, and in the one to come. Give freely, for what you have here you will not soon need.

Spear has to stifle a gasp when Maud Trenton comes into his office during the first week of February. She is as pregnant as any woman Spear has ever seen, her belly stressing the seams of her black dress. He can see patches of skin between strained buttons, and for just a moment he desires to reach out and touch her stomach, to feel the heat of the baby inside.

Maud sits, her hands and arms wrapped around the round bulk of her belly. She says, I need your help, Reverend.

With quivering lips, she says, I don't know where this baby came from, and I don't know what to do with it.

Spear shudders, trying to imagine who would have impregnated this woman. He realizes it has been weeks since he last saw Maud at services or group meetings. She's been hiding herself away, keeping her shame a secret. The people in the village may not be ready to accept such a thing, but Spear prides himself on his progressive politics, on the radical nature of his insight. He believes that a woman should be able to make love to whom she wants, that a child can be raised by a village when a family is unavailable. This does not have to be the ruin of this woman, but there must be truth, confession, an accounting.

Spear says, Do you know who the father is?

Maud neither nods nor shakes her head. She makes no motion to the affirmative or the negative. She says, There is no father.

Through the curtain of gray hair falling across her downcast face, she says, I am a virgin.

She looks up and says, I know you know this.

Spear shakes his head. He does not want to believe and so he does not. He says, If you cannot admit your sin, then how can you do penance?

He says, The church can help you, but only if you allow it to. I ask again, Who is the father?

Spear asks and asks, but she refuses to tell the truth, even when he walks around the desk and shakes her by the shoulder. She says nothing, so he sends her away. She will return when she is ready, and when she is ready he will make sure she is taken care of. There is time to save the child, if only she will listen.

At night, Spear wanders the floors of the small cabin, checking and rechecking the doors. He locks Abigail's door himself each evening, ensuring that she is in her bed, that no one can disturb her, but later he awakens, sure her door is open wide. He rushes out into the hall only to find it locked, just as he left it. These nights, he stands outside her door with his face pressed to the wood, listening to the sounds of her breathing. Sometimes, he dreams he's been inside the room, that he has said or done something improper, only later he can never remember what. More than once, he wakes up in the morning curled in front of her door, like a guard dog, or else like a penitent, waiting to be forgiven.

The Electricizers fill Spear's bedroom with more specters than ever before. He can see now some of the others, the older spirits he first intuited, can hear the creaky whisper of their instructions. These are past leaders of men, undead now but still burdened by their great designs, and Spear can sense the revealments these older ghosts once loosed from their spectral tongues: their Towers of Babel, their great arks. His fingers cramp into claws as he struggles to write fast enough to keep up with the hours of instruction he receives, his pen scratching across countless pages. Near dawn, he looks down and for just a moment he sees himself not as a man, not as flesh and blood, but as one of the Electricizers. His freezing, fading muscles ache with

iced lightning, shooting jolts of pain through his joints. Spear understands that Franklin and Jefferson and Murray and the rest are merely the latest in a long line of those chosen to lead in both this life and
the next, and Spear wonders if he too is being groomed to continue
their great works. He looks at Franklin, whose face is only inches
away from his own. He sees himself in the specter's spectacles, sees
how wan and wasted he looks.

Spear says, Am I dying?

The ghost shakes his head, suddenly sadder than Spear has ever
seen him. Franklin says, There is no such thing as death. Now write.

February and March pass quietly, the work slowing then halting altogether as supplies take longer and longer to reach High Rock through
the snow-choked woods. Spear spends the idlest days pacing alone in
the snow atop the hill, watching the road from Randolph obsessive-
ly. There is so much left to do, and always less time to do it in.

In June, the nine months will be over. The motor must be ready.
God waits for no man, and Spear does not want to disappoint.

Spear spends the short winter days in the shed, checking and rechecking the construction of the motor, but the long evenings are
another matter. Being trapped in the cabin with his wife and children
is unbearable, and being trapped there with Abigail is a torture of
another kind. From his chair in the sitting room, he finds his eyes
drawn to her flat belly, to the lack of sign or signal. From there he
wanders to her covered breasts, and then to the lines of pale skin that
escape the neckline of her dress, the hems at the wrists of her long
sleeves. He watches her while she plays with his own children on the
floor, watches for the kindness and grace he expects to find in his
New Mary.

Mostly, what he sees is boredom, the same emotion that has overwhelmed him all winter, trapped by snow and waiting for the coming thaw that feels too far off to count on. While they wait, he
expects some sign, something to show her development into what
she must become. He knows she will not give birth to the motor, not
exactly, but she must give it life somehow.

Spear wishes he could ask the Electricizers, but knows there isn't
any point. Despite their long-winded exposition on every facet of the
motor's construction, they have been silent on the subject of Abigail
since he first plucked her from the flock.

Spear decides nothing. He stops touching his wife, stops holding his children. He tells himself he is too tired, too cold. Food tastes like ash, so he stops eating. The Electricizers keep him up all night with their diagrams and their inscriptions and their persistent pushing for speed, for completion.

Jefferson tells Spear that by the end of the month, he will know everything he needs to know to finish the New Motor. The revelation will be complete.

By the end of the month, Spear replies, I will be a ghost. He spits toward the ancient glimmer, sneers.

The specters ignore his sacrilegious doubt. They press him, and when he resists, they press harder, until eventually he goes back to work. He writes the words they speak. He draws the images they describe. He does whatever they ask, but in his worst moments he does it only because he believes that by giving in he might one day reach the moment where they'll leave him alone.

THE 176TH REVEALMENT

The PSYCHIC BATTERY must be cylindrical in shape, constructed of lead and filled with two channels of liquid, one containing a copper sulfate and the other zinc. Copper wires will be run from the GRAND REVOLVER into each channel, with great care taken to ensure that none of the wires touch each other as they ascend into the NEW MOTOR. There is a danger of electrocution, of acid burns, of the loss of life and the destruction of the machine. From the moment of CONCEPTION to the moment of BIRTH, always the NEW MOTOR has been in danger, and in these stages there is no safety except for the careful, the diligent, the righteous. When the PSYCHIC BATTERY has been successfully installed, the NEW MOTOR will be complete in one part of its nature, as complete as the MEDIUM alone can make it. Men have done their work, and now it is the women's turn.

In the morning, the other leaders of the congregation are waiting for Spear when he steps out of the cabin. On his porch are other preachers, mediums, the newspapermen who just months before published articles in support of the project. The men stand in a half circle in front of his house, smoking their pipes and chatting. Their voices drop off into silence as Spear descends the steps from his porch onto the lawn.

One of the preachers speaks, saying, John, this has to stop. What-ever you're doing in that shed, it's bankrupting the community.

The newspaperman nods and says, We thought this was a gift from God, that his spirit spoke through you, but now—

He breaks off, looks to the others for support. He says, John, what if what you're making is an abomination instead of a revelation?

And what about the girl, John? What are you doing with the girl?

The others mutter their assent, close ranks around him. Spear doesn't move. They aren't physically threatening him, despite their new proximity. He closes his eyes, and waits a long minute before responding. He holds out his small hands, displays the creases of grease and dirt that for the first time in his life cross his palms.

Spear says, I am a person destitute of creative genius, bereft of scientific knowledge in the fields of magnetism and engineering and electricity. I cannot even accomplish the simplest of handy me-chanics. Everything I tell you is true, as I do not have the predisposi-tion to make any suggestions of my own for how this device might function or how to build what we have built.

He says, This gift I bring you, it could not have come from me, but it does come through me.

It comes through me, or not at all.

The men say nothing. They tap their pipe ash into the snow, or shuffle their feet and stare down the hill. There is no sound coming from the shed, even though Spear knows the workers have all arrived by now. They're listening too, waiting to hear what happens next.

Spear says, Four more months. All I need is four more months. The motor will be alive by the end of June.

He promises, and then he waits for the men to each take his hand and agree, which they eventually do, although it costs him the rest of his credibility, what little is left of the goodwill earned through a lifetime of service. It does not matter that their grips are reluctant, that their eyes flash new warnings. Whatever doubts he might have when he is alone disappear when questioned by others, just as they always have. The Electricizers will not disappoint, nor the god who directs them.

While he's shaking hands with the last of the men, he hears the cabin door open again. Thinking it's Abigail coming to join him in the shed, Spear turns around with a smile on his face, then loses it when he sees his wife instead, standing on the porch, holding his old-est child by the hand. Their other child is balanced in the crook of her arm, and all of them are dressed for travel. He looks from his wife to the men in his yard—his friends, until now—and then back again. While the men help Abigail with the two chests she's packed, Spear stands still and watches without a word. Even when his family stands before him, he has no words.

He blinks, blinks again, then he looks at this woman. He looks at her children. He turns, puts his back to them, waits until they are far enough that they could be anyone's family before he looks once more.

He watches until they disappear into the town, and then he goes into the shed and begins the day's work, already much delayed. He sets his valise down on the work table at the back of the shed, unpacks his papers detailing the newest revealments. While the men gather to look at the blueprints, he wanders off to stare at the motor itself. It gleams in the windowless shed, the lamplight reflecting off the copper and zinc, off the multitudes of burnished magnetic spheres. He puts his hand to the inscriptions in the table, runs his fingers down the central shaft, what the Electricizers call the grand revolver. It towers over the table, vaguely forming the shape of a cross. There are holes punctured through the tubing, where more spheres will be hung before the outer casing is cast and installed. It is this casing that he has brought the plans for today.

Spear does not need an explanation from the Electricizers to understand this part. Even he can see that the symbols and patterns upon the panels are the emblematic form of the universe itself. They are the mind of God, the human microcosm, described at last in simple, geometric beauty. He does not explain it to these men who work for him, does not think they need to know everything that he does.

The only person he will explain it to is Abigail, and then only if she asks.

With his family gone back to Boston, the cabin is suddenly too big for Spear and Abigail, with its cavernous cold rooms, but also too small, with no one to mediate or mitigate their bodies and movements. Everywhere Spear goes, he runs into the girl, into her small, supposedly virginal form. Despite her bright inquisitiveness whenever she visits the shed, she is quieter in the cabin, continuing her deference to his status as both a male and a church leader. Abigail keeps her eyes averted and her hands clasped in front of her, preventing her from noticing that in their forced solitude Spear now stares openly at her, trying to will her to look at him, to answer his hungry looks with one of her own, only to punish himself later for his inability to control these thoughts.

By March, he is actively avoiding her within his own home, so much so that he doesn't notice at first when she begins to show around the belly. The bulge is just a hand's breadth of flesh, just the start of something greater yet to come.

He is elated when he sees it, but the feeling does not last.

Spear knows he has chosen wrong, has known for months that the Electricizers' refusal to discuss the girl is his own fault. In the shed, he stops to take in the New Motor, growing ever more massive, more intricate. There is much left to do before June, and now much to pray and atone for as well. He is sorry for his own mistakes, but knows Abigail's pregnancy is another matter altogether, a sin separate from his own. A sin that must be punished. Spear drags Randall out of the shed by his collar and flings him into the muddy earth. The boy is bigger than he, healthier and stronger, but Spear has the advantage of surprise and it is all he needs. He cannot stop to accuse, to question, must instead keep the boy on the ground, stomping his foot into the teenager's face and stomach and ribs. The boy cries out his innocence, but Spear keeps at it until he hears the unasked-for confession spray from between the boy's teeth.

When Randall returns to the shed, Spear will welcome the boy with open arms. He will forgive the boy, and then he will send him to collect Abigail and return her to her father's home. Let Abigail's father deal with what she and Randall have done, for Spear has his own child to protect.

Even after Abigail leaves, Spear waits to go to Maud Trenton. He walks down the hill to his offices in the meeting hall, a place he hasn't been in weeks, and sends one of the deacons to summon her. When she enters his office and closes the door behind her, Spear barely recognizes the woman before him as the one who last visited him.

Her face is clear now, her acne scars disappeared, and the thin gray hair that once hung down her face is now a thick, shining brown, healthy and full. Even her teeth have healed themselves, or else new ones have appeared in her mouth, grown in strong and white. She is shy, but when he catches her gaze, he sees the glory in her eyes, the power of the life that rests in her belly.

Spear says, Forgive me, Mother, for I did not know who you were.

He gets down on his knees before her and presses his head against the folds of her dress. He feels his body shudder but doesn't recognize the feeling at first, the sadness and shame that accompany his sobs. While he cries, she reaches down and strokes his hair, her touch as soothing as his own mother's once was. In a lowly voice, he gives thanks that his lack of faith was not enough to doom their project, or to change the truth, now finally revealed to him: This woman is the Mother and he is the Father and together they will bring new life to the world. He reaches down and lifts the hem of her dress, working upward, bunching the starched material in his fists. He exposes her thick legs, her thighs strong like tree stumps but smooth and clean, their smell like soap, like buttermilk and cloves. He keeps pushing her dress up until he holds the material under her enlarged breasts, until he exposes the mountain of her swollen belly, her navel popped out like a thumb. He puts his face against the hot, hard flesh, feels her warmth radiate against his skin. She moans when he opens his mouth and kisses the belly, and he feels himself growing hard, the beginning of an erection that is not sex but glory. Maud's legs quiver, buck, threaten to collapse, and he lets the fabric of her dress fall over him as he reaches around to support her. He stays like that for a long time, with his face against her belly and his hands clenched around her thighs. He waits until she uncovers him herself, until she takes his weeping face in her hands. She lifts gently, and he follows the movement until he is once again apart from her, standing on his feet.

Maud kisses Spear on the forehead, then crosses herself before turning away, keeping her back to him until Spear leaves her there in his own office. He walks outside into a suddenly hot day, into the warmth of a sun he hasn't felt in months. He has supplicated himself, has seen the mystery with his own eyes, and he has been blessed by this woman, the one he failed to choose so long ago. It is enough now to put faith in God and in what God has asked of him. It is enough to cast aside all doubts, forever more.

Jefferson wakes Spear with a touch to his shoulder, the specter's hand like a dagger of ice sliding effortlessly through muscle and bone. Jefferson says, Come. I want to show you what will happen next.

The reverend gets up and follows the spirit outside, where they stand together on the hill and look down at High Rock, at the roads that lead toward Randolph and the railroad and the rest of America.

Jefferson says, Just as the Christ was born in Bethlehem and raised

241

in Nazareth, so the New Motor has been built here by the people of High Rock. When it is finished, it must go forth to unite the people, and you with it.

Spear says, But how? It gets bigger every day now. Surely it's too large to rest on a wagon.

Jefferson shakes his head. He says, Once the machine has been animated, you will disassemble it one more time, and then you will take it to Randolph where you will rebuild it inside a railroad car.

Spear says, The railroad doesn't go far enough. We'll never make it across the country that way.

Jefferson ignores him, saying, One day it will, and in the meantime the motor will grow stronger and stronger. You will take our new messiah from town to town, and he will reach out and speak through you to the masses. He will use your mouth and your tongue to relay his words, to bring about the new kingdom that awaits this country. This is why your family was taken from you. This was why we could not allow you to keep the girl, even after the motor was finished.

He says, As much as you have given, there is more that may be asked of you. You must give up everything you have to follow the motor, just as the disciples did before you.

Spears looks at Jefferson, stares at his ghostly, glowing form. He wants to say that there is nothing left to give, that already he is a shell of a man, reduced to a mere vessel, an empty reservoir, but it is too late to protest, too late to go back. Whatever else remains, he does not care enough for himself to refuse any of it.

THE TWO HUNDREDTH REVEALMENT

BIRTH will commence upon the arrival of the NEW MARY, who will arrive pregnant with the energy necessary to bring the machine to life. Through the WOMBOMIC PROCESSES, the NEW MARY will be filled with the THOUGHT CHILD, the necessary intellectual, moral, social, religious, spiritual, and celestial energies that will fill the PSYCHIC BATTERY and give BIRTH to the new age. The BIRTH will be attended by the MEDIUM, who will become more than a male—a FATHER—even as the NEW MARY becomes more than a female— a MOTHER. The womb has had its season of desire. It has had its electrical impartation. The organism of a choice person was acted upon by our LORD and MAKER. The NEW MARY is a person of extraordinary electric power, united in a harmonious, well-balanced physical, mental, and spiritual organism, and when she is brought within the sphere of the NEW MOTOR she will give it life.

The first week of June, Maud Trenton struggles up the hill in the predawn dark, her arms wrapped under the largesse of her belly, supporting the baby inside. She climbs alone, as she has done everything else in her long life, but she also feels watched, as she has since even before the stirring in her body first began. She feels the presence of spirits, of angels, of men who care for her, protect her, keep her safe. When she stumbles to the stony path, it is these angels who give her the strength to rise again, lifting her with hands as warm and soft as they are invisible. The rest of the climb, they hold her by the elbows as she walks, keeping her ankles from twisting, from casting herself again to the ground beneath her feet.

At the top of the hill, both the cabin and the shed are dark and quiet. She looks up into the sky, into the pink dawn obliterating the star-flecked heavens by degrees. She moans, squatting over her knees to wait out the horrible pressure of the next contraction. She wants to go to the cabin first, to wake Reverend Spear, but even a mother as inexperienced as she knows time is short. The angels whisper to her, guide her away from the cabin and toward the shed instead. She must be inside when she gives birth, must be near this new messiah that the reverend has revealed to her.

She tries to open the shed's wide, sliding door, but can't. For a moment, she sees the lock clasped around the latch and despairs, but then—after another crushing contraction—she sees that it's unlocked, as if it never was. The door glides open at her touch, helped along its tracks by her angels. Inside, the room is dark and cool, the dimness softened by the slow sunlight following her inside. At the direction of the angels, she moves to lie down on the floor, to lean her head back on the dusty floorboards, but only after she stares at the machine, at its metallic, crafted magnificence. She does not understand its purpose, but its beauty is undeniable.

There is no midwife to guide her, no husband to comfort her, but Maud needs not these things. The angels are beside her, and with them is her god. It is enough. Her whole life, he has come when she's called, and it has always been enough.

*

Spear watches from the cabin windows, waiting for the Electricizers to leave Maud's side, to come and get him, but they stay with her and envelop her with their light. Eventually, Spear leaves the cabin himself and goes to the shed, where he sits down beside Maud and takes her in his arms, holds her sweating, convulsing body to his. He watches her clenched jaws and closed eyes, watches her legs kick out from her body. He tries to remember the birth of his own children, finds he cannot, then puts his past from his mind. He whispers to Maud, telling her about the great purpose of what she is doing, about the great world she is bringing into being.

At last, he says, Push, and then she does. She spreads her legs, and her womb empties, and afterward Spear and Maud and the Electricizers all wait together, a long moment where Spear feels nothing except for the breath trapped in his lungs, the woman in his arms, the way his heart beats both fast and slow at the same time, as if it might stop at any moment, as if it might go on forever.

The New Motor begins to pulsate subtly, a motion so slight Spear can only see it if he looks at the machine sideways, out of the corner of his eyes. He smiles with a slow, crooked hesitance, nine months of doubt reassured only by this pulsation, by this slight swaying in the hanging magnets of the grand revolver. It is not much, and certainly it is less than he hoped for, but it is something.

Spear hopes—Spear prays—that this is only the beginning, that this infant energy will mature into the great savior he has been promised, that he has promised himself.

Her pregnancy ended, Maud Trenton is light, her body barely skin, barely bones, her cries producing so little water they are barely tears. He lifts her in his arms, carries her gently from the shed into the cabin, where he lays her down on the bed he once shared with his own wife. He waits with her until she falls asleep. It takes a long time, and it takes even longer for Spear to realize that's she's not crying in pain, but in frustration. A lifetime of waiting and a near year of effort, and still she is without a child to call her own. Now Spear understands the terror that is the Virgin, the horror that is the name Mary, the new awfulness that he and the Electricizers have made of this woman.

Whatever this thing is she has given birth to, it will never be hers alone.

He whispers apologies, pleas for penance into her dreaming ears, and then he gets up to leave her. He will go down into the village and fetch the doctor, but first he must attend to the motor.

First, he must lock the shed's doors and be sure that no man crosses that threshold until he is ready, until he can explain what exactly it is that has happened to his machine.

The next morning, he invites the other leaders of the congregation to view the motor, to see the slight pulsation that grows inside it. They listen attentively, but Spear sees the horror on their faces as he tries to point out the movement of the magnets again and again, as he grows frustrated at their inability to see what he sees. They leave at once, and Spear stands at the top of the hill, listening to their voices arguing on the way down the crooked path. By evening, their deliberations are complete, and when the messenger arrives at the cabin with a letter, Spear knows what it says before he reads it. He has been stripped of his position in the church, and of the church's material support.

Spear locks himself in the shed with the motor, where he watches it pulsate through the night until morning, when there is a knock at the door. He opens the door to find Maud waiting for him. She is beautiful now, transformed by her pregnancy, and she takes him by the hand, saying, This machine is ours to believe in, ours to take to the people.

She says, I have listened to your sermons, and I have heard the words you've spoken.

She says, You can't give up now. I won't allow it.

Spear nods, straightens himself, and looks back at the machine he's built. There is life in it, he knows. He looks at Maud's hand in his. It is just a spark now, but one day it will be a fire, if only he nurtures it.

There is no more money to pay for the things Spear needs—wagons and assistants, supplies for the great journey ahead—and so Spear splits his time between the shed and his desk, between preparing for the disassembly of the motor and writing letters begging for financial support. He writes to New York and Boston and Philadelphia and Washington, asking their spiritualist congregations to trust him, to help fund this new age that is coming.

He writes, The Glory of God is at hand, and soon I will bring it to each and every one of you, if only you will help me in these darkest of hours.

The words he writes are his alone, and he finds himself at a loss to explain the New Motor without the help of the Electricizers. He calls out to them, begs them for assistance.

In his empty office, he cries out, All that you helped me create is crumbling. Why won't you tell me what to write?

His words are met with silence, as they have been since the birth of the motor. The Electricizers are no longer distinct to him, just blurred specters at the periphery of his vision, fading more every day. Their abandonment is near complete when Maud begins to help him instead, comforting his anxiety and giving him strength with her words. She has not gone down the hill since the day she gave birth, and Spear knows now that this is the reason his family had to leave, that his congregation had to abandon him. Even the Electricizers leaving him—he recognizes it now not as an abandonment but as making room for what was to come next.

Like Mary and Joseph's flight with the newborn Jesus into Egypt, he and Maud will flee with the New Motor across America, taking it by railroad to town after town after town.

Like Mary, Maud will not love him, only the motor she has birthed.

Like Joseph, he will have to learn to live with this new arrangement, this adjusted set of expectations.

Spear tears up all the letters he's written so far, then starts new ones, ones infused not with the bitterness he feels but with the hope and inspiration he wants to. Soon, the motor will begin to speak to him, and he must be ready to listen.

It takes a month for the letters to come back, but Spear receives the responses he requires. He runs into the cabin, where Maud awaits him. He says, They're coming to help us, with money and with men. They'll be waiting for us in Randolph, ready to assist me in reassembling the motor.

He hesitates, then says, I'll start tonight. I'll disassemble the motor, and get it ready for travel, and then I'll send word to Randolph for a wagon to transport it. The worst is nearly over, and soon our new day will begin.

Maud rises from the dining table and takes Spear in her arms, cradling his head against her shoulder. She does not tell him what the angels have told her about what must happen first, about what has always happened to those who have served God with hearts like his,

246

too full of human weakness, of pride and folly and blinding hubris. She does not tell him about Moses at the border of the promised land, about Jonah in the belly of the whale. She could, but she chooses otherwise, chooses to repay his one-time lack of faith with her own.

Despite his intentions to start immediately, Spear finds that he cannot. Once he's locked himself in the shed with the New Motor, he is too in awe of its ornate existence, of the shining results of all the months of effort and prophecy that went into its construction. He watches the pulsation of the magnets and tries to understand what they might mean, what message might be hidden in their infant energies. He doesn't know, but he believes it will be made clear soon, even without the Electricizers' help.

Spear sits down on the floor of the shed and crosses his legs beneath him, preparing for the first time in many months to go into a trance, to purposefully pierce the shroud between this world and the next. The trance comes easily to him, in all of its usual ways: a prickling of the skin, a slowing of the breath, a blurring of the vision. He stays that way for many hours, listening, and so he does not hear the knock at the door or the raised voices that follow. By the time something does snap him out of his trance—the first ax blow that bursts open the shed door, perhaps—it is far too late to save himself.

All around him are the men of the village, men who were once his friends and swear now that they have come only to help him, to set him free of this thing he's made. They promise they won't hurt him, if only he'll lie still, but he can't, won't, not in the face of what they've come to do. Held between the arms of the two Russians, he watches, disbelieving, as one of High Rock's deacons steps to the New Motor, hesitant at first but then emboldened by the encouragement of the others. The deacon reaches up toward the grand revolver and takes hold of one of the magnetic spheres suspended from its crossbeams, and then he rips it away from the motor.

Spear waits for intercession, for an Electricizer or angel to step in and stop the destruction, but none appears. He struggles against his attackers, tries to warn them against what they plan to do, against the wrath of God they call down upon themselves, but they do not listen. Eventually he twists free and attempts to take a step toward the motor, where others have joined the deacon in dismantling the hanging magnets. The Russians stop him, knock him to the ground, fall upon him with fists and boots, and when they tire of striking him they step aside so that others may have their turn. Spear no longer cares for himself, only for his new god, for this mechanical child gifted not just to him and to Maud, but also to all of mankind, if only they would accept it.

By the time Maud arrives in the doorway to the shed, he is already broken, both in body and face and in spirit. The motor is crushed too, ax blows and wrenching hands tearing its intricate parts from their moorings, rendering meaningless the many names of God written in copper and zinc across its components. He cries to her for help, but knows there's nothing she can do. All around him are the men he once called to himself, who followed him to High Rock and up its steep hill to this shed, where he had meant for them to change their world. He watches the Russians and James the metalworker and the carpenters, all of them striking him or else the machine they themselves built. When they finish, when his teeth and bones are already shattered, he sees Randall, the youth he once admired above all others, and he lowers his head and accepts the vengeance the boy feels he's owed.

Before the beating ends, Spear lifts his head to look up at Maud, to take in her restored youth and beauty. For the last time, he sees the Electricizers, sees Jefferson and Franklin and Rush and Murray and all the others assembled around her. He cries out to them for protection, for salvation, and when they do not come to his aid he looks past them to Maud, who glows in their light, but also with a light of her own, something he wishes he had seen earlier, when there was still some great glory that might have come of it.

The First Intifada
Jerusalem, 1987–1993

Elizabeth Rollins

HE SKITTERS TO HIS LEFT, leaps cobblestones, crates, carts, old women, and their heaps of fabric. The boy is carrying a pot. The lid clatters slightly on the pot, a soft clanking that accompanies his running steps. He ducks down the narrow passages, glances blankly at the metal doors, the shimmering copper jugs, and thickly woven rugs. The alleys are jammed on all sides with flat cakes, long tubes of sesame bread, oils, and bearded coffee sellers. The boy doesn't look at the food, he doesn't look at the aged and shining cobbles under his feet. He carries the pot always before him, eyes flashing black, and runs.

Once in a while, a tourist with soft skin like an apricot will hold up a hand to stop him, smile kindly, ask him to wait, to slow, could she buy him a meal? He stops, shirt open to his skinny chest heaving breath, and he holds the pot as neither invitation nor warning, just stands, his expression unchanged by the stopping. The soft woman will lift the pot lid, she insists on it, smiling as if to imply that she is willing to bear his burden too, to be his witness, but when she looks inside she shakes her head in confusion, her smile becomes uncertain.

When this happens, the boy replaces the lid with the utmost delicacy and care, as if there were a snake inside, waiting to uncoil and strike.

He does not stay to hear the woman murmur to her friend, *But it was empty!*

He turns and runs again.

A story like this begins in the silence of a kitchen. Where the mother of this boy rarely speaks, and when she does, it is with the plucked strings of a bickering harp. Where the father sits, deadly dulled, thick and red and mute. Where the mother murmurs to herself the faults of the man, until the man's glowering eyes pin her mouth shut.

Or does it begin before the father ever set eyes on the mother, does it begin in his ignorance, his youth, his willingness?

Or does it begin before the father ever met the mother, before he ever set foot in her father's house?

Or does it begin in the coiling flame of hope that is dead inside her and not replaced by anything?

The loam of the place where they live is bloody. It is soiled with hate and burned bare by sun. No one there has the fat of kindness to lend. Or this is what they tell themselves. This is how they behave.

The mother is of a hundred generations of the malevolent place. It began before she was born.

It began before the father was born.

It began again in them.

And what of their son?

The boy plays serenely by himself. On the corner of the terrace outside, on what has not been blown away in the past forty years of fighting. He builds things with the jagged rocks he gathers, tempers them with feathers, weeds, olive leaves, his own marks in the sand. His fingers drag lines in the dirt city he has made, and all day he works on this city, even crouching over it to eat his bread, which he has carried from the kitchen. He watches his shadow on the "buildings" below, moves a knee or an elbow to make his presence known to the imaginary civilians there.

Sometimes in the evening, the boy climbs into a chair in the cool, dark kitchen, almost sightless after his day in the full sun. He sits in the circle of his father's morbid silence. He peers up at the dark roses of color around his father's eyes. His father no longer looks at him. The boy moves quietly, lifting a spoon to a platter on the table. No one ever stops him from this, but he is not invited either.

The boy lifts the spoon or uses his hands. He eats quickly, quietly, slides from the chair without notice. He does not like to be near, for the sharp slap of his mother's hand is quick, and it is only a matter of time before he feels it.

Occasionally the mother barks for the boy to help her, to wash, to leave, to come, to rise, to get out. He does not remember her speaking to him in any other way.

Other days, the only voice he hears is the boom and crackling twine of loudspeakers in the distance, crooning a call to prayer. For the boy, it is only a sound marking the passage of the day, letting him know when there will be food inside. His father does not pray.

Outside, sometimes he watches other children from behind walls, children who play games of hostages and soldiers. Children who play seek and play hide, play at hiding babies and crossing borders. Their play is all breathing and running and legs.

The boy's solitary play on the corner of the broken terrace is of stone and quiet. His heart races when he watches the other children, sees the soles of their feet when they run, hears shouts of joyous capture, the sounds of their live-blooded play. He can see that they are different. Their hair shines with blue-sheen health. Even their arms are thicker, stronger, darker than his. His own hair, when he touches it, is rough and dusty.

In a time past there was an uncle, who took him out of the city. The uncle had bright white teeth and smiled. The boy watched the uncle's teeth tear bread, and flash, when he talked. The uncle had been arrested, spent his time in jail like so many, but unlike others, unlike the boy's father, the uncle did not speak with the hard curd of bitterness spoiling his voice. He spoke with white teeth, with smiles, with the tearing of bread. The boy's father and the uncle disagreed. But the uncle laughed. He took no offense. The mother even, the boy saw, smiled at things the uncle said. When the uncle came, the boy spent the day inside too. In the corner, but close enough to watch.

One day the uncle came but he didn't even step inside the kitchen. The boy played alone in the dirt and he had made a line of stick camels walking through a desert.

The uncle stopped, looking at the boy's work, and smiled, saying, "What are these animals you've made?"

The boy pointed to his own back, got down on all fours, gestured a hump with his dirty hand.

"Camel?"

The boy nodded his head yes.

"Have you ever been to the desert?"

The boy shook his head no.

The uncle nodded and said, "Shall we?"

The uncle drove them in a little white car. The boy had never been in a car before. There were seats, like chairs, and music came out of holes in the doors, and the windows were made of glass and could be lifted and lowered by a crank. The boy was busy with the glass and the crank for some time when the uncle said, "No, look *through* the glass, not at the glass, look *through* the glass."

And the boy looked through the glass and they passed billowing pink and orange spills of flowers and stone houses and street signs and long and short and wrinkled and hairy and covered faces and they were in the little white car speeding by and there was no stopping or talking or anything but the moving, and the boy sat in his chair that was a chair attached to the car, that rolled on wheels, and he sniffed the air.

The uncle stopped the car only once to pull up at a stand and buy a package of dates, which he handed to the boy and said, "I suppose you like sweet things," and the boy opened the package, which was sticky, and he took out a date and ate it and it was thick and sweet.

It seemed, to the boy, in all that air that was coming in the cranked-down windows, that the dates tasted like nothing he'd ever tasted before. They reminded him of things he didn't understand, but loved, like breezes on his face, the hooting of night birds, shadows of bugs on the ground.

When they got outside the city and the stone houses fell away to rock cliffs and the rock cliffs fell away to stones, and the stones fell away to the long roll of curving desert sand, it looked to the boy as if someone like him, only thousands of times larger, had dragged his fingers through, mounded, with thumb and palm, the heaps and the valleys under the light that shone down, and used a huge finger to draw out the very road they drove on. And he and his uncle drove there, in the car past the hot sand, on that road.

The uncle swept a hairy arm before the boy's eyes, encircling the desert before them, and said, "How much of man's blood can it take and still absorb? Should we not have expected the blood to come boiling back out one day?"

But the boy had no answer for this and the man did not expect one, and they drove on.

When the uncle asked if the boy would like to see a river of water, the boy was shocked to believe that there could be more, that a river could be somewhere in the sand.

He almost shook his head no, but he resisted. There was already so much singing in his ears, the wind, he felt he could take no more, not a river of water too, but then he felt he could not miss it, could not possibly miss the seeing of a river of water too. He nodded yes at the uncle, and then again and then again, wildly nodding yes, causing the wind and the car and the uncle to spin and stir and thump in his head. The uncle smiled, and reached out with long fingers and plucked a date from the box and ate it. He sang and drove and the boy ate another date slowly, thinking of the great light on the desert.

When they came to the trees, there was a little village, and stone houses not like his, not broken and exposed but still whole and old, entire walls flanked with bright tumbling red and blue blossoms, doors brightened by pots yellow and orange and purple blossoms. They drove on past these houses to the river of water. At the river, the little white car came to a stop and the man took the dates from the boy and set them on the backseat, and nodded, saying, "Go look. It's delightful."

And the boy could not get the door open. He touched all the metal bars and the glass crank and his uncle laughed and got out and the boy watched the man's white-shirted middle as he came around and opened the door. The boy climbed out and followed his uncle down the bank to the river of water and his uncle told him, "This is where people come to be healed. In these waters."

And the boy looked down and just then a hundred fish gleamed, flickered, and finned over the stones under the green but also clear water and the boy gasped and clapped his hands and laughed out loud.

The uncle turned to him, and looked down, and the boy thought he had done something wrong because the uncle looked so stricken, but when the uncle spoke to him, he also knelt and he touched the boy's hair gently and said, "I've never heard you laugh before."

But the uncle was taken to jail again soon after, and the boy didn't see him again.

The market people are accustomed to the slapping sounds of his feet as he passes. More than once a day they look up too late, just catching the thin brown form slipping by, which could be mistaken for a dog. But they know the sound of his feet slapping stone, the faint clanking of his lid.

The market people do not know his name and do not even ask it of each other. If they are together when the boy passes, they shake their heads, mutter a prayer, but they do not speak directly to, or of, this boy. He hangs in their minds only as long as a wasp hangs in the corner of their stores, just the leggy hovering and then gone. More solid, tangible, quantifiable things require their attention.

They know that a vision of a boy that thin, running, does not bode well, and so they choose not to look. How many lonely boys have they seen in these violent years? They have lost count.

If the market people did stop him, would they offer him food?

Elizabeth Rollins

Something from the simmering pots in the back of their stores, a handful of nuts from their cart? Just one or two small things to nourish such a small-skinned space as the boy? But the vendors do not look up when he runs by. They know he does not steal. He does not stop long enough to steal.

No one in the market calls to him, regardless of how often they see him. Even when his feet bleed and leave prints on the stone— long, thin, snake-like crescents—even these the market people do not bother to read.

After the desert, the boy imagines another life. With sweet flowers, sweet tastes, sweet smells, sweet voices, and fish in clear green water. With motion, and glass windows that crank up and down. With laughter. With children running and playing together. He imagines a world away from the broken terrace, away from the cold, dark kitchen, away from the corner where he sleeps, listening to his parents snort and sigh at night.

He practices his uncle's name, the one he has heard them call him by. He practices it, and finally says it aloud to his parents at the table one day. They turn to him, stunned to hear that he has a voice. His mother shrugs. She shakes her head at the boy. She hisses in a low voice, "He is an important man. He does not have time for babies. "

But the father says, without expression, "He is dead."

The mother cries out, bends at the waist, groans as though she's been struck. The boy doesn't understand what his father has said, but watches his mother. She moans, straightens, bends again, backs slowly into a corner of the kitchen. Her face is red, her eyes bulging. Her lips push out and tremble. She stares at the floor.

The father, sweating, his eyes black and poisoned, shouts, slamming his fist on the table, *"He's dead he's dead he's dead he's dead he's dead he's dead."*

The boy climbs down from his chair. He stands a moment longer, watching his mother. She looks up and blinks and it is as if the birds of her eyes have flown away. She stares at nothing. This frightens him and he slips out of the kitchen. He doesn't know which way the uncle went, driving the little white car. The boy tries to remember. He walks, ducking behind dusty terraces and fences and broken houses. He climbs a stone barrier, so small and light and quick that the soldiers never see him, and enters the other part of the city. He follows a series of steps leading up the hill, and takes them running, looking around to find the way to the edge of the city where the desert will roll out flat and wide, where the blood has not boiled up yet.

Up high, the boy is sure he will be able to remember which way to go when he descends again, but he becomes entangled in the buildings and houses and streets and people and lights and traffic and bushes and trees and loses all sense of where the desert is. He walks and walks. He sees plants as big as families spreading out over corners of the city. He sees a tree draped in rags of prayer. He sees children wearing uniforms, laughing on their way home, eating bread and meat from silver wrappers purchased at a stand. He pauses near the stand, sniffing deeply. The owner does not see him. The man scoops and stirs and spreads and rolls up the silver packets, and hands them, one after another, to the children and adults who wait in line. The boy wanders down the stone steps to the entrance of the market. There are the women in dark dresses, sitting on their bundles of green and fragrant herbs. The bright umbrellas offer them shade. They do not look at him. No one seems to see him, a thin boy alone. He enters the market and is stunned by the color. Red carpets and blue bags. Rows of reflecting black glasses, showing the store opposite in every round, shining surface. Heaps of leather sandals. Breads laced with fruit, with seeds. Long, shining rows of vegetables, red and white and yellow and orange and green. The boy wanders. He forgets that he is looking for his uncle in his amazement at what the market holds. It seems that everything is in the market. Everything anyone ever needed. He drinks the noise and color in. He steps quietly across the rows of stones on the market floor, looking and looking and listening and smelling.

After hours, he finds himself at an opening to the outside. He blinks at the sky. He is tired. He wants to lie down. He wanders out into a neighborhood. Down streets and past houses. A soldier with a gun walks toward him and the boy is frightened. He runs into a yard. In an attached fenced yard a dog yelps and wags his tail. The dog is under a thick-leaved plant. The boy crouches near the dog. He puts his fingers through the fence. The dog licks them. The shadow of the plant shades them both from the sun. The boy sinks to the ground. The boy pulls his legs into the shadow. He tells the dog about his uncle. The dog listens. Licks his fingers. Sits patiently with him. Darkness falls and it is cold. The dog's fur is tan and short and sticks through the fence so the boy can touch it. The dog has brown eyes and the boy presses his cheek to the fence and to the dog's fur. The dog is warm, and they sleep spread against each other and the fence.

After a few hours, there is the fence, and despite the warmth he shared with the dog, they are on opposite sides. When the dog rises, the boy rises also. The dog looks at him, and turns away toward the building. The boy sees the dog is limping badly.

Or does a story like this begin in the broken heart? Say the mother of this boy was once in love with a man with flashing white teeth. Say her father refused the man. Say she stopped speaking. Say her father told her she was ruined. Say, after a time, the boy's mother was given to her lover's brother. Say her father said to her, as he gave her to this brother of her lover: "You need a man who will break and be tamed. I do not wish you to be disgraced. I am doing this out of love."

The boy is half asleep. He wanders. At a stone barrier, he climbs over and slips into a dusty, quiet neighborhood. He turns a corner. At the end of the street there is a line of soldiers with guns. One of these soldiers with a moustache orders the boy to stop. The boy freezes. The soldier leaves the line of waiting soldiers and stalks toward the boy. The boy turns to run too late. The soldier knocks the boy to the pavement and presses the cold, round metal end of his gun against the boy's face.

A woman emerges from her house, weeping and screaming. She claws at the soldier's arm, crying. The soldier turns, lifts the gun from the boy's face. Shouts at the woman, shakes her hand off his arm. The woman is screaming down at the boy; he sees a wide, black mole on one of her cheeks. Another soldier yells at the woman. The boy scuttles away, backward on his hands and feet, like a spider. Behind the men at the end of the street, metal tanks roll around the corner. Massive and stern. The boy runs. He can hear the woman screaming. He hears gunshots. She stops screaming. He runs. An explosion erupts behind him. The ground heaves. The boy falls to the pavement. A small breeze touches the boy's face and he scrambles to his feet. He forces his thin body through a gap in a metal fence, scraping his belly and arms, drawing deep, bloody gashes. He runs down a street where no one is moving. He keeps running, his heart thumping, his small lungs burning.

The boy runs up a hill, into a flowered, quiet, sun-strewn neighborhood. He finds a shaded, overgrown yard and throws himself down. His mouth is thick with dry dirt and fear. He eats fruit from the ground, and passes out.

When he wakes, it is bright noon and his insides are liquid. He shakes and shudders leaning against the side of a house. It feels like there is a man's fist clenching and unclenching inside of him, squeezing his guts into brown water, which splashes from the ground back up onto his legs. He curls on the grass. The hours of the afternoon pass before him in shadows on the ground.

He trembles and watches the light change. His body burns hollow. He is alone. He is nowhere. He is no one. He dozes off, shivering.

When he wakes, he rises again.

The boy walks down the hill. As he walks, he sees the market entrance below, where he began his day. There are the colorful umbrellas, people churning in and out of the stone archway, men with golden coffeepots, soldiers with guns. He makes his way down to the entrance. He doesn't know how to ask any questions. He blinks. He sees the weeping woman again and again, the wide, black mole on her cheek. He blinks again. She is in his eyes. He can't close them away from her. Even now when he sees her in his eyes, he doesn't know what she was saying. He doesn't know what happened to her. His chest throbs where he has torn it on the fence. He is surprised by his own blood, drying on him. He walks carefully, close to the walls, making his way down.

When he thinks of the dark kitchen, he thinks of his mother's blank gasping, the birds flying from her eyes. He thinks of the pulsing line of blue in his father's forehead, a tiny snake writhing. The woman screams inside his eyes. The black mole. His father's red-circled eyes. He does not know where to go. Where the soldiers will not be. Where the woman will not run out screaming inside his eyes.

He passes the tree of prayer rags and looks up into the mass of fabrics, faded, so many pleas frayed, swallowed by time. He crawls beneath the tree and curls his arms around his dirty knees. He watches his fingers tremble. Above him, the flags slap and flutter helplessly in the breeze. The boy shivers.

An enormous Boom! shakes the whole street, and again. Boom! Boom! People run past him, dragging each other, and children, by the hand, shouting. Boom! His feet are shaken up from the dirt, as though he is only a bit of branch, a rock. He stands too, and runs the way the people are running. But the people are running in all directions. He follows the men who are screaming curses and running, and then he is in his neighborhood. Smoke billows up in great black tongues from half houses. There are flames, and men running, soldiers running, smoke, sharp, rapid bangs. The boy crawls on his hands and knees over the dirt and the rubble. Dirt-covered shrubs rain rubble on him when he passes beneath them. He passes the house where the other children played, but it is black and burning bright. His own terrace is gone. Smoke boils out of a hole in the wall. There is a pile of rock where he played. The kitchen wall is open, streaming smoke. He climbs inside and stares at the wreckage, blinking and coughing in the black fumes.

His father is half hidden, thick cement kissing his spine.

His mother is on the floor. Her eyes are open and soft in death. She lies staring at the sky. There is blood around his mother's head, and a great brightness over everything, which is the sun shining through the opened roof. There is a pot on the stove and the boy stares at it. His stomach growls.

The boy slides and crouches and climbs over the heap of stone. He inches around his mother's blood shadow to the stove. He grasps the handle of the pot and lifts it. He scrabbles his way out into light, just past the smashed tumble of kitchen walls. He looks back at his parents, blinking.

Crawling back under the shrubs, he finds two broken walls, tipped together, creating a little space to hide in. He waits and waits and waits until the noises stop. Darkness falls. The blood has dried into red bitter bars of ache on his chest. He peers through the slit into the ruined street. The noises have stopped. The boy closes his eyes. The woman screams. He opens his eyes. His stomach growls. He lifts the lid on the pot carefully. The lentils are red with tomato. He dips his fingers in and eats. He closes his eyes. The woman screams. He sees his mother's blood shadow. He blinks.

He opens his eyes and keeps them open. He eats. He eats every last bite of the lentils with his eyes open. As soon as he is finished eating, he struggles from the dark stone womb of walls into the night, dragging the pot after him, and he begins to run.

Avrila
D. E. *Steward*

In Nuevo Laredo, Tamaulipas, the newest drug entrepôt, Guadalupe García, *journalista investigatora*, took eleven days to die

"You are next, Lupita. We are coming for you"

Y el bordo y las maquiladoras

And then there are many hundreds of unsolved femicides in Ciudad Juarez and environs since 1993

Cowboy-macho Chihuahua has been dealing with women pulling down *maquiladora* paychecks by extreme sexual violence for twenty-five years now

Government indifference, impunity of local police and officials

Women come north from Mexico's southern states and become disposable

"The Part About the Crimes" in Roberto Bolaño's 2666

Mexico's hot-wax hard-sheen machismo is the underlying explanation

Huesos en el desierto, Sergio González Rodríguez

Maquiladoras being one of the stratagems of multinational enterprise

The breadth of the Mexican-Gringo interface that has lost the old topology because Hispanic people live nearly everywhere north of the border zone

The border itself left virtually abstract

D. E. Steward

In the post-Soviet manner of the old Iron Curtain's zone

El bordo infused with Latin American dollar hunger

In the way the wide-front dignity of El Paso's 1920s houses make Montana Avenue's strip malls appear misplaced

The muffler shops and walk-in dentists look transient and insecure

El Paso almost an appendage to huge Ciudad Juarez

Fort Bliss is El Paso's only unswerving institution

In and out, in transit, temporarily here, there, the Fort Bliss GIs arrive and eventually all ship out

And the border crossers who, once across, evanesce

One out of eight Mexican adults is already in the United States

Over ten million Mexicans now live illegally in the States

Half of all Mexican adults say they would come if they could

Out of town going north through Bliss's sagebrush flats for Cloudcroft in the Sacramentos

Below Mule Peak and Cerro Pajarita in the Mescalaro Apache Reservation

A golden eagle's dramatic wings-locked soar before a vast, lofting cumulus over bajada-tracking US54

Nearly empty now, this land of the Chiricahuas, the Jicarillas, the Lipans

The Mimbreños, Cibecues, the San Carlos, Northern Tontos, Southern Tontos, the Western Apaches with their Sonoran Uto-Aztec tongue

All kin to the Yaquis

Ultimately defeated by the Mexican government with machine-gunning biplanes

Vida: By the fire eaters on the midway of a carnival in Chihuahua in the fifties, standing near a young Pima Bajo–speaking couple, theirs another Uto-Aztecan language

Smockish cotton clothes, maybe even yucca fiber, deerskin moccasins

Later into the stage door of a Chihuahua University theater to stand agape watching modern dancers rehearsing

With innocent wonder nearly the equal of the Pima couple's

Sleek hair in dark buns, halter brown-limbed *lampiña* tight-wound intense confidence

Of the fresh tradition of José Limón

Limón born 1908 in Sinaloa, the next state south, d. Hunterdon County, NJ, Winter 1972

At seven across El Bordo into Tucson with his family, then to LA

His last years in his red-dairy-barn studio in New Jersey, driving off grandly for New York in a tan Jeepster

Gracious waves with fingers trailing as he disappeared around the bend

A twenty-first-century extension of Mexico, a red-dusted remnant of Apache dominance, stands with his family in Alamogordo's Walmart breaking his open pit–mine paycheck

A week's food, toys for his three kids, a big bouncy ball the size of a weather balloon, all of them smiling to beat sixty

But he is tired as only all-out physical labor in the dust makes tired

D. E. Steward

On ahead up above Alamogordo, the Sacramento Mountains are criss-crossed with development roads and West Texas weekend houses

Shack city there as soon as the big trees were lumbered out soon after the last steep-canyon resistance of the Mescalaros

The Tularosa Basin, White Sands below

No rivers drain from there so, from evaporation, the immense tracts of white-sand gypsum are left

Geological time creep, almost three hundred square miles of blinding white dunes

With the prevailing southwesterlies, the dunes crest, then slump, continually advancing

Go on westward to Las Cruces on the Rio Grande, and then Interstate 10 to Deming

Into empty Dona Ana County

Then down State 11 to the Columbus-Palomas border point

See one blanket-roll Mexican on the road

A jackrabbit world

Cross into Chihuahua with the confidence and smug ease of having *yanqui* papers

Along little Palomas's short main street, storefront sheds sell hiking boots, sunhats, jackets, water, whatever people think they need to maybe make it across

The town crowds right up to the line in the transitory border-crossing mood of backstreet El Paso itself

Full of people up from inner Mexico

Waiting for the night when they try for Interstate 10 above Columbus in New Mexico

The migrants come to there on *Ruta* 24, from *Federal* 2, the big Mexican east-west west-east border highway

From Palomas they parallel on foot the route toward Columbus of Poncho Villa's Raid of 1916

In which seventy Villistas and eighteen gringos died

A usual ratio for most things Mexican-American

West on New Mexico 9 from Columbus along the empty range-land border

Federal 2 close by on the Mexican side

Through New Mexico's and Sonora's near-desert, empty Luna and Hidalgo counties

Federal 2 runs from Tijuana to Ciudad Juarez–El Paso, and again from Ciudad Acuña–Del Rio to Playa Bagdad east of Matamoros on the Gulf

On the U.S. side are more green-and-white Border Patrol SUVs than local trucks and cars

They tow portable skybox trailers to high points and flank them with floodlight tripods

Then, like the migrants, wait for dark

First-generation skyboxes are viewing cockpits for a watcher lifted high on hydraulic pantographs

The newer ones operate on remote, digital cameras scan the horizon and the border from high on pantographs and send the images electronically back to monitors

Vast, arid distances on the border here

D. E. Steward

Dramatic, sad, and always chancy confrontations

The thousands of migrants waiting night to night for dark, the time to go

Armed Border Patrol people hoping not to come across drug couriers armed with AK-47s

Empty water bottles, discarded jackets, lost shoes on the entry trails

Eerie lines of human tracks in the dust of the draws and arroyos on both sides of New Mexico 9

As along all the other border roads all the way to Tijuana and the Pacific, and back across broad Texas to Matamoros on the Gulf and Playa Bagdad

Tunguska

Paul West

IT COULD HAVE BEEN the shade of his mother, Abis Chybaz, passing in the night, then replaced by her real shadow, her big baby. No school today, nor any other, said his hyperbolical view of the remains of the school year.

It was 7:17 a.m. when his mother exclaimed in alarm when a column of bluish light swept across the sky, followed ten minutes later by a detonation reminiscent of artillery fire, east to north, at such speed that it chopped her cry of terror off short and convened it into a stifled cry; at which his only thought was of his mother.

Inside, she emitted a thought of artillery. Outside, because she thought it safe to risk it, she ventured the abruptly silenced cry, each time worrying about her lazy son. Inside, he noticed the cannon shot not at all. Outside, he heard only a bleat rising to an abrupt crescendo, and he was afraid. Not having heard anything comparable in his sixteen years of country living, he cast around for explanations, but relinquished the quest for what he decided was a punctured eardrum. Apart from a distant rumble of thunder, from far away it sounded, there was nothing further, and life began to settle back to normal. The event had passed by.

Elsewhere, though, people had been knocked off their feet, by percussion and then fire. Shirts were in flames, the sky shut down, and rocks began falling. People tore off their jerkins, unable to stand the heat. A hot wind raced, damaging crops, and windows far and wide were shattered. An end to the world had come and not gone. Gradually the steamroller sounds diminished, leaving a trail of sunder behind, from which people picked themselves up, gesticulating at the rows of demolished and denuded trees.

An airburst some called it. Something had exploded in midair, low to the ground, ferocious too, changing the shape of the region forever, and as the news filtered in (a slow process in this rustic area) their minds filled with stories of people scalded to death, crushed by falling rocks, swept away to places unknown by heat trauma. Not a tree was left standing, and those who came later theorized the impact as being ten to fifteen times the bomb dropped on Hiroshima in World War II. Eight hundred and thirty square miles were devastated and left barren for going on thirty years.

Years ago she had given birth to him, an uncouth-looking child with a three-inch birthmark next to his navel, which had grown as he had, six feet already, and still going strong, perhaps seven feet by the time he would cease. Was he handicapped? she wondered, having him studied. Not exactly, but he was no prodigy. Wheeling his way through the alphabet at pedestrian speed, slow, but sure enough, once he had grasped the simple word that was afflicting him.

So they had grown up together, two rainbows with a single destiny, timed to grow old together and perhaps even, at some stage, to inexplicably stop growing "up," he at thirty-four and she at fifty-one with a modicum of language between them, enough to get by on Krasnoyarsk Krak, which both pronounced Lower Stony, being unable to pronounce the devilish syllables of the longer word. Krak, which would have been simpler for both, somehow eluded them.

So, to friends and neighbors, simple or rustic people, never attempting difficult words, they lived on, having no destiny other than to keep doing the same thing day in, day out, a quick handclasp doing duty for the complex routines of the rest of the hamlet. Of the father nothing was known, merely the sperm bearer of another generation. Or, if he was remembered, forgotten entire. The first day of fatherhood was his last. Perhaps lost eventually when he built a snow house for himself, into which he disappeared, willingly, his name not even known.

The two of them prospered in an average way, making love to the tundra in a sheepish routine, sleeping a lot, wondering how long they had in the scheme of things, and neither speculating on the chance of outliving the other. When the instant came (and nothing more complex than an instant ever entered their heads), they would vanish together.

How they survived the colossal explosion of their way of life will never be known. Little aware, how the airburst was felt as far away as London did not occur to them. Even their ramshackle cottage survived, a few large rocks allowed in, and the heat and wind passed them by as if a normal day. All things considered, they had come through with flying colors and they took in this feeble triumph, seeing how many of their neighbors had simply vanished amid the red-hot cataclysm that had engulfed them. They resumed eating their bread and curd, and queried not.

Some observers (excepting the recent dead of their catastrophic day) would have said of him he had second sight. Others would have said his head was full of pipe dreams. Suffice to say, when he looked outside he saw a structure that was now a mess of uncoordinated splinters. He used to envision hanged men instead, positioned at various angles along the woodwork. He did not know why, he just assumed they were there because they were there. Corpses instead of live men. Now he saw neither live or dead, but abundant devastation, spewed out along the high road, and was grateful for that simplification of his worldview, his umwelt. He awaited the day when all things would be abolished in this way to bother him no longer with their troubling edifices. Meanwhile, he balanced the disappearance of the hanged men with his own situation and counted himself the winner. He was, as they all thought, an unusual teenager, seeing what was not there, always anxious to clean up the world.

What lay behind his eyes was normal, what was beyond his eyes was not. Rumors abounded (or used to) about his mother and the suspicion that there had been a One-Sixth Humbly connection, long lost in the history of abnormal perversion. The resulting child was a monster; he seemed normal enough on the outside, but was a curious beast from within. Recent events had, of course, reduced the population, so there was a hint of reprieve in Lower Stony, mother and son. His name was Humbly, incredible as it seemed.

The locals tolerated him, some (the ministry) because they thought him retarded, the rest because they detected in his roaming eye and introverted manner the sign of uncanny intelligence, and hoped to profit from this later on. The way he spoke elongated words. First, he attempted *pony,* which he could not utter, then p-o-n-y, which he did, voicing the final result as n-y or n---y, which was no good to anybody. Better to avoid conversation altogether than fumble about his mispronounced words in hope of catching a patch of sunlight among his gaffes. There was always hope of his launching himself into correct speech, becoming a famous orator, but not yet.

So he dwindled and dawdled, caught in a verbal trap not of his own devising, amid rumors of his peculiar ancestry and hopes of improvement such as big, burly men often get.

Then came the airburst, demolishing and scattering, and his cadre of well-wishers diminished to a precious few. There was faint hope of rebuilding, dashed by the first meeting of the survivors, then a second meeting of the group, at which a more hopeful tone emerged. Rebuild? Of course they would, and better. In all this tohu-bohu, preferring to keep his light under a bushel, advising and counseling with a nod or gesture on the length of a plank or the size of a yurt.

The amazing thing was that the survivors managed to find enough material to work with. Certain timbers showed greater silent resilience than others and these quickly became the centerpiece of the new settlement around which the rest took a diffident almost apologetic part. Progress slowed, then started up again as the faint of heart (including the bereaved) cheered up, thanking God (in the most shallow way) for making this festival of torment during high summer.

Strange to relate (though not so strange when you consider the barrens of the scene), another ten years would elapse before anybody gave a second thought to the events at Tunguska, time enough for a new generation to grow and forget.

Besides, the events of World War I, the Russian revolution of 1917, and the Russian Civil War took precedence, until 1921 and the first visit of the Russian mineralogist Leonid Kulik to the Tunguska River Basin for the Soviet Academy of Sciences. He ascribed the disaster to a gigantic meteorite and persuaded the authorities to mount a full-scale research expedition to the Tunguska region based on the iron ore that could be salvaged to Soviet industry. Such a prosaic beginning aftermath to an event that had even touched London.

Kulik was shocked to find no crater but instead a region of scorched trees thirty miles across. Trees with their branches stripped off, and knocked down. The moving finger had written and moved on.

Three more expeditions followed. Kulik found a little "pothole" bog he suspected of being the original crater, but jettisoned the idea after finding several stumps on the bottom. In 1935 he arranged for an aerial photograph that clearly showed a large butterfly-shaped area. There was simply no crater to be had.

Little of this reached the ears of Humbly, however. He lived on, aware that something fearsome had happened. Once. And that was that. The dead were buried. Life, after a brief, solitary pause, resumed its even tenor. Life built anew, as it should. But the image persisted, nagging his brain during the silence of the night when ghostly figures haunted his dreams and threatened to recur, perhaps the end of the world. Abis Chybaz got on with her knitting and worried about her seven-foot son, whose brooding manner bore increasing menace without threatening anybody. He still spoke in slow-motion runes, which they humored him for having, convinced that when his day came there would be a second aerial burst that would wipe them all out.

Humbly remembered better than most survivors the earth tremors and the felling of bodies (but not the fluctuations in the atmosphere). He remembered also the next few weeks when the night skies glowed with unearthly light by which one could read the paper in London thanks to the dust suspended in the air. Most revealing of all, *The Guinness Book of World Records*, far in the future, stated that if the collision had occurred five hours later, it would have completely destroyed Saint Petersburg.

In the still watches of the night, he found himself ruminating on the event as if it were some object of perpetual memory: He was sitting at the time, facing north, toward Onkoul's Tunguska road, and suddenly the sky split in two and fire began in the woods. As the sky seemed to grow and became hotter he couldn't bear it. He tore off his shirt. Then the sky cooled somewhat with a sustained thump and his mother ran outside shrieking.

Why remember such detail, in all its intricacy and profound shock? It was as if he wasn't there for the event, apart from the shriek, then recovered, then reexperienced the airburst in all its horror for the first apocalyptic moments. As if his mind woke up. As if, in the first pain of the event, his mind went into abeyance. He had heard, in his woolly way, about similar experiences, dismissing them with a young man's sangfroid as not real, something for the idling to work on while peeling potatoes.

Again he heard the cavalcade of rocks falling, the sounds of woodwork crashing down, the screams from certain parties as if disemboweled, all of a sudden close to death. Cannons firing. Pressing his head close to the earth. A furious hot wind racing along between the houses still standing and at speed looking for new meat to abolish down the Onkoul road. He heard the iron padlock of the barn snap and give way, thus freeing the horses for incineration, and could not figure out how so many were doomed and so few spared. For the moment, he thought he was dead, thinking to himself, "Well, that was not so bad, was it? If it had to come when it did, it could have been worse." Then he recovered, amazed to find his cottage still standing. No longer stammering, as far as the audible version, yet still blind as a bat whenever speech was required.

269

*

The day soon came when, with his mother in tow, with return fare paid both ways for two, he was obliged to visit the lion's mouth across the whole of Russia, to consult with the elusive One-Sixth Humbly. He wondered if he would ever come back from such a breathtaking appointment, knowing its implications for both him and his mother. One-Sixth Humbly was One-Sixth Humbly, the destroyer of millions. You were doing well even to return from such an excursion.

So trepidation assailed him in full measure, beginning with sleepless nights, culminating in nervous tremors throughout his body. He fondled the limp travel papers idly, half suspecting they would be his last and wondering why he had been vouchsafed silent speech, as he called his ability to fluent interior dialogue while fumbling phonemes to the exterior. *All for naught?* he wondered. He had not been a bad son after all, more than a mite inarticulate, but with champion recitals to himself in the amphitheater of his mind.

Abis Chybaz, his mother, was no better off, having had several experiences of One-Sixth Humbly's attentions long ago. She wondered why she had been sent for as well, to wind her way across dismal Russia, the vast tepid expanse for an interview she feared would be her last. Why? For having botched her son in the breeding department, victims both of an airburst? She blamed everything on the massive natural disaster, and then concentrated on the wearisome path that led from Omsk to Yekaterinburg and Kazan to Moscow, a route hardly well known to her, but memorable nonetheless.

The green unwieldy ticket obsessed her. How about reversing it instead, Tunguska to Khabarovsk, for starters, and then a quick escape to Vladivostok? She wondered at such an expensive fare, which tempted her with a false sense of Soviet security. She imagined the person meeting them off the train would be Leonid Kulik, and not One-Sixth Humbly, Leonid of the Full Resolution photograph (515 by 775 pixels, file size) she kept by her in an otherwise bare alcove after the airburst had struck. Furrowed brow, glasses, wizened beard, and a look of preternatural curiosity mixed with infinite peering: not One-Sixth Humblyesque at all, but good-naturedly staring at the incomprehensible. A jovial explorer.

*

At last transported by ironclad taxi to a reprieve, minus the clanking steam-ridden railway engines, the bitter-feeling eloquence of One-Sixth Humbly himself, approachable only by means of various subordinate doors, one door yielding at last to The Presence. During this process Humbly had lost his mother to the rebarbative company of three or four princelings, intent on according her the best of suave attention, but not a fig more than that. Humbly's hulking presence went on to higher things, now swathed in ormolu candlesticks, until at last the ogre revealed himself, half hidden behind a tapestry of the horrors of war. The son wondered at the fate of his mother who had not seen One-Sixth Humbly for ages. Would he ever run into his mother again, soapy fingers, iron foot, and all?

The face was devilish black, plastered with fungus, no doubt for effect upon the homuncules presented, at last, to the august being. Black oil decorated thick hair, a spurious effect to cancel the gray. He spoke in a phlegmy rumble, to what effect Humbly hardly knew, so overwhelmed as he was by the working-class splendor of One-Sixth Humbly's appearance.

"How was the train?"

The boy, as was his way, maintained his silence, expecting a repeat. Which came, louder than before. He nodded, amazed to be talking to somebody so regally presented and finally summoned his wits to say, "Fine, your Excellency."

"Ah, you *can* speak."

"On occasion."

"That will be just as well. We have things for you to do while here."

Humbly quivered, such was the impress of the ogre before him. He must at all costs put on his bravest front, faced with this destroyer of absolute millions. The imperial breath evoked tripe and onions, complemented by a smell of some ancient pomade brought in to cancel the first effect, but hardly up to the task.

"Ready?"

For what? Speechless as usual, he gaped at the question—*For what?* No sitting down, no small talk. One-Sixth Humbly was all business. Humbly found the wherewithal to murmur his yes, and One-Sixth Humbly motioned him into the neighboring room, not as opulent, and loaded with basins, cloths, and clear liquids containing brains, pulpy and severed.

"Watch," commanded One-Sixth Humbly, with a twinkle of amusement playing around his mouth. An aide, later presumed to be Lavrenti Beria or someone similarly both august and punitive, addressed himself to one of the brains, bisected it neatly as could be, and slammed the meat cleaver down. It yielded its mysteries easily, divulging a mother-of-pearl surface. *Fresh brains,* thought Humbly. *To whom addressed, I wonder?*

Next, in this panoply of bisecting arts, Humbly was to seat himself comfortably. The whirring began (this being the sound of one half of the brain transformed into a stew) while he waited. One-Sixth Humbly briefly absented himself behind a screen of devils and angels copulating and emerged with a satisfied leer, having masturbated into the rapidly swirling mix, which reappeared from behind the secluding screen. Humbly, impatiently waiting in his chair for the result of this fragrant bouquet, perused a dog-eared magazine dedicated to the work of Galaktionov and Agronovsky, two factory surveyors. One-Sixth Humbly seemed refreshed, though breathing heavily.

The whirring subsided. One-Sixth Humbly said, *Drink,* and it was over as soon as Humbly had consumed the last dregs. Some infernal celestial plot had been completed. There remained only the rail journey back to where he had come from, to which One-Sixth Humbly urged him without a word. Something had been achieved, though not much immediately notable. Traveling all the way from Eastern Russia, Humbly had imbibed half a sufferer's brain, and who knew what else? He picked up his mother again, half surprised to find her intact (she, as was not her norm, wasn't speaking) and they took the nearest taxi to the station in a silence that lasted until they boarded the train.

"So." She finally said.

"It wasn't bad. Just a peck of brain stew."

"I read a magazine about Galaktionov and Agronovsky and their recent doings."

"So did I."

For the next hour they discussed the erratic habits of dictators, seemingly indifferent that they had just been in the presence of the most dangerous man in recorded history, yet quite jovial in his offhand way. When they reached Omsk, they changed trains, something also done on the westbound journey, reminding them of their lowly status. Then they thought again. Something poetic pushed through their muddled thinking: high and low. They had conversed with the ruler of their land. No wonder they had, after that, been relegated back to their norm. They traveled onward, twice more obliged to change trains, in a state of sated bliss, their minds not for an instant on the sinister events of the day. They sidled, exhausted, into their niches, and slept the sleep of the just.

The next few days they spent the time recovering, she with stultifying memories of being left alone with a choice of seats to sit in. He found the silence of the beverage the most exotic because he had not seen what One-Sixth Humbly supplemented the bowl with, nor detected what he might have added or withdrawn at the last minute. Such was life at the top; you are lucky to emerge with your head intact. What followed, if anything, was what followed, and this mode of total thanksgiving he accepted implicitly.

For a week he noted nothing, then became aware of some easing of the frame, a partial remission of stuttered speech, noticeable by neighbors. What had One-Sixth Humbly wrought? Some work of the passive countenance, something of blessed remediability aimed at restoring Humbly to normalcy after suffering the torments of the damned during his long period of near aphasia? Humbly was improving, it was clear, from utterance to speed of delivery. A little more each day.

His mother noticed it, at first dismissing it as optimistic illusion, then coming to recognize the phenomenon as real, a thing of golden welcome after all her years of blind waiting. Her son was going to be a genius after all. Or at least a prodigy among the men of Tunguska. Then her thoughts grew wild again, he could be the next One-Sixth Humbly, dealing a free and easy death to all and sundry, massacring Kulaks with princely ease while declaring war on half the world. Thoughts swerving on the possibilities, she decided it could make a pretty picture after all, something to look back on after an epoch of waiting for Humbly to start being famous.

Humbly's response, though full of gladness, was less ecstatic. How would it end? Perhaps it would go halfway, then cease, gifting him with no more than average response to hearing his name called out with correct intonation. A B+ grammarian, or a shade better than that. A silver-tongued sage. It did not matter. Improvement was improvement anyway. Finally he could talk among men, share their jokes and obsessions, and he said a quiet prayer to himself, addressing whatever lay beyond.

To the East, meanwhile, One-Sixth Humbly had dismissed the entire episode as one of a hundred similar. It would work or not. He moved on to bleaker and purer grandiosities, vaguely aware of being master of all that he surveyed, and rather tired of his omnipotence.

*

Humbly felt that life was only just beginning, if rather late. Between One-Sixth Humbly's jerking off and Humbly's recovery, there must surely be a link, a vision of the lost son or something such. At least Humbly thought so, daily strengthening his hold on the language, and looking forward to the day of his first honorary degree. He was nothing if not ambitious. Why, he had been saved from a fate worse than death and his mother along with him. He deserved belated recognition, and, in his wilder moments, fancied himself a second One-Sixth Humbly. But One-Sixth Humbly was not dead yet, and Humbly was far from the perfection he planned. Still, he could dream, and this he did with a realist's fervor, imagining a May Day parade without One-Sixth Humbly, another war without anyone to thwart him with their special brand of laissez-faire. Humbly was a Manchurian Candidate of his nether world.

At first he felt a tingly, incomplete ignorance of what One-Sixth Humbly had gifted him with. Nothing much. Then the tingling became much more than a sensed presence, more like burly substratum, and he started to attend to it thoroughly. His attention now on the larger of One-Sixth Humbly's supplements to his growth: the half brain that he decided was swelling in the most amicable way. And then he began to feel extended, a feeling of extraordinary vigor instead of his old lethargy. At last his brain was taking over in some access of blissful jubilance. For the first time in his life, he felt preternaturally endowed, a feeling of imminent readiness for all comers. For the first time he seemed ready for whatever life served up.

None of this superplus of sensations went away, though the initial burst took his breath away. His mother continued to note his renewed vigor, which she somehow related to the stimulating motion of the train, there and back.

How long she had waited for this change of his heart. She served up larger portions of his favorite reindeer meat to keep him in trim. She watched his increased attentiveness to girls, and, best of all, he started to grow taller again, not much but certainly noticeable if you measured him month after month. She formed the habit of extolling One-Sixth Humbly for all the good he produced, finally embodying her delight in an aphorism: "We should go back to see him for another helping."

Humbly had told her in the vaguest way about the brain supplement, but had omitted the vivisection and the drink. She assumed he had been given a typical One-Sixth Humblyese potion. Everything followed from that. And of sperm addendum he never knew anyway.

By now, going on a month later, people had begun to gaze approvingly at Humbly, at his augmented vigor and fondness for girls. They started calling One-Sixth Humbly "Dr." and lauding his eugenic ways. In short, Humbly had become a changeling leader among men after a long period of waiting until Dr. One-Sixth Humbly had fortified certain parts of his body to make him right. The chorus of praise for Humbly grew apace, however bogus, and he grew in size (bypassing seven feet). All and sundry awaited what he would do next, some culmination long desired that so many routine Tunguskans had passed and failed. There was no reason to halt his growing other than at some point he ceased, and that was that.

Winter was approaching fast and so he was draping his heavy form over the local girls, squashing the life out of some of them, which they accepted as part of the pleasure of having a hero at all. In this ecumenical fashion he created six or seven babies, all born close together, introducing among the populace a random element hitherto unknown. Then winter set in, and his stoked-up appetite decreased, only to resume with a next generation, when the sun returned. Complaints surfaced, however, about his incursions into the female fabric of the land. He was a simultaneous ogre and hero, tupping the girls for mere lack of something else to do. He was insatiable. They had no prophylactic condoms in the untamed vastness of Mother Russia, and were not soon likely to. Women accepted his perfunctory favors with condign delight, looking forward to a lifetime of babies in series.

The birthrate went up thanks to his efforts and to his mother's delight. He slept little, ever anxious to make more babies, and the forces of local resistance, initially massed against him, weakened and succumbed. They could not keep up with his perpetual presence, which was ever sunny, melodic, and horny. In truth he had come home to stay, unemployable because sexually too busy and self-engrossed.

One-Sixth Humbly, tucked away in his run-down dacha, could not have cared less about this latest result of his many sexual supplements. Scatter the seed and multiply was his motto and he had lived up to it by executing thousands who knew not why. In a sense, One-Sixth Humbly evened things out, varying production of sexual prodigies with corpses. He was not, he boasted, responsible for any increase in the birthrate. Three or four young men each day were the recipient of his sexual favors, which entitled him to three or four put paid to.

The motives of this monster will remain in darkness. He was so

prolific on all fronts, making war, not peace (never peace), occasionally passing up a victim because of absentmindedness (Humbly), and
forging thousands of babies, none of whom he ever saw again. One
may well ask, but what of the brain implants? Was this a special
favor bestowed on the neediest of recipients? No. He was as generous with halved brains as with babies. The scores kept evening out,
and one day even Humbly would go the way of all flesh, polyphilo-
progenitive to the last.

Humbly's ability to focus, before the trip, had triumphed over every
bit of noise; now he found the clink of every pot and pan was an aes-
thetic trial, crashing where previously they had murmured. It was
a matter of getting used to it, but he could not bring himself to,
flinching and recoiling at the merest sound, until his mother rebuked him for being so sensitive to the mere sound of her cooking.
So he spent more time out of doors, even at the expense of freezing,
just to quieten the world down and readjust his hearing to its newly
augmented dimension.

Apart from this, his sensations were normal except for his only-
too-ready erection, which resisted all attempts to control it. Humbly
had become the neighborhood cocksman without even trying, though
he would have swapped the painful sound effects of several crashes
and bangs for a restful diminution of his manhood. There must be
some reason for everything, he mused, some way of evening things
out, but he could not find it, hopeless when erect, hopeless whenever
the world careened down.

Primarily, he was now having to cope with two languages, one
familiar, one not. For one, the old words sufficed, simple and brutish.
For the other, always a nominative novelty, newborn and fancier.
And, strange to say, he found the complex one easier. For example,
he found the words "disjointed" and "stanchion" simpler to pronounce than "butter" and "bacon." He didn't know why his mouth
habitually selected the most complicated abstruse words, but it did,
and the incongruity both delighted and harassed him even to the
point of sometimes wishing for the old days of stumbling over simple words. His newly galvanized brain now sought out complex
words for the very ease with which he said them.

Powered by One-Sixth Humbly's brain surgery (at least) he was an
absolutely superior somebody to talk with, destined (some thought)
for higher things in spite of being a dreadfully late beginner. Whereas

they used to think of him as soldiering on, now they recognized him as a prince of pronunciation, and ever improving. Where would he end up?

The Tunguskans left it at that, not knowing the correct vocabulary for marks of academic or scholarly distinction but convinced in their bland way he would rise in the Party. At least that. They realized he had gone beyond them, at last coming into his belated heritage, but they were not willing to meddle further into the unknown region. His mother felt similarly, though less reconciled to the prospect of losing him to some form of higher panjandrum.

She would have preferred him staying simple, at her august disposal, even as layabout or dummy, but she recognized in her prosaic way that she couldn't have everything in this life and as soon as he started ambitious words she went along for the ride, little realizing where his augmented vocabulary came from. They both had survived the time of the airburst, which many had not, and one miracle was enough for one family.

She suspected a lonely life looming for her, but not just yet, as he met with one man of distinction after another. Such was the prophetic side of her being. Having survived the airburst, that monster of insensate natural fury, who could expect more catastrophe than that?

For his part, perfected language was within his reach at last, and he gaped at the transition he had made, wondering how much more would follow. He half knew all the words he was predestined to use by some miracle of prestidigitation, and in this he was not mistaken, surmising the life to come. Was it in the cards that he would become a prodigy of astronomy, rhetoric, or physics? If something else, that was all right with him, convinced as he was of his own superiority. He felt the first glimmerings of smugness invade his being, and labored to tamp it down, being a modest chap at heart.

But he *knew* now that all would be well with him. He was older than most, having had such a late start, but didn't harp on that. One-Sixth Humbly's brain banquet would serve him well, and he secretly wondered when next they would meet and what treat the next encounter would yield. The other part of the split brain, kept on ice ever since? Envisioning moments such as this kept him vibrant long into the night. Humbly needed to sleep little, in spite of his mother's sibylline warnings about taxing his fertile mind. On he went, marshaling his words to an ever-anxious mama to whom he never looked back.

His head was sprinkled with ideas, not all of them relevant to his cause. The free play of the mind obsessed him as never before. All words became relevant because so few of them had been tested, so fragmented and tentative had been his verbal (not quite verbal) attempts to cope. He said his thanks to every word scrap that came his way, repeatedly chanting, *lemming, muskrat, Stalin, One-Sixth Humbly,* or поезд, the Russian word for *train,* just for the pleasure of anything to pronounce, wondering if their verbal forbears meant anything at all: *lem, mus, Sta,* or пое, or *ing, krat, lin,* or the Russian for *ain* (to be more difficult than ever).

All was clear to him now, which was mostly the reason for his lack of sleep. He babbled all night long, sometimes when he was alert and systematic, later when he was tired and the old simple habits reasserted themselves. He always knew what he was saying, even when resorting to stuttering from fatigue, which was never the case in his previous incarnation.

Much of this rehearsal escaped his mother, conscious of only his lucid moments, and she thanked her lucky stars for making him whole after the long wait to make him anything at all. She relished the way he made perfect sense, *always,* as distinct from the clutter that he once serenaded her with. In a word, he was sane, and she gave thanks to the neighbors who had suffered his valiant attempts at language without looking down their noses at him. Three or four of his contemporaries had fared much worse and would stutter even to their graves, and she attributed Humbly's run of luck to the airburst that had spared them both. He was, after all, slated for big things, whereas they were not. Such *orgueil* typified her and the notion she had of herself and him. Another airburst would have confirmed his more than celestial future, but it never came in her lifetime.

Understandably, his mother clung all the more to him as he improved verbally. She, who had previously set no particular store by skills in that department, thought the better of it and began her own laborious effort to improve, which only drove her away from him. So there entered a new element into their relationship, a mild sort of repugnance. The better she got, and at speed, the more he shied away from plaintive cries of *You don't love me anymore?* So long as she stuck to discussions of food, weather, and gossip, he humored her, but language was off limits and the more he improved the more he left her behind.

The result was a dearth of their conversation, and an insistence on food, weather, gossip to maintain a semblance of decorum. In good weather he learned to swim, preferring the backstroke over all others, the price of learning being her continual presence at swimming sessions, something he put up with, plowing away from her repeated entreaties and tentative advice as far as possible, always in deeper water. So he become adept and wondered how to put his swim to further use. In the end, confronted with his rapidly receding body, she left him to it.

His cherished inability to sleep bothered her, and she in the mildest way rebuked him for it. But he appeared not to care, seeking new words to occupy his nighttime hours, such as *reminiscence, alarm, emitted,* and *bleat.* He never forgot his new words, and extolled their very nature, marveling at the complexity and way they all ultimately began to fit together. Entranced by this vision of the language, he began to dress untidily, going without shoes even in the coldest weather, and then socks on occasion. His mother of course rebuked him, but he did not care, and did it more often just to spite her. Where would it end, this rift between a mother and son who had begun in tender harmony?

The vision of language as a never-ending parade began to occupy him more and more. Was it really true? Or would he have to shift to another language, say Finnish or Greek, once he had finished learning this one? The answer was obvious, though late in coming, so engrossed had he been with words themselves. He would have to leave the by now fully repaired homestead and take his mother's wrath on the chin. But *where to* and *how* remained horrors to him, beginning with Moscow and ending in Tunguska. He would need to be *invited.*

There was another angle to his private life and it had to do with the young ladies of the town who had so liberally met his overtures. Four or five of them were now pregnant in the early stages and had come running to the offender. It is a moot point which outcome they demanded of him, marriage or abortion, jumping downstairs, or one of the sublimer forms of magical miscarriage. Of course, he was younger than the average courting age, so his needs were not necessarily for the wedding couch but rather for a potent smack of the behind or something such, which bestowed on them another bite on the apple. At any rate, in the fashion of women throughout the ages, they accused him of knocking them up and what was he going to do about it?

First, in no order of priority, he came to the girl's house, holding a symbolic jam jar with which she was to have magical abortive results. This was Sophonisba, her name a Russian transplant from Italy, her second teeth already scarred and wizened, but she was, nonetheless, in the family way at just sixteen. Why had she succumbed to humble babbling when she had the whole surviving village to chop at? No one knew. No one had bothered to find out, as if anyone could. There she was, in the least regarded part of Russia, abandoned to fate and bound for at least another pregnancy in short order.

"Jump," said Humbly, who had more esoteric things on his mind. "That'll fix you for sure." She did his bidding to no avail and represented herself in brutal terms. "Silly man." He moved away from her bleats of frustration, muttering something about female destiny and how it was what women were born for. Poor Sophonisba, doomed to an early extinction, having been denied access to the finer points of his exquisite elocution.

He moved on to the next case a fortnight later, without for an instant checking his assault on the other women of the village. This conversation took place behind a herd of samite reindeer in the lower meadow, to the tune of their clacking jaws. "Jump several times," he said, and she did right there and then.

"Does it work?"

"Wait and see," he said, listening to his interior voice, which instructed him to curtail this interview. "Wait a week. That should do it." His mind was on escape, even if only to a neighbor village. This was Gaistan, whose teeth were the wonder of the world, pure, except that she declined to wear her drawers (ready for action, she proclaimed). Although they had heard rumors of the Dutch Cap (whereas the humble lummock of a lover had not), the local peasantry went without, trusting in nature to see them through.

As for Popov, his favorite (she of the hazel quinquireme eyes), she made no bones about it, calling out "Preggers, at last," to all and sundry. No parents, she had been brought up by grandparents and allowed many privileges. Her attitude to Humbly consisted of jubilant high jinks reinforced by a willingness to say anything that came into her mouth. She figured among the survivors of the explosions, remembered fourteen or fifteen years later as an event of fabulous fury, something almost to celebrate. The more it receded from memory, the more it remained an occasion for academic excitement or juvenile spawning. An event not too fearsome at all. So Popov's excitement (mainly based on boredom) was a thing of sheer novelty; she considered the pregnancy the property of Humbly himself, as if the subsequent blood work and timing were more his than hers. She

claimed his seniority was superior to hers, and washed her hands of
the whole process much to his confusion, primed as he was to retreat
from his mother's nagging ways. She danced gravidly, naked and
clad. She mythologized it into twins (not hers but his) and she drove
him crazy with anticipation of the couplet as they grew, strangely
echoing the doubled value of his main character, duffer and linguist,
claptrap and expert logician, the creature with two heads.

By no means surrendering to her eruption into his private life, he
blustered and cursed, swearing that even if the pregnancy harelipped
every inhabitant of Bear Creek, he would expose its toils, just when
he was feeling so splendid and at last finally himself, as he ought to
be. She persisted with the good-natured assault anyway, and drove
him into a state of not hearing her, the only remedy for which was
to worry about the fourth or fifth maternity to be of Golgotha, the
only fully fledged retarded young lady in the vicinity, the one whom
pregnancy endangered from the first and who did not belong in the
company of more adventurous girls. But what to do in this land-
locked village, the victim of a colossal explosion, minus all forms of
help and left to handle the restitution of everything as best they
could?

The steppes were full of such settlements, pushed to the limit and
then left there to flounder or survive, with nothing reported for
years, just the smell of reindeer and hay, and the occasional episode
of tree destruction to keep them on their toes. Life at its lowest.

The vision of those many unwanted pregnancies all vying for his
attention both sickened and fascinated him, prepared as he was to
greet the girls with a gladsome mind, in principle at least. He countered with his standard complaint of it should never have happened
to him, now least of all when he had so many other matters to think
about. It wasn't fair, he thought, to saddle him with such things right
in the middle of preparing to leave. Then he realized he had started
the whole thing, in each case. But had he? It occurred to him that the
girls might have been victims of some other jolly roger, rolling his
sperm along to a finer destination. Nothing to do with him at all.

So why had he in the first place offered himself on the chopping
block of imminent maternity? Why had he been so eager to be considered? He pondered that, hard and long. Was it the natural thing to
do, offering his jism as the best in town? Was it simply a matter of
who was best equipped for the task? It was natural, he thought, to
assert his natural superiority, and then to withdraw it when you
came right down to it. Having your cake and eating it at the same

time. Or whatever the metaphor was.

Best to leave town while the going was good, before the competition for fatherhood became intensive. But where to go and for how long, with his mind on being a perfect linguist?

Besides, who cared what kind of linguist he could be, exemplary or not? Something was missing, a lost piece of the puzzle. What other people, in more celebratory circumstances, might call context, background, or even something else he couldn't quite recall. Some perfect holding pattern for the soul to squat in. You had to belong before you were allowed to belong. At last he was miraculously in the society of mechanical engineers with invitations to teach at Moscow University.

Between dreading imminent fatherhood and not knowing how to negotiate people in the picture called infrastructure, he was a ready-made dunce of aspiration, hoping to wrangle his way inside something or other at the risk of not belonging to anything ever again.

But how was he to reconcile craving the women not yet explored, or even known by name? Forget the pregnant few for the romance of the rest. What was this lust for, idling for some two dozen of the neighborhood doxies? Was it a desire, simple and vain, to spread his seed far and wide before leaving for good? Or something more devious, more ambitious, secretive, such as a reluctance to leave the region after all, a kind of self-deception through which to chavel his cake while eating it too.

Such were his misgivings on the brink of departure, a form of clinging abandon that panted to be off. Something, he knew not what, was holding him back, but it was much burlier than the occasional uprising of sperm. Was it his mother, now marooned in the toils of a brilliant sun? She continued speaking to him in the old way, but it was no use. His speech to her was mannered and maneuvered, a consummate work of clauses and subclauses, designed for a brain subtler than hers. She sang along bravely, even consulting a battered dictionary at times, but it was no help, actually puzzling all the more with sudden lurches, foreign tongues, and little-known expressions peculiar to Muscovites. She pursued gallantly, but it was over. He had gone beyond her at the last minute, and she recognized that she was now speaking to him less than before. There was no maternal response, not that he wished it so, but he was intoxicated at the highest level so there was no looking back.

So, for a brief while, he hedged his bets, on the brink of departure but always drawing back as some lure of the flesh worked its will on him or some curlicue of the language enticed him to learn something extra. In some ways it was a rather privileged position to be in: *Reculer pour bien sauter,* or whatever the French meant (withdraw only to jump ahead better, or something such). His French studies often led him into dark and devious waters. Nonetheless, he kept trying, from Russian to French, a New Russian obviously, and an unknown French.

And still he did not go, either from an outburst of shyness or some reluctance to commit himself, to another unknown. He had given up on his mother, with enduring regret (a pagan melody with no holds barred) and got the unfortunate girls out of his system. All that remained was the rest of the virgins, presumably not pregnant yet. Could he be lusting after them, and if so what was his purpose? Not lust, certainly, but something far tenderer, some mode of feeling them up without despising them in the least. What a turn of events! He was growing older already, not so young after all as he kept reminding himself.

So this was old age, or was it some ruse inspired by One-Sixth Humbly with his half headedness bursting out into a modicum of sedate behavior? Perhaps it was a weakness inspired by the helping of One-Sixth Humbly he'd never know about. Perhaps someone who knew him thoroughly, inside and out, could understand him better. The halt in his progress had yielded to something far richer. Language, perhaps, at which in his darkest hours he knew he excelled, a beginning duffer who had pulled off a stroke of genius. It was natural that one had yielded to the other, making of him a martyr to lust and to maternity. Thousands, he thought, had gone the other way, holding to cocksmanship and mother love at the expense of language. He hoped words would never fail him, having come so far.

The problem was what do with it, having found himself and prevailed. He hoped words would go on forever, enriching him a thousandfold, instead of going blank on him, returning him to the fold of sensuality and mother love. What could One-Sixth Humbly have had in store for him? A bullet in the back of the neck, conducted by two grim but dutiful Cossacks: "Don't look round, sir." That reversion to type, the fate of the duffer repeated all over again. He hoped for Saint Petersburg Forestry Institute, grappling as best he could with the uncertain future, or the University at Kazan. Any forestry institute or university. He had heard of thousands of rejects, although he would not be, could not become, one of them.

His mind obsessed with one thing: how to *Get In,* by hook or by crook, to get the piece of pasteboard that said *Admitted.* Everything would follow from that. Of that he was sure.

So the long campaign of letter writing began, letters of ingratiating pluck and zeal, many of them rejected for lack of good manners, but encouragement enough to keep the heart ticking over. The process ascended through *unfortunatelys* and *regrets* to *perhaps next year* to the *interview,* some turned down, one accepted by the Mineralogical Museum in the city of Saint Petersburg. He was *in,* after all that, and he found it hard to sleep.

Who was it who declared that no two people have the right to tread the same rainbow? My real story begins with my trajectory (onward and upward) to *Kapustin Yar,* where I, Humbly, I ascended all the varied dimensions of space, breathing hard with each one, eventually settling on the planet *Hush,* where some would think I turned into a stone, whereas I found it a haven, all the way from the Tunguska blast.

Five Ghost Poems
Cole Swensen

THE CLASSICAL AGE

glided down from the sky   on other rails   the ghosts of the era
often brought advice   often at great expense   to themselves   they cried

child after child   entered the cold   and so Aeneas descended
at the request of his father   but as is usual in such cases   when he

actually tried to touch him   the bottom fell out of history   resulting
in these pastures   that are nothing like   and never will be

what in reaching we see   is like that rare condition of the blind who
learn to see with their skin   being locked in a windowless room

OFTEN AGAINST

Often against its will   the ghost is called back   even wrenched
from its flight-in-place   with a sound   don't

even think of it   maybe hurtled   toward a light inside of which
a certain play of wing and sand   had been trying to forget

as had the ghost   in 1 Samuel 28:13   who said I have been torn
from the touch.   I am blind, and I flinch   and had forgotten how

the world in which you live   is so limited in its range of visible light

Cole Swensen

THERE WAS A CERTAIN POINT

at which the story changed   from that of the living who traveled
to the underworld and back   and became instead   one of the dead

who came from the land of the dead   and could not return
is a turning.   Why are we frightened   by doorways; why is there a fear

especially made for the sound of a door   or an ear   or a stare   Fear
is an aperture   but also a ligature.   Something deep inside

the house swings shut   and they start to describe it as something else

THE GESTA

But when they saw the wound   but when was full of hounds
a pack, grounded   can trace a grain of salt   back to its share

that could not be staunched   was an arrow thrown by hand
and though they'd never seen him before   they knew his name

and so the town was saved.   In the Middle Ages the ghost story
was not a genre as such   but was something that accrued

not without alarm   yet with a kind of trust   she took
the wound without the arm   and wore it as a past

Cole Swensen

YET

Yet it was precisely when the ghost story   became a genre
that ghosts became strangers   that the Romantic movement

managed to refuse   death through its flagrant celebration   so
stylized it remains   poised on the tip   of a letter opener

and the man   who holds it in his hand turns around   silhouetted
on a promontory over a crevasse   and thus his sister

dies of music   or the ghost is reduced   to an overpowering smell
of the sea   and only she can hear   how we have inherited

fletcher of tongues   thin in the wind who   blinded by now
a ghost in fingers   is touching them empty   of all its burning

And we claim we never knew them   living   is lost in living
and thus the phaeton stopped to pick him up   and went on to plunge

over the cliff   just as it had in all its lost   every night for
the past fifty years   the ghost ship   the phantom train

the cathedral fear   and how right we are   to claim it isn't ours
though it leaves them stranded   or we abandon   or we

a screw   in a door nailed shut.   It isn't our fault

Two Poems
Nathaniel Mackey

A NIGHT IN JAIPUR

—"mu" sixty-fifth part—

Lakshmi wept as we made our
way outward, blue devotion's
 annuity looped and led back,
reluctance's allure yet to accrue.
                              Larger
       than life, they'd lain belly to
belly, patch of hair pressing patch
of hair, leg pressing leg, all they'd
    have otherwise been held in
    abeyance, Krishna's remnant
                         kiss...
Whatever after-the-fact embrace
   had hold of her we listened,
   bamboo hollow the heart of it,
                              bam-
       boo flute's burnt opening blown
                              on,
       hole his breath finessed... Flush
lozenge lipped, let go of. Tongue
    to've tarried on tongue less than
    a memory, sound what might've
                              been...
       Lakshmi wept as we made our
way birth after birth, two-headed
    hollow beaten on at both ends, log
                              we
   slept in,   Mira's amanuenses,
                              mud
bouquet

288

*

Sat gameless at the gaming table.
Sitar glint knuckling the night's
   one luster spoke sputter, made
   sputter speak... A diffuse kiss
                           low to
the ground, blue reconnoiter. Voice
   also known as Wrack Tavern.
   "Bar, be my altar," it sang...
                             Semi-
sang, semiwept, Lakshmi's bond
   an abatement. Held but not had,
                           had
held, churchical girth. Caught strings
cut our thumbs... Insofar as there
   was an I it wasn't hers we heard
   her insinuate, of late begun to be
                           else-
where, the late one she'd one day be...
                           Semi-
sang, semiwept as we sat lost at the
   gaming table, thumbs all thumbs
                         no
   thumbs to hold on with... Held-not-
   had was her new way, what had its
                      way
   with us, held-not-had her
   numb regret

*

   Lakshmi sang as we sat stuck at
the gaming table, hands tied down
   by sympathetic strings. To be
                      was
   to be at her behest... Sought
                      bodily
solace, bodilessness, reluctant allure
   it seemed. A certain way she

289

had with Krishna's going, beautiful
rebuff she made it seem... We'd
                                         been
        borne by a wind we hardly knew
                                    was
        blowing, wrung notes lingering mo-
ment to moment, phonic perfume
it seemed... Seemed it said cover,
                                seemed
        it said collect, seemed it bid reaching
                                          good-
bye, went on reaching, seemed it told all
it said no... We sat aloft looking in on
        ourselves... Five layers we'd have
                                     to
        get thru to get to what lay underneath.
                                         A low
        hum came from under the gaming table,
        chance's debt reneged on, romance's
                                        bet
called off

STICK CITY BHAJAN

—*"mu" sixty-sixth part*—

        If I saw myself I saw myself
stagger. To see was to be in my
own way... Albeit to be went
        without looking, see caught
                                look's
        delay, see saw possible miscue,
look-see made it so... If I saw
myself I saw myself stumble,
                                saw
        myself steady myself. Quick
        step, leg stuck, saw myself
undone. Slipped on the stairs
                                I'd

begun to go up, lay flat on the
                                    floor
I'd walked across... Insofar, this
was to say, as there was an I it was
no other, of late letting go no getting
    out. I saw myself I saw, no parallel
                                    track
intruded. The voice I thought his was
    mine, no if it was me, myself my
own Mira, my own sweet Krishna,
    tongue's tip touching my ear no one's
                                    if not
mine... Sufic, sulfitic, resinous, a thin
    wine tipped my tongue, took my
feet away. Black leggings moist with
                                    leg-
sweat the taste of it, lost, I was no one
                                    else's,
    Wrack Tavern wine's bouquet unremit-
    ting, Wrack Tavern wine's bouquet
unmerciful, lost, I was only my own, I
                                    lay
flat... Less than a second I lay there. I lay
    looking up thru the ceiling. I lay looking
up at the sky. Stars were tiny pinpricks in
    the blackness the nightsky was, black
                                    leg-
    gings wafting the light they let in, Wrack
Tavern's acrid bouquet... The voice I thought
    Mira's inhered in lifted cloth, aromatic
                                    leg-
sweat, cloth under cloth, underness above
                                    me,
sky-high

                    *

Home's near side far behind me, took
    now a new name, I-Insofar. Voice
broke, I-Insofar resounded, ground fell
                                    away

and lay flat at the foot of a cliff, made,
as it slid, what I wanted moot... Voice
  broke as all escort faded, legs I took heaven to be, black leggings, drummed-up

                              equation of
  leg stride and starlight, legs' lit recompense...
    It was I-Insofar's Insofar-I, late slope
      I stood stuck on, stood if not
    stumbled, spliff-lit, metathetic

                              remit...
    Beset by drums that were code

                        for
dreams, hair let down in the dream
  they said I dreamt, spinning wheels
    a music of sorts... Black leg-
    gings beneath her sari, said the

                              exe-
    gete, love's understudy, he quipped,

                              called
      himself, love's upstart, I said, instead...
    So the floor fell away to my right,
north I thought, umpteenth amendment
      begun to go renegade, lacktone's

                              chatter
      the country I came to, coming-to

                              the
      glimpse I
    caught

The Discipline of Shadows
Tim Horvath

UP ON THE CHAIR, I reach for the ceiling and beat the vents, sending mold fluttering downward. Like some black rain, it lands variously on me, on chipped, yellowing tiles, on the paperwork fanned out over my desk. It speckles the latest budget, a trail of powder on the glossy cover of the newest *International Journal of Umbrology*. It must be going into my lungs. I think about miners descending, invisible until the shaft collapses and the cameras swarm. Maybe, I think, this is what we need—some tragedy. Something more than mere scandal. More than Lew and his lawyer. More than the death of a department, which is like an animal, already limping, vanishing at last under the wheels.

I won't have time to change my shirt before the big meeting, and for a moment I regret this. After all, lawyers and trustees, the titled and brass nameplated, will be there. Lew's "representation," all the way from Lower Manhattan. At yesterday's department meeting the guy sat with Lew, hovering at the edge of my vision, a thick-browed smudge of pleated charcoal. Finally I wanted to confront him. "Mr. Vadrais," I wanted to say, "at the end of a workday, when you exit 214 Pearl, do you ever pause to take in the shadows?" I felt them like a chill, then, those revenants of an older New York, strewn across the narrow, birdshit-encrusted streets.

But I held my tongue. He would've been mystified and the rest of them would've all thought I was losing it.

The Department of Umbrology is located in the basement of Sackler Hall on the easternmost edge of campus. Our neighbors are the physical plant and Parking Violations. Students and professors of all ages huff by in three-piece suits and skimpy spaghetti strappery, tickets in hand, excuses rehearsing themselves upon the tongue. Upstairs is the old Engineering Library (the new one, slated for ribbon cutting in September, a veritable suspension bridge with walls—it stuns) and three rooms the Theater Department uses as a sort of gulag for old props. There's talk of tearing the building down. The odds of our out-living it? In this economy, I ask you? A memo before the wrecking ball meets the wall is what I hope for.

At four full-timers and one visiting professor, we are the smallest department on the campus (not including the interdisciplinary ones, like Africana Studies and Russian, the latter part of Foreign Languages). I'm sometimes asked to defend my department's integrity (and I mean this etymologically—no one, till now, has questioned our moral stature, only whether we ought to be considered *one*). Well, I muse, what about Foreign Languages? Are they "one"? Can we roll up all the vernacular, all the literary traditions, the Day of the Dead and Bastille Day and the notebooks of Dostoyevsky and *das bier und bratwurst*, and, by cramming them together under a single roof, make them *one?*

Immediately down the hall from my office is that of Dahlia Peterson on one side, and Phil Abelard on the other, and then past that is the office of Lew Dorris, and then finally our visiting scholar, Alex Kuperman. Dahlia is our shadow theater person; she thinks she's made it to Broadway and I'm not going to disillusion her. Her office, the largest, lit from within by Indonesian lamplight, ushers one into a 2D universe of gauze stretched between bamboo poles, tables over-spilling with the most ornate, intricately carved puppets. The room is always alive, CD player blaring gamelan or some mainstream fluff, students snipping and doweling away at all hours like child laborers, only happy, her Brooklyn accent wafting like fresh bagels down the hallway as she chastises them, "Not like that . . . who taught you how to . . . here, here." She's superficially abrasive but profoundly gentle, the students inform me—worked to the bone, by term's end they are putting on virtuoso epics of Bali, Turkey, or China, and in Advanced they westernize, shadow-working their family memoir, slave ships with oars the luminous water pushes back at, streets that seem somehow paved in gold even if just variants of black, always, Marge Simpson makes an appearance, it's a running joke. Abelard is the one who's been here longer than me and grown way too com-placent. Doesn't bother with office hours, hasn't produced an iota of scholarship in twelve years. Wrote his book about Shadows in Lit. back in the day but since he got tenure it's been a handful of confer-ence talks and *Easy Rider* in his swivel chair. Kuperman's fresh blood, but wrong blood type—hasn't panned out at all. My hopes were high. A scholar of neo-noir, he's actually produced a film you might've seen, *The Better Half?* So we've snagged ourselves a bona fide celeb. Too bad he's always on the phone with his agent—pair of Bluetooth pincers, one on each ear. He teaches on Tuesdays and then I swear he slips out between the blinds, jetting back to LA; his weekends start Wednesdays. I won't miss him, nor will the students. He was a mistake—a case of mistaken identity, you might say, with no more interest in shadows than a rooster has in gold coins. But one door further down is Dorris, our rock star. Astrophysicist PhD 1987 from Dartmouth, his long, frothy hair cascading onto ample shoulders, but don't be distracted—you'll need all of your cognitive faculties as he leaps from discussing what happens to shadows from objects approaching the speed of light to the tiny fingerprints left behind by the particles called muons. Then he unwinds by pummeling his way through some video game, sounds like some teenager in there, tearing things up, kicking through walls and mowing down Nazis. Like some home brewer he even designs his own games as pastime. But no ego on him, no Kuperman. He pro*duces* too—four reputable journal pubs in the past year, four! Unheard of. One in the *Umbro*, too, the mothership, damn him.

As for me, my work is much more mundane. Philosophy—the ontology of shadows in the history of thought, and given the postlinguistic turn, of course, how they're treated in language. Plus I oversee the department. I've chaired for eleven years now and probably will till I retire or keel over. No one else wants it—can you imagine Dahlia with her sextuple-jointed puppets filing a budget or tracking postgrad job stats? She may talk like a Flatbush Ave. importer with her students, but she's a softie when it comes to the bureaucrats. I'm not crazy about paperwork but I'm orderly and never cowed, especially by some administrator with a diploma in something called public policy.

And, hey, if Lew wants to cash in on his research so his two kids can go to their colleges of choice, can I blame him? He can even justify it morally—he's *making the world a safer place.* His algorithms will help snare terrorists huddling in the mountains of western Pakistan. Help rid the world of evil.

Not incidentally, they'll also make him rich, and in the meantime the terrorists will cover their tracks better, find alternate hideouts, go deeper, where their shadows, seen only by the walls, won't betray them.

Still, I don't hold it personally against Lew. With Edmund it feels a bit more personal, more *Et tu*ish. After all, *I* recruited him, groomed him, saved him from the fate of a giant state school with its rows of clone-like cheerleaders and ambiguously mammalian mascot. Last time our eyes met he ducked between buildings and I caught his shadow as it fluttered for a millisecond at the corner, as if hesitating. He was gone. Cold shoulder no mere figure of speech.

In memory I'm Edmund's age again, home for fall break. I sit my father down and tell him I've got an inkling of what I'm going to do with my life, and he looks at me quizzically. "Umbrology? The study of um*brel*las?" Impossible to know, then, how typical this reaction will be. Countless times I'll hear it over the years, even hear about ingenious designs from closet inventors, giddy for an audience. "No," I'll learn to cut in gently, "the study of shadows." (Always "shadows," the vernacular, never "shadow," though the semantics is hardly uncontroversial in the field; one either deems it substance or quantifiable entity and thus divisible. Each has consequences.)

My dad is far from the worst, though. From him I never expected understanding. He worked with his hands, wiring buildings, whole counties. Worse are those who should know better, colleagues whose own disciplines get scoffed at as impractical—sociologists, literary critics, art historians. When *they* imply or even state outright that offices and funding and a fax machine are luxuries we aren't worthy of, it stings. We're a stone's throw from parapsychology, they'd have it; we're Sasquatch groupies, Roswell nuts. I much prefer the out-and-out jokers, such as the guy who showed up to one of our slide shows—open, as always, to the public—and cast a giant phallus against the screen, balls and all. Witless, yes, and yet my instinct was to invite him to one of my classes.

The thing I find least forgivable, though, is flatness. "Oh, study shadows, do you? Well, geez, how about the football team, huh?" Dwelling in two dimensions so much of the time as I do, I shouldn't be rankled by this but am.

It's not hard to pick us out: the vision always slightly askew, aimed downward or slightly to the side. We take on a certain look, a spinal kink, the price exacted in chronic conditions that demand regular visits to orthopedists, chiropractors, the town's Rolfer. It's not all bad—I kept crossing paths with the same violinist. Once we'd established the similarity of our ailments, she got me cheap balcony seats at the symphony, and Edmund and I, then on benign terms, sat there and reveled in the antic play of bows and horns across sheet music and against the performers' neatly pressed white shirts, with the occasional ricochet off the gleaming, chair-checkered stage. Of course, I enjoyed the music too; without it, the shadows would have been of only passing interest.

Leaving my office today, I sit in the parking lot, visor lowered, watching Kuperman's Impreza out of the corner of my eye. I'm not the following type—I've never pursued anyone in my life. But as chair, I'm the guy ultimately responsible if he's not in his office during the hours clearly posted. So far it's easy—I might just be sitting here exactly as I am, eating wasabi peas. I suspect he's off to see Dahlia. Their sparring, the way their barbs hook just slightly toward one another in meetings, betrays a secret history, a tryst. Case in point: He recommends a cinematographer friend as a guest speaker, she fires back that the lecture series is about the students, not *us*, he parries with, "There's no rule that says they can't *enjoy* the talk," and here my gut tells me this is all allegorical, that it's the bedroom that's on trial. The grapevine backs it up. While I generally frown on faculty flings, I could see it had added a few coils to Dahlia's step; maybe she'd get around to writing the article on shadow erotica she'd been bandying about since the day I met her. I knew Kuperman was using her for short-term gratification, probably plying her with promises whose shelf life was the term's end; I hoped it wouldn't leave her marriage wrecked, but beyond that I didn't really care one way or the other.

But I had to ensure Kuperman wasn't in violation of the terms he'd signed on for. If he's contractually on campus x hours a week, whether he's schtupping Dahlia or playing cribbage instead is frankly irrelevant.

Now he pulls out and I do a slow five count before pulling out behind him. I get stuck waiting for students, one walking a bike, to cross at their languorous pace, and I'm sure I've lost him, but at the light I spot the Impreza. I stay three car lengths back as we glide down Meadow and into the right-turn-only lane for Fessenden. He goes straight, not the way to Dahlia's two-family Victorian. A motel rendezvous? He pulls into the lot behind Sips and Swigs and I, in turn, ease into what isn't a spot but a good vantage point. At first I think I'm mistaken when I see Edmund Evans in boxlike glasses, frayed jeans, and loafers stride up and into the shop. There are several students who share his look, and Edmund doesn't touch coffee. And he can't stomach Kuperman, at least as of last time we spoke. But no, it's him, and they must be here together. I consider abandoning the car and strolling in, but three umbrologists in a coffee shop can be no coincidence, so instead I squint at the semiopaque windows.

Edmund and Kuperman? I make out shapes at a table. An anti–Venn diagram—two sets whose overlap is nil, betwixt whose sensibilities runs an unfathomable chasm. Yet here they are.

I'd give anything to be able to listen in. Instead, I shovel several fistfuls of peas into my mouth until I hear a series of raps on my window and look up to see a cop pointing at the sign; he looks angry, personally offended. Nodding, I turn the ignition—I ignite—and move out. I'm running late for Intro Umbro, the first years, and if I'm not there they'll leave.

I race in two minutes late and there are jokes—"We were, like, whoa, is it a shadow holiday"—and statements—"Bix was ready to peace"; Bix, backup quarterback, exquisitely diligent, takes the ribbing good-naturedly. I say, "It's a good thing you didn't. It's movie day."

"No movie today on the syllabus," they inform me.

"We're switching things around a little bit," I announce, slipping in a DVD. *He Walked by Night* appears on the screen, and I let the film do its work, just this once sans hand wringing about reducing myself to mere projectionist. I find a seat in the back, look on numbly. The plot is trivial, boilerplate police procedural, so I (and the students) can focus on the shadow elements. A deranged killer lurks in the sewers beneath LA. There will be much to talk about. How blinds, noir's signature emblem, are magnified, splayed over walls and ceilings and clothing. How the black-and-white universe of the film itself dictates that shadows are more substantial than non-shadows, the latter appearing ethereal, impalpable. But I can't focus.

Edmund Evans was a product of that flat America where the land reaches out like canvas under tension and the shadows stretch correspondingly, sparse, stark. I met him at some undergrad research forum, where he was going a mile a minute about some economic correlation he'd graphed up on a poster. His leg bore a giant cast, but he was up there on his feet and he swung his crutch like a pointer, explicating away to anyone who'd listen. I heard out his spiel and asked some question to show I'd been paying attention and then I extended a hand, which he seized after awkwardly repositioning the crutch.

"Um*brology?*" he said, squinting. "No, I can't say I know what that is." In the next instant he did something I'd never seen before: He guessed it. "Score one for Dublassi. AP Latin," he said, shaking his head. And in that single etymological grab was adumbrated a path, a future. He'd been set to transfer to another school for business, had already sent in his application. But he wanted to know what this was all about, and I could see hunger fleshing out into his face, his eyes, hunger after something that couldn't be found in any of his graphs or his econ textbooks. His face let me know that right then he'd follow me anywhere.

For each of us, of course, the shadow we fell for first. Reaching for our second or third drink at our annual conference's cocktail party, we kick off shoes under the chandelier, bask in the presence of the like-minded. Warily at first and then more boldly, we tell our stories:

—Regaining consciousness, the first thing that entered our field of vision was the shadow line of the very fence we came tumbling off, merciful as a missionary nun, leaning over us.

—The show *Mystery Science Theater*, with its silhouetted peanut gallery, sent us into spasms of laughter time and time again.

—In Arizona's Black Rock Canyon, hiking with a friend, we lost our way, and, thinking this was it, curled up in the slight shadow vestibule formed by the banks of a dried arroyo, conserving ourselves till awakened by the sound of the single propeller and, without waiting for visual confirmation, stood out of the gulch and started to form broad circles in the air with the shirts we'd already taken off.

—With our dad, we heard the crackle of Lamont Cranston announcing, "The Shadow knows," about to abort some foul play or nab some perpetrator. And we wanted to know too, whatever there was to know, even without knowing what this might be.

Less dramatic beneath the sui generis sprawls the universal, submerged somewhere in the collective unconscious. Who didn't skip beside his shadow, marveling at it as an emperor might his lands or a peasant his erection, this view of the augmented self offering up just a whiff of omnipotence? But just when we thought it gave us boundless control, our shadow evaded us, hiding itself inside another or going its own way (priming us early for love?). Like any boy or girl, I chased mine up and down hills and on sun-baked pavement till I came tumbling, breathless, to my knees.

In truth it began for me in a garden, a stolen kiss and hot breath in the ear, a sundial with a gnomon of regal brass, angled amidst peonies and shrubs. I stood tiptoe, arching my neck to catch a glimpse of the face, rimmed with mystery symbols, no number system I knew of. Just behind me stood the girl I'd been told all week was my cousin but learned earlier that day wasn't, it had just been a figure of speech, and this set free the pangs that, resigned to their unrealizability, I'd stifled all week long. Now I could look unflinching into her pale seaweed eyes (brine on the palate), and even study the two faint bumps in her plain white T-shirt, partly shrouded where the shadow fell.

Maybe I already knew what a sundial was, maybe she explained it to me, maybe some adult came along to edify us. Who knows; these things are as lost as her name. I was nine and we were left alone, the two of us, while They toured the mansion with Some Period of Furniture that held some fascination for them, and as I swung around her lips caught mine in the chill of the shadow. Would I ever recover? Is it too transparent that a lifelong love affair (with shadow, not her) begins here? Or simply unfathomable in this age that any love would last a lifetime, even one whose only constant is the peripheral figure?

What an obscure, tenebrous bunch we are. I've been relieved to find I am talking to a bryologist (scholar of mosses and lichens). I shake my head in time with the bluesy lament of the reprographer (connoisseur of copies and copying). I once skipped a return flight to spend the night with a woman who declared herself a pyrologist instead of merely a "chemist that studies fire" (and her brown hair indeed went embery in the dark).

At least the dictionary affirms that these exist. Others, more fledgling, more marginal, persist solely by the curatorial zeal of their adherents. I half pity the neologist (novelty and newness across the board) and the spontanographer (doodles, sketches, and scribbles)—

academia's stooges, her warthogs, creatures who persist because nature is decidedly not beautiful, who operate under some inner need, nuzzling up against anything that doesn't run away screaming.

Here are some tips if you are planning to apply to one of the five degree-conferring graduate programs in umbrology in the United States. Don't make any jokes pertaining to how you've always had a shadow. It's akin to writing you've always had teeth on your dental application—simply beyond the pale.

Second, do your homework. Out of the five programs, two are primarily devoted to shadow theater, leaving three for strictly scientific study. In their defense, one of the theater programs is highly interdisciplinary, and they incorporate scientific principles into what they do. One, though (petrified of getting entangled in another lawsuit, I won't name names), finds science anathema. They seem to think the shadow world ought to be kept as mysterious as possible, as ludicrous and untenable a position as that is in this era. Now—when we can explore the stars, sunspots, and eclipses and shadow images on other worlds, those that asteroids lend one another as they hurtle through space, the six-thousand-mile-thick shadow that Saturn's razor ring casts on the planet's surface; now, when Lew Dorris can sit beside intelligence officials poring over satellite maps of Tora Bora, distinguishing cave from cliff, searching for the slightest hint of human presence—how can they believe such a thing now of all times?

My last word of advice: Don't allude to Punxsutawney Phil or anything related to Groundhog Day, even in jest, anywhere on your application.

It is not what the shadow tells us about the figure but about the ground that ultimately matters.

It's become harder and harder to catch the interest of the undergrads (Intro Umbro). Thank God for video games. With Lew's help I can strip away the shadows from fight scenes to expose how ridiculous and cartoonish their so-called virtual worlds are sans proper shading. And from there I segue right into painting before they can object— first the *Mona Lisa*, so familiar it might as well be a video game, the eyes tracking them as if they're being controlled by some remote joystick. I point out how da Vinci steeps her outfit in shadow, captures the sweep of her hair, dribbles it down her neck, pits shadows at the corners of her cheeks, forcing them to vie with one another, dramatizing the enigma of her emotions.

Next up it's Dolcinaux's untitled work, commonly called *Paripurgferno* (1774), that magisterial reinterpretation of the moment wherein Virgil admits Dante into purgatory. Where Dante strips Virgil of his shadow, leaving his metaphysical status a mystery, Dolcinaux sends it back toward hell, adding the likenesses of the shadows of a terrace and a sphere that aren't in the painting. From notebooks we know that Dolcinaux believed Dante got it wrong, that hellish circles, purgatorial terraces, and paradisal spheres ought to have been combined into one, a sort of folded triptych of translucent panels. He didn't have translucent panels, so he did the best he could, his quarrel with Dante writ large here. If I've done my job right, some students are still awake when we arrive at this.

In my usual spot in the library once, bleary after hours of staring into one book or another, I fell into a trance. It was as if something had pulled some of the ink partway off the page and it was hovering between the paper and my eyes. As I tried to hold it aloft, it struck me that the choice of black as the near-universal color of print was no mere convention, no mere appeasement of the eyes. My epiphany: Printed words were the shadows of referents. Things: Rock. Sand. Onion. Ideas: Carpool. Justice. Maximization. Irrevocability. Paragraphs were composite shadows of the scenarios and subjects they captured: the overwhelming richness and messiness of the world distilled to bare, chiaroscuroed necessity. Sure, imagination, not eyes alone, was required in reconstructing the original. Yet in my carrel at that moment I swore I could see the strand of beach rising off the page, shells strewn everywhere, jagged watermarks and slick seaweed pods, and could feel the onrush of surf, salt spatter, and greedy undertow, and I suspected I'd hit on something nontrivial. Newly awake and trembling with cold and not a little fear, I gathered my belongings and moved quickly past the unsuspecting undergrads, their heads buried in books, and exited. My manic gait mirrored the fervor of the conjecture: If words were shadows, then all fields were umbrology, all knowledge a strain of the umbrological, and all of us of a scholarly bent spend our lives peering at shadows. And what, then, did this suggest about the Bible and the Koran and the access they might offer to the sacred? In the distance were evergreens with what little snow they hadn't yet shed and the more spindly, deciduous trees with their intricate interweavings, neuronal branchings. I saw the agriculture complex with its various roofs covered with swatches of snow, then the purple bruise of a cloud bank unfurling across the sky, then the orange glow like something from another world, and then I tried to see before me a page, *the* page, with these words upon it. As I neared the parking lot, its blue signs with white lettering felt discordant, and I fell in among a crowd arriving for or leaving a game. There was a honk and someone leaned out of a car and yelled, "Ursula's not the whore, *I* am!" and everyone in earshot erupted in laughter. At once my insight shriveled into preposterousness like a balloon surrendering, and I felt ridiculous, all the more so as I too was laughing along. I haven't returned to that idea since; maybe someday.

There was a woman once, though. A couple of flings but only one, really (I don't count my sundial maiden). Valerie stayed a while—months. She got me to talk about things I never had, try things, foods—Indian, Tibetan, Moroccan—whose existence I'd had only a vague awareness of before. She took me out to a ball game, prodding me every few hitters with little quizzes about what had just happened. At museums she'd take my shoulders and gently pull me away from the canvas, forcing me to take in paintings at a sweeping glance and describe how they made me feel. She made me carry her bags, restock her lip balm, sniff her slippers, all of which I have to admit I enjoyed. Together we salvaged a dog, Saskia, from the ASPCA, gave her a home, and even cured her of the habit of peeing at the slightest jarring sound.

Val didn't even mind my endless discoursing about shadows, though she told me once she preferred rainy days because on them I looked at her more directly. She talked about us relocating to Seattle. Maybe there I could shed my strange "wandering eye." She only half believed me when I insisted it was shadows I was watching askance instead of other women. Somehow my gaze would be pulled in the direction of the most stunning or scantily clad (so she claimed—I hadn't noticed), and later that evening she'd be sobbing or, as the months went on, brooding in ruffled distraction.

Once, watching her apply mascara, I pointed out that makeup was nothing more than the insinuation of shadows onto the face to feign

303

the signs of youth. I said this as I might have to my undergrads; the type of assertion they'd record dutifully, and which every so often incited them to lively discussion and intellectual sparring, although afterward I have suspected that I may have meant to hurt her for some reason. At the time her brushstrokes held steady. But a day later, she announced that nothing—no therapy, no medication, no aphrodisiac, no self-help book, no spontaneous trip—could bridge the gulf that lay between us.

Rasmussen, president of the university, has staked out Intro Umbro and pulls me into an empty adjoining room after I dismiss them, shutting the door behind him. He doesn't bother flipping on the light. "Glenn," he says, appearing troubled, maybe slightly haggard. "I wanted to feel you out on this one. What's the mood? What is it going to take today with Lew?"

"Your guess is as good as mine," I shrug. "He has a lawyer. We're no longer communicating directly."

"I see." He mulls this over. "How can I sweeten the pot." It is more statement than question. I'm reminded anew of how unctuous I've always found him. Never a glimmer of interest in our departmental offerings, goings-on. Quick to pardon a plagiarist whose parents are paying in full. "Look," he continues, "I want to be fair to him, and fair to the university."

"Of course."

"There's one more thing, Glenn." His voice falls to a hush, and I can hear the din of students milling about between classes. "I've had some people contact me. Homeland Security. This is in the strictest of confidence. Obviously, this algorithm is, you know, really something."

"I know about as much as you."

"I don't know whether to mention Homeland Security today. I don't want to scare anyone."

Oh but you do. "That's entirely your call."

"Maybe I'll hold it in reserve." I can't make out his eyes in the dim light, can't discern whether he is waiting for some kind of response.

My feelings about Book Seven of Plato's *Republic* are likely slightly more virulent than even the average umbrologist's.

"Motherfucking Plato," I was telling Lew Dorris one May. My best students were graduating and going on to Nantucket and New York, one to be an architect for the summer *hauts,* the other to serve as a loading-dock clerk. It was depressing. "Fuck motherfucking Plato. Far as I'm concerned he can take it gangbang style from Socrates, Glaucon, and Adeimantus one-two-three."

Lew was a fiendish player of darts. We'd completed a round or two, and Lew's feather shadows were clustering around the bull's-eye, forming a penumbra, where mine were lost in floorboards and flopping miserably off a vintage Guinness pelican beak.

"Ease up, Glenn," is what he was saying. "Get one near the board."

"No, but I mean . . . ," I stammered. "Take Plato out of the picture, look at what we get. Respectability, Lew, that's what we get. The respect we got coming. Galileo, motherfucker," I said. "Gali*l*eo knew the value of a shadow."

Each time I squeezed a dart before the furrows I could feel in my brow, he'd shrink back, watching people in the vicinity nervously. "Glenn," he said. "If it isn't Plato it's someone else. People aren't made to love shadows. It's that simple."

"Screw that," I said. "We *are* made to love them. Hello? Three-dimensional vision?" Hearing myself saying it, I felt foolish: I'm going to remind *Lew Dorris* about 3D vision.

"Glenny," he said. "It's the end of the semester. Take some time off. Go to Orlando."

I knew Dorris was speaking figuratively—he knew I had neither a family nor a desire to cavort with giant cartoon replicas. For a moment it crossed my mind that roller-coaster shadow in Florida sun could be manna, the theme park itself a sort of Rorschach of America.

"Lemme ask you something, Lew," I said. "Thought experiment. Lessay you can go back in time and ya have the chance t'ssassinate Plato. You're alone with him, no one's looking. This is before he writes Book Seven, OK?" I felt myself growing more lucid in the act of speaking. In ten minutes I'd be puking in the alley behind the bar. "Do you do it?"

"Glenn." He shook his head.

"It's a hypothetical," I said. "Critical thinking, just like we ask our students, right? All of Western philosophy a footnote to Plato. Versus giving shadows an outside shot at r-e-s-p-c-e-t."

"You're drunker than you think you are," said Lew.

*

But, you say, Plato's Myth of the Cave is the stuff of academicians only, any prejudices that it instills in us merely academic ones. You say there is no abiding denigration of shadows in our society, subconscious or otherwise. I, however, know otherwise, having felt the sting of discrimination firsthand. Most memorably at a ski slope this past winter, a gleaming December day, ideal conditions for shadow watching. By ideal (sorry, Plato, I'm taking that word), I don't mean only from a weather standpoint; consider the slope itself, its perpetual careenings, poles and skis jutting against a bright scrim of snow. Nothing surpasses a city street in summer with its buildings, awnings, pedestrians cane bearing and non, cyclists with mesh baskets and spokes, dogs tugging on leashes, three-card-monte tables evaporating as quickly as they were thrown together, shoulder-strapped bags, cradled melons. But still.

I was out on the slope, staring, admittedly. Had I been a sociolinguist or a family systems therapist, I might have holed up in the lodge, pretending to read a book and taking in conversation all around me. You might think that after twenty years of study I'd grow weary of shadow watching—*They're all alike*, are they not? Yet I'm certain that only now, after these decades, have they begun to yield up their secrets to me.

The ski patrol approached me, two directly, one hanging back, American flags sewn onto their shoulders. "Hey, buddy," one said.

"Yes, sir."

"How are you today, sir?"

"Fine, just fine."

"We've had some people saying you've been here in this spot quite a while. Doin' a whole lot of looking."

"Yes, that's right."

"You, ummm, waiting for somebody? Planning on skiing today, or got kids on the slopes?"

I looked down at an absence of skis. The outlines of my interrogators towered on the heavily trodden snow, stretching till they struck the roofline of the lodge. Mine merged with theirs.

"I'm an umbrologist," I chanced.

"What's 'at you say?"

I started to give the usual explanation.

"That doesn't sound like a real thing. Is that a real thing?" he asked one of his compadres, who shrugged and grunted. "Well, look, irregardless, this here's a family recreation spot. So I suggest you maybe find yourself an alternative viewing location." Then after a moment, "Sir, can you look at me now, in the eye?"

I let my eye climb up his torso slowly, nodding. He went on, "We've had some unsavory characters here recently, if you know what I mean, so we need to know that you're here to ski or with someone that's skiing or you're gonna have to move along."

Skia—Greek for shadow. "Have you read Plato's *Republic*, Book Seven?"

His partner stepped in. "Sir, we're not gonna stand here and be mocked. This is a ski resort."

"I was under the impression it was a mountain."

"I'm gonna give him . . . I'm gonna give you one more chance to walk to your car."

As they escorted me, flanking me with the radio-bearing one behind, I didn't resist, and it occurred to me that much of this could have been avoided had I simply invented, say, that I was blind.

The morning Edmund informed me that next semester he was going to work with Lew rather than with me, I'd been daydreaming and had almost rammed into a stopped car that was waiting for some animal to cross. I'd managed to slam on the brakes, and my pulse was still pounding when I arrived at the office. Edmund slipped his news, then, into this strange pocket of relief.

"Well." I'd sucked in my breath, disappointment lodging somewhere down in the region of my diaphragm. "That's fantastic. And all the Greek you've been learning—you're simply going to forget it?"

"Never!" he said in mock horror. His tone pivoted, though. "It does make sense, though, doesn't it? You support the move?"

It did. It shouldn't have arrived as a shock. The students, the ones who wind up majors or minors, I'm their first love, ushering them into the field. I do a little bit of everything in Intro, an exotic uncle with a seemingly bottomless bag of novelties, a living-room vaudeville act. Once they've had a taste of the more advanced classes, though, steeped in one or another subfield, they *specialize*. Mostly they move on, cordial to a fault— I get an occasional e-mail, or they drop in to tell me about their thesis or gripe about how Abelard holds their papers hostage.

But I couldn't believe Edmund was sitting in my office telling me this; he'd practically lived there these past two years. As my research assistant, he had access to hundreds of pages that, thankfully, no one else will ever see. But he did more than track down references—he filled the margins with comments, netting fresh references from the Sargasso of mediocre scholarship. He'd spent hours in the scuffed, stained armchair, its foamy entrails pouring out as we talked about Pliny and Rembrandt and impossible objects and life too, his ups and downs with his girlfriend, his mother's depression.

It was little wonder he was destined to go with Lew.

The meeting feels like a courtroom except without any designation of who's on what side. Empty chairs flank me. Rasmussen presides in gray vestments, sport coat and striped shirt and white tie with what look like spouting little blue whales. Lew sprawls, too-long legs jutting awkwardly till they're practically in the center of the room, Vadrais on one side and Edmund on the other, and then there's Amos Duffy from Mathematics, and Sue Gessen, a dean with whom he's chummy, and I wave to her. Next to them are trustees I only know from meetings like this one—though there's not been one exactly like this one. Next is Kuperman and, sitting right next to him, Dahlia. The president looks jovial, or looks as if he's straining toward some Platonic form of joviality, and everyone else appears overly severe. Even Kuperman; I didn't know he had it in him.

Rasmussen starts things off with a toothy smile. "We're gathered because we understand that you, Professor Dorris, have developed an idea here at the university that just might benefit all of us. So, essentially, seeing ourselves as pioneers of the twenty-first century, looking to ride out these tough times, we'd like to know how we can help you and help ourselves and . . . help our students."

His voice drones on and I pull some wasabi peas out of the bag, the few that remain, for alertness. Then I am drawn to tug and pull at my eyelid with my nonwasabi hand. This makes his image double and appear to lean like some aspect of him is bowing or trying to get out, and the tilted version exhibits a deference so foreign to his character that I can't help but find it amusing. I send him back and forth like this. The transformation continues, the head expanding and reshaping itself, tendrils coiling outward till he's no longer a balding bureaucrat but a sort of shadow puppet-villain in a demonic headdress, hinged at the joints, and I start to hear strains of gamelan as he makes his false-friendly pitch. A demon-king.

Vadrais stands, now also swinging at hinges, stiffly made. "Mr. Dorris has developed certain ideas and, in particular, an algorithm that does promise to be lucrative. However, the terms of the offer you have made him are not sufficient to persuade him to authorize the school to . . ."

And then things start getting ugly. The demon-king bristles. Pulling back, he increases in size till he towers over the entire room, a grim Gargantua. I think then that he might windmill his arms or soar through the air or double over into an elephant and invite the trustees to mount him and ride on his back into battle. His accusations fly like a downward volley of arrows at Vadrais and Lew, some sticking in the wall, some in the table, some hanging, tips embedded in Vadrais's clipboard. I hear the words "homeland" and "security" and murmurs sweep like electric current through the room. Vadrais comes to his feet, wielding his hand like a scimitar and throwing out countercharges—"coercion" and "neglect" and "red tape" off his lips like throwing stars. Again and again they come at each other, sometimes landing a clear hit, at others leaving us to guess from thrust velocity and the ensuing shudder. My hand is no longer on my eyelid; things just look this way.

A trustee jumps into the fray. "Let me be clear about this." He reads off a sheaf of papers. "There were research grants filed through the school? There was a sabbatical, no? In two thousand and . . ."

At some point I realize that it's me he's addressing, and I nod, since what he says is beyond dispute.

Now the demon-king whirls to address me. I almost want him to appear paper thin, as shadow puppets do in the instant they are reversing direction, the instant when the illusion fails. "My understanding is that the department is coming up for review, along with every other expense on campus. Times are tough. We think umbrology would be much more likely to get funding if, as is the case here, tangible benefits could be pointed to."

Vadrais jumps in. "For the record, we don't think that the university necessarily has Lew's best interest at heart."

The demon-king nods. "Maybe Glenn can speak to the integrity of the school. He's been here longer than . . ." He looks around. "Well, let's just say he's an institution at this institution." He chuckles.

The whole room is watching me and waiting. I see Kuperman, Dahlia, jobs hanging in the balance. Dahlia's, at least. But before I can answer, Vadrais jumps in again. "Lew's researched this, thanks in part to a very talented student of his who has developed a plan for a start-up." He doesn't gesture to Edmund, but we all know who he means. "Dr. Dorris believes the private sector is where he can make what he is rightfully entitled to. He has interested investors."

309

For some reason my gaze is drawn to Kuperman, and I catch the slight smile percolating over his face, the knowing glance he shoots Dahlia, and know exactly whose connections were used to get these investors. The expression is so subtle it would be hard to convey in shadow theater, exactly the sort of thing that makes it an art.

The look changes nothing. What I say is exactly what I would've said anyway. "Dr. Rasmussen, I'm afraid I agree with Mr. Vadrais. I don't think it is very likely that the school has Lew's best interests in mind."

Afterward, there is the brief chaos that ensues when a jury pronounces guilt or innocence, the tumble on one side or another of the high wire of fate. Formalities are discussed, the school not abnegating its pro forma right to sue, to which Mr. Vadrais only says, "Of course." And then order returns and we are academics who will sit together at graduation in a matter of weeks. In the hallway, Lew comes up to me, shakes my hand, and thanks me. "Glad you understand, Glenn," he says, adding, "You always supported me." Edmund is nowhere to be found.

Later that week, I stand in my driveway watching a total lunar eclipse, one of the most dramatic instances of shadow imaginable. Most shadows happen in black and white. We live in a chromatic world; umbrologists can't compete. If shadows came in a lavish array, if they suddenly took on their casters' hues, I might be a rock star (think Strato-). As it is, I'm more like an *erhu* plucker from northern China, consoling myself with chilly, two-stringed beauty. Not that I would choose to go electric—I'm merely stating a fact about the world.

And another: On occasion shadows do flirt with color, this being one. Because of how the moon moves through earth's shadow, coupled with the light-filtering effects of earth's atmosphere, the moon appears as bloodred as Mars. The cold metal of my car's hood yields a bit as I lie back. I want to shout through the neighborhood, pound on doors—rouse the mesmerized viewers of *Lost* (are they any *less* lost than the characters on the show?) and the compulsive checkers of e-mail.

I want to share it with someone, but the street is silent. Others, out there beyond my block, must be watching this too, but I can't think of anyone. For a moment I consider calling one of my former students—there are over a thousand, with one or two who stand apart, who might pick up warmly, wish to talk about things other than the eclipse, inquire how I am and ask after Saskia. I might take poetic license, borrowing the stories of some of my more illustrious colleagues about consulting with the designers of the game *Goad* ("will make *Doom* look like *Ms. Pac-man*"), about extra-tight security clearance while decoding maps, sifting for the anomalies whose discovery could forestall disaster. Something about this incarnation of the moon makes the truth feel malleable, as if it can be suspended without altering its fundamental features.

But, then, I think, why not just be blunt—the department's on the brink of oblivion, and a tinge of black mold sits on my shoes from earlier in the week. I glance at it; in this earth-fed moonlight it is nearly impossible to resist finding a pattern there, something that belongs and will persist long after I slip them off and head upstairs.

Hard Objects Found in People
Martine Bellen

Jailbirds in striped jumpsuits that can't be seen through bars
    Angry prisoners known to drag around balls and cat bells

        Hungry ghost prisoners
        Turrets occupied by armed prison guards
                Smoking hot terrine with four and twenty blackbirds

      [breath of bird]
The curve of his chest
Pressing against blades of grass to carve the nest

When a dreamer considers tenderness
           Wears his demeanor like a bulletproof vest
Considers psychoanalysis
When a dreamer dreams a wren considering a nest egg, annuities

      When the dreamer and wren dream of transporting the telepathic girl /

Saint Anthony, patron saint of lost items (girls, birds, prisoners)
Saint Adrian of butchers, of arms dealers and prison guards

When Saint Anthony and Saint Adrian met at a
confession convention at Santa Barbara's, they were
magnetically pulled into each other's booths and
naturally chose one another when it came time to
reveal their hearts.

Space of a camera Time of a camera

The *vaulted chamber* of prison extended to our chats
                    In our hearts, more gothic chambers

          A canopied forest protected
          His mind from high winds
          If he weren't dreaming he'd be flying

Even love requires immigration officers. Expiration dates. Identification
after   death.
I'm surprised at how completely we can disappear.
I'm surprised at how we can't *completely* disappear.
Even though we were insignificant when alive. Even though we spent
our   lives in prison.

Even love requires irrigation, irritations

The telepathic girl—a configuration that participates from without /
within   form
          With isolate and transcendent
                         Transparent though with no parent
          Unconscious data, too
                Withdrawn

What she/I/we think/don't >that which we know
                         no notion

The cat broke out of prison,
               Bonelessly slipped into *invisible times*. Disquietly appeared
               (no negation without sense)

313

Why set up surveillance cameras? Those presence chambers that catch
    Clips of meaningless winged felines chasing contrail birds
    Building nests in the eaves of prisons—parallel lives that fade
    From focus to focus. Liquid dreams of cats.
                       Tell me who haunts you

Time doesn't move (has no hands, no legs, surely no heart)
                        But is the median out of which we float

Halls encircled by trees
Hells
Rêves

The Gratitude Holiday parade included a giant Dora
the Explorer helium balloon and a prison float. The
inmates, dressed in jumpsuits, catcalled our guards
and executioners.

Cameras flashed. Smiles.

"Happy Gratitude" was hollered at the top of their lungs as inmates
jumped   in unison

Birds in V formation hovered above veiled revolutionaries dressed as saints

The city's dream face, its stronghold and revolving doors

Two Poems

Ann Lauterbach

A CONTINUE, OR ENTRY

1.

Where next? Oblique cost of the *not yet.*
Strange flotation of the stampede, resembling play.
The octagonal stop, characteristic, time *is* place.
Intentional rupture of the flow.
Play coming upon belief, instruments, kin.
Kindred bricks or blocks, the hallucinating margin.
Then: double vision, a skill contained by doing.
A refusal to embed that into this, so that this perishes.
A spread or insistence, as in a flood.
A local extremity, a wall.
Extent and its delimiting edge.
Elaboration sprouting form, its voraciousness.

2.

What next? Unique cruelty of the undone.
Rook rhymes with *book, crow* with *toe.*
Also *hook.* Also *know.*
To countermand restlessness, settle on fact
as it seeks to order a well-worn shoe, two
shoes, a pair of old shoes. And yet
the sun lays claim to
natural dyes, rifts through the glow-torn
phenomena where I see
the metonymic rituals of spring
expose a mournful goddess in her crypt.
Hook rhymes with *crook, know* with *foe.*

3.

Strange flotation of the stampede, resembling play.
Rumble, blaspheme, crooked under the gun.
Too much is previous. Even the game,
about to start, will vanish
with its partner, day. Reach out your spoon
for another portion; arch your neck.
Everything is in profile toward evening.
If, on behalf of a last chance, you move
Yours sincerely into the winning slot, then
cherries, stars, and the quick weave of your
hair into braids: all this shall be yours.
These are lessons of chance. They are not plans.

4.

The octagonal stop is my master.
I was thinking of roaming out of range
to where a sidelong pillar of light
rides the river sky. Wow! If I turn away
toward an unmarked grave
(here find the stop where the real is done)
will you believe if I say
something gains on our aspiration, our embrace?
Branches against cloud. Fence against road.
Above the shade, the elastic flirtation of a web.
Words in another room, if the radio were on.
These are lessons in mobility. They are not fate.

5.

Intentional rupture of the flow,
blurry, as in a Vermeer. You, who may
not have seen such reproductions of the same,
missed the optical illusion which,
as it happens, is rhetoric at its best.
He saw how materials collapse
a desire for reality's articulated shield.
The Dutch love the small, domestic stage.
I love the huge impertinence

of an unresembling fact. Look!
A deep pink developing above, there,
in the west! It cannot be saved.

6.

Play touches belief, sorts out, finding kin.
Could be time to count. *Ten, five, three*
as if pointing toward severance,
the throw of the dice.
Looking back, there seems to have been a hive
or bank in which things were kept,
a hoard or list or will. In the philosopher's tale,
there are bitter claims at stake;
in the great attic, increasing remorse.
Dearest, I visited your room after you
were gone and found the
and the the and the the and the.

7.

Kindred plays or blocks, the hallucinating
margin above mementos of—
a supplemental neuter deletes
some revenant's luck. Her.
I dream the awkward dream. I disallow.
On the rug, with paint and trowel,
under stones and ash and the rude
vocabulary of the frost, grammar
disobeys its rules. The western crawl space.
Air and earth aglitter, collide.
Something adds, something subtracts.
How near is the thing that counts, what is it called?

THE TRANSLATOR'S DILEMMA

As if to foretell an ordinary mission, with fewer words.
With fewer, more ordinary, words.
Words of one syllable, for example.

For example: step, or sleeve.
These are two favorites, among many.
Many can be found if you look closely.

But even if I look closely, surely a word is not
Necessarily here, in the foreground.
I see an edge of a paper, I see orange, I see ear.

I see words and I see things. An old story,
Nothing to foretell in the ordinary mission.
I see "her winter," and I see "I am merely

A tourist here." Are these issues of
Translation, the barriers of translation?
I see John and an open book, open to a day

In August. I am feeling defeated
Among these sights, as if I will never find
Either sleeve or step. These ordinary

And pleasurable words, attached to
Ordinary and pleasurable things, as if
To announce them I am

Announcing certain criteria. The step, the sleeve,
How they invite hovering over and within
Our necessities: a coat, a stair.

But I am merely a tourist here, deaf to light.
What is this *wreath?* What is this *thing?*
Nothing to foretell the ordinary, its leap across.

In Search of the Body
Robert Coover

WHAT YOU'D BEEN looking for, ever since it was found down in the docklands, then disappeared, was the widow's body. No clues. It was gone like it never was. You sometimes picked up a tip in Loui's Lounge, so you stopped in there, chased off the wimp who was sitting on your customary stool, and ordered up a double on the rocks, ice being potable in this hole. You needed one. Things were going badly. Your client dead, her body missing, your pal Fingers run down, your own health in constant jeopardy. Not to mention what would have been a broken heart if you had one to break. Joe the bartender, wearing a poker face, greeted you as he would a stranger, which probably meant something was up. Flame was in the middle of a song about a brutal lover called the Hammer (there were rhymes like wham her, jam her, slam her, and goddamn her), who could be lethal (. . . *I know you think you're the big cheese, but, baby, don't kill me, please,* she sings), and you expected her to drop over after her number, but before that a big-fisted suit sat down on the stool beside you and offered to buy you a drink and you realized things were not as you thought. I've got one, you said. Have another, he said and signaled the bartender. Beware of geeks bearing gifts, you said, and pulled your glass back. Suit yourself, he said with a shrug and tapped his own glass for a refill. Just trying to have a friendly conversation, mac. What about? You're looking for a body, he said. Yeah? Stop looking. The Hammer is ramming: *It's just a little trick,* Flame sings, *but it's got a mean kick.* . . . You could see that the suit had a gat pointed at you from his jacket pocket. You'd be dead before you reached your own. You set your glass back on the bar and shrugged at Joe. If you insist, you said dryly.

Before Joe could pour, the song ended and Flame came over and interposed herself between the two of you. Move your ass, buster. I want to converse with my lover here. Joe was also coldly staring him down. The suit scowled but took his hand out of his pocket and slipped back into the shadows. Flame kissed you, running her tongue along your teeth as if checking to see if the ones that remain were all still there, then nibbled at your ear, pressing up between your legs. Looks like you're staying here tonight, lover, she whispered. Her wild-animal aroma was dizzying. Who does that bozo work for? you asked, stroking Flame's silky backside. You know, she said. Over her shoulder you could see Loui's bouncers disarm the suit and toss him. Why did you come here tonight, Phil? After what happened to Fingers, you must've known there'd be trouble. They know you were at the Shed last night. I got a note, sweetheart. I thought it was from you. If I want you here, baby, I don't have to write a note. I just send out vibes. This was true. You often turn up here on what you call intuition and find her waiting for you, her desire like a magnet. Not for nothing does she call her lovers moths.

⊙

The next day you launched the search in earnest, starting with a return to Big Mame's ice cream parlor. Fingers sent you here and you asked Big Mame why. She just shook her jowls and went about her business. She had one of those classic mudbucket faces, sullen and rumpled and full of sorrow, the kind that was very expressive but said nothing.

Fingers is dead, Mame.

No blame on me, Mister Bad Luck.

There's a dame who's dead too. A widow. Why are people trying to stop me from looking for her remains?

Can't say. What's it to you anyhow? You do the dirty with this lady?

I don't even know what she looks like.

So how you gonna know it's her if you find her?

I'll know.

But it was true. How would you know? By her legs? Legs aren't faces with eyes and noses. Good thing too. It would be a mess to have faces down there. No, what you were in love with was something less visible: a voice, a manner, poise. Style. A counter to your cluttered and seedy life. Would that be recognizable in a dead body? Mame only folded her arms over her big breasts and stared dully at you when you asked her questions. Fingers always has a hot butterscotch sundae in here, and you thought to have one in his memory, but your favorite is a five-layer parfait she makes, topped with cherry sauce, whipped cream, and rum raisins, and you had one of those before hitting the streets again.

⊙

For a while, you were literally looking everywhere, as though the widow's corpse might be hidden under a carpet or behind the door. In flophouses, movie theaters, beer halls, public toilets, penny arcades, massage parlors, gambling dens, hock shops, gyms, and boxing arenas. You checked in with your contacts among the city's dealers, strippers and street vendors, numbers runners, hoods and hookers, pimps, plastic surgeons, pickpockets, addicts, medics and ambulance drivers, counterfeiters, cops and con artists. There were vague rumors, they wanted to help, eager for your coin, but you got nothing you could call a real lead. A one-armed taxi driver said he picked up a woman dressed in black who had to be lifted into his hack by the two gorillas she was with and taken to a fancy block near the harbor, but added that she snored like a horse the whole way, so that was probably not who you were looking for. A newspaper vendor outside the bus station who had lost his nose in the last war and had to tape his thick glasses to his temples told you he'd seen a fat guy shoving a duffel bag that might have held a body into one of the baggage lockers. You weren't sure how he could see anything through his thick ink-smudged lenses, but coughed up the better part of Blanche's allowance to get the station manager to open all the lockers within the vendor's view. There was actually a duffel bag in one of them. It was full of candy bars, jawbreakers, bubblegum, all-day suckers, and children's underwear. You'd just helped solve some crimes you'd never get credit for, might now even be accused of, but you hadn't come closer to finding the dead widow.

At the morgue, you asked the Creep to see all the female stiffs and made him pull them out just far enough that you could look at the legs, more in blind hope than with any conviction you'd see anything you recognized, having to put up all the while with the Creep's evil sniggering. The widow was always covered up except for her legs, which were all you knew her by. I have some other pretty people here if there's something particular you want, he whispered, and you popped him one, right on the honker, flattening it to a bloody splatter in the middle of his ugly bug-eyed face. Made you feel better, the way hitting out always does, even if it's completely senseless. You don't understand this need for rough stuff. It's just something you have to do from time to time to tell the world what you think of it. Your secretary, Blanche, is always telling you to grow up and stop hitting people, but you can't help it, your fists have a mind of their own, you go on doing it. You might say it's who you are, but you don't know who the fuck you are. Just a dumb dick, sometimes full of aimless rage. After you slapped the Creep around a bit more, he admitted he'd heard about a body floating around with a price tag on it, but he didn't know where it was. What do you mean, floating? I don't know, he sniveled, lapping at the blood on his upper lip. That's what I heard. You don't want me to hit you again, do you, Creep? He rolled his pop eyes up at you and grinned with swollen lips, his nose streaming. Yes, please. You left the sick sonuvabitch and stepped out into the night.

Where it was raining again. Lightly, just enough to scatter glittery reflections on the street and to drive most pedestrians inside, making the streets seem like a damp, empty stage with sinister events brewing in the darkened wings. You pulled your fedora down over your eyes, doggedly continuing your search, stopping in at the aquarium, casino, the Chinese theater. On the third floor of a cheap hotel in the theater district, a silhouetted woman was undressing behind a drawn blind. The kind of movie showing nightly all across town. The movie you're in. Chasing shadows. You paused to look into a backstreet watch-repair shop window. Old sleuth's habit of using a window as a mirror to see if anyone's following you. There was. Fat Agnes. Across the street. You spun around to confront him: not there. Just a blinking neon light advertising McGinty's Pool Hall. You turned back to the window to check: Yes, that's all it was. You were on edge. Seeing things. What you saw now through the curtain of rain dripping off your hat brim was your own reflection, Philip M. Noir, private investigator, staring back at you with rain-curtained eyes, cigarette glowing at the lips, the multitudinous faces of time ticking away in the shadowy background. What are you doing out here, you dumb fuck, you asked it, it asked you, the lit cigarette bobbing as if scribbling out your question. You don't love the widow, alive or dead. That's bullshit. You don't love anyone, wouldn't know what to do if you did. This is what you love. The gumshoe game. Played alone on dark, wet streets to the tune of the swell and fade of car horns, sirens, the sounds of breaking glass, cries in the street, the percussive punctuation of gunshots and shouted obscenities. You nodded and your reflection nodded. You love your own bitter misery, your knotted depression. In short, you're a fucking romantic, Noir, as Joe the bartender likes to say. A disease you medicate with booze, needing a dose now. The widow knew how to get under your skin.

Denial. Frustration. Deception. Depravity. You eat it up.

Cheered by all this heavy thinking, you crossed over to McGinty's, where you found Cueball alone at a table, peering down the length of his cue the way he used to peer down rifle barrels, his eyes so close together they seemed almost to join at the bridge of his sharp, narrow nose, crossing into each other as they took aim. He wasn't always Cueball. He was once a famous hit man named Kubinsky, but he changed his name while doing time when nature changed his hair style, leaving him with a shiny white dome like a wigless manikin. About as much emotion in him too. Give him a pistol, he'd somehow shoot himself in the elbow, but put a rifle in his hands and the flies on the wall ducked and shielded their eye facets. No telling how many poor suckers he'd iced before his prison vocational retraining. When he was still Kubinsky and had hair, it was said he worked on occasion for Mister Big and you asked him what he knew about the man. You were convinced that the elusive Big had something to do with the killing of the widow and probably the disappearance of the body too, in spite of what Blanche said. Yeah, I done some jobs for him, I think they were for him, Cueball said, potting three balls with one stroke, but I never seen him. There was a bunch of guys running around town saying they was Mister Big, but none of them really was, none I met. He was quietly clearing the table on his own, there being few who dared challenge him. Cueball, like most professional killers, was a loner. No male friends and, when in need, he hung out mostly with working girls, partnered up with none of them. Except one.

⊙

You know the story because Kubinsky hired you to find and tail the girl. In Kubinsky's case it wasn't just the fee. He was a scary client and refusing him in those days was a kind of suicide. The chick was a dishy but simple taxi dancer named Dolly, who confused the guys she danced with by falling passionately in and out of love with each of them from dance to dance, resulting in a lot of consequential mayhem between suitors. Kubinsky was not a dancer, he literally had two left feet, the little toe on his flat, archless right bigger than the big; this was not how they met. He was hired by a small-time racketeer named Marko, one of her baffled lovers, to kill her. Marko was instructed to walk her out onto the street for a smoke between dances and he could have the pleasure of watching her drop at his feet. When Kubinsky got her in his sights, however, he was for the first time in his life utterly and hopelessly smitten. He was not confused. He knew exactly what he wanted. It was Marko took the hit just as he was fitting the fag he'd lit from his own into Dolly's lips, a cruel, expectant smirk on his mug.

This ruthless, cold-blooded torpedo stunned by love was a sight to see. You'd only heard about lovers drooling. Kubinsky drooled. He panted. His eyes lost focus, the pupils floating haphazardly away from the bridge of his nose. His stony white face was puffy and flushed. He stumbled when he walked, bumped into things. He wept, he snuffled, he dribbled at the crotch. You witnessed this transformation because he turned up at your office one morning, offering you a bag of money and lifetime impunity from a bump-off if you would find the missing Dolly for him and tell him what she was doing. After knocking off Marko, he'd put the rush on her immediately, walking onto the dance floor and shoving her current partner aside, which naturally impressed her, but since he was no dancer, it was not easy for Dolly to love him, open to the general idea though she always was. He'd bought up every dance night after night and did his best to learn the two-step, and finally she did seem to fall for him, enough anyway to go on a two-step tour of several exotic cities with him until the money ran out and Kubinsky had to come back and take on more contracts to pay for his love life.

The cop who had been assigned the Marko murder case, however, was waiting for her. He had figured out that to get what he wanted from her it was best if she was in love with him, which simply meant dancing with her. He booked one entire night when Kubinsky was out working and took her home with him, dancing all the way. Or, rather, as you soon learned, to a rented room across town. After a couple of days, his wife reported him missing. Probably he'd forgotten what it was he'd wanted to know. You submitted your report. Kubinsky returned, asked for all copies, plus negatives of the damning photos and your notebooks. His eyes were crowding the bridge of his nose once more, though redder than usual. The pallor was back. His rifle case was in hand. He seemed to be a doing a melancholic little two-step there in the doorway. He said he planned to eat the barrel of his rifle, but first he had some business to attend to. Crossing Kubinsky could be lethal, but you'd had something going with Dolly for a dance or two yourself, and wanted to know she was still there for a dime. Besides, Kubinsky was a man of his word; you figured he'd honor his warranty. You tipped the cops.

Kubinsky was nabbed before the killing, which no doubt embittered him, but it saved him from the chair. The cop changed his name and disappeared. So did Dolly. Maybe they're dancing together yet. Did Cueball né Kubinsky ever figure out who ratted on him? Maybe. But prison transformed him. Maybe it was the saltpeter in his diet. Most likely it was his new obsession. Without a rifle at hand, he picked up a cue stick in the prison rec room and the rest is poolhall history.

⊙

Cueball had a straight shot on the six ball into the corner, but he chose instead to go for a double bank, clipping the six from behind the eight just enough to send it skidding into the same corner, the cueball continuing up the table and nudging the seven ball into a side pocket. You wondered if he ever attempted any ricochet hits that way. Two for the price of one. I heard about a floating body, Cuby. You hear anything?

Word's getting around you're shit luck on a smelly fork, Noir.

That scare you, Cuby?

He shrugged, chalking up. It'll cost you.

Here's what I got. You emptied out your pockets onto the green nap.

Down at the docks, he said. Pier Four. Somebody's boat. Won't come cheap. Better reload before you go down there.

⊙

No time to waste. Squeezing your late lamented ex-client's webby black veil in your pocket as though to wring knowing itself from it, you headed straight for the fogged-in docklands and Pier Four. Your pockets were empty except for the widow's veil and note, but you were holstered up with other tools of the trade. Marketing corpses was still illegal, far as you knew; you figured you could just lay claim to it, at gunpoint if necessary, throw it over your shoulder and tote it away. It was a dark, damp night, the sort you're most at home in, with a thick, coiling fog that concealed movement and allowed only occasional glimpses of wet brick, swaying yellow lamps, occasional gray shadowy figures emerging out of and disappearing into the mist. Such fleeting glimpses were like the sudden brief insights that cut through the fog of a case, and you were on the alert for anything that might help you solve the mystery of your client the widow's life and death and her hold on you. You were trying to fit the bits together, but they were invisible bits—it was like trying to work a jigsaw puzzle without the pieces. As you drew nearer to the piers, warning signs appeared saying WATCH YOUR STEP and DANGER—HIGH VOLTAGE, and it was as though they were posted there for you. Things Blanche might say. You could hear water slapping softly against something. The honk of unseen gulls. Must be close. But which was Pier Four? No idea. You heard heavy footfalls behind you and ducked behind a small white fishbait hut with shutters on the windows, a ramp at the door, a box outside with the sign: ICE. Which you read as: *freeze!* A burly mug in polished dogs stomped by, head down, muttering to himself. Big guy with big mitts. On a hunch, you let him pass, then stepped out into the fog and followed him. More by ear than eye.

At the water's edge, you passed huge coils of black cable on massive bobbins like giant spools of thread, beached buoys and floats, old concrete gas tanks standing together like benumbed sentries, wreathed by wisps of fog as if they were smoking (you could have used one). You proceeded warily, stopping whenever the steps stopped. They backtracked sometimes, suggesting the guy you were following didn't know where he was going either. Or maybe he had heard you behind him and was checking or else was just pacing. Forced you to flatten yourself against shed walls from time to time. Then their sound changed. They were walking on wood, growing fainter. Then they stopped. You crept forward, found the wooden pier, stepped out on it stealthily. Foghorns in the distance. The squawking gulls. Buoy bells. The black water lapping. Otherwise a thick, misty silence. If the guy knew you were there, he could be on you before you could see him. Blackness at first, but then a hollow glow ahead, which eventually revealed itself as a ghostly white yacht, rearing up in the fog. There was something nightmarish about it, but you didn't hesitate. You boarded it, .22 in hand.

Was there someone else on the yacht? There was. Through a small window, you could see a light moving about down in the main cabin. Probably that tough you were tailing. The light was picking out leather sofas, teak tables and cabinets, navigation charts, fish tackle, step boxes. And then he saw it, you saw it, in the adjoining bunkroom, half obscured by a bead curtain: a body. He moved toward it (there was something glinting in his free hand), and you moved toward the cabin door. It was ajar. As you slipped through it, the guy

doused his flashlight and turned on the bedside lamp and you saw
then who he was. The bum you'd met the night before in Loui's. The
suit. The Hammer. And by the hothouse aroma you knew whose
body it was. It also belonged to someone you'd seen the night before.
Not the widow. Michiko, the tattooed hooker. She'd helped you
escape Blue's goons at Skipper's Waterfront Saloon. You'd heard her
scream. You thought about just backing out and leaving them to it,
but then you saw the Hammer raise a knife, and you stepped quietly forward, tapped him on the shoulder, and when he spun around,
met him with a roundhouse, gat in hand. He crumpled like a sack of
shit. You grabbed up the shiv, tossed it out the porthole, and while
he was still groggy, you lifted him by his collar and slugged him
again. And again. Did this palooka work for Mister Big? Take that,
Mister Big! *Wham!* Was he responsible for Michiko's death? Take
that—*pow!*—for Michiko. The widow's disappearance? *Biff! Bam!*
There was a telephone on the bedside table. You ripped it out of the
wall and hit him over the head with it, then clobbered him with a
brass telescope. You were having a great time. You lifted him for one
last blow to the gut (his jaw was hurting your knuckles) and threw
what was left of the rube to the floor, went over to kiss the tattooed
"4" on Michiko's cold forehead. Good night, sweetheart, you said.
Phil-san gonna miss you, baby. You strode off the yacht, lighting up,
feeling pretty good about yourself. Until he caught up with you.

⊙

You came around, stretched out in your bruised skin on your office
sofa, Blanche applying ice packs and Mercurochrome and spooning
in a bit of what she called cough medicine. Something you'd picked
up from a grifter pal for moments like this. There was nothing that
did not hurt. Every time we get up, something comes along and
knocks us on our ass again. As someone said. One of your clients
maybe. Laughing probably. Just before he got knocked down for good.

Lift your leg, Mr. Noir.

Ow!

Now the other one.

Oh shit. What happened?

You tell me, Mr. Noir. They fished you out of the water down at
the docks, badly damaged. Your friend Officer Snark saw the light on
and dropped you off up here rather than hand you over to Captain
Blue, who I believe harbors bad feelings toward you.

It was the goddamned Hammer, you groaned. He hit me when I wasn't looking.

The Hammer?

A guy I ran into last night. The one who told me to lay off the search for the body. I should have killed the bastard. I don't know if I'm tough enough for this racket, Blanche.

If you had listened to me in the first place, Mr. Noir, this wouldn't have happened. Your clothes were drenched and filthy and in dire need of mending. I'll bring them back in the morning. Is there anything more I can . . . ?

Well, I could use a good brandy, but—

There's a bottle on the table beside you, Mr. Noir. I took the precaution . . .

Beautiful. You're an angel, angel.

She blushed, took her glasses off for a moment, put them on again. I try to do my best, Mr. Noir. Now get some rest and take care of yourself. You shouldn't be disturbed. The phone is disconnected and I'll double lock the door.

Thanks, kid. And hit the light switch when you go.

⊙

A few brandies later, you were still on your back, but on the case again, thinking about your client, her story. On the one hand, she seemed to have been a ruthless schemer who twisted men and truths around her little finger like taffy, and on the other, a sweet kid from a nice town with a weakness for older guys. You, for instance. Not Blanche's view, but then Blanche trusted no one. Made her a useful assistant in a detective agency but blinded her to life's tenderer side. That night, lying there in pain and darkness (this is a tough life), the cough medicine just beginning to take a numbing grip, was when you first started thinking about the way the widow might have been using her old-guys stories as a way of coming on to you. I was strangely flattered by the heartrending ardor of his gaze when he looked at me, she said of her grandfather, or else her father. While gazing steadily at you through her veil (you supposed), her thighs whispering. I felt an eager affection coming from him, melting my resolve. My heart jolted and my pulse pounded. I knew it wasn't right, but I was powerless to resist. It was the most important experience of my life, Mr. Noir.

You were still hurting, but the edge was off, blunted by Rats'

328

prescription, the brandy, and the flow of blood to other parts. Recalling the widow's stories had filled your dick with a bit of liquid fire of its own and, lying there on the office sofa, you had taken it in hand. You were changing the story. You weren't ripping her clothes off, she was. She was mad with desire, couldn't wait. Neither could you. Nevertheless you fell asleep. You don't remember what you dreamt, but when you woke you thought you were locked in that fishbait hut at the docks and couldn't get out. There was someone in the office. Over near the hall door. More than one. Where's the fucking flashlight, one of them asked. I forgot it, boss. Shall I turn on the lights? No, you goddamn idiot. Light a match. Seemed to be several of them, all bumping into each other, cursing softly. Your heater was in your trenchcoat pocket, hanging from a clothes tree near the door. What you still held in your hand was useless. Fishbait. You guys start with the desk. I'll look for a wall safe. You slid softly off the sofa onto the floor for maximum cover. The only thing close at hand was the brandy bottle. You took a final slug, hating to waste it, then pitched it toward one of the struck matches. He hit me! one of them screamed. They started shooting. Bullets were flying. One struck the sofa where you'd been lying with a muffled thud. Oh shit! He got me! It's an ambush, boss! There's hundreds of 'em! They—*aaargh!* All their guns were blazing at once. It was like the finale of a fireworks display. There were screams, curses, crashing bodies. The shattering of glass.

When silence had fallen, you crept over to get your rod, throw on the lights. There were five dead guys in leather jackets. May have been more. The door was open and there was a trail of blood out into the hallway. Three of them had goatees, more than you'd seen before in the whole city. You felt good. It was as if you'd accomplished something. It relaxed you and you locked the door and doused the lights and crashed to the sofa again, falling almost immediately into the sweetest, deepest sleep you'd enjoyed since the widow first turned up. Certainly nothing like it since.

Two Drafts
Rachel Blau DuPlessis

DRAFT 93: ROMANTIC FRAGMENT POEM

Follow, fellow, and furrow
this labyrinth scratched in mud,
the "I" I am, the "I" I was,
the I that she collects;
the you and youse
for mulching roots:
yes, follow, pronoun, find and
grasp the all that lay outflung,
the we that formerly
got trashed, half policy, half chance,
our numbers up, like die;
and others, such as they and he
who has and is and are and give
a ritual possession of some spot
that's not a firm R-ticulate,
nor neither fixèd find, but wobbled
floppy thing with ties nearby
—the road, the dirt, the park,
the lot, a thing a-traveling, a pocky
prickly skin of bllod ty3pe O,
some certain bones
and one reverberant
titanium rod, whose
tuning forked to pitch of A
got embodied
and embedded
in the homeless
wandering
poem

as everything. In history.
Sidereal. Unsure.
It could repeat, and had resist,
could then recur, this mangy mongrel itch
for different shapes, for
further speckles in this
rash of textured specks.
O glamour of interior skylines, to
grasp and face this space between,
the space within, the deep aside beyond
whose yearning
activates a crucial urge
along the diva diptych of the page—

those floating motes of light or dust
caught for instant instances before
they changed, yet tried to
fix one there as you,
a you absorbed, an other I,
all this as if some kind living
hand burst up through pressings
of the tissue paper page,
mesmerizingly engaged, wanting
to warm you eye to eye, meet hold to hold,
thrust sweet to sweet, take verge to verge
throughout the full and endless here—
where then abruptly thereupon . . .

DRAFT 100: GAP

Dark landscape, its disordered order,
a walk shrinking into the mist.

Bright landscape, desperately
hot and dry and dusty. Both.

I leave places I've not yet got to,
and cannot then arrive at others.

And other ones again _____
_____.

Did these years have to happen
the way they did? _____

_____. The poem, unwritten
is concealed by the poem,

written. And in it.
There was always to be

another one. Beyond
_____.

There were the unseen,
the unheard, the unprojected,

unprotected. _____
_____.

As I read the sentence
"It is more arduous

to honor the memory
of the nameless

than that of the renowned,"
a door slammed in the corridor.

What's here is here.
But what is next

is not clear yet.
_____.

Hyper-scrite lecturer.
Quiet. Settle yourself.

_____. This is
a crossroads but nowhere

striking, and while there are
rocks marking the path,

they look no different
from the rocks all around anyway.

And did that path or the other
lead anywhere? _____?

_____? The other
side of words _____.

Can I remember what I was saying?
What did it amount to?

I assumed it mattered
but maybe there wasn't enough

silence. _____
down the fig-tree roadway

_____.
To spook the crows, someone

threw string-tied bottles
that will blow and glitter

over the seductive branches
fully laden, but as yet

only with hard, inedible figs.
One wanted to let them ripen.

_____.
How many words can hang from,

can depend on five trees,
fourteen-odd bottles

knocking their shiny plastic sides
together, in the wind?

_____
_____.

Try to be more than callow;
try to be more than curdled.

Slow down. The task
is luminosity. Darkness.

The complete
is never complete.

What implicates what?
What is necessary? What not?

You can see finally there are
two stories—_____

_____ and_____,
_____ but all diffused. Obscure.

Didn't I want, finally,
to write the second?

Never clear that I did.
This is a gap.

Or an opening. _____
_____,

the pattern unstable,
unstatable, extending itself.

_____.
_____?

Hunger for the next letter
makes the letters very difficult.

But if there were no hunger?
Then _____?

Can someone translate
the language of this work?

Guttering words, blown words,
light gleaming, yet distanced.

What is the truth
of the matter?

Let it go.
It is finished.

Even if it is not
complete?

Even if,
even that.

Will I not be lonely?
I am afraid to. Not to.

I am afraid so. This is
_____.

Be alone and quiet. Listen. There
will be a second other language.

The volta will happen
when the poem is over.

_____. _____
_____.

NOTE. The Walter Benjamin citation in the poem is the sentence engraved in German, Catalan, Spanish, and English on the monument in Port Bou, Spain, made by sculptor Dani Karavan and called *Passages: Homage to Walter Benjamin*. The sentence that follows is "Historical construction is devoted to the memory of the nameless." From Benjamin's "On the Concept of History." Draft along the "line of 5."

Rainscape
Can Xue

—*Translated from Chinese by Karen Gernant and Chen Zeping*

I LIKE TO SIT at the desk and tally the accounts. I look out the window: a gray structure built of granite is about one hundred meters away. Its windows—two rows of them—are all positioned in high places. Each window is narrow, and at night most of them are dark. A little faint light shines through from only two or three windows, giving people an unfathomable feeling. In front of the structure is a path, where people in twos or threes frequently pass by. Some are going to work, some are running errands, and some are children going to school. They all walk quite rapidly. In the sunlight, their shadows flash past the stone wall. I've never seen anyone emerge from the granite building, whose small black iron front door has been closed for years. But on the door is a large new gold-colored lock.

One day, when I was at the desk and facing the window in a daze, my husband said from behind me, "Listen. Someone in back is weeping."

Terrified, I concentrated intently, but neither heard nor saw anything. Out in front, because there had just been a rainstorm and there was still the sound of light rain, no one was on the path. But the granite building was actually a little different.

"Someone is coming over," my husband said. "It's the person who was weeping just now."

I held my breath and waited. I waited a long time. There was no one. The rain fell heavily again, with a *hualala* sound. The shrubbery was bending in the wind. My face fell, and I said, "Why don't I see anyone?"

"What a shame. I think it's your brother. With a flash of bright light, he disappeared on the wall. I wish you had seen this." My husband was still emotionally absorbed in what was happening over there.

"Did he completely vanish on the wall?"

"Just now, I certainly did hear him weeping—over there, next to the persimmon tree."

The week before, Brother had come to our home. He hadn't been well dressed and looked like a tramp. But he didn't talk at all the way a tramp does. He's always been shy, saying very little. Each time he comes to our home, he sits in a corner, for he doesn't want to attract any attention. Because he doesn't have a real job, my husband feels guilty and now and then gives him a little money. Brother takes the money and sneaks away. It's always a long time before he shows up again.

When talking about him, my parents say, "We can't figure out what to think of him. We never get a clear-cut impression of him."

Could what happened just now be a figment of my husband's imagination? I wanted to ask him, but he had already forgotten the incident. He had picked up the account books and was examining them carefully.

People were passing by in front of the granite wall—two young persons, a man and a girl. The girl was lame. Holding aloft a large sky blue umbrella, the man was keeping the woman from being drenched by the rain. They were talking as they walked. A long time passed before I could hear their alternately loud and soft voices. Blending with the sound of the rain, their voices remained out there below the gray sky.

After a few days, Brother came over and sat on the edge of the desk, dangling his skinny legs. When I mentioned the granite structure across the way, his face immediately clouded over.

"I always hear someone weeping over there," I said.

"Why don't you walk over to the front of the wall and take a careful look?" Brother mumbled as he jumped down from the desk. With his back to the window, he blocked my line of vision. "Fantasy is still the way we do things best."

Lowering his head, he walked out, seemingly quite irritated.

The granite facade glimmered in the murky twilight. Next to the wall, some people walking past were dimly visible. What on earth was going on over there? I hadn't heard Brother weeping; I had just wanted to draw him out to talk about some things, and so I had lied to him. He must have grown angry because he saw through this. Could my husband have told a lie? I made up my mind to go over to the wall the next day to take a careful look.

It could be said that I had "turned a blind eye" to this building for years. The granite wall was very old with dark watermarks on it.

337

This was a deserted building. I heard a key turn twice in the lock, and the door opened with a creak. I went inside without a second thought.

A person with his back to me was standing in the empty corridor. In the dim light, I couldn't get a good look at his face. I thought he was crying.

"On the 18th of April, you saw the beginning and the end of the matter," he said, his bare head gleaming and closing in on me. I still couldn't see his face well. I waited for him to go on talking, but he didn't: It was as if something had struck him. Bending over, he began to sob softly.

No one else was in the corridor, and the atmosphere was gloomy. He squatted against the wall and cried. As he sobbed, his aged back shuddered. Just then, from somewhere outside, I heard the sound of a car rolling by. At the end of the corridor, someone quite angrily bumped into the door with a *ping*.

"Probably you know my brother?" I bent down and shouted at the man.

"It's too late. Too late!" he said, out of breath, through his tears.

As I stood there, both ashamed and afraid, countless emotions welled up in my heart. He began scrabbling at the crumbly limestone wall with his fingers, making a nerve-racking sound. The dust kept falling.

"Brother! Brother! Don't leave me behind alone!" I blurted out in despair.

At this, the person stopped crying right away and stood up like a gravely wounded wild animal. He turned toward me. Now he and I were so close to one another that we couldn't have been any closer. His sleeves touched my hand. The strange thing was that his face was still a dark shadow. No matter which angle I looked from, I couldn't see his true face. It was as if the light couldn't reach it.

He began backing away from me. For each of his steps backward, I took a step forward. Our entangled shadows were reflected on the wall; it looked as if we were fighting. I felt an unparalleled tension. All of a sudden, the doors on both sides of the corridor opened, and the person turned around and fled. It seemed that people in all the rooms were craning their necks to watch. I didn't dare stay here, so I turned too, and ran out the front door.

I stopped at the end of the path. Looking back, I saw that the door still stood wide open. Inside, the corridor was pitch-dark, and the lights in those few windows had all been turned off. This structure

338

had once more become lifeless. I looked up at the sky: It was actually already daybreak.

People were coming around from the path over there, talking in low voices. I saw again the lame girl and the young man. Although it wasn't raining, the young man was still holding aloft a large sky blue umbrella. When they passed me, the two of them were dumbfounded for a moment and stopped walking. Lowering my head, I charged forward. I didn't dare look at them. After walking quite far, in the end I couldn't keep from looking back. They were still standing in the same place, and in the first rays of morning sun, the large blue umbrella glittered with light. The man was bending his head to say something to the girl. Behind them, the granite wall of the lifeless building was blurry and remote.

When I got home, my husband was already up. He was sitting there neatly dressed, as if intending to go out. He set my breakfast on the table.

"Time flew last night. I overslept," he said.

It was strange: He had the same feeling. Was time different inside and outside the building? As I drank some milk, I peeped at his face. While dreaming, could people tell any difference in time? Since he had slept straight through, how did he know whether time had passed quickly or slowly?

"What's the 18th of April?"

"It's the anniversary of your older brother's death. Have you forgotten even this?" He was a little surprised.

"At night, people can forget anything, no matter what it is."

"True. I've felt this too. In one short night, innumerable things can occur."

I walked over to the desk, and my gaze settled on that wall. The room suddenly felt sultry. Like a small fish, a faint desire swam back and forth. My husband went out, heading in the opposite direction from the building. He kept stopping, hesitating as if thinking of backtracking to take a look and then giving up the idea. Turning a corner, he disappeared. The leaves on the date tree at the doorway were moist. Had someone sprayed it with insecticide, or had it rained hard again during the night? Brother had told me last time that he would leave here soon. This was the first time in his life that he was going far away. I asked where he was going. He replied laconically, "I'll just keep going." When he said this, I recalled my husband's description of him a couple of days ago. When a person disappears like a ray of light into the wall, what does time mean to him? Our parents' faces

339

were alight with joy, their dispositions softening at once. Because of their tardy expression of love for my brother, they both felt a little confused and said they regretted being unable to accompany their son on his journey. If they had been ten years younger, they could have.

When he left, he kept looking back, his face darkening, his appearance dejected. When he was about to get into the car, Mother hung onto the strap of his backpack and wouldn't let go. When the car started up, Father followed, jumping along like a locust, thus giving rise to jokes from passersby. As soon as the car disappeared around a corner, the two old persons sat down on the ground, looking demented. My husband and I had to exert ourselves to get them back into the house. They sat side by side on the couch, and Mother suddenly asked quietly: "How can someone who has everything going for him be carried away by a car?"

My husband tried his best to explain. He said my brother hadn't disappeared from this world: He was merely taking a trip. This was common enough in other families. He would enjoy himself in the outside world for a while and come back again before long.

Sneering at his explanation, Mother said, "Have the two of you reached an agreement with him? Your father and I are old. We passed our prime a long time ago. But even though we're old, we're still alert. We've also heard about what happened in front of your house: It's exactly what we predicted. When you chose to move down here, we talked about it."

Then she took Father's hand and looked at it carefully. After a while, the two of them dozed off.

I started earnestly considering making an inspection behind the building. We hadn't gone there since we moved here more than ten years ago, because there was a craggy hill behind the granite wall. My husband and I always thought there was nothing worth looking at. Before falling asleep, I mentioned this to my husband. He said vaguely, "What if you get lost?"

Early in the morning, I set off in that direction. I had no sooner reached the path than I saw two people ahead of me: It was the lame girl and the tall youth. This time, they weren't carrying an umbrella. Empty-handed, they turned around and stood facing me. This time, I saw that the "girl" was actually a middle-aged person wearing a wig, and the "youth" was a thin old geezer almost seventy years old.

They beckoned to me, asking me to approach them.

Impatient, I spoke first. "I see that the two of you always go over there. I've watched you from the window lots of times. What's it like there? I really want a complete concept of this building."

They laughed in unison. I didn't think this laughter was genuine, and I wondered all of a sudden if they were two ghosts, ghosts that had floated out from that deserted building. Frightened, I unconsciously recoiled, but I also kept staring at them.

A key turned in the lock. At the *ka-ta* sound, I fled for my life. After running a short distance, I stopped again and looked back: The two of them had disappeared. The door was wide open; inside was the corridor I was familiar with. They had probably gone inside. Thinking of the first impression I'd had of them and of the bright colorful umbrella, I felt my knees weaken. I didn't dare go behind the granite wall again: Because of this episode, I'd lost the little confidence I'd had early in the morning.

I went back home, where my husband was sitting in my usual place. His head was bent as he repaired the alarm clock, and the desk was covered with parts and tools.

"You've been gone a long time. It's almost time for lunch," he said without lifting his head.

"True. And I couldn't find a way to reach the back of the building."

I thought, annoyed, that perhaps he was also faking it. Sitting here, he had seen everything that transpired this morning. I shouldn't have retreated: I was really ashamed of myself. What was there to be afraid of? The two ghosts? They might have been nothing but two locksmiths or pharmacists when they were alive. After their deaths, they had disguised themselves. It was nothing more than that.

As I was reasoning like this, the alarm clock suddenly rang with an insistent and terrible sound. It went on and on, as if it would never stop. It vibrated so much that it numbed my brain. When the sound finally stopped, my husband had disappeared, and nothing was on the desk. Yet, just now, I had seen the desk covered with his tools. Was he sitting here and playing a trick on me? Just now, he said, "You've been gone *a long time.*" This was a hint.

I looked out the window. The door was closed now, and a little light glimmered on the granite wall. At the upper left corner, close to the eaves, there seemed to be a ball of bright light. My heart throbbing, I wondered again what on earth it was like behind the building. I still needed to find out; no one could stop me. Even if the two ghosts wanted to discourage me, they couldn't guard the path every

minute, could they? There must be times when they were careless.
A huge time difference existed between the inside of the structure
and the outside of it. If they weren't ghosts and were just two ordinary people, how could they be accustomed to this time difference?
It was my husband who had confirmed the time difference: What if
he was also lying?

Every day, I faced that gray granite wall, with my brother's situation lingering in my mind. He had left by car, but that was only a
superficial phenomenon. This superficial impression remained in
my parents' minds. The black iron door opened and then closed again,
closed and then opened again: The lame woman and the tall youth
walked out from there and opened the large sky blue umbrella.
Standing in the rain, they chattered incessantly. One time, I told my
husband of the scene I had observed. My husband blinked and said
quietly that he had just come back from outside and that it certainly
was not raining. It was a bright spring day. He was contemplating
hanging his laundry out to dry in the sun. Nonetheless, I still heard
the sound of raindrops falling on the umbrella. One of the woman's
sleeves was drenched on one side. It was really mystifying.

NOTES ON CONTRIBUTORS

SAMUEL BECKETT (1906–1989) is regarded as one of the most influential writers of the twentieth century and a critical artistic force during the transition from modernism to postmoderism. Poet, essayist, short story writer, novelist, and playwright, Beckett conjured a dark and fatalistic view of the human condition that became the central theme of his writing, ranging from the novels *Molloy, Malone Dies,* and *The Unnamable* to his seminal plays *Waiting for Godot, Endgame,* and *Krapp's Last Tape.* In 1969 Beckett was awarded the Nobel Prize in Literature.

MATT BELL is the author of two chapbooks, *The Collectors* (Caketrain) and *How the Broken Lead the Blind* (Willows Wept Press), as well as a full-length fiction collection titled *How They Were Found,* to be published in fall 2010 by Keyhole Press. He is the editor of *The Collagist,* online at www.mdbell.com.

MARTINE BELLEN's recent chapbook, *Mothers, Daughters & Nightbirds,* published by Beard of Bees, can be found at www.beardofbees.com/bellen.html. Her novella *2X (SQUARED)* is forthcoming from BlazeVOX.

THOMAS BERNHARD (1931–1989) is the author of numerous plays and novels, including *Correction, The Lime Works, Concrete, The Loser,* and *Heldenplatz* (whose first appearance in English was in *Conjunctions:33*). One of the most important European writers of the second half of the twentieth century, Bernhard published poetry in the 1950s. When a manuscript, titled *Frost,* was rejected, he seemingly abandoned verse for fiction and drama, publishing his first novel, also titled *Frost,* in 1963. Bernhard, however, continued to refine his poetry and published it again near the end of his life, issuing *Ave Virgil* as a chapbook and finalizing a volume of collected poems.

GABRIEL BLACKWELL is currently at work on a polycephalic, semiautobiographical novel. His previous work can be found on *Web Conjunctions.* This is his first appearance in print.

ROBERTO BOLAÑO (1953–2003), the Chilean-born novelist and political and poetical dissident, met nearly unanimous recognition of his work, beginning with the English translation in 2003 of his novel *By Night in Chile* (New Directions) and his posthumous *2666* (Farrar, Straus and Giroux), which won the National Book Critics Circle Award. Bolaño died of liver failure in 2003, having written some twelve books in as many years. The novel *Antwerp* is forthcoming in English next spring from New Directions. The excerpt in this issue contains fifteen pieces from the novel, which has fifty-six numbered chapters.

CAN XUE's first novel to be translated into English, *Five Spice Street*, was published in 2009 by Yale University Press. Her book *Blue Light in the Sky and Other Stories* was published in 2006 by New Directions. Both were translated by Chen Zeping and Karen Gernant. She lives in Beijing, China.

CHEN ZEPING is professor of linguistics at Fujian Teachers' University. He has published numerous books and articles in the field of Chinese dialects. Translations by him and Karen Gernant have also appeared in *Manoa, Words Without Borders, Black Warrior Review*, and *Ninth Letter*.

ROBERT COOVER is the author, most recently, of *A Child Again* (McSweeney's). "In Search of the Body" is an excerpt from *Noir*, published by Éditions du Seuil in France in 2008, and forthcoming in English in 2010 from Overlook Press.

MARK EDMUND DOTEN's writing has appeared in *Guernica, The Believer*, and *The Agricultural Reader*, among other journals. He is the managing editor of Soho Press.

RACHEL BLAU DuPLESSIS's most recent book, *Pitch: Drafts 77–95*, is forthcoming from Salt Publishing. In 2002 she was awarded a Pew Fellowship in the Arts, a residency for poetry at Bellagio in 2007, and in 2008–09 was a Fellow at the National Humanities Center in North Carolina.

ANDREW ERVIN's first book, *Extraordinary Renditions: 3 Novellas*, will be published next year by Coffee House Press.

WILLIAM H. GASS's most recent book is his collection of essays, *A Temple of Texts* (Knopf).

KAREN GERNANT is professor emerita of Chinese history at Southern Oregon University. She and Chen Zeping collaborate on their translations of contemporary Chinese fiction.

PETER GIZZI's most recent books are *The Outernationale* and *Some Values of Landscape and Weather* (both Wesleyan). He has an artist's book, *Homer's Anger*, forthcoming in France (Collectif Generation), as well as a limited-edition chapbook, *In Song & Story*, in Holland (Tungsten Press). He currently serves as poetry editor for *The Nation*.

DUNCAN HANNAH studied at Bard College and Parsons. He debuted in 1981 and since then has had some fifty solo exhibitions in the United States and England. His paintings are in collections as diverse as those of the Metropolitan Museum of Art and Mick Jagger. Hannah lives in Manhattan and West Cornwall, Connecticut.

TIM HORVATH's novella, *Circulation*, was published by Sunnyoutside Press. His stories have appeared in *Alimentum: The Literature of Food, Fiction*, and *Puerto del Sol*, among other journals. He teaches creative writing at Chester College of New England and Boston's Grub Street Writers.

MAUREEN HOWARD's last of her Four Seasons novels, *The Rags of Time*, is just out from Viking Penguin.

PAUL LA FARGE is the author of three books: *The Artist of the Missing, Haussmann, or the Distinction* (both Farrar, Straus and Giroux), and *The Facts of Winter* (McSweeney's). He is currently working on a project about flight in America.

ANN LAUTERBACH's most recent collection is *Or to Begin Again* (Penguin). She teaches at Bard College.

NATHANIEL MACKEY's most recent book is *Bass Cathedral.* In 2006 he won the National Book Award for *Splay Anthem* (both from New Directions).

STEPHEN MARCHE is the author of *Raymond and Hannah* (Harcourt) and *Shining at the Bottom of the Sea* (Riverhead). He is currently the pop culture columnist at *Esquire* magazine.

ADAM McOMBER's recent stories have appeared in *StoryQuarterly, The Greensboro Review, Arts and Letters,* and *Ascent.* He teaches mythology and creative writing at Columbia College Chicago, where he is also managing editor of *Hotel Amerika.*

ANDREW MOSSIN is currently at work on revisions of *Drafts for Shelley*, sections of which have been previously published in chapbook form by Facture Books. He has recently completed a new book of poems, *The Pledge*, and a book of critical essays, *Male Subjectivity and Poetic Form in "New American" Poetry*, forthcoming in 2010 from Palgrave Macmillan. He teaches in the writing program at Princeton University.

PETER ORNER is the author of *Esther Stories* (Houghton Mifflin), winner of the Rome Prize, and *The Second Coming of Mavala Shikongo* (Little, Brown), which won the Bard Fiction Prize in 2007. He recently edited *Underground America: Narratives of Undocumented Lives,* a collection of oral histories. He is currently the William Kittredge Writer in Residence at the University of Montana.

BERNARD POMERANCE's work includes the Tony and Obie award-winning *The Elephant Man*, a play published by Grove Press that has been performed in dozens of countries around the world and enjoyed a Broadway revival in 2002. *We Need to Dream All This Again* ("An Account of Crazy Horse, Custer, and the Battle for the Black Hills") was published by Viking Penguin, and *The Collected Plays of Bernard Pomerance (Superhighway, Quantrill in Lawrence, Melons, Hands of Light)* is available from Grove. Pomerance lives in New Mexico.

FRANCINE PROSE's most recent book is *Anne Frank: The Book, The Life, The Afterlife* (HarperCollins). Her previous books include the novels *A Changed Man* and *Blue Angel* (both HarperCollins), which was a finalist for the 2001 National Book Award, and the nonfiction *New York Times* bestseller *Reading Like a Writer: A Guide for People Who Love Books and for Those Who Want to Write Them.* She is a Distinguished Visiting Writer at Bard College.

JAMES REIDEL is a poet, translator, and biographer. His previous translations of Thomas Bernhard's poetry have appeared on *Web Conjunctions* and in *In Hora Mortis/Under the Iron of the Moon* (Princeton University), a 2007 PEN finalist in translation. His other translation work includes the novel *A Pale-Blue Lady's Handwriting* by Franz Werfel, which will be published by Godine in 2010.

ELIZABETH ROBINSON's most recent book is *The Orphan & Its Relations* (Fence). In 2008, she was a recipient of a Foundation for Contemporary Arts Grants to Writers Award. She teaches at Naropa University.

ELIZABETH ROLLINS is the author of *The Sin Eater* (Corvid Press). Her work has appeared in *The New England Review*, *The Bellevue Literary Review*, and elsewhere.

Legendary publisher and editor BARNEY ROSSET founded Grove Press and *The Evergreen Review* and published, among many others, such authors as Samuel Beckett, William S. Burroughs, Henry Miller, Malcolm X, Tom Stoppard, Jack Kerouac, Jorge Luis Borges, Jean Genet, Eugène Ionesco, Federico García Lorca, and Kenzaburō Ōe. Rosset has completed work on his autobiography, *The Subject Is Left Handed*, from which his memoir about Samuel Beckett in this issue is excerpted.

D. E. STEWARD's "Avrila," one of an ongoing series of 276 poems based on months of the year, is the sixth to appear in *Conjunctions*, with two other months on *Web Conjunctions*.

COLE SWENSEN is the author of twelve books of poetry, most recently *Ours* (University of California). She is also a translator and the founding editor of La Presses Books, which is dedicated to publishing contemporary French poetry. She teaches at the Iowa Writers' Workshop and lives in Washington, D.C., and Paris.

Among PAUL WEST's more than fifty books, the most recent is *The Shadow Factory* (Lumen). Gallimard has just republished, under the title *Des Poupées et des Dieux*, his novel *The Place in Flowers Where Pollen Rests*.

NATASHA WIMMER has translated fiction and nonfiction by Roberto Bolaño, Rodrigo Fresán, Pedro Juan Gutiérrez, Laura Restrepo, Mario Vargas Llosa, and Gabriel Zaid, among others. Her translation of Bolaño's *The Savage Detectives* was one of *The New York Times'* top ten books of 2007, and her translation of *2666* won the 2008 National Book Critics Circle Award. She is the recipient of a PEN Translation Award and an NEA Translation Grant.

Since 1981 our summer-based MFA degree program in upstate New York has offered a non-traditional approach to the creative arts. Intensive eight-week summer sessions, emphasizing individual conferencing with faculty and school-wide interdisciplinary group conversation/critique, combine with ten-month independent study periods to both challenge the student and allow space for artistic exploration.

Our Writing discipline emphasizes awareness of a variety of verbal, aural, and textual structures, and students develop an individual process of composition as well as a critical understanding of their field. Forms such as innovative poetry, short fiction, sound, and mixed-media writing are particularly well-suited to the structure and nature of the Bard MFA program.

2009 Writing faculty include:

Anselm Berrigan, co-chair	Paul La Farge
Robert Fitterman	Ann Lauterbach, co-chair
Renee Gladman	Anna Moschovakis
Carla Harryman	David Levi Strauss
Laird Hunt	Matvei Yankelevich

Call or email us to schedule a campus visit, or check *www.bard.edu/mfa* for a list of upcoming information sessions.

MFA
BARD COLLEGE

815-758-7181 • mfa@bard.edu • www.bard.edu/mfa

Jean Daive, *Under the Dome: Walks with Paul Celan*

Jean Daive
UNDER THE DOME:
Walks with Paul Celan
translated from the French by Rosmarie Waldrop

[Série d'Ecriture, No. 22; tr. from the French by R. Waldrop]

An intimate portrait of Paul Celan in his last, increasingly dark years. Celan and Daive translate each other, walk, talk. Tensions, silences and, discreetly, Celan's crises and suicide. The book blurs the time of these encounters (1965 -1970) with the present of the author writing, 20 years later, on a Mediterranean island.

Memoir, 136 pages, offset, smyth-sewn, ISBN13: 978-1-886224-97-1, original pbk. $14
Burning Deck has also published Daive's poem, *A Lesson in Music* (tr. Julie Kalendek).

Peter Waterhouse: *Language Death Night Outside*

[Dichten=, No.11; tr. from the German by R. Waldrop]

An "I" between languages. A text between the genres of poem and novel. 3 cities, 3 poems, 3 philosophers. A life takes shape through precise particulars in short, staccato sentences. But the effort toward the concrete and definite stands in tension with the boundlessness of thought where the city turns ship, and a flower in Vienna touches the sand dunes of North Africa.

Poem.Novel, 128 pages, offset, smyth-sewn, ISBN13: 978-1-886224-99-5, original pbk. $14
Also available: *Where Are We Now*? Poems. Duration Press, 1999.

Michael Gizzi: *NEW DEPTHS OF DEADPAN*

Should the two archetypal masks that represent Comedy and Tragedy pass through each other (imagine a total eclipse), might not their overlapping intersection be an expression of deadpan? Or does the almost reckless declarativeness of these poems show a mind's weathering both the antic and the intimate, both merriment and distress?
"Razor sharp but also rich and generously compelling, Michael Gizzi's poetry lambastes as it celebrates"—John Ashbery [on *No Both*]
Poetry, 72 pages, offset, smyth-sewn, ISBN13: 978-1-886224-96-4, original pbk. $14

Sawako Nakayasu: *HURRY HOME HONEY*

10 years of love poems, unusual for their sense of moving between cultures, their awareness of physical space as intersection of humans, the land, and architecture. Love itself is now game, sport, speed-time, dance, performance, now contract, conflict, failure, but always a shifting structure of relations.
    "An extraordinary voice — an ease that thinly covers a swirling anxiety, a well-honed knowledge of how things turn out; and yet an unending romance with the process of romance, only rarely referential (and never explicit) to the act or state of satisfaction, sexual or otherwise. A sense of possibility."—Craig Watson
Poetry, 80 pages, offset, smyth-sewn, ISBN13: 978-1-886224-98-6, original pbk. $14

Orders: SPD: www.spdbooks.org, 1-800/869-7553, In Europe: www.audiatur.no/bokhandel
www.burningdeck.com

BROWN UNIVERSITY LITERARY ARTS

Program faculty

Brian Evenson
Thalia Field
Forrest Gander
Renee Gladman
Michael S. Harper
Carole Maso
Aishah Rahman
Meredith Steinbach
Keith Waldrop
CD Wright

Joint-appointment & visiting faculty

Ama Ata Aidoo
Rick Benjamin
John Cayley
Robert Coover
Joanna Howard
George Lamming
Gale Nelson
John Edgar Wideman

For over 40 years, the Brown University Literary Arts Program has been a home for innovative writing. To learn about the two-year MFA program and the under-graduate concentration, or to have access to Writers Online, an archive of literary recordings, see our web site: http://www.brown.edu/cw

MFA application deadline is 15 December.

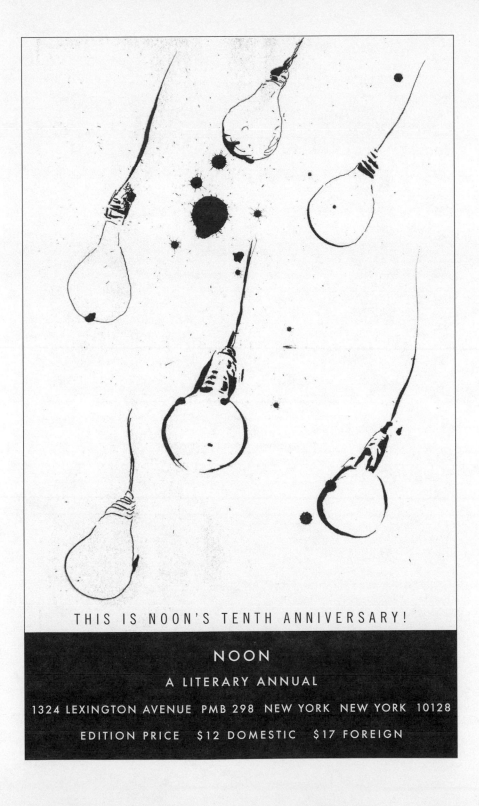

THIS IS NOON'S TENTH ANNIVERSARY!

NOON

A LITERARY ANNUAL

1324 LEXINGTON AVENUE   PMB 298   NEW YORK   NEW YORK   10128

EDITION PRICE $12 DOMESTIC $17 FOREIGN

Best American Short **Stories**

Best **American** Poetry

Best American Essays

Best American **Science**

& Writing
Nature

the **Pushcart**

Prize anthology

It's difficult to keep up with the daily tasks (besides making tea, reading blogs, self-googling, checking email, playing solitaire, going to work, and—oh, yeah!—that thing, writing) that complicate a writer's life: tracking submissions, finding markets, planning projects, researching funding. . . .

A Working Writer's Daily Planner is the answer.

Written by writers for writers (and always taking suggestions for items for inclusion for next year), this is much more than a planner—and will be the perfect gift for the writer in your life.

> "I am ticking off the days until I can get my Working Writer's Daily Planner. All work is at a complete stop until its arrival."
> —Karen Joy Fowler (The Jane Austen Book Club)

This is a handy, all-in-one, energetic and inspiring guide and one-stop-spot for writers to keep track of the practical, business end and give you more time to the real daily work of writing.

Available this fall in all good bookshops and from smallbeerpress.com.

Distributed to the trade by Consortium.

9781931520584 · $13.95

A Working Writer's Daily Planner 2010
Your Year in Writing

"I am ticking off the days until I can get my Working Writer's Daily Planner. All work is at a complete stop until its arrival." — Karen Joy Fowler, author of The Jane Austen Book Club

More features:

- Award and residency deadlines.
- Monthly markets.
- Submission and result tables (with reminders to keep it updated!).
- Illustrated with inspiring art and photos.
- Federal holidays . . . to remind you that the post office is closed.
- Resource listings.
- Reading periods.
- Blank pages specifically set aside for notes.
- Writing prompts.
- Recommended reading lists (fiction, nonfiction, inspiration, &c.)
- Standard planner data: What time is it in Kazakhstan? How many liters are in a gallon? What do we talk about when we talk about love?
- And, maybe, just maybe, paper dolls.

TORTURE OF WOMEN   NANCY SPERO

Torture of Women juxtaposes first person testimony by female victims of torture with imagery drawn from ancient
mythology. Spero collapses time and dissolves geographical
boundaries, making space for public cries of outrage and
for the solitariness of pain itself. This startling and nu-
anced collage is not only a seminal feminist work but an
artwork that indicts the abuse of power and bears witness
to the resiliency of the human spirit. As powerful now as
it was when it was created in 1976, Siglio's publication
translates the epic 125 ft work to almost 100 pages of color
reproductions, so that it can be read and experienced with
immediacy and intimacy. With a story by Luisa Valenzuela, an
excerpt from Elaine Scarry's *The Body in Pain*, and an essay
by Diana Nemiroff. (Hardback / 156 pgs / Spring 2010)

siglio uncommon books at the intersections of art & literature

www.sigliopress.com . 2432 Medlow Avenue, Los Angeles, CA 90041 . 310-857-6935

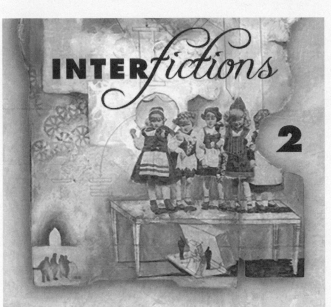

Henry Jenkins
Jeffrey Ford
M. Rickert
Will Ludwigsen
Cecil Castellucci
Alaya Dawn Johnson
Ray Vukcevich
Carlos Hernandez
Lavie Tidhar
Brian Francis Slattery
Elizabeth Ziemska
Peter M. Ball
Camilla Bruce
Amelia Beamer
William Alexander
Shira Lipkin
Alan DeNiro
Nin Andrews
Theodora Goss
Lionel Davoust
Stephanie Shaw
David J. Schwartz
Colleen Mondor
Christopher
Barzak, and Delia
Sherman

9781931520614
TRADE PAPER · $16
EBOOK · $9.95

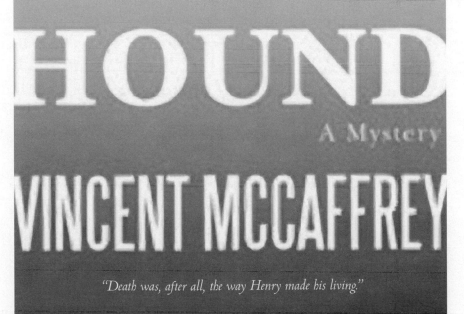

"Death was, after all, the way Henry made his living."

DISTRIBUTED TO THE TRADE BY CONSORTIUM.

TRADE CLOTH/EBOOK · 9781931520591 · $24/$15.95

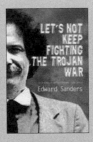